Blood Shadows

by Tessa Dawn

A Blood Curse Novel
Book Four
In the Blood Curse Series

Published by Ghost Pines Publishing, LLC
http://www.ghostpinespublishing.com

Volume IV of the Blood Curse Series by Tessa Dawn
First Edition Trade Paperback Published
10 9 8 7 6 5 4 3 2 1

ISBN-13: 978-1-937223-06-9
Printed in the United States of America

Author may be contacted at: http://www.tessadawn.com

This is a work of fiction. All characters and events portrayed in this
novel are either fictitious or are used fictitiously. Any resemblance to
actual persons, living or dead, business establishments, events, or
locales is entirely coincidental.

 Ghost Pines Publishing, LLC

Acknowledgments

For Harold & Goldie, my celestial stars...

A special thanks to the following contributors:

Lidia Bircea, Romanian Translations

Miriam Grunhaus, Cover Art

Reba Hilbert, Editing

Ghost Pines Publishing, LLC

Additional Credits

A Tale of Two Cities by Charles Dickens (1859)

"Unchained Melody" (1955), lyrics by Hy Zaret

The Blood Curse

In 800 BC, Prince Jadon and Prince Jaegar Demir were banished from their Romanian homeland after being cursed by a ghostly apparition: *the reincarnated Blood of their numerous female victims.* The princes belonged to an ancient society that sacrificed its females to the point of extinction, and the punishment was severe.

They were forced to roam the earth in darkness as creatures of the night. They were condemned to feed on the blood of the innocent and stripped of their ability to produce female offspring. They were damned to father twin sons by human hosts who would die wretchedly upon giving birth; and the firstborn of the first set would forever be required as a sacrifice of atonement for the sins of their forefathers.

Staggered by the enormity of *The Curse*, Prince Jadon, whose own hands had never shed blood, begged his accuser for leniency and received *four small mercies*—four exceptions to the curse that would apply to his house and his descendants, alone.

Ψ Though still creatures of the night, they would be allowed to walk in the sun.

Ψ Though still required to live on blood, they would not be forced to take the lives of the innocent.

Ψ While still incapable of producing female offspring, they would be given *one opportunity and thirty days* to obtain a mate—a human *destiny* chosen by the gods—following a sign that appeared in the heavens.

Ψ While they were still required to sacrifice a firstborn son, their twins would be born as one child of darkness and one child of light, allowing them to sacrifice the former while keeping the latter to carry on their race.

And so...forever banished from their homeland in the Transylvanian mountains of Eastern Europe, the descendants of

BLOOD SHADOWS

Jaegar and the descendants of Jadon became the Vampyr of legend: roaming the earth, ruling the elements, living on the blood of others...forever bound by an ancient curse. They were brothers of the same species, separated only by degrees of light and shadow.

Prologue

Nachari Silivasi gripped the iron stakes on either side of his hands and shouted his pain as the harsh lash bit into his skin again and again. And again.

He would not beg.

He would not give them the satisfaction.

His body shook against the hard granite beneath him, and his back arched in unnatural contortions as his spilled blood pooled beneath his naked belly. It felt warm against the otherwise cool stone.

It had been three long months.

Three terrible months since he had descended into the Valley of Death and Shadows—and entered hell—in order to save the Vampyr king of the house of Jadon from a dark possession.

It had been three agonizing months since he had seen his brothers.

The lash struck again, catching him off guard on a violent exhale, and he almost passed out. His amulet, the one Shelby had given him, was cutting into his skin—it always did when they laid him facedown against the stone for his lashings—but he didn't dare take it off. Once, a minion of the dark lord had tried to wrench it from his neck, and it had burned the demon's hand like a hot branding iron.

As the lash struck lower this time, falling somewhere between his upper thighs and his buttocks, he heard himself whimper, and he cursed his momentary weakness. If only he could die. If only his brothers would renege on their promise to continue providing life support to his body until he returned. If only he could be free.

If Nachari could have laughed at the irony—which he couldn't—he would have: In their desire to keep him alive, to hold him to the earth, his brothers were keeping him in a vampiric version of purgatory instead. As long as his earthly body remained safe and healthy, awaiting his spirit's return to Dark Moon Vale, he could not fully die. Once dead, his corporeal body, which was holding his soul at bay, and his ethereal soul, which was projecting a corporeal form in order to sustain the endless torture, would merge. He would be one entity in one place, and the Dark Lord Ademordna could no longer enslave him.

Granted, he would be dead, never to return to his precious valley in the Rocky Mountains, never to see his Romanian homeland one last time, never to meet his *destiny,* but he would at least be at peace—for the dark lord who had taken him into the Valley of Death and Shadows could not hold him as one integrated being. His eternal soul would find its solace in the Valley of Spirit and Light where it belonged. With Shelby.

As the next stroke of the lash fell into the exact groove as the previous one, Nachari inadvertently bit his tongue: *Great Celestial gods,* how much more could he endure? Day after endless day. Knowing his body would regenerate again and again only to prepare him for more torture.

Unable to withstand another moment of his torment, Nachari chose to take the only way out available to him…however temporary. Indeed, it was an escape he had taken one hundred times before. He threw back his head, his glorious mane of thick, raven hair spilling around his face and shoulders in wild waves of blood-crusted locks, and slammed his forehead against the stone.

The pain was indescribably profound.

Literally and figuratively stunning.

And then—mercifully—he collapsed against the stone, and the entire underworld went black.

Deanna Dubois knelt on her living room floor in deep concentration, rocking back and forth on her heels as she stared at the new set of drawings in front of her. She sighed in frustration and more than a little trepidation. The only reason she could call these drawings *new* was because she had drawn them last night—as opposed to the night before…

Or the night before that.

There was nothing new about her disturbing, ever-growing obsession.

She twirled a thick lock of ash-brown hair around her finger, noticing a particularly stark amber highlight, before turning back to the paintings.

Dear God, what was wrong with her?

She needed help.

And it was getting harder and harder to deny it.

She reached for the thin, lightweight computer beside her, drew it on top of her lap, and used the mouse to enlarge the webpage she had opened—and left open—almost two weeks ago: Psychiatric Clinics in New Orleans.

Just pick one, Deanna, she told herself. *You need help!*

She glanced once again at the pictures before her and tried to see them in a new light, maybe, with an eye for self-analysis—it was time for some serious introspection. Setting the laptop aside, she laid the drawings out in order, sort of like a progressively animated comic strip, and then sat back and studied them.

On the far left was the most beautiful man she had ever seen, a tall, incredibly well-built Adonis with deep green eyes and a face so utterly perfect she wasn't sure God could actually create such a being—let alone endow her with the ability to draw it. His hair was unnaturally thick and silky, and there was a strange air of confidence swirling around him even in the drawing—not quite arrogance, but definitely pride—a regal-like quality. He was simply breathtaking. Actually, more than that: He was arresting…almost disturbing in his appeal.

The next sequence of drawings was more benign, and she drew them the same every time: pine trees, rock outcroppings, skies filled with dark, mottled clouds, and endless miles of forest. Nothing especially interesting or disturbing there. They reminded her of pictures she had seen of Colorado.

She turned to the next drawing, the one immediately to the right of the last forest picture, and she shivered. In this frame, the ground had opened up beneath the handsome man, and he was falling into a dark, endless hole, being sucked into some evil netherworld. The hands that were reaching up to grab him were skeletal and demonic; and, of course, this is where the metaphorical comic strip began to deteriorate and her own mental health came into question: In the subsequent set of photos—the largest sequence that she drew night after night— the ungodly beautiful man was depicted in all kinds of horrific scenarios and positions being tortured.

And by *tortured*, she meant hideously tormented in ways that no stable human being could possibly come up with—let alone draw in such brutal detail—unless that artistically disturbed woman was seriously going insane.

She rubbed her face with her palms as if she could scrub away the anxiety and stared apprehensively at the farthest picture to the right. Something in her gut turned over as her eyes connected with the images.

It was as if it were real.

As if it were happening right now.

As if, right this second, the man was lying facedown against a cold stone, bound by four heavy lengths of chain, with diamonds—of all things—embedded in the links. And God almighty, was he writhing in pain as his flesh was literally torn from his body by a spiked lash. Yet never—not even once in all of her drawings—did the guy beg his tormentors for mercy. For lack of a better term, he took it like a man.

A man forged from iron.

Whoever her phantom captive was, he clearly had the heart of a lion.

Deanna reached out and swept the drawings into a haphazard pile, purposefully disturbing the order in a desperate

Tessa Dawn

attempt to erase the madness that had become her nighttime—and more and more often, daytime—obsession.

"Who are you?" she whispered, pleading with heaven-knows-what for just a moment's peace. "And why are you haunting me?"

One of the earlier-sequenced drawings seemed to rise to the top as if it were trying to answer her question by floating above all the other images...speaking in some cryptic, metaphysical way. "It's just random, Deanna," she reassured herself. "From the way you messed them up—you are not *that* crazy!" She emphasized the last five words while momentarily squeezing her eyes shut. And then she began tapping the back of her foot nervously against the floor in a frenetic, repetitive rhythm as she cringed. "What's wrong with me...what's wrong with me...*what's wrong with me?*"

She continued to stare at the most prominent drawing.

"Fine," she finally spat, reaching for the picture and lifting it up to study it more closely. "I'll bite. Show me some great hidden meaning, then." Shaking her head, she whispered, "Show me just how psychotic I am so they can lock me away forever."

As she turned the drawing over and over, observing it at different angles, she began to notice a strange pattern in the sky: There was something hidden within the shadows of the dark clouds, the ones that loomed ominously over the forested valley, the place from which the man always fell into the black hole. And the hidden pattern wasn't something Deanna had added to the picture; rather, it was a deliberate omission—white space that remained empty, uncovered by pencil marks.

An outline emerged in the absence of color.

Frowning, Deanna leapt up from the floor and went to get her magnifying glass in order to take a closer look. As she held the drawing beneath the lens, she bent way over to study the vacant space...and froze.

What in the world?

The spaces were letters.

And the letters spelled very distinct words.

BLOOD SHADOWS

Wondering if she wasn't about to open Pandora's box—and whether or not she might be better off leaving well enough alone—Deanna reached for her pencil and flipped over another drawing in order to transcribe the letters on the back, one at a time.

DARK-MOON-VALE-CLINIC.

She sat back and stared at the words, and then she picked up the magnifying glass and verified each one a second time, making sure she hadn't overlooked anything. Yep, that's what they said all right: Dark Moon Vale Clinic.

She set down the magnifying glass and shrugged. At least they hadn't spelled out Sybil or Three Faces of Eve. At least they hadn't spelled out *Redrum, Redrum, Redrum* over and over and over: "All work and no play makes Deanna a very dull girl," she whispered, shivering at the inappropriate reference to *The Shining*—a terrifying book written by Stephen King in the 1970s that was later made into a movie. That was later remade at a remote Colorado hotel...

Near the Rocky Mountain National Park...

Just outside the Roosevelt National *Forest*.

Deanna swallowed a lump in her throat, set the magnifying glass aside, and slowly reached for her laptop again. This time, she ignored the intimidating list of local psychoanalysts in favor of trying a different search: Colorado Clinics. When she didn't find the one from her drawings, she began to breathe easier. *Okay, this is good. The clinic isn't real.*

Even as she thought it, an uneasy feeling grew in her belly, and she continued to try various word combinations in the search engine, absently seeking to discern whether or not the *place* was real, even if the clinic wasn't.

And there it was.

Right beneath Mountain Hotels and Accommodations: *Dark Moon Vale Lodge.*

Damnit! she thought, her trepidation growing. It was time to research the place in depth.

Despite some frantic voice screaming deep within the

recesses of her mind, *Stop! Don't go any further. This is one of those forks in the road—one of those ominous moments in life from which there is no turning back—don't do it!* she was helpless to stop herself.

Because something far deeper within her, something far more fundamental and compelling than fear, was spurring her on, inexplicably drawing her to the suffering man in her sketches. To the haunted eyes of that masculine figure.

And nothing in this world—or the next—was going to keep her from solving the mystery...if, in fact, it could be solved.

Even as Deanna clicked on the link and prepared to read further, she already knew she was headed for Colorado: She was going to Dark Moon Vale.

Somewhere...the victim in her drawings did exist. And she was going to find him even if it killed her.

If she had harbored even the slightest doubt before, it was now completely gone: Deanna Dubois was absolutely—*certifiably*—insane.

one

Dark Moon Vale

The sterile room in the private clinic was as orderly as it was disheartening. Kagen Silivasi dragged his chair closer to his brother's bedside and rested his elbows on his knees. He let out a gentle sigh and stared at Nachari's peaceful face, wishing Nachari would open his eyes. "How are you doing today, little brother?" he whispered, knowing there would be no response. "Everything seems to be in order…at least physically."

Kagen frowned. Nachari had been like a vegetable for three months now: His vital signs were good; his heartbeat was steady; and his complexion remained vibrant and flawless—albeit lacking the young vampire's customary lighthearted smile—and his eyelids rested gently closed over his typically vibrant green eyes. Wherever he was, whether in this world or the next, he appeared to be at rest.

At peace.

Kagen rubbed his jaw in contemplation, wondering for the millionth time what had gone wrong the day Nachari had traded his immortality to follow their sovereign king beyond the realm of the living, to save Napolean from the Dark Lord Ademordna, who had possessed the king in a plot to impregnate and destroy the king's *destiny*. Had Nachari followed the evil being into the Valley of Death and Shadows? Had he chosen the afterlife over his ceaseless existence on earth? Or had he been derailed in some other horrific fashion?

Only the gods knew.

And they weren't talking.

Kagen cleared his throat and tried to put some pep into his voice. "So, let's see: What's new today?" He spoke to the sleeping vampire the same way every morning, casually and with

1

deliberate hope, praying his faith would one day get through. "Oh yeah, we worked out a new schedule for you." He absently took Nachari's hand. "It looks like Nathaniel will be hanging out from two to eight every evening; Marquis will sit with you from eight to three AM; and, of course, I'll get up with the chickens to be here every day from three until noon." He tried to chuckle but it sounded as insincere as it felt. "Nurse Katia will take the noon-to-two shift, just to give us a short break, but don't worry, Jocelyn, Ciopori, and Kristina will be dropping in on a regular basis during that time…more than likely to talk your ears off." He absently brushed an errant lock of hair from Nachari's forehead. "Braden would come more often, but we're trying to protect him from too much exposure to the situation—limit his time in the clinic and keep him busy."

He set his brother's hand back down, and then he shrugged away his guilt.

The two-hour window—120 minutes without Kagen, Marquis, or Nathaniel at Nachari's side—still felt like too much time: Nachari needed to know that his brothers were there every second, pulling for him, standing by him, willing him to live.

That they fully expected him to return to the family—both mentally and physically whole.

It was the women who had finally convinced the Silivasi brothers that they simply couldn't spend every waking hour at Nachari's side, that their fatigue also projected a tangible energy; and if they didn't take a break, make an effort to fortify their own souls, none of them would have anything left to give Nachari. Pretty wise, Kagen thought. Nevertheless, two hours out of twenty-four were all the Master Healer would concede. Luckily, the women were wise enough not to push it any further.

A smile warmed his expression, and he chuckled softly. "Speaking of the women, Marquis is treading on some very thin ice these days." He leaned in conspiratorially and lowered his voice. "Ciopori finally drew a line in the sand about Marquis's constant roughhousing with Nikolai—after all, the child is all of what? Just over four months old now?" His voice deepened. "So

2

what did Marquis go and do? He gathered all of Niko's rattles, hollowed out the centers, and filled them with lead. *Lead.* Basically, he turned them into barbells, so every time the boy teethes and reaches for a rattle, he's forced to lift weights." Leaning back in the chair, he crossed one leg horizontally over the other and placed his arm on the back rest. "Nathaniel thinks Ciopori is going to kill him this time when she finds out. Frankly, I think she already knows but is waiting for the best time to use it as leverage." He leaned in as far forward as possible and added, "If you ever repeat this, I'll deny saying it, but Marquis no longer runs things over there...even if he thinks he does. I swear to you on my honor, our newest sister has that male wrapped around her little royal finger." He smiled without restraint. "It's priceless. It truly is."

All at once, the steady line on the monitor dipped for a moment and a shrill beep sounded, drawing Kagen to immediate attention. His breath caught as he checked the screen, processed all of the numbers quickly in his head, and prepared to jump at a moment's notice if necessary. After thirty seconds or so passed without incident, he relaxed his shoulders and chalked it up to the normal fluctuations of technology. And then he sternly chastised himself for overdramatizing the moment. *By the gods, he had never been this antsy before with a patient.*

Of course, Nachari wasn't just any patient...

Still, Kagen couldn't help but wonder whether or not he was even capable of providing his youngest brother with ongoing, competent care anymore. Clearly, he could not remain objective, rational, or detached. Perhaps he could no longer see things from a true healer's perspective.

Perhaps he should have another healer step in for him.

The second the thought crossed his mind, he dismissed it.

Good, bad, or indifferent, there was no way in hell Kagen Silivasi would ever relinquish Nachari's care to another. The mere thought made him cringe. Nachari would either wake up, come back to the land of the living with gusto, or he would slip away quietly—or not so quietly. Either way, it would be with

BLOOD SHADOWS

Kagen at his side.

Kagen rose from his chair.

He crossed the room and opened one of two windows that looked over the whitewater river below. A crisp breeze swept through the night, bringing with it the fresh smell of pine and juniper, clean mountain air. As the invigorating scent filled his nostrils, he inhaled deeply. He thought he had worked through most of his guilt. At least he had tried to put it in its proper place—which wasn't in the Dark Moon Vale Clinic, interfering with his one-on-one time with his patient. Even if the patient was his beloved brother.

Looking at it rationally, he knew he had done all he could for Nachari. From the moment events had first begun to unfold, Kagen had acted with infinite care and meticulous precision: He had overseen the draining of his little brother's blood with expert timing; and he had treated the wizard's dying body with the utmost respect, going out of his way to preserve the dignity of the sacrifice Nachari was making.

Correction: the *temporary* sacrifice Nachari had made.

It had never been intended to be permanent.

Kagen stared out the window at a towering group of Ponderosa pines as he recalled that fateful, horrific day: Salvatore Nistor had conjured a parasitic demon from hell in an attempt to destroy Napolean Mondragon, actually brought the monster to earth from the underworld. Since none of the Dark Ones were capable of getting anywhere near Napolean on their own, they had relied upon every trick in the book—literally, in the Book of Black Magic—to bring the formidable king down, to exact revenge for the day Napolean had single-handedly slain eighty-eight of their warriors in the underground colony as punishment for Salvatore's capture of Princess Ciopori. Meanwhile, Nachari had agreed to try and save the king—to allow the warriors in the house of Jadon to drain his body of blood and force him to flatline in order to free his immortal soul from his body. It was the only way Nachari could enter the Spirit World and do battle with the demon on behalf of their king.

And Kagen had brought Nachari back to life immediately, just as he had promised.

He had started Nachari's heart and pumped oxygen to his brain, all the while keeping him viable so that his traveling soul could return to his body the moment their king was out of danger—just as soon as Napolean was safe, back in his own healthy body, and no longer possessed by the Dark Lord.

But nothing had gone as they planned.

Nachari had never returned.

Something had gone horribly…horribly wrong.

Kagen shook his head to dismiss the memory. It stung to think of the way the Dark Ones had snuck a possession worm into their king, tried to use Napolean to destroy his newfound mate—and then himself—and cost the Silivasis their beloved brother in the process.

Kagen was infinitely proud of Nachari.

And endlessly ashamed of his inability to do something more to bring the Master Wizard back.

He rolled his head on his shoulders to release some tension and looked back at Nachari, noting how peaceful he appeared on the bed. If three months had not already passed, he would have sworn his little brother was just sleeping soundly. That any minute now, he was going to jump up, flash that broad, endearing smile of his, and saunter across the room with that rare, almost arrogant swagger that Nachari wore like a second skin—the one that had women swooning, gasping, and begging for even the slightest glance in their direction, just hoping to get a look at *those eyes*.

Truth be told, Kagen thought, underneath it all, Nachari was one of the kindest, most sincere males he had ever known.

Kagen walked leisurely back to the bedside and tilted his head to the side, studying every nuance of his brother's face.

Remembering.

Decades of teasing. Centuries of endless jokes played on the family by both Nachari and Nachari's late twin, Shelby. Endless antics—some planned, some accidental—but all evoking silly smirks, childish chortles, and raucous laughter in their wake. So much animation in those arresting features.

Kagen shook his head.

There was so much more life left to live for the young, 500-year-old vampire. So much more of the world to see. So many more experiences to enjoy.

Like Kagen, Nachari had yet to meet his *destiny*. Unlike Kagen's, Nachari's woman would undoubtedly become the most envied woman on the planet. Not that women didn't swoon and pant over the only brown-eyed, russet-haired Silivasi brother in the bunch as well, but Nachari was...well...Nachari. And Kagen never wanted to see that change.

He shrugged, tapping the sleeping male lightly on the shoulder. "You know what, brother. I almost forgot to tell you about Storm." He held both hands in front of him and toggled them up and down as if measuring two invisible weights. "Now, keep in mind, of course, that parents tend to exaggerate; however, this little guy is actually starting to babble already and make some words. If I'm lying, you can sue me."

Although all vampire children developed far more rapidly than their human counterparts, at only four and one-half months old, Nathaniel and Jocelyn's industrious child was already showing an unusual level of intelligence.

"The other day," Kagen continued, explaining the outlandish claim, "Jocelyn was strapping Storm into his car seat in order to bring him to the clinic for a visit; and apparently, the little guy was so accustomed to coming here to see you that he looked up and said, 'Unka Chari?'" Kagen felt his eyes grow moist. "*Unka Chari*, can you get over that? The boy knew that he was going to see his uncle Nachari." He looked away as the last words caught in his throat; and then he cleared it, took a deep breath, and slowly blew it out. *Damn it all to hell—why did this have to be so hard?* For the love of all that was holy, what did the gods want in exchange for bringing Nachari back? There was no price the Healer wouldn't willingly pay, regardless of any cost to himself.

Suddenly, from somewhere far away, deep in the recesses of

his mind—someplace where unspoken doubts lurked in the shadows, threatening, always threatening, to come into the light—Kagen felt the subtle stirring of fear. Waiting. Prowling. Ever ready to pounce. And it spoke in a terrifying voice: *"Your brother is gone, and there is nothing you can do to bring him back! He will never walk this earth again!"*

For all intents and purposes, Nachari was dead, and that which remained now was only a picturesque shell of a life that had once been vital. Just like his twin Shelby, Nachari was forever lost to the grave.

Everything inside of Kagen resisted the voice.

He steeled his determination and stuffed the thoughts back down, forcing the wretched voice back into the shadows where it belonged, because the alternative, to listen and to *hear*, was unthinkable.

Unfathomable.

Inconceivable.

Not. Going. To. Happen.

Shaking it off with steely determination, Kagen jumped to his feet, drew his cell phone from his pocket, and quickly dialed the number of a human female who lived in Dark Moon Vale, the daughter of a loyal family who had served the vampires with honor for years. As the phone rang several times, he tapped his foot impatiently against the floor.

A woman in her mid-twenties answered. "Dr. Silivasi; is this you?"

Caller ID, Kagen thought, and then he rolled his eyes. He hated the title *doctor*—humans had doctors; the sons of Jadon had healers. They spent 400 years at the Romanian University studying infinite theologies and practices in order to become *healers*—anatomy, biology, and pharmacology did not even tap the surface of where they went in their quest to understand the countless nuances of regeneration and wellness—so advanced was their craft. Kagen Silivasi understood the flow of kinetic energy at a quantum-physics level. He could manipulate the subtle interplay of mind, body, and spirit, measure the subtle influences of nature on a vampire's body rhythms. He understood life to be an interconnected system of living energy as well as fundamental elements; and he knew how to influence each one at the most basic, atomic level. And that was on top of mastering the general medicine practiced by humans.

Whoa, Silivasi! he thought, stopping the irrational mental tirade. *Defensive much? Get a grip.* Feeling like an overly temperamental idiot, he forced a smile in order to put some warmth into his voice. "Just call me Kagen, or even Mr. Silivasi, Shelly. Okay?"

The woman sounded nervous and far too apologetic. "Oh, gosh…yes, of course, I'm sorry, Doctor Sil—I mean, Mr. Silivasi. Do you…" She paused as if searching for the exact, right word. "Do you need my…services…this afternoon, Master? I'm…I'm always here, at your service."

Kagen switched the phone to his other hand. *Master?* He decided to let it go. "I'm afraid I do, Shelly. It has been a little over a week since we last—"

"Yes, yes, of course!" She rushed the words, cutting him off in midsentence. "Oh, I'm so sorry—I didn't mean to interrupt you." She groaned, sounding totally exasperated. "Forgive me."

Kagen fought back a chuckle. As far as he knew, no vampire in the house of Jadon had ever punished or harmed a loyal human servant for not genuflecting sufficiently, yet Shelly Winters had always responded to him the same way: like she was afraid he might just put her six feet under—perhaps come steal her in the night, whisk her off to a dark Romania castle, and drain her body of blood—if she didn't pay sufficient homage every time she heard his voice. For the love of Auriga, he had no idea why she still behaved that way after so many years of serving the Vampyr, of living within their generosity and beneath their protection. Surely, she had to know them better by now. Her family had to be one of the few who had been with the house of Jadon for more than five generations.

"Mmm, I see," he purred, deliberately inserting a low, rumbling growl into his already raspy voice. It was awful to toy with her like this, but she had sort of invited it. "I will overlook the indefensible...this time." His voice was deep, hypnotic, and practically dripping with menace. Dracula on steroids.

Shelly didn't respond.

And he could have sworn he heard her heart pounding through the phone, rising to a frenetic rhythm, even as she swallowed reflexively several times in a row. Without actually seeing her, he imagined her delicate hand protectively covering her throat as she shivered.

"Shelly?" he said, his voice now calm, steady, and reassuring.

"Y...Y...Yes, Mr. Silivasi?"

He chuckled softly. "I'm *teasing* you, sweetheart. You don't have anything to apologize for. I'm just trying to loosen you up."

She sighed audibly. "Oh...yeah." And then she tried to laugh along with him—tried but failed. "You got me. You're very funny, Mr. Sil—"

"*Relax*," Kagen drawled. This time, he placed a hint of compulsion in his voice, not enough to override her perceptions, just enough to take her heart rate down a notch. "Breathe, darling."

She breathed heavily into the phone. "Okay...I'll try."

Kagen chastised himself for toying with the poor female: Not everyone understood his unique sense of humor, and Shelly Winters had a good soul.

She was a sweet, innocent young lady with a true heart for service. She practically radiated love for her fellow man— although, when Kagen considered the behavior of most human men toward their women, only the gods knew why—but Shelly was one of those rare types who always saw the best in everyone because she looked for it. There wasn't a fake or pretentious bone in her body, and that was why Kagen had chosen her to nourish Nachari while he was...inanimate. Shelly's soul was a perfect match to Nachari's goodness. And the human female had come to the Dark Moon Vale Clinic on a weekly basis, as requested, ever since the day Nachari had been admitted. While Kagen couldn't speak for Nachari's eternal soul, he could absolutely certify that his brother's physical body was in top condition, and Shelly Winters was a big part of the reason why. "You are ready, then? To feed him today?" he asked.

He was referring to the practice of drinking plenty of fluids to flush her system of impurities, adding vitamins and minerals to richen her blood, and generally avoiding all processed foods in order to raise her overall vibration. While vampires could consume any human blood, ward off diseases, and still find nourishment, this was Nachari they were talking about. And as long as different elements projected different frequencies, nothing but the best would go into his brother.

"Absolutely," she assured him. "I'm always very diligent. Ready at a moment's notice." Although she spoke with confidence—perhaps courtesy was the better word—her hesitance could still be heard.

And Kagen couldn't really blame her.

Under normal circumstance, the vampires in the house of Jadon did not call upon their human allies to provide blood; they hunted like all other predators, choosing their prey in the moment, inoculating them against the pain, and wiping their memories. But Nachari couldn't hunt right now. As it stood, the fresh human blood had to be taken from a vein and fed to the male through a tube. It was awkward at best, intimidating at the least.

But it shouldn't have been scary.

"I really do appreciate this, Shelly," Kagen said sincerely. "I know that the situation is…difficult."

Shelly sighed. "No, not at all." She obviously lied for his benefit. "I am more than happy to do it." At least the last part was true.

"So you can come now?" he asked, changing his manner to a business-like tone.

"Oh, yes, of course," she said. "I can leave in ten minutes…be there in twenty if you'd like, Dr. Sil—Kagen."

He smiled then. Progress had been made after all. "Very well; I will see you when you get here."

"Absolutely," she said. "Is there…um…oh, never mind. I'll see you soon, then."

"What were you going to say?" Kagen asked, curious.

She hesitated. "Nothing, really…just…"

"Just?"

"Just…is there anything else you need? I mean, *anything* at all?"

There was a strange, unfamiliar note in her voice, a peculiar emphasis on the word *anything*, and suddenly, Kagen wasn't at all sure what she was asking…or offering.

Shelly Winters?

Surely not.

"I don't think I know what you mean, Shelly," he said, getting straight to the point.

She sounded mortified. "Oh…oh…um… I don't…I didn't…can I get you anything…from the grocery store or anything?"

The corner of Kagen's mouth turned up in a wry smile. *Well, I'll be damned.* "No, sweetie, thank you." He almost added, *Vampires rarely eat human food—and certainly not a Healer*; but then Shelly already knew this, so he decided to leave well enough alone. "Your generosity toward Nachari is more than enough. I am eternally in your debt, Miss Winters." Perhaps a little more formality between them was in order, after all—although it was a little hard to pull back all the *sweethearts* and *darlings* at this point—what could he say? Kagen had grown up in a different era, and his innocent dallying with the opposite gender was as natural as breathing and walking. "Just drink a glass or two of orange juice before you come, and be prepared to stay for at least an hour afterward."

Although he was very careful with the amount of blood he took in any one feeding, Kagen never took unnecessary chances with human charges. An hour was more than enough time for Shelly to recover from the process, but he would rather be safe than sorry. Especially now, after the loss of Joelle Parker: after Valentine Nistor had schemed to take the daughter of one of

11

their most loyal human families, violate her, and use her body to father his dark twin sons under the guise of pretending to be Marquis Silivasi. The evil one had known the young woman was naive and in love with Marquis, and he had used it to his own hideous advantage, causing her inevitable death in less than forty-eight hours after the deception. The loss had sent shock waves through the house of Jadon and the interconnected human community alike—the privileged few who were exposed to the truth about the vampire species…as well as the dangers that came along with that knowledge—and now, the vampires had to be ever more diligent. The humans needed to know, under no uncertain terms, that their vampire benefactors did not take them for granted or consider their health and safety lightly.

Not ever.

"Okay," Shelly whispered, sounding mildly deflated. "For what it's worth, I also…I'm always here for you as well, to talk…if you want."

Kagen grew deathly silent.

When after thirty seconds or so he still didn't respond, she pushed forward. "I don't know if that's really appropriate or anything. I just know that it must be truly awful, what you're going through, and I'm…I just want you to know I'm always here if you need an objective ear." She swallowed hard, betraying her nervousness. "Even if I'm human, I do care, and I'm just very sorry about—"

"Thank you," Kagen said curtly, cutting her off mid-sentence. "We will see you when you get here, Miss Winters." With that, he hung up the phone and slipped it back into his front pants' pocket. He knew that Shelly meant well—of course, she did. But she was treading on very thin ice. And he would not be crooned to like a child…by a human.

He glanced at the bed—at the peaceful yet lifeless-looking male lying on top of the crisp white sheets—and slipped a careful, protective mask over his emotions. *I'm sorry if that came across as rude*, he thought, *but it just isn't a subject I'm going to discuss with you, Shelly. You…or anyone else.*

Tessa Dawn

He walked to the cabinet, opened the pine door, and began retrieving the apparatus he would need to facilitate the blood transfer in business-like fashion. It wasn't that he was cold or unfeeling. In fact, it was quite the contrary. It was just that, as a human, there was simply no way someone like Shelly Winters could possibly understand…

All of the sleepless days.

All of the second-guessing.

Had he done right by Nachari? Was he prolonging his brother's life or withholding his peace? Could he have changed the course of events by doing something differently, and if so, what? Was there a medical answer to why Nachari remained in a comatose state? And if so, why wasn't Kagen wise enough to figure it out? Should he step aside and let someone more objective assume the wizard's care? Could he ever…possibly…live with the loss of another sibling, knowing that he had given his consent for the action that led to his death?

No, Shelly Winters did not understand.

That vampires were intrinsically connected to the earth, and their emotions brought about immediate changes in the same. That, for the sake of her kind, the rivers needed to continue to flow…without flooding. That the sky needed to remain tranquil…without thundering. That the earth needed to remain solid…without trembling and splitting open beneath their feet.

And it would if Kagen were to ever give voice to his feelings.

It most certainly would.

Kagen glanced down at his hand and the dual rivulets of blood flowing across his skin, realizing that he had unwittingly bitten into it with his fangs. He slowly licked the blood away and closed the twin wounds with his venom before forcing his fangs to retract.

He drew in a deep breath.

Steady. Calm. Focused.

Turning to the male on the bed, he smoothed back Nachari's hair and laid the back of his hand lightly against his cheek. "Shelly Winters is coming to feed you soon, my brother. To help

13

you keep up your strength." He watched for the response he knew wasn't coming, and then he nodded. "You *will* return to us, Nachari, and when you do, I expect you to be in perfect health. Do you hear me?" His voice was as calm and dispassionate as a still pond.

Yet his soul was on fire.

As always, his words were a prayer, beseeching all the gods and goddesses in the heavens…and beyond.

By all that is holy, bring this blessed one back to me.
Please!

two

One week later

After a long, exhausting drive from Denver International Airport, Deanna Dubois arrived in Dark Moon Vale around 4:00 PM, exactly one week after the revelation she'd had about the mysterious man in her drawings. She immediately checked in at the main lodge, retrieved a map of the local area, as well as a set of keys to a small remote cabin she had rented for the week, and headed for her final destination: 116 Forest Hill, Cabin B.

Now, slowing her rented four-wheel drive to a creep, she pulled over to the side of the road and turned the map upside down on the steering wheel in order to visualize the route from an exact point of view. For some reason, the GPS was completely lost; it simply didn't work on this side of the mountain. Thank goodness she'd had the foresight to take the map when it was offered to her.

She placed her finger on a familiar geographical marker and stared out the window.

There.

Right behind that grouping of trees was a steep embankment that should lead down to the Snake Creek River. If she was reading the map correctly, the cabins would be located just on the other side of the creek, after crossing an old stone bridge.

Deanna pulled back onto the roadway and drove slowly over the uneven, rocky ground, relieved when she finally saw the approaching bridge in front of her. She rolled down the window in order to take in the melodious sound of the rushing water as she crept across the stony bridge and breathed in the fresh mountain air. It was truly heavenly. There was nothing like it in New Orleans. She glanced at the map once more to regain her bearings at a fork in the road, and then she wove to the right and

15

drove about 500 yards farther before suddenly coming to a screeching halt.

Her foot slammed against the brake pedal.

She dropped the map and gripped the wheel with two iron fists as she stared dumbfounded out the rearview mirror at an eerily familiar clearing. Her heart thudded in her chest; goose bumps appeared on her arms; and a light wave of nausea swept over her body. Struggling for air, she released the wheel and pressed a taut hand against her stomach.

"*My God,*" she whispered.

Reaching to release the vehicle's locks, she opened her door, shrugged into a lightweight jacket, and bounded out of the SUV, practically sprinting toward the clearing. In the distance, she could just make out the Snake Creek River and a small cluster of guest cabins on the other side, but that no longer held her attention: She was too entranced by the endless miles of forest. The frighteningly familiar setting. The particular coloring, angles, and juxtaposition of the various elements: pine trees, rock outcroppings, skies that were blue today but had once been filled with dark, mottled clouds.

In her drawings.

This was the place.

The haunted clearing where the beautiful man had been sucked under the earth by something—what?—so evil.

She slowed her pace and approached the scene with caution, if not reverence, stunned by the exact likeness to her drawings. As she drew closer and closer to the very spot that had haunted her for months now, something inside of her turned almost electric—it practically hummed with pulsing energy—and she wasn't sure if she could handle all the metaphysical sensations.

Still, she kept on.

Drawn as if by an unseen force to a particular spot on the ground.

Deanna drew in a sharp breath as her eyes swept over the barren earth. It had been cleared away, no longer natural, leaving evidence that something...or someone...had, in fact, been right there. And there was a dark, ominous stain in the center.

She squatted down to touch the dirt. What was this? She immediately backed up with a jolt and stood upright.

It was blood.

Earth that had been soaked—no, practically bathed—in blood.

For reasons beyond her comprehension, she felt like crying.

Screaming.

Falling to her knees and weeping.

What the hell?

There was such an overwhelming sense of grief enveloping her that she staggered where she stood. Unable to bring it under control, she knelt in the dirt and placed the flat of her palms over the bloodstained earth. "What are you?" she whispered, distraught. "*Who* are you?"

She lifted her hands and brushed the bloodstained dirt through her fingers. "And why do I feel like I'm going to die because of you...like I wish I could?"

She wrapped both of her arms tightly around her middle and started to rock back and forth, inexplicable tears streaming down her face. When finally she had shed her last teardrop, she wiped her eyes with the back of a dirty hand and stood. "Come back to me." She mumbled the words nonsensically. "Please...oh, please...come back to me."

Fearing for her sanity, she turned to run to her car but was stopped short by the presence of a skinny, brooding redhead sitting on the hood of her SUV. The woman had parked a pink Corvette behind Deanna's Ford Explorer and was watching her with piercing, angry eyes like those of a tiger. Everything about the otherwise small woman screamed danger.

Just one more thing that made no sense.

Deanna appraised the stranger from head to toe as she raised her chin, held out her keys, and approached with caution. She hadn't grown up in a perfect suburban world, and she knew how to handle herself if necessary. Under ordinary circumstances, she would never fear another female of such small stature, but these weren't ordinary circumstances. And somehow, although she didn't know how she knew, the woman sitting so brazenly on the hood of her truck was no ordinary person.

"Hello," Deanna called pleasantly, figuring it might be best to get on the woman's good side up front.

The girl popped a piece of gum, pushed away from the hood, and took a large, measured stride toward Deanna, kicking off a beautiful pair of spiked black heels as she stepped forward.

Oh shit, this isn't good.

The redhead narrowed her eyes. "Two questions: Who the hell are you? And what the hell were you doing underneath that tree?" She took out her gum and tossed it on the ground. "Speak now, skank, or forever hold your peace."

Kristina Riley-Silivasi watched with suspicion as the human woman rocked back and forth, crying like a ninny, directly over the spot where Nachari had died. The chick felt the earth, touched her adopted brother's blood, and held it close to her heart.

What. The. Heck.

The only ones who knew about what went down in this meadow were the sons of Jadon and, of course, the sons of Jaegar. No one else. And since Kristina knew damn well that this girl wasn't a *destiny* to one of the Jadon vamps—or a convert, since there weren't any converts other than her—she quickly did the math and figured the Dark Ones had sent the woman…

But why?

As the girl approached her car with more confidence than Kristina appreciated, Kristina gave her a once-over. Granted, the chick was very pretty—exotic-looking actually. Strange. Some kind of indecipherable racial mix that definitely worked for her, that was for sure. And she had a lot of confidence with her five-foot-nine or -ten, clearly toned body.

But…oh well.

Kristina was Vampyr now, ever since Marquis had converted her under the unwitting protection of the dark lord Ocard—which was a whole other story—and only because Marquis had mistakenly believed Kristina was his *destiny* at the time. It really wasn't his fault, though; Salvatore Nistor has used a black magic spell to switch Kristina and Ciopori in a ploy to kill Marquis. Luckily, the plan had failed, but not before Marquis had claimed Kristina, converted her, and almost made her…*his*…in every way.

She shook her head, dismissing the thought.

Back to the matter at hand…

The flipped-out female sent by the Dark Ones to do something…to Nachari? Anger swelled in Kristina's breast, and she jumped down from the hood of the car, kicked off her shoes, and strolled right toward her. "Two questions," she said, feeling her anger rise to even greater proportions. "Who the hell are you? And what the hell were you doing underneath that tree?" *Where Nachari died?* She took out her gum and tossed it on the ground, willing her eyes not to turn feral and her fangs to stay put. "Speak now, skank, or forever hold your peace."

The beautiful lady stopped dead in her tracks and took a step back. "Excuse me?" she said, with way too much metal.

"You heard me," Kristina snapped. "I don't believe I stuttered."

The woman smiled then. Actually smiled. "I don't believe I gave you permission to sit on my truck." She strolled confidently forward and hit the *unlock* button on her key fob. "Pardon me," she said, waiting for Kristina to step aside.

Kristina reached out and grabbed the chick by the arm, squeezing just hard enough to let her know she could crush her bones at will if she chose. Placing an implied threat into her voice—something she had just learned recently in Jocelyn and Nathaniel's self-defense class—she shoved her way into the woman's mind. "Tell me what the hell you were up to and who sent you. *Now.*"

The woman yanked her arm free and took a step back, but there was definitely a wash of fear in her eyes. "I...I'm a guest staying at the cabins." She turned around and pointed in the direction of the log cottages.

Kristina scowled. "Show me your room key."

The woman frowned, but she did as she was told. Well, actually, as she was compelled. "Here," she said angrily, pulling one of the unmistakable lodge key-cards out of her pocket. "Satisfied?"

Kristina frowned. *What the hell?* "You're a guest?"

"Yes," the woman huffed, "that's what I said." She squared her shoulders. "I'm Deanna Dubois. I'm here from New Orleans...for the week, but I have to say, if this is how the people around here treat visitors, then don't expect any repeat business from me."

Kristina looked off into the distance toward the clearing. "What were you doing over there—all playing around in the dirt and crying and shit? What the heck was that?"

The lady looked embarrassed now. Unsettled. "I...I honestly don't know. I just felt something really powerful...and terribly sad...and it drew me to that spot. Sorry if it was private property or something. I didn't mean to trespass. I just...I don't know what came over me. That's the truth."

Being as new as she was to the species, Kristina wasn't especially good at vampire tricks, but this was just too important—she had to try. "Look right in my eyes, Deanna."

The woman blinked, and she even frowned; but she did as she was told.

"Now tell me straight up: Are you telling the truth?"

The lady nodded.

"You're actually a guest here, and you just felt something powerful that drew you to that spot? And made you cry like that?"

Deanna nodded her head again, this time more slowly. "Yes." When she reached up to rub her temples as if she were getting a headache, Kristina figured she'd better back off a little.

No point in giving the chick a lobotomy. "Did the Dark Ones send you?"

"Who?" Deanna asked, genuinely confused.

Kristina shook her head. "Nothing...forget it." She looked deep into Deanna's eyes. "Really, *forget it*." She took a step back and waited. When Deanna shook her head back and forth, like she was all of a sudden unaware of where she was or what they were talking about, Kristina swallowed with relief. "It was nice meeting you, Deanna. I hope you enjoy your stay in Dark Moon Vale." *Amazing*, she thought as she slowly backed away. The chick had to be one of those real psychics or something; too bad she didn't read fortunes.

Deanna blinked several more times and nodded. "Yeah, thanks. Nice meeting you, too..." She paused. "I'm sorry; I don't remember your name."

Kristina held out her hand. "Kristina," she said, smiling wide enough to flash her pearly whites. "And that's okay. My memory sucks too most of the time."

Deanna nodded then. "*Kristina*. Great, I'll remember next time." She offered an insecure, confused smile.

"Cool. Take it easy, and enjoy your stay, okay?"

Kristina didn't turn around to watch the woman climb into her SUV. She'd had enough of the Twilight Zone for one day and didn't care to see any more of the chick's confused expression. Besides, she figured if she had done everything right, the lady would forget most of the conversation, take a couple of aspirin for her headache, and be on her merry psychic way.

If not, then she could only hope that Marquis and Nathaniel never got wind of it. They both took the whole business-industry-in-Dark-Moon-Vale thing pretty seriously, and it wasn't like Kristina was anyone's favorite person around there anyway. Well, maybe Braden's—at least since Nachari had been gone and the two of them had ended up saddled with each other—but even the adorable boy couldn't save her if news of this fiasco got back to one of her new brothers. Or worse, Napolean.

She cringed as she climbed into her Corvette and put the key in the ignition: Better to keep the whole incident to herself for now. After all, who really needed to know about a strange, clairvoyant lady from New Orleans who ran around in the trees, sensing psychic energy?

No one.

That's who.

three

The Valley of Death and Shadows

Nachari Silivasi came awake with a violent shudder and a horrible shout of agony as his bruised and bloodied body was dropped into a cold saltwater bath to awaken him. His arms and legs were quickly chained to the four iron posts that encased the porcelain before he could react or orient himself.

They had done it one hundred times before, so he should have been used to it by now; yet every time it happened, he still reacted with the same shock, disorientation, and agony. He shivered, trying to regulate his body temperature. That was always first. He couldn't remain alert if he was delirious with cold. And then he gasped for breath, trying to force his lungs to work through the pain—inhale and exhale in regular, forced increments—so he could tune in to his surroundings and see who was in the room.

Who the Dark Lord Ademordna had chosen to share him with today...as a meal.

What day was it, by the way, he wondered. It seemed like a Saturday, but it could have been Monday...or maybe Wednesday...

Sunday?

Oh hell...who knew?

And who cared.

His eyes began to focus—there was a buxom blonde in a tight leather suit standing in front of him—and he grimaced. *Her again. Noiro.* The twin, sister-energy of the Celestial god Orion, a shadow demoness who lived in the Abyss.

She loved to watch him being tortured; and more and more often, Ademordna seemed to enjoy inviting her to the festivities. But this was unusual. Feeding was usually proffered to

23

Ademordna's minions, his loyal, pathetic servants, whom Ademordna abused as often as he pleased. One pleasure was the same as the other down here, Nachari figured.

"You're alone today?" Nachari grit out through chattering teeth. He may as well find out what was coming next—not that it made a lot of difference in the end—but sometimes being prepared helped...a little. "And blond."

Noiro sidled up to the bathtub in a seductive, devilish walk. "Mmm, do you like it, my sweet wizard?" she purred like a cat.

"Not especially," he muttered.

She jumped back, indignant, all at once morphing her shape into a slender redhead. A cautious smile curved her lips. "Better, my lovely?"

Nachari braced himself against the salt seeping into his wounds and counted backward from ten to one just to give himself something to concentrate on. "Whatever."

"Pooh!" she huffed like a spoiled human rather than a powerful demon. "I do so want you to play with me, Nachari. I don't know why you won't cooperate."

He watched her through the corner of his eye and let his head loll back against the tallest point of the claw-foot tub—fairly appropriate for demons, he thought—refusing to respond.

She stooped to sit on the edge, reached into the bath, and splashed a small trickle of water on his face. When he looked at her straight on, she smiled. "That's better." She moaned. "By all the dark lords, you are the most beautiful creature ever created." She ran the tips of her fingers over his lips, his cheekbones, and then she fingered his hair. "My brother, Orion, was so infatuated with your twin, and now I can see why. What was his name? Shelby was it?"

"Still is," Nachari growled.

"Yes, yes...whatever." She waved her hand in dismissal. "I have very little interest in what happens in the Valley of Spirit and Light." She leaned forward then, placing her lips inches away from his so that the heat of her breath scalded his skin. "But here, among our own, I find that I understand my brother's…devotion…more and more each day. To own and control one such as you…oh…lords…I would give my soul…if I had one." She shrugged, and then she bent to kiss him, leaving his lips cracked and bloodied from the acidic property of her saliva. "How was that, my soon-to-be lover?"

Nachari coughed and spit into the tub, expelling whatever Noiro had left in his mouth. "Eat shit and die," he snarled, and then he chuckled. "Oh yeah, I guess I already did both…just in reverse order."

"Excuse me?" Noiro thundered.

"I died, came here, and just ate—"

"How dare you!" Noiro flew backward from the tub like a crazed, winged creature, her face transforming into a hideous, serpent-looking monstrosity. Her nostrils flared wide and shot fire; her forked tongue snaked in and out of her mouth in quick succession, and her beady eyes narrowed even further into tiny yellow slits. "Don't test me, boy. Never forget, I can have your testacles for breakfast if I choose!" She slowly approached the tub on legs that were suddenly balanced on hooves.

"Do your best," Nachari whispered, either unwilling or unable to relinquish the only control he had left in this damnable inferno: his dignity and his free will.

He would not grovel.

He would not kowtow.

And he would not give respect to a demon. No matter the cost.

Noiro licked her thin, reedy lips and tsk-tsked him with her tongue. "You are lucky, my naughty wizard, that you are so *damn* beautiful. If I didn't need your seed to reproduce a dark lord of my own someday, I would rip your jewels from your body and add them to my chicken soup…as dumplings." She cackled, a shrill, high-pitched sound. "As it stands, I will just have to settle for nibbling on your ears." She snapped her teeth at him, displaying a full set of jagged, razor-sharp fangs, each one more hideous than the last.

Nachari didn't blink…or wince…even though he knew what

Noiro meant by *nibble on your ears.*

She would lick his skin with her acidic tongue until it began to melt away from the bone. She would wrench out large patches of his thick, wavy hair for her demented pleasure, and then she would eat away at his flesh until he no longer had any ears, sticking her snake-like tongue into the holes left behind to burn the inside of his skull—all the while, she would wait for everything to grow back so she could do it again.

If and when she finally grew tired of the game, she would call Ademordna, who would come and do his worst—and it was always far, far worse—before removing Nachari to the throne room to let the courtyard *play with him* for the rest of the evening.

If only he could die.

Nachari's focused gaze narrowed on Noiro's steps as she, once again, drew closer and closer to the tub. "Tell me you love me," she whispered, cocking her head to the side like an unaware animal. "Tell me you love me, and I'll spare you…at least one round of torture."

Nachari met her steely gaze and held it with contempt, saying nothing.

"Very well," she snarled.

And then she wrenched his head back by the hair and bit down on his throat.

Salvatore Nistor knocked twice before entering the stuffy, formal office, with its high stone walls and thick, expensive floor-rugs. He sat down in the large leather armchair opposite Oskar Vadovsky's desk, placed his legs on the matching leather ottoman before him, and crossed them at the ankle.

Oskar Vadovsky stared pointedly at Salvatore's legs, leaned forward to rest his elbows on the mahogany desk, and frowned.

"Excuse me, High Council," Salvatore said in as pleasant a voice as he could muster. "Sometimes I forget myself." *What the hell is an ottoman for then?* he snarled inwardly. He removed his feet and politely planted them on the floor. "Better?"

"Thank you," Oskar said gruffly.

Salvatore inclined his head. "Of course, my liege."

"Now then…" Oskar cracked his knuckles slowly before folding his hands back together. "I am trying…*very hard*…to remain objective and calm about the outcome of your latest scheme. Especially considering the price."

Salvatore nodded. *Why don't you try going after Napolean—or any of the other sons of Jadon— yourself then, you smug, clueless bastard?* "I understand, Oskar," he said, "but with all due respect, the matter was brought up before the entire council; and, if you recall, we all agreed to go forward with the plan. Furthermore, a colony-wide vote was taken on the proposal to sacrifice a firstborn son from our own ranks in order to gain the demon's favor. The measure passed, and the plan came very close to working: The human pawn was able to implant the possession worm in Napolean, and Ademordna did manage to get to the king's *destiny*. Who knew that the sons of Jadon would be willing to flatline their king in order to release the spirit inhabiting his body—which just happened to be the demon lord we beseeched? Or that Nachari Silivasi would be willing to give his own life in order to follow the king in death? That the arrogant young wizard would actually confront Ademordna in the netherworld and keep him from repossessing Napolean's body when the sons of Jadon brought him back to life?" He stared at the chief of council incredulously. "Honestly, was I to foresee all those events?"

Oskar waved his hand. "Of course not, but our loss was…so great."

Salvatore knew that Oskar was referring to Victor Dirga and Rezak Brodske, the young, vital males who were sacrificed right there in the colony in order to win Ademordna's favor. Never before had the house of Jaegar been willing to go that far, to slaughter one of their own in order to appease the dark lords, just to oppose the house of Jadon; but it had been Napolean's demise they were seeking, after all. And the opportunity, however slight, was too good, and too rare, to pass up.

"It's not as if all was lost," Salvatore said.

"How so?" Oskar asked, barely concealing his irritation.

Salvatore chose his words carefully. "It is true, Napolean's possession by the dark lord Ademordna cost us the precious blood of our favored brothers in sacrifice, a loss that will reverberate through these halls for decades to come. And in the end, Napolean did not die, nor did his *destiny*. But one thing—"

"From what I am told, Napolean Mondragon is healthy, happy, and more powerful than ever. And why shouldn't he be? He has a new mate and a son—the long-awaited heir to his throne and our future archenemy." Oskar shook his head with disgust.

Salvatore suppressed a snarl and struggled to keep his fangs from extending. "May I continue?"

Oskar nearly rolled his eyes. "Very well…"

"Thank you," Salvatore said, his words clipped. "Now then, as I was saying, we may not have destroyed the king, but Nachari Silivasi is another matter altogether."

Oskar looked off into the distance. "Go on."

Salvatore leaned forward with increased interest. "It has been over three months now, and the Master Wizard has yet to return to his people. I hear his brothers are preserving his body like some ancient mummy, ever hoping and praying for the fool's return." He licked his lips with obvious pleasure. "This, at least for me, is incredibly rewarding."

Oskar pursed his lips together and tipped his head from side to side in consideration until, at last, a slow, maniacal smile curved the corners of his mouth. "The wizard who dared to take the Ancient Book of Black Magic; yes, I would have to agree, Salvatore." His harsh features relaxed a bit then. "What do you think became of the arrogant lad?"

Salvatore shrugged. "I don't know. My cube shows me nothing, but my guess is that he found the Dark Lord Ademordna after all. And let's just say his wizardry was no match against the demon lord's powers." He shivered, remembering the short time he had spent in the demon's presence after conjuring him from the spirit world. There was nothing he had ever seen or experienced, in all of his infinite years on the earth or indulging in black magic, that came close to that breadth of power. Or that depth of darkness. He felt lucky to have escaped with his life.

Oskar nodded his head. "Let us hope you are right, sorcerer. At any rate, I agree: Nachari Silivasi is a significant loss to the sons of Jadon. Without him, I do not believe there is another practitioner of magic who can directly challenge your power."

Salvatore raised an eyebrow in surprise. "Excuse me, councilman, but did you just give me a compliment?"

Clearly unable to concede even the smallest commendation to Salvatore, Oskar changed the subject. "So what now?" He made a great show of straightening his collar and sat back in his chair. "What do you foresee as our next move?"

Salvatore shifted in his own chair, sinking deep into the dark leather. He placed his left hand in his lap across his knee, while tapping on the arm of the chair with his right. "What I have in mind," he droned, "is not so much large-scale revenge as humiliation...coupled with insult."

Oskar smiled and raised his eyebrows in anticipation. "Go on."

"I say we hit them where it counts," Salvatore began, "something bold, arrogant, and in the full light of day, so to speak. Something like Valentine did when he took Dahlia and caused Shelby's death—when he pretended to be Marquis to strike out at the warrior's human servant, Joelle. The more I think about my brother's antics, the more brilliant they seem. At least Valentine never came away empty-handed. And neither will we—not anymore." He flicked a piece of lint from the arm of the chair and sat up straight. "You see, Valentine struck when and where they were least expecting it; he slithered right in through the cracks in the walls, exploited those relationships that either didn't mean as much or weren't as well protected. Right now, the most vulnerable member of the Silivasi family is the idiot redheaded girl Kristina something-or-other; I believe, Riley. The girl is an accident waiting to happen: vulnerable, impressionable, and foolish as the day is long. A prime target, indeed. I say we go directly after the girl. Use her, then destroy her. Send another message to the Silivasis. Let them know that we can come in anytime…anywhere…and pluck anyone we wish from their ranks."

Oskar licked his lips, clearly contemplating Salvatore's words. After a short time had passed, he cleared his throat. "You would have the girl impregnated by one of our rank, a dark son of Jaegar, in order to cause her death in forty-eight hours? Like Valentine did with Dahlia and Joelle?"

Salvatore rotated his hand in a *sort of* gesture: Oskar was close, but there was more to his plan than that. "Yes, Oskar. Once pregnant, the girl will face a slow, tortuous, imminent death. And, of course, we both know her brothers will never allow her to suffer like that, so they will put her down like the dog she is." He chuckled at the thought of it. "They will euthanize the worthless female to spare her the slow, unrelenting agony. In the meantime, we get as much information out of her as possible…kill two birds with one stone. She's the perfect target."

Oskar's eyes lit with possibility. "I would agree—she is certainly malleable. So how, then, do you intend to get to her? Do you really think her brothers will allow a Dark One—any Dark One—to come within fifty feet of her? Even she cannot be that gullible."

Salvatore sneered then. "No, of course not, but Nachari Silivasi is not the only practitioner of Magick who can hold a cloaking spell for another being. He was able to cloak Marquis in the persona of Joelle Parker in order to finally capture…and kill…Valentine; well, I would be happy to return the favor. I will cloak one of our most persuasive, seductive, and heartless soldiers in the body of one of their most trusted sentinels. Kristina will swoon at the attention; it will never cross her mind that it's a ruse—that the male is not who he appears to be. Trust me."

Oskar raised his eyebrows and shrugged. He slapped his hand against the desktop like a gavel as if to say, *Very well then. It's done.* "For the record," he quipped, "who is the male that will have this honor?"

Salvatore laughed, more than just a little pleased with his choice. "I intend to use Saber Alexiares," he said with authority.

Oskar tapped his forefinger against his lips several times in consideration. "The male who was taken and tortured by the Lycans? The one Nathaniel's woman saved from the guillotine?" He rubbed his chin. "Hmm. Why him?"

Salvatore crossed his arms in front of his chest confidently. "He is ruthless, without conscience, and easily bored. Plus, he is one of the few males who is rumored to seduce his female prey before he drains them. To waste days, if not weeks, toying with them like a cat with a mouse before he kills them. I think he might enjoy the game."

Oskar stood up, cleared his side of the desk, took a step toward Salvatore, and ushered him toward the door. "Very well then. Have a full plan ready to present to the council this evening, and we will go forward."

Salvatore nodded like he was pleasantly surprised. *Of course they would go forward.* Without him, the rest of them could hardly find their own rear ends. "I will have all the information necessary, and if luck is on our side, I will even bring Saber Alexiares with me to the meeting as an honored guest."

Oskar nodded, satisfied. He strolled to the office door, opened it, and waited while Salvatore rose from his chair. Before Salvatore could pass through the threshold, Oskar spoke in a barely audible tone. "Sorcerer?" His eyes were as keen as they were malevolent.

"Oskar?"

"I like this plan…very much." He nodded his head—once. "In fact, I look forward to watching the games unfold."

Salvatore chuckled in spite of himself. "So, do I, Vadovsky.

So do I."

four

Three days after she arrived in Dark Moon Vale, Deanna Dubois stared at the front door of the remote medical clinic, somewhat astonished that the place actually existed. It seemed more than a little odd that an unlisted medical facility would be built into the face of a canyon at the end of a dirt road, beyond a narrow bridge that crossed a forceful stream of water, or that the entrance would be placed at the top of a vertical incline following a steep series of stone steps. Glancing around, she couldn't help but feel that the proprietor wanted to keep people away—especially people who were sick or injured. Go figure.

Just the same, the clinic was real.

And the surroundings were as cryptic as they were in her drawings.

Deanna coated her lips with a soft layer of lip balm to protect the sensitive skin against the unusually dry climate and took a deep breath in an attempt to steady her nerves. Figuring *there's no time like the present*, she made a fist and knocked vigorously on the door.

An attractive young woman with skinny arms and legs answered—she appeared to sniff the air, and then she frowned.

Really? Deanna thought. Did this woman just *sniff* the air? *Okay…* "Hi." Deanna smiled broadly. "I'm Darcy Dubois. I'm a certified nurse practitioner who just moved to the area—Silverton Creek to be exact—and I was wondering if you might be hiring."

The woman looked at Deanna like she had egg on her face. "No," she said brusquely. "We never hire from the outside." Her stare went from disapproving to suspicious, and Deanna had to gather all the courage she had not to just turn around and run. What was it with the women in this town, anyway? They were odd, to say the least. Deanna cleared her throat. "I understand, but would you mind if I just filled out an application and left it with the administrator? It would go a long way to convincing my unemployment counselor that I really am out here trying to find a job. I promise I won't take much of your time." Just then, a cool breeze swept over Deanna, and she shuddered.

What in the world?

"Listen here, lady," the woman said, with more than a little disdain in her voice, "I don't know what kind of game you're playing, but you are knocking on all the wrong doors. Trust me. I suggest you turn around and go somewhere else…while you can."

Whoa, Deanna thought. *Now that was just downright…Texas Chainsaw Massacre;* but then she thought about the beautiful man in her drawings, just how far she had come to find him, and the improbable fact that the Dark Moon Vale Clinic was real. No, she could not turn back now. She was too close to…something. She could just feel it.

She reached into her back pocket, pulled out a thin gray wallet, and, using only one hand, flipped it open with a flick of her wrist. "You're right, ma'am. I'm sorry. My real name is Deanna Dubois, and I'm with the Department of Health and Human Services. There have been some recent complaints about this establishment, and I'm afraid I need to take a look around and speak with your director."

The woman smiled and drew in a slow, yawning breath. Her eyes narrowed and her voice dropped to a silky smooth lilt. "You've had complaints? From whom?"

"Patients, ma'am."

The lady's mouth turned up in a wry, wicked smile. "Patients? Patients who were served at *this* clinic?"

"Yes," Deanna said, wondering why that seemed so implausible. She tried to sound confident. "If you could just—"

The lady waved a leisurely hand in dismissal and sneered. "Oh, well then, by all means; let me go get the owner for you. I think he will be *very* interested to hear of this. Please, come in." She stepped back from the door, and for some bizarre reason, it suddenly felt like Deanna was being asked to enter Dracula's castle. Like she was stepping through a portal from which there was no return.

Deanna hugged her chest and shivered. Careful to keep her attaché case in front of her, she ran her palms up and down her arms to generate heat against the sudden chill. Man, she had to be stone-raving mad to persist with this, but it was a little too late to turn back now.

As the woman slowly walked away—smiling eerily like a cat who had just consumed a naïve canary—Deanna looked around the room. The clinic was definitely five-star: It was tiled with expensive slate tiles, decorated with custom-made furnishings, and outfitted with everything from an unobtrusive flat-screen TV, mounted inconspicuously on the lobby wall, to a classy beverage station inside the waiting room. Fashioned art-niches were spaced out evenly and filled with unique, rustic sculptures or framed scenic photography, each reflecting the local topography; and the entire space gave off a sort of peaceful, Tibetan monastery vibe. That is, if one could overlook the beautiful yet cold bride-of-Dracula nurse who had so recently answered the door.

A warm breeze wafted down the hall—the kind that masks a gentle summer's day right before it unleashes a horrific storm that turns into a violent tornado—and Deanna spun around, feeling suddenly tense. Strolling directly toward her, with a poised and commanding gait that almost seemed unnatural, was the most exquisitely handsome, yet unquestioningly dangerous, man she had ever seen—perhaps with the exception of the man in her drawings.

Deanna's breath caught in her throat as the man quickly closed the distance between them, still moving with a sleek confidence that bordered on predatory. Animalistic. His enchanting brown eyes were backlit with specks of silver that gleamed like distant stars in a midnight sky, and his rich, golden-brown hair outlined his strong masculine face like an antique picture frame, both elegant and timeless. His narrow hips supported a strong, muscular frame that practically screamed power—and dominance—even as it exuded sensuality. The entire picture was one of a man clearly accustomed to absolute control.

Deanna stepped back.

This wasn't right.

This man wasn't…normal.

Suddenly, she felt as if she were in grave danger.

"Ms. Dubois." His voice was like silken fire, burning its way through her ears. "I understand you are here to take a look around my clinic."

Deanna's heart skipped a beat.

The door.

The front door.

It was five…maybe six…feet away. *Just get to the door, open it, and run.*

Nothing else mattered.

"Um…I'm sorry to have bothered you," Deanna murmured quickly. "I…I've changed my mind. Just…please…forget I was ever here." She tried to take several calm steps backward, but the palpable sense of danger overwhelmed her, and she couldn't maintain the ruse.

She turned around and ran.

"Stop." His voice was steady and controlled, yet it echoed through the hall like a distant crack of thunder. And it was as if her body simply slammed into a brick wall.

Deanna's legs froze beneath her. Her feet stuck to the tile as if suddenly anchored in concrete, and her arms fell to her side, sending the attaché case flying to the floor, where her drawings spilled out in a random, desperate pile.

"You are neither looking for a job nor inspecting my clinic," the terrifying man growled. He caught up to her then, grasped her by the right shoulder, spun her around, and stared into her eyes. "Who are you?"

His last three words hit her with such force that, if she didn't know better, she would have sworn he had just struck her between the eyes with a pick-axe. She reached up to grab her throbbing forehead. "Stop!" she yelled, intuitively knowing he was somehow causing the pain. "Please, stop. I'm sorry I lied. I'll go."

He smiled a cruel, wolfish grin. "You'll stay right where you are, and you will do whatever I tell you." He absently glanced down at several of the drawings that had spilled onto the floor, and then slowly, frighteningly, tilted his head to the side. His eyes dimmed almost imperceptibly, and then he froze.

Deanna waited in suspended horror, unable to think or speak, just watching him…watching the drawings.

"What are these?" he whispered.

Deanna trembled with fear. "Nothing." She swallowed hard. "They're just…drawings." Looking up into his eerily placid face, she followed the movement of his eyes as he took a closer look at the sketches, one by one, examining the morbid details. Blinking several times, he regarded her coolly, and then he finally squatted down to pick up a particularly disturbing sketch—the one of the beautiful man being sucked into the ground by a multitude of demon hands.

He lifted it and stared fixedly without appearing to breathe.

When at last he drew in air, he turned the sketch this way and that, considering every detail and nuance, and then he slowly licked his lips, not unlike a lion about to devour its prey. Standing back up, he thrust the drawing out in front of him, where she could clearly see it, too. Pitching his voice low and lethal, he whispered. "What's your real name?"

"Deanna Dubois *is* my real name," she whispered.

"Did you draw these?"

"Yes."

He looked momentarily perplexed as he studied her face. "Are you human?"

She hesitated. What kind of question was that?

"Are you human?" he repeated.

She nodded. "Yes…of course."

"Who sent you?"

37

She shook her head and shrugged. "I don't understand."

He rolled the drawing up in his hand and, with a lightning quick flick of his wrist, smacked her sharply against the forehead with the curled paper. "Listen very carefully, little lady. I am not playing games with you, so do *not* make me repeat myself: *Who sent you?*"

Deanna cringed. Although she had never been the type of person to become easily rattled, let alone faint of heart, she suddenly felt the overwhelming urge to pass out. "No one...sent me. I swear. I came on my own."

"Why?" he asked, his piercing eyes practically carving holes in her soul with their intensity.

She cleared her throat and bit back tears. "I don't know." He frowned, and she knew he was about to lose his patience. "I don't know!" she repeated. "I swear...*I don't know.*"

He paused, slowly unrolled the drawing, and then pointed to the tortured figure in the center. "Who is this man to you?"

Afraid of something she couldn't name, Deanna tried to bite a hole in her tongue. For reasons beyond her comprehension, she desperately feared the man's *question*. It was as if there was something hidden in the answer, something intrinsically life-changing and primal, and whatever it was, it posed a much greater threat to Deanna than the dangerous man in front of her. As she struggled inwardly to repel whatever purpose had brought her to this point in her life...to this place...to this terrifying man, she felt as if she wrestled with fate.

Fought with the truth.

Resisted an inevitable collision in time where all that had come before would be forever separated by this one defining moment.

Yet, in it all, she remained utterly powerless to do anything but obey her inquisitor's demand: to answer the question. "He's...he's...someone," she whispered the words, trying to find the least offensive way to say it, "who's being tortured...in hell."

The man jolted in surprise, and his face drew taut with anger.

"What did you just say?" His voice was nearly inhuman with loathing.

Deanna winced, fully expecting him to strike her at any moment. She drew in a deep breath for courage and slowly repeated the words. "He's a man who's being tortured in hell."

He nodded.

Simply nodded.

And then he dropped the drawing, snatched her by the arm, and dragged her down the hallway with dizzying speed.

Deanna flailed her free arm and shuffled her feet, trying to regain her bearings. They were moving so quickly…too quickly. Her surroundings whizzed by like a passing blur, and the breakfast she had eaten earlier threatened to come back up. As the vertigo promised to engulf her, she caught hold of the man's shirt, grasped it with a tightly clenched fist, and struggled to maintain her equilibrium. "Stop!" she cried out, not sure if she was speaking in her mind or out loud.

Either he didn't hear her—or he didn't care.

When at last they stopped, it was in front of an exam-room door. The man let go of her, turned the knob, and thrust her inside the room, forcefully. "Enough of these games," he bit out. "Tell me who he is to you. And what is the meaning of those drawings?"

Deanna struggled to focus. She needed to catch her balance, regulate her breathing, and make the room stop spinning—and quickly—before she provoked the angry man any further. Holding both arms out to the side, she stared at a fixed point on the wall until she was at last certain that the ground was securely beneath her. Slowly…carefully…she began to turn her head and look around the room, blinking repeatedly as the contents slowly came into focus.

Now then: What was it he had asked her to do?

Tell me who he is to you. And what is the meaning of those drawings?

Deanna continued to look around the room, scanning the contents for any meaningful clues that might help her give the man what he wanted. She desperately wanted to answer his questions honestly, but she truly didn't know how. Her eyes swept across a sterile countertop filled with miscellaneous medical supplies; they took in a wooden frame surrounding an open window, and then, they finally shifted to a slightly raised hospital bed…and a strikingly handsome man lying lifeless between two crisp white sheets.

Air shot through Deanna's diaphragm like water escaping a swirling geyser, and a cry of inexplicable anguish escaped her throat. "Noooo!" Reaching up to cup her face in her hands, she stared wide-eyed and horrified at the ungodly handsome man sleeping in the bed.

It was him.

The man from her drawings!

And he was *real.*

Tall, muscular, surreal…perfect.

She had found him.

Tears began to pour out of her eyes in rivers of anguish she could barely comprehend or contain. "No, no, no…" she whispered again and again, all at once gasping for air. "Oh God, no!" She rushed toward the bed. She needed to take his hand. Touch his face. Feel his flawless, smooth skin. She needed to know he was alive. "Is he okay?" she asked, turning to glare at the cruel doctor even as she made her way to the mysterious man's bedside.

The doctor moved so quickly she never saw him stir.

"That's far enough," he cautioned, holding his arm out as a barrier between Deanna and the unresponsive man in the bed. "Don't touch him."

She stopped short. "But…" She hesitated, and then she shook her head to clear away the cobwebs, feeling unbelievably disjointed, almost as if she were no longer in control of her thoughts and emotions. "Please…I just need to know that he's alive."

The doctor continued to use his arm as a barricade, all the while pushing Deanna gently away from the bed. He looked almost as confused as Deanna felt. "Who are you?" He spoke softly now. "How do you know my brother?"

Deanna blinked rapidly. "Your brother?" She looked back and forth between the two men several times in quick succession. Of course they were brothers. The resemblance was so obvious now. And then, like the sudden gush of water breaking through a dam, the words began to spill out of her mouth as if of their own accord. "I see him in my mind...always." She turned to face the doctor, gesturing furiously with her hands. "I have for months now...day and night...those pictures...my drawings..." The tears fell unbidden. "They haunt me like ghosts, and I don't even know what they are...where they're coming from...why I'm drawing them." She rubbed her hands briskly up and down her arms to keep her chilled blood flowing. "I didn't mean to lie to you, but I had to come here. I saw this place—this clinic—I guess in my imagination because I drew it." She took a deep breath. "God, I know I sound crazy. Trust me, I do, but I can't help it." She sagged from the weight of her words. "I can't eat. I can't sleep. I can't think. I feel like I'm dying...with him."

She stumbled back, and the doctor caught her by the arm before she could lose her balance. Any residual anger seemed to drain from his face like water through a sieve; and then, to her immense surprise, he pulled her gently into his arms and held her against his chest. "Shh," he whispered, as if crooning to a child. "It's okay. I believe you. *It's okay.*" He ran one gentle hand through her hair and slowly rubbed circles on her back. "We're going to figure this out, Deanna, all right? It's going to be okay."

Both stunned by his words and relieved to have finally spoken the truth, Deanna slowly nodded her head—someone had heard her bizarre story, and someone believed her—no, not just someone: *his* brother. Pulling away from the doctor's arms, she looked into his haunting brown eyes, and for the first time, she recognized the true reflection of compassion. While his confusion persisted, there was no longer any anger etched into his brow. *Thank God.*

"Do you...do you understand any of this?" she ventured

cautiously. "Do you know what's happening to me?" She turned to regard the mysterious man in the bed. "Can you tell me what happened to...to your brother?"

The doctor nodded and slowly exhaled as if gathering his own courage. "His name is Nachari." He spoke matter-of-factly.

"Nachari." Deanna whispered the word with reverence. She tried it out on her tongue again: "*Nachari*." She implanted it in her heart and buried it in her soul...*his name was Nachari*. "And what's yours?" she asked tentatively, half expecting him to refuse to answer.

"Kagen," he replied.

He was still wary. Perhaps even distrustful—maybe even dangerous—but there was something else there in those keen, predatory eyes now. Something that resembled hesitance mixed with...hope.

He wouldn't hurt her.

Not now.

Not yet.

Not until he had the answers to his unspoken questions.

Deanna sighed, trying to slow her heart rate down. "What now?" she asked, knowing that however things proceeded, the brother—Kagen—would be in charge.

Kagen gestured toward the counter full of medical supplies. "First...before we do anything...I need to draw some of your blood."

"My blood?" she asked, immediately concerned. "Why? What are you looking for?" Was mental illness detectable through a blood test? Was he going to drug her? Maybe even kill her after all? What in the hell was—

"Deanna, you will sleep for a time, while I run some tests, try to figure some things out."

"Sleep?" Deanna echoed. "I don't think—" He caught her just as she staggered forward, her head lolling to the side. "What did you do?" she whispered.

"Shh," he responded. "You will sleep without dreams, and you will not awaken until I call your name."

"But what…what…" Her words trailed off as the entire world began to fade into various shades of gray.

"Don't be afraid," he answered as if from a great distance. "I'm going to test your blood for traces of Celestial DNA."

And then the entire world went black.

five

Kagen Silivasi laid Deanna Dubois down ever so gently on a clean hospital bed in the empty room next to Nachari's. As he carefully unwrapped a plastic hub, a hypodermic needle, and a vacuum tube from a blood draw kit, he called out telepathically to his eldest brother Marquis and his twin Nathaniel: *Brothers...are you there?*

Marquis responded in less than thirty seconds. *What is it, Healer? Is something wrong with Nachari?*

I'm here, brother, Nathaniel chimed in, his psychic voice appropriately concerned.

Kagen sighed, searching for the right words to convey all that he needed to tell them, hoping to bring them up to speed succinctly and with minimal drama. *Nachari is fine...there has been no change in his physical health. However, something rather...unusual...has come up.*

Unusual? How so? Nathaniel asked.

Marquis remained silent, listening attentively, assessing with a keen ear as always.

Kagen sat down beside the hospital bed, rolled up Deanna's sleeve, and applied an alcohol wipe to her inner arm, just above her brachial artery. *I'm not sure exactly how to say this, but a human woman came to the clinic today looking for Nachari.*

Does she belong to one of the human families that serve the Vampyr? Nathaniel asked. *Perhaps she just wanted to visit—*

No, brother, Kagen interrupted. *She came to the clinic pretending to be a CNA looking for a job: She had no idea what we were or what the clinic was all about. When Katia tried to scare her away—rather forcefully, I might add—she changed course and pretended to be a government agent following up on patient complaints about the clinic. At that point, Katia came to get me.*

Nathaniel whistled low beneath his breath. *Humans,* he said absently.

Go on, Marquis barked, a hint of impatience in his voice.

Kagen inserted the hypodermic needle cleanly into Deanna's vein, added the vacuum tube to the end, and began to draw a vial of blood. *Needless to say, I knew something was up. And actually, so did the human—the moment she saw me. For whatever reason, my presence spooked her, and she decided to take off running. That's when she dropped a case full of drawings on the floor. They were pencil and charcoal sketches of Nachari, depicting him quite accurately on that...horrible day in the meadow.*

What did you say? Marquis asked, grunting his concern. The Ancient Master Warrior's hearing was both heightened and flawless, so Kagen knew he had heard him clearly the first time.

I said the woman had a series of drawings portraying Nachari in the meadow the day he followed Napolean to the Spirit World. She also had some other pictures of him—scenes I haven't really had a chance to look at yet—not sure if I want to.

What kind of scenes? Nathaniel asked. His voice was laced with dismay.

Kagen shook his head as he rose from the chair and plopped the vial in a sterile plastic bag. He placed a small cotton ball over the needle-prick and applied pressure; then, he covered the wound with a Band-Aid and left Deanna in the room to sleep while he headed for the lab to analyze the blood. *The drawing I saw was of the ground opening up and swallowing our brother; the woman depicted several demonic hands reaching up to grab him.* He didn't want to repeat what Deanna had said to him, but there was no point in mincing words—his brothers needed to know the full scope of what was happening. *When I asked her about it, she said Nachari was a man who was being 'tortured in hell.'*

A low, feral growl rumbled in Marquis's throat, even as Nathaniel inadvertently hissed.

What the hell was that supposed to mean? Nathaniel asked.

Who is she? What is she? Marquis demanded.

Kagen sighed. *She's human, rest assured.* By way of explanation, he added, *My immediate concern was that she had been sent by the Dark*

Ones—perhaps she was being used as a minion…or worse: Perhaps she was a tool for some sort of Black Magick, another possession spell or gods-know-what, sent here to mess with our heads…or get to Nachari.

And how do you know that's not the case, brother? Nathaniel asked.

Because I dove very deeply into her mind, Kagen answered emphatically.

As a vampire, the ability to dissect a human's brain, to discern the truth of their actions and words, was an inherent ability; however, it often caused pain or distress for the human and was strongly frowned upon by Law as a breach of free will. Unless it was absolutely necessary, the sons of Jadon tried very hard to respect a human's right to privacy. However, the good of the people always came first, and as a Master Healer, Kagen had been trained to move more swiftly and deeply than most, leaving very little trace of the invasion as he entered. Had any other vampire scrutinized Deanna's mind as deeply as Kagen had in those first critical moments, she may have passed out—or even suffered an aneurism. But as it stood, a piercing headache was all he had left in his wake.

The moment I suspected she was here to harm Nachari, I took her memories.

And? Marquis asked.

And, toward the end, she was telling the truth. She is a human female who has been drawing these strange illustrations for months now. She's confused. She's terrified. And frankly, she thinks she's going mad because the images won't stop haunting her. She came to Dark Moon Vale to try and find answers, and her search led her to the clinic. He paused, remembering Deanna's reaction to the sight of Nachari lying in the hospital bed, connected to so many monitors. *And, you should have seen her reaction when I took her into Nachari's room. She was…devastated.*

What do you mean? Nathaniel asked.

She recognized him…from her drawings…the images in her mind. And she was absolutely grief-stricken by his condition. There was nothing fake about it. Her emotions were far too real…incredibly raw.

Where is she now? Marquis asked.

BLOOD SHADOWS

She's sleeping in exam room one.

Under compulsion? Marquis asked.

Of course, Kagen answered.

Nathaniel sighed. *So what do you make of it?*

The truth? Kagen asked.

No, lie to us, Marquis snorted, his impatience finally getting the best of him.

Kagen let it slide. They were all accustomed to Marquis's *special* personality, and they all knew that underneath the harsh, brusque exterior was an endless well of hyper-protectiveness. And love. *I think this woman is deeply connected to our brother,* Kagen said. *And I haven't looked at all of her drawings yet, but I think she may know more about what is happening to him—why and how his spirit is stuck—than the rest of us.*

How is that possible? Nathaniel asked. *I mean, it's true; we have met some humans with unique psychic abilities lately, but this? Seems a bit much to me.*

I agree, Marquis snorted. *This kind of information can only come from the source…perhaps Salvatore Nistor…or the Dark Lord Ademordna. Are you sure she isn't connected to our dark brothers from the house of Jaegar somehow? What if she—*

Is his destiny? Nathaniel interrupted.

The psychic connection went momentarily silent.

I'm ahead of you, twin, Kagen said. *I don't see any other way for the two of them to be so deeply connected.*

There has been no Blood Moon, Marquis argued.

True, Kagen said, *but think about it: Our* destinies *are chosen before their births. We are connected the moment the gods and goddesses select them.* He absently ran his hand through his hair, massaging the base of his neck. *Even though we don't meet them—have any way to recognize them—prior to the Blood Moon, the bond is already established. It's…inbred.* He paused, searching for the right way to express his thoughts more clearly. *What if whatever has happened to Nachari— whatever is occurring on a spiritual level—is so strong…so elemental, so to speak…that it has somehow awakened or tapped into the bond between our little brother and his chosen female.* He thought more about it, and

48

another idea suddenly came to him. *Nachari is a wizard,* he said. *That means he plays in a realm we don't even begin to understand. What if—somehow—he is reaching out to her, using that primordial connection, or even her existence, to try to get through to us from whatever realm he is in. I don't know, but I'm telling you: You had to see her face. Feel her emotions. She was driven…and devastated.*

Nathaniel blew out a long, contemplative breath. *Okay, so…what next?*

There is no definitive way to tell if a female belongs to a vampire before the Blood Moon, Marquis insisted. *There is no way to prove your theory.* Marquis Silivasi was a brilliant tactician and thus, a male of logic. He preferred to stick to the facts—and *only* the facts.

True…and false, Kagen said.

True because? Nathaniel prompted before Marquis could argue.

Because only the Celestial deities know the true identity of each male's destiny: Marquis is right about that.

And false…why? Nathaniel prompted.

Because every woman destined to be the mate of one of our males is both chosen—and marked—by the gods before birth. As we all know, they are human but not. They are compatible to us through their—

Celestial DNA, Marquis supplied the answer. *Have you tested her blood yet?*

Doing it as we speak, Kagen responded.

And if it's positive, Nathaniel quipped, *then we know for sure that she is a human* destiny, *but we still don't have proof that she belongs specifically to Nachari.*

Correct, Kagen said.

Marquis sighed. *If it's positive, then the combination of physical corroboration and circumstantial evidence is adequate for me.*

Kagen rolled his eyes: And Marquis was always ordering everyone else to speak plainly? *Yes,* he said. *Good enough for me, too. Certainly enough for us to act upon.*

Keep her detained, Marquis said adamantly, issuing the statement as a direct order. *We will be there immediately.*

Actually, give me ten minutes, Nathaniel said.

BLOOD SHADOWS

You will not take ten minutes—you will go now, Marquis barked.

Marquis… Nathaniel sounded slightly exasperated.

Chill, big brother, Kagen added. *It can wait ten minutes. It'll take me a little while to finish analyzing this sample anyhow, and I'd like to collect the rest of those drawings as soon as I'm done.*

Five minutes, Marquis said, brooking no arguments.

Kagen shrugged. Marquis was intense as usual, but it did make sense…sort of. If Deanna was Nachari's *destiny*, then her life was Nachari's life. She could not be permitted to leave their sight, and she certainly needed protection from their enemies while they sorted things out. Marquis was no-nonsense about those kinds of matters, especially since the loss of Shelby, and there was nothing anyone was going to say or do to change his perspective. *Very well,* Kagen said. *I'll see you both in five minutes.*

Nathaniel chuckled, his laid-back, relaxed manner emerging in the end. *As you have spoken, Master Warrior,* he said, using the formal language of the house of Jadon to goad Marquis.

I see no humor in this, Nathaniel, Marquis replied.

Ahh, Nathaniel quipped. *And this surprises me…not at all.*

And then they all grew quiet…

Because it occurred to each of them at the same time that this was the point where Nachari would have stepped in with his lighthearted humor, had he been there, to tease Marquis relentlessly. Perhaps he would have suggested that Marquis seek professional help; or maybe he would have sought to appease Nathaniel with some off-handed story about some silly command Marquis had given him in the past. One way or another, Nachari would have made light of the whole situation, bonding the brothers together with humor, while smoothing over the rough edges, because that was what he did.

Nachari was the peacemaker.

The calm within the storm.

And he brought the warmth of the sun into their tight-knit family. At times like these, his absence was felt profoundly. And didn't that just bring Marquis's domineering protectiveness back into perspective for all of them?

Tessa Dawn

I will be there in five, Marquis, Nathaniel repeated, piercing the silence. This time, his tone was both acquiescent and respectful. *Be well, Master Warrior,* he added with formality.

And you, Nathaniel, Marquis responded in kind.

Brothers, Kagen said in parting.

And then he closed the telepathic connection.

six

Marquis Silivasi sat back in the large leather armchair in the clinic's waiting room across from the terrified woman and crossed his muscular arms. They had been at it all day: questioning Deanna, digging for information, feeling her out for subtle inconsistencies in her story.

There were none.

She was exactly who she said she was, and her story matched the information Kagen had taken from her mind earlier that day...to a tee. He rubbed his chin lightly with his thumb while measuring the woman for the umpteenth time, categorizing every nuance of her personality—the way she moved, the fluctuations in her voice, the peaks and valleys of her heartbeat...the body language that revealed far more than her words ever could.

Deanna Dubois was an exceptional woman but in an understated way. To begin with, she came from an unusual mixed heritage. Her flawless skin was the color of coffee, heavily loaded with cream, and the splendidly exotic nature of her features spoke of at least three different racial influences: Her heavily-lidded, bluish-gray eyes reminded him of those he had seen on the original Spanish Conquistadors; her imminently straight, sculpted nose and her full, heart-shaped lips spoke of more than one French ancestor; and her long, deep brown tresses, littered with natural brushed-gold highlights, had just enough texture to betray some African-American ancestry as well. Overall, it was a devastating combination—not unusual to find in New Orleans—and Deanna carried it all on her five-foot-ten frame like an international model. If the Celestial deities had tried to match Nachari's rare good looks with a human female's, then they had done a stellar job.

But Deanna was more than just an exotic beauty. She was

supremely confident, despite the unsettling situation she found herself in, and she had an insightful, clever mind that revealed a great deal of intelligence. She was both articulate and smooth, like one who had been educated in the back alleys of life as well as the stuffy universities. However, she was only twenty-three years old, so much of her astuteness had to be innate. Again, she would be a perfect match for Nachari—if, in fact, she was his *destiny*.

Her blood test had come back positive for traces of Celestial DNA.

And even though the brothers had suspected as much, they had still stared at the results with both shock and awe. After all, randomly testing human women had never been done before; the concept just didn't make sense. Not only would the sons of Jadon have to sort through millions of women before they found one single match, but the positive result would tell them nothing about whom the human female belonged to—which vampire she was destined to mate. Seeing such results before the Blood Moon's omen was as astonishing as it was unsettling.

The woman straightened her back and forced an insincere smile. "It's getting dark outside," she said, gesturing toward a window. "I really need to get going."

Marquis sighed and shook his head. "No."

Kagen leaned forward in his seat and cleared his throat. "I think what my brother means to say is we haven't sorted through all of this yet; we would appreciate a little more of your time."

Marquis shrugged impatiently. "I think what I meant was *no*."

Deanna narrowed her eyes and gave Marquis an angry, albeit frightened, glare. "You can't keep me here." She put it as a statement, but the inflection in her voice made it a question.

Marquis didn't flinch. "We haven't decided yet...where you will be allowed to go."

Her face paled, and unconcealed fear washed through her eyes. She looked from one male to other, pleading with her gaze.

Nathaniel licked his lips and shifted languidly in his seat.

"Ms. Dubois," he purred in a faintly seductive tone, though absent of compulsion, "you don't need to be afraid. We don't mean you any harm. It's just"—he paused as if searching for the precise words—"it's just that Nachari's well-being is our foremost concern, and you must admit, there is something…unusual…going on here."

"Unusual?" Deanna said, her mouth falling open. *"Unusual?"* She stood up abruptly. "You guys are scaring the hell out of me!" She turned to face Kagen. "I'm sorry I came to your clinic, and I'm sorry I lied to you to gain access." She placed the palm of her hand against her diaphragm as if to force herself to calm down. "Obviously, I was little freaked out myself by my drawings…and your brother. But I've answered all of your questions. More than once. And you haven't answered any of mine. So, as far as I'm concerned, we're not going to get any further tonight." Her shoulders sagged. "I'm tired. I'm hungry. And I just want to go back to my cabin and get some rest."

Marquis started to speak but was quickly cut off by Nathaniel, who held out his hand in a *stop* motion. *Brother,* he said telepathically, so all of them could hear, *we can't keep her here like a hostage. There has been no Blood Moon to alert our enemies of her existence; perhaps she will remain more…amenable…to our desires if we make her feel more comfortable. Allow her to feel safe at the least. What harm is there in letting her return to her cabin for this night only? We can place a hidden guard on her tail so she goes nowhere.*

Kagen shrugged. *I'm okay with that—for tonight,* he qualified. *But eventually, we're going to have to tell her something.*

Marquis waved his hand in dismissal. *At this point, what the human does or does not want is of no consequence to me; what matters is Nachari's safety and figuring this out.* He rubbed his brow in frustration. *I can't believe I'm saying this, but I think we need a wizard.*

Deanna threw her arms up in the air. "What in the hell are you guys doing?" She took several steps back from her chair and shuffled in the direction of the front door. No doubt, she had seen the body language and hand gestures…in the absence of speech.

Kagen stood slowly. "We're just considering your request," he said.

Deanna shook her head vigorously. "It's not a request. This is America, and last I checked, I was free to come and go as I please." She raised her purse strap on her shoulder and hugged her attaché case to her chest. "So if you gentlemen will excuse me, I'm outta here." Without looking back, she started to walk briskly toward the front door. Her heart was practically beating out of her chest.

Marquis immediately rose to cut her off.

Let her go, Marquis, Nathaniel said.

Marquis glared at him angrily.

"Call Ramsey," Nathaniel whispered in a voice so slight only another vampire could hear. *Ask him to meet us at the cabins. The moment she pulls out of the driveway, we will cloak our appearances and follow her while remaining invisible.* He turned in the direction of Nachari's room. *Kagen, of course, will stay here with Nachari.*

Marquis thought it over. He would never understand why his brothers went out of their way to see to the comfort of humans. Perhaps this Deanna was Nachari's *destiny*, perhaps she was not; but either way, she had answers they needed in her drawings. What she couldn't explain—because she honestly didn't know— perhaps another wizard, or even Napolean himself could discern.

It will be as I say. Marquis spoke with authority then, making it clear that he was pulling rank as the eldest brother and the most senior Ancient Master Warrior in the room. *She will return to the cabin tonight under the protection of Ramsey and Nathaniel. She will be brought back to the clinic at first light tomorrow to meet with our wizards, Jankiel and Niko. Until then, the drawings will remain here at the clinic where we can study them. I do not care to waste an entire night waiting for the girl to get her beauty sleep.*

As you wish, Nathaniel responded. And then, flashing a brilliant smile, he called after Deanna. "Ms. Dubois?"

Her back stiffened and she looked over her shoulder, but she didn't stop walking.

"You will stop walking now," he said in a low, melodic tone. She froze in place.

"You will hand me your collection of drawings willingly."

She blinked several times, glanced down at her attaché case, and held it out to Nathaniel.

He moved at the speed of light, all at once appearing before her, and gently removed the case from her arms. "Thank you," he whispered. "Now go home and get some sleep. And do not think to leave Dark Moon Vale—as you will gladly return to the clinic tomorrow morning."

Deanna stood before Nathaniel like a statue as his words were absorbed into her consciousness—as his will became her own. She slowly nodded her head and smiled. "So, I'll see you all in the morning, then?" Her brow creased in confusion.

"That would be perfect," Nathaniel responded, releasing her from his compulsion.

She gave him a harsh look of suspicion. "Good night," she clipped. And then she turned and nearly ran to the front door.

Deanna threw open the front door to the clinic and took a deep breath of cool night air, trying to fill her lungs with as much as she could. Trying to return sanity to her befuddled mind.

If someone had told her that her name was Alice and she had just fallen down a rabbit hole—or that she was actually Dorothy from Kansas and finding the Wizard of Oz was her only way back home—she would have believed it without question.

What in the world had she gotten herself into?

She shuddered, thinking of the three predatory men who had kept her in the clinic all day long, hurling question after question, hour after hour, in her direction: When did she first begin to sketch the drawings? What went through her mind when it happened? What was she feeling? Did she dream about the sketches? Had she told anyone what she was doing? How had she found the Dark Moon Vale Clinic? What did the clouds in the pictures mean to her? Whose hands were reaching out of the ground for the mysterious man? What did she feel when she thought about the man lying so lifeless in the hospital bed?

She placed her hands over her ears and fought so hard to stifle a scream that the resulting sound came out as a long, drawn-out moan. She had come to Dark Moon Vale for answers, to convince herself that she wasn't, in fact, crazy. And now, all she believed was that the whole world was crazy right along with her.

The hair stood up on the back of her neck, and she quickly spun around, fully expecting to see someone standing right behind here. There was no one there. She glanced nervously around the parking lot as she took the stone steps in front of the clinic two at a time, all the while digging for her keys at the bottom of her purse.

A branch broke from the limb of a tree overhead, and she jumped.

She could have sworn she heard a second set of footsteps right beside her.

The heat of another body drifted tangibly around her, and it felt as if her left arm were brushing against an invisible person. She yanked her arm away and accidentally dropped her purse. "Who's there?" she called, squatting down to gather her now scattered belongings.

In her mind's eye she could still see the giant, terrifying man—the one who called himself Marquis—scrutinizing her with his penetrating gaze. His eyes were such a dark black that they practically shone blue; and his huge, rock-hard body dwarfed everyone who stood near him, not just in size but in power. In presence. He was like a living, breathing pillar of stone: harsh, unrelenting, and deadly with purpose. There was no give in that man, no soft edges. Like the rest of them, he was ungodly handsome, but there was something harsh and unforgiving in his style. Something that made Deanna want to scream and run...all the way back to New Orleans.

And the seductive, charming one—the guy named Nathaniel—he wasn't anything to play with, either. In fact, the word that came to mind was *panther*: sleek, powerful, hypnotically beautiful, and oh-so-very dangerous. He had the charm of a Lothario yet the stealth of a hunter. Like he could sidle up to a woman, purr enticingly in her ear, and then pounce and rip out her throat all in one graceful motion...without ever abandoning that beguiling smile. He was the kind of man who could make a woman weep for his favor...or beg for his mercy.

Deanna sat on the last of the stone steps, bent over, and hung her head between her knees. She needed air. She needed to get a grip. She did not want to freak-the-heck out—not now. She did not want to do anything that might bring the good doctor out of the clinic to her rescue.

Or demise.

The good doctor.

What in the world did she think of him?

The thought made her picture the brown-haired, brown-eyed physician, and she wished she'd had the good sense to avoid the clinic altogether in the first place. Too late.

Kagen Silivasi.

He was the least outwardly intimidating of the three brothers, the most casual and restrained; yet in his own way, he frightened her more than the other two—there was just something about his carefully controlled demeanor.

He was eerily calm...too calm.

His nonchalant behavior was too easy, too refined, too measured.

Like the quiet before a storm, Kagen Silivasi was all bottled-up ferocity just waiting to happen. As far as Deanna was concerned, dealing with Kagen reminded her of the Old West warning about dealing with an Apache: If you ever find yourself cornered by one, save the last bullet for yourself.

Deanna dropped the last of her scattered belongings, a thin

tube of rose-pink lipstick, back into her purse, and sat up straight, raising her head from her knees. Normal men were just not that threatening, at least none of the men she had ever met, and certainly not without trying to be. And they were never that handsome.

They were never that…feline.

Something was so wrong with this whole picture. So why was she planning on returning in the morning? And why had she chosen to sleep hours of the day away in the room next to Nachari's?

In a pit full of vipers?

Nachari.

His name played over and over in her mind.

Oh God…Nachari.

Why, in spite of so much danger, when every warning bell in her head was going off—screaming *Run! Get away!*—did she want to march right back into that room and wake that beautiful man up? See his eyes.

Save him.

It made no earthly sense. Surely, he would be as strange, intimidating, and dangerous as his brothers. Not someone she wanted to meet.

But still…

Forcing herself to stop thinking about it—and ignore the very real sense of danger she felt all around her—Deanna rose from the steps and made her way to her SUV. She opened the door and was just about to toss her purse onto the seat when she felt a sudden, inexplicable tingling on the inside of her left wrist. It was as if her skin were on fire…but not…burning without pain. She held up her arm and rolled back her sleeve; perhaps she was having an allergic reaction to something she had come in contact with in the clinic…

And that's when the sky turned black.

The lights in the heavens simply went out, leaving the world in utter, terrifying darkness.

Deanna held her breath. She waited, motionless, as her mind

tried to make sense of what was happening around her: Was it a lunar eclipse? Some rare, astronomical phenomenon she had never heard of? She could hear her own heartbeat as she stared up at the sky, waiting for the stars and the moon to return to the heavens.

And then they did—only not at all like they were before…

The moon was the color of fresh blood, a red so vivid that it looked like an artist had climbed a ladder to the sky and painted it by hand. And the stars were back, but they had shifted their position in the sky—was that even possible?—to form a very clear and distinct image. Deanna had loved astrology in high school, and she immediately recognized the constellation: It was Perseus, the Victorious Hero, holding his sword in one hand and the head of the Gorgon in the other. Despite her trepidation, she was awestruck. Fascinated. What in the world was happening?

She ducked into her car to retrieve her cell phone from her purse. She wanted to use the camera—she just had to snap a picture—and that's when she noticed the unusual markings on her arm. Jolting in surprise, she traced the vivid lines and dots along her wrists, comparing each and every one to the same vivid lines in the sky: Perseus, the constellation, was indelibly etched into her forearm.

Deanna set her phone down on the seat.

She was scared now. Really. Scared.

She didn't want to go back to the cabins. She didn't want to try and figure this out. She just wanted to head back to New Orleans on the next plane out of DIA and check herself into a hospital where she could get the help she needed.

To hell with this.

Her danger meter was registering off the charts. If ever there was a time to throw in the towel, this was it.

"Calm down, D," she whispered to herself. "Just get in your car and go. It's going to be okay…you just need to get somewhere where someone can help you." She ran her fingers gently along her wrist and trembled. *It's not cancer. Diseases don't just suddenly appear out of nowhere. It's probably not even real—after all, the sky doesn't just change out of the blue; and if it did, those changes wouldn't just suddenly appear on your arm. There's gotta be some rational explanation.*

Maybe those guys drugged you…

Maybe that's why you slept so long…

Maybe you're just hallucinating…

Of course, that was it. The emergency room. She just needed to find a local emergency room and get some help.

"Deanna." A soft male voice interrupted her thoughts, and she nearly jumped out of her skin.

Where the heck did he come from?

"Nathaniel?" she gasped in shock. Then just as quickly, she shouted, "Get away from me!"

She shoved at his chest and turned to duck into her car, but he blocked her with his arm. "Deanna, don't."

She quickly ducked beneath the obstruction and took off running across the parking lot, kicking off her two-inch heels along the way so she could really pump her arms and put everything she had into her stride.

"Deanna," he called after her, his voice never rising above a conversational pitch.

To hell with you! she thought.

Every breath burned like fire as she pushed her body to the limit and strained her lungs against the altitude. And then, a piercing scream escaped her throat as she looked up to find Marquis Silivasi standing like a brick wall in front of her, as if out of the clear blue sky.

Now where had he come from!?

Circling her arms in a backward rotation to stop her momentum, she pulled up short and took several steps back. Suddenly, the doctor was standing to her left, both of his hands held out in front of him like he was trying to coax a frightened jumper down from a ledge. "Deanna, slow down…just breathe," he whispered.

She whipped her head to the side: Nathaniel was now on her right.

Impossible!

The brothers were the three points of a triangle, practically surrounding her, and she had never seen—or heard—any of them approach. "Leave me alone!" she cried out, completely reversing directions in order to run back to her car.

As she neared the SUV, Nathaniel suddenly appeared again, standing in front of the driver's side door, as if he had never left.

She whirled around, utterly frantic. Nathaniel was in front of her. Marquis was behind her. And Kagen was quickly approaching from the side. She spun around in hysterical circles. She ran a few steps this way, then a few steps that, heading wildly in all directions, only to find one of the brothers blocking her path no matter which way she chose to run.

"Oh my God…Oh my God…Oh my God," she chanted desperately. She shifted directions yet again, this time heading for the stone bridge. If only she could get to the water, leap into the river, the current would carry her downstream, and…and…maybe they couldn't follow. And that had to be better than—

"Noooo!"

She shouted so loud it hurt her throat as Nathaniel's iron arms closed around her from behind. Once again, he had simply appeared out of nowhere.

She kicked and struggled in earnest.

"Deanna, please…don't." His smooth, raspy voice terrified her even more than his sudden, inexplicable appearances. He had used that voice…many times…to do what? To make her do things against her will? Like give him her drawings?

"Oh…*shit*," she uttered as the realization hit her: Kagen had put her to sleep earlier—with his voice. Marquis had compelled the answers to his questions—with his voice! Nathaniel had taken her drawings and ordered her to come back the next morning…

With his voice!

"What are you?" she demanded. And then, before Nathaniel could answer, she clasped her hands to her ears and began reciting the word *No* in an attempt to drown out his voice. That powerful, dangerous, *inhuman* voice.

Nathaniel pried Deanna's hands from her ears easily. "Deanna, I am not going to compel you…again. But you must listen to me."

"*Compel me? Again?*" she repeated. Then it was true. "How? Why?" She took two careful steps backward, and he let her. "What are you?"

"Deanna—"

"What the hell are you!"

"We are Vampyr." Marquis Silivasi spoke evenly, having swiftly closed the distance between them.

Deanna felt her knees go weak. "Did you just say *vampire?*" She almost laughed. Almost. "As in Count Dracula? Blood-sucking monsters?" She heard herself giggle for real then and knew it was from hysteria.

"No," Kagen answered, all at once standing before her and reaching out his hand. "As in a separate species from humans that has existed on the earth for over twenty-eight hundred years."

She shook her head in disbelief.

He sighed. "Deanna, you are strongly connected to our brother Nachari. That is why you felt compelled to draw sketches of him. When he was…hurt…you must have sensed it."

Deanna listened as if from a great distance away, the words floating around her more than sinking in. It was more like eavesdropping on a conversation than participating in one. Absently, she looked at her arm. "What is this?" she asked.

"Perseus," Kagen whispered. "You recognized the constellation the moment you saw it."

"No…what does it mean?" she heard herself say.

Nathaniel took a step toward her. "Perseus is Nachari's reigning constellation. He is the Celestial god who chose you for my brother long before you were born."

"Chose…me…for…for what?"

"You belong to Nachari," Marquis said in a stern voice. "It is that simple, and now you must come back inside with us."

"*Marquis*," Kagen chastised, sounding clearly irritated, "let Nathaniel and I do the talking...*please*."

Marquis grunted. "It is what it is, and we can't stand out in the open all night. She's Nachari's. Period. Bring her inside."

Deanna blanched, looking back and forth between Nathaniel and Kagen. Would they obey Marquis and just snatch her? Kidnap her? "Wait," she said, turning her full gaze on Kagen. He seemed to be the most reasonable one. "How did you know that I recognized that constellation? That I knew it was Perseus? Were you...reading my thoughts?"

"Yes," Kagen answered, holding her gaze. "I was."

"And I was following you to your car," Nathaniel added. "That is the presence you felt around you."

"But...how...why?" she asked.

Nathaniel sighed. "Because we suspected that you might be Nachari's *destiny*, and we needed to keep you safe...and close by." He held out both hands palms up. "That is the truth, Ms. Dubois."

"And," Kagen added, "your drawings...we don't understand them any more than you do, but we have been desperate to try and save our brother...to hold him to us, keep him on this earth. Perhaps you have answers that can help."

Deanna shook her head vigorously as if she could simply erase the reality of what she was hearing with the motion. "No...this isn't possible. None of this is possible...people don't get sucked down through the earth...or belong to other people—"

"We are not people," Kagen said softly.

Deanna looked up at him then, noticing that his golden-brown eyes, with their deep silver speckles, were practically glowing. "You're...you're a vampire?" she repeated, half disbelieving that such outrageous words were even coming from her mouth.

Kagen nodded slowly, and there was an emerging kindness

in his eyes.

She smiled almost sarcastically, feeling suddenly light-headed. "Then show me your fangs, Mr. Vampire."

Kagen looked at Marquis for permission, and the huge one nodded almost imperceptibly. He took a step back then, almost as if he were trying not to frighten her, and his eyes flashed a solid red before two long, razor-sharp points began to extend from beneath his upper lip, causing it to curl back in a wolfish snarl. A barely discernible growl escaped his throat, but Deanna heard it for what it was—raw, animalistic, and not at all human.

The ground dropped out from beneath her feet.

As the doctor glided forward to catch her, it no longer mattered that she might be insane. It no longer mattered that she had come to Dark Moon Vale of her own volition to find the mysterious man from her drawings. It no longer even mattered that she felt inexorably drawn to Nachari—or that a part of her needed to help him.

It only mattered that she escape these creatures.

As Deanna's terror continued to mount, she fought and screamed like a madwoman. She clawed at Kagen's face with unrestrained ferocity. She bit and kicked him violently as if her very life depended on it. "Let me go! Let me go!" she shouted as she landed blow after furious blow.

"Oh to hell with it," she heard the huge one Marquis grumble. "Sleep, woman."

"No!" she shouted in protest—

And then the turmoil went away.

seven

The Valley of Death and Shadows

The Dark Lord Ademordna stormed into the large marble bathroom and made his way to the deep claw-foot tub, his tangled hair streaming behind him as if blowing in the wind, his hooved feet pounding against the cold tiles. "Have you fed well?" he said to the small audience of demon subjects that surrounded Nachari, blood still dripping from the corners of their mouths.

"Yes, master," a small winged creature with the face of a lizard hummed, sounding imminently satisfied.

"And you, Noiro?" Ademordna said. "Did you enjoy the show...again?"

Nachari's stomach turned over as he waited to hear the evil demoness's response. Of course she enjoyed the show. She always enjoyed...the shows.

Noiro rotated her hips in a sultry motion, taking a cautious step toward Ademordna. "Immensely," she purred, licking her fetid lips.

Ademordna nodded, and then he abruptly reached down into the tub, yanked Nachari's head back by his thick mane of hair, stroked his jugular three times as if petting a kitten, and sank his fangs deep into the wizard's neck.

Nachari jerked, and then he quickly braced himself to keep from reacting. He could endure this. He had done it before. He chanted several soft refrains in Latin, using a separation-spell to release his mind from his body—to drift away from the tub, where he could watch the scene like a spectator. The pain would still be acute, but the awareness of it would be lessened. And at least he could feel like he wasn't directly in the putrid demon's grasp. Illusion. Wasn't that a huge part of what magic was anyway?

Nachari waited for what seemed like eternity for Ademordna to drink his fill, and then having been abruptly released, he slumped down into the tub and tried to maintain consciousness.

The dark lord licked his lips. "Exquisite. You are that, my dear wizard."

Nachari stared straight ahead without answering.

"Look at me!" Ademordna shouted, growing instantly angry at Nachari's insolence.

Nachari blinked, but he didn't turn his head. He was thinking about Shelby now, clutching his twin's amulet in his imagination and remembering a particular day in the valley when they had raced a pair of ATVs. Shelby had left Nachari in the dust, pushing his Arctic Wildcat to the outer limits and beyond. A high-pitched humming interrupted his thoughts, catapulting him back into the moment.

"You will acknowledge me, boy," Ademordna growled, low and insistent. "By all that is unholy, you will meet my eyes, and you will call me lord!"

Nachari cringed inwardly. What now? What manner of indescribable punishment would the dark lord dream up...now? And why couldn't Nachari just give in and comply—become obedient—at least try to lessen the frequency and intensity of his daily tortures?

Ademordna reached across the tub to a low, free-standing table that stood just beyond the raised base and retrieved a four-inch-wide iron bit. He grasped Nachari's jaw with two long talons, forcing his mouth open so that he could insert the bit, and then forced the wizard to clamp down on the crude device.

Nachari trembled inside: a bit...between his teeth? *Dear Celestial gods, what was the demon about to do to him?* He swallowed his fear and waited, desperately willing his mind to become a blank slate. In this one fleeting moment—if he could only escape from his shadowed body—he could at least enjoy the sensation of being pain-free...

Until the next moment arrived.

It was how he lived. How he endured.

One torturous moment at a time.

Ademordna waved his hands erratically over the tub, threw back his hideous head, and began to laugh between harsh, guttural syllables—some sort of dark, summoning chant. Before Nachari could interpret the words, he felt the result: spiders and scorpions.

They filled the tub like smoke rising from a damp fire.

Nachari held his breath as the spindly legs and claws clambered for perch against his skin, crawling along his legs and arms, huddling above his chest, clinging for perch on his jaw, his neck, his fingers. He held himself perfectly still as he felt the creatures enter his mouth from around the bit...and grab hold of his manhood, further down.

Great God Perseus, please...please let me die, he prayed inside. *Kagen, brother...*

He projected his soul as far outward as he could, pleading with some unknown force to carry his words, his feverish plea, to his brother's ears. *Release me, Healer,* he begged. *Please let my body die...oh gods, Kagen...help me.*

Ademordna beckoned to Noiro to come closer. "Come, Demoness; watch your lover writhe in pain."

Noiro smiled as she sat on the edge of the tub, clearly unafraid that the creatures would touch her—either that, or not caring if they did.

Nachari glared at her with such hatred and fury in his eyes. One day. Somehow. He would kill that witch...if it was the last thing he ever did.

And then he clamped down on the iron bit, grunting in pain as the spiders began to bite and the scorpions began to sting him all over his body. His eyes rolled back in his head, and sweat began to pour from his brow, even as his body convulsed to the left, then the right, writhing desperately in pain, uselessly trying to escape his porcelain cage.

Oh gods in heaven, he could not endure this any longer!

He shook his head from side to side, grunting, screaming,

and resisting the need to vomit. There was no end in sight. No way to force himself to pass out. No escape. He pulled at the thick diamond-coated chains linked to his ankles and wrists, calling upon all the strength he had as a vampire to break free.

Nothing.

And it was not just because of the diamonds.

It was this place. The Abyss: The *Valley of Death and Shadows* that kept him so helpless and weak. So defenseless to his captors.

There was a different set of rules in hell—the laws of physics were altered—and everything bowed to the will of the demon lords. His knees clattered together, causing water to swish over the edges of the tub—*please gods, let just a few of the hideous creatures wash out of the tub…away from my flesh.*

He bucked. The poison was mounting in his bloodstream now, burning like fire, eating away at his body from the inside out. He felt his sanity slowly ebbing away, and he greeted the inevitable fracture of his mind: Any break from reality would be welcome.

No, no, no! he shouted inside, angry at the tears he could feel welling up in his eyes. *Think, Nachari! There has to be a spell…an incantation. If death of your mortal body is the only way out, then so be it. Conjure death. Command your body on earth to die! You are a Master Wizard. Concentrate!*

Grim Reaper, Death, Eternal Sleep,
harken to my voice;
Beseech the gods on my behalf,
grant me now, this choice:
Extinguish breath; expunge my life—
to earth from lands below;
return my heart to join my flesh,
At last, release my soul.

Just then, a powerful current shot through him like an enormous pulse of electricity, and he felt his soul hurtling forward, traveling at enormous speeds, even beyond that which he knew on earth as a vampire. The sound of wind was deafening, the feeling of being encased in a tunnel beyond what his senses could comprehend, and then all at once he was there!

At the Dark Moon Vale Clinic...in the parking lot...his ethereal body less than fifty feet away from his mortal flesh. If only he could get to his body, repeat the refrain one last time, he could end his life for good—once and for all.

Yes, he could do it. He *would* do it.

Grim Reaper, Death, Eternal Sleep,
The hour's drawing near;
return me to my resting flesh—

Just then, something caught his attention.

As he drew closer to the ground, in an effort to locate his body, a startling scene swept up to meet him, commanding his attention and bringing him up short.

His brothers...all three of them...they were standing in the parking lot, surrounding a woman; and she was the most beautifully exotic creature he had ever seen. Instinctively, he drew closer.

They called her...Deanna.

"You belong to Nachari," Marquis said in a harsh voice. "It is that simple, and now you must come back inside with us."

Nachari jolted, awestruck. Somehow, his vision suddenly came into clear, dramatic focus, and he instinctively glanced up at the sky...and then at the woman's wrist.

Perseus: his reigning constellation.

A Blood Moon.

Was this really happening?

His heart stopped beating for a second: The woman was his *destiny;* and she was there in Dark Moon Vale, at the clinic.

And his brothers had her surrounded.

She was in their care.

His determination instantly faltered, and he abruptly lost his focus, launching back into the tub in the Abyss, descending into an otherworldly body covered with spiders and scorpions, convulsing in pain. He screamed in agony as the pain seized him like a long lost lover, and his teeth clamped down around the thick bit of iron. As he grappled for air, forcing his lungs to expand and contract, he tried to process what had just happened.

If only for a moment, he had left his prison in the Valley of Death and Shadows. He had traveled, however briefly, to earth, and he had seen…

His *destiny*.

Nachari locked eyes with Ademordna and nodded his head in vigorous compliance, trying desperately to gain the dark lord's attention.

"What's this?" the dark lord snarled. "Do you wish to speak?"

Nachari nodded again.

Shrieking his delight, Ademordna waved his hand over the tub, and the creatures immediately ceased their assault. He reached down and yanked the bit out of Nachari's mouth. "Speak now, Wizard—and do not try my patience."

Nachari stumbled over his swollen tongue and fought to keep the dark lord in focus as he slowly bowed his head. "I…I acknowledge you as…my lord," he stuttered.

Ademordna froze, clearly taken aback by the unexpected entreaty.

"Say it again!" he thundered.

Nachari steadied himself. "I acknowledge you, milord."

Ademordna cocked his head to the side, and then he bent over and licked Nachari's cheek with his long, slithery tongue, leaving acid-burnt skin peeling away in its wake. He held Nachari's gaze, eye to eye, on the same level. "Good boy," he whispered. And then he patted him on the head.

Nachari did not turn away; rather, he averted his eyes in a pretend gesture of respect.

Noiro jumped up then, looking both shocked and disappointed. "But I was just starting to have fun." She stuck out her bottom lip and stamped her foot against the ground. "He's soooo beautiful when he screams." Her ridiculous red hair swayed in time to her emphatic gesturing.

"That is enough…for today," Ademordna said, his voice full

of self-satisfaction. He turned to the winged creature standing in the background panting with excitement. "Clean him up, Devion, and bring him to my throne room. He will rest for an hour or so. And then we will begin his torment...again."

Nachari dropped his head and held his tongue, fighting to stop his body from convulsing.

Yes, he would accept an hour or so of rest. As often as he could.

He would comply with the revolting bastard, and he would gain strength.

He had used his Magick to escape the Abyss once—if only for a fleeting moment—and that meant he could use it again.

It could be done.

As Noiro bent to kiss the top of his head, he forced himself to remain perfectly still.

Not to shudder.

And not to pull away.

As her acidic lips touched his scalp, he let out a barely audible moan of contrived pleasure, low enough that only she could hear. Her shocked, hopeful expression told him all he needed to know; yes, she would be his pawn...to use and command, eventually.

Blinking rapidly, she stepped back and stared at him in yearning desperation. He winked, allowing her a moment's reciprocated gaze into his deep emerald eyes. *Not too much too soon*, he thought. And then he abruptly looked away, leaving her forlorn.

If the foul female thought she loved him—as sick, twisted, and demented as the freak of evil nature was—then so be it. At the least, she needed his seed to sire her idea of some beautiful, vampire-wizard-demon super child.

As if!

Well, two could play that game.

It was time to stop resisting and start planning. It was time to become strategic. Nachari Silivasi had a *destiny*. And she was alive and on the earth...already in Dark Moon Vale.

BLOOD SHADOWS

He had thirty days to return to her—less than that, really, if the required sacrifice was to be made in time—so he would use Noiro, Ademordna, and every demon in hell if that was what it took to make it back home to his female.

Yes, he would rest for an hour.

And then he would begin...anew.

eight

Dark Moon Vale

Kagen, Nathaniel, and Marquis sat in the Healer's second-story office above the clinic's main floor in deafening silence, each one staring off into the distance. The rustic, corporate feel of the large, majestic space with its wide-plank wood flooring and two-story stone fireplace provided the perfect backdrop for what they were feeling: overwhelmed and powerless to act against the whims of nature.

Why had the gods chosen now—this time—to bring Nachari his destiny? Kagen wondered. He shifted uncomfortably against the soft velvet chaise and met the eyes of his brothers for the first time, each one in turn, as they sat across from him in large, leather armless chairs.

Marquis practically glowered with anger. He cleared his throat. Twice. "Did anyone make an official record of the time?"

Nathaniel stirred. "Seven o'clock PM."

Nachari's Blood Moon had occurred at precisely seven o'clock PM on Monday, January 25th, which meant the male had until precisely seven o'clock PM on Wednesday, February 24th to make the required sacrifice, or—

Or what?

Marquis seemed to read Kagen's thoughts. "And if he and Deanna have not...come together...by then, we are to wheel him in on a stretcher to the chamber of sacrifice so the Blood can exact its pound of flesh?"

Nathaniel whistled low beneath his breath but didn't respond.

"That's insane," Marquis added.

"Agreed," Kagen said. "But I don't think—"

"Perhaps it is time for a war between heaven and hell,"

75

Marquis grunted, cutting Kagen off in mid-sentence. "Because all hell will break loose before I turn Nachari over for failing to appease the Blood…when he isn't even conscious!"

The earth began to shake beneath them, causing the furniture to slide gently to the left before settling back in place on the wooden floors.

"Brother," Nathaniel cautioned, staring into Marquis's phantom-blue eyes. "Please…check your emotions. It will not help Nachari to have the clinic fall down around him."

Marquis's large chest rose and fell with the weight of his breath—and his burden—but he managed to calm down.

Kagen spoke up then. "I spoke to Napolean briefly. Our king will visit the clinic first thing in the morning to discuss the situation with us, perhaps to add some deeper insight." He paused. "In the meantime, there are vital matters we must discuss."

"Indeed," Marquis grumbled.

"What are you thinking?" Nathaniel asked, resting further back in his chair and raising his eyebrows curiously.

Kagen sought to rein in his own emotion before continuing. "I think we need to approach this…challenge…in stages. Take it one issue at a time." He nodded appreciatively at Nathaniel. "Thank you for being mindful enough to make note of the time; with all that was going on, it never occurred to me to begin making a record of events." The internal calculations made by a male vampire the moment he encountered his Blood Moon were as instinctive as sleeping and breathing. The instant the Omen began, the male automatically recorded the date, the time, and the…deadline: When, exactly, would the thirty days be up? Exactly how much time did he have left to fulfill the edicts of the Curse? It wasn't something one thought about. It was simply imprinted on a cellular level; but Nachari hadn't been there to internalize the information. Nathaniel's reaction had been wise and proactive.

"Of course." Nathaniel nodded. "Perhaps it is because I have gone through it myself."

"What now?" Marquis demanded, quickly changing the subject.

Kagen angled his body toward Marquis. "Well, first I talk to Napolean…and the other wizards. Find out if they can divine any information: Why Lord Perseus chose to bind Nachari to the human female at this time, knowing he is helpless to act upon the revelation. Perhaps it was an act of intercession."

"How so?" Nathaniel asked.

Kagen shrugged. "I don't know, but maybe she holds the key to getting through to our little brother—wherever he may be—perhaps having his *destiny* here will act as a magnet of sorts, drawing him back into his body. Certainly, there could be no greater motivation. Perhaps her presence was needed right here, right now, for reasons we don't yet understand."

"Perhaps," Marquis agreed. "But in the meantime—assuming the worst-case scenario—what can we do for Nachari?"

Kagen nodded and clasped his hands together, rubbing his thumbs against each other in agitation. "We can do what we can to foster the relationship with the belief that Nachari will wake up in time, and we can even act on his behalf with regard to the Curse if necessary."

"Explain," Marquis said.

Kagen leaned forward. "The woman—Deanna—was drawn here on her own accord. There is already a very powerful connection between Nachari and his mate, if only by the grace of the gods; so I think we nurture that. We feed it." He stood up and walked to the window, staring out at the spectacular view beneath him of the southern cliff face and the low-hanging clouds. "We let her look through photo albums; we answer all of her questions; we tell her stories about Nachari's life—his childhood, his time at the University, his guardianship of Braden." He turned to face his brothers. "We allow her to spend time alone in his room…with his things…with him."

Nathaniel cocked his head to the side, slightly uncomfortable.

"I know," Kagen said, "it makes me nervous as well, brother. But she won't harm him. She is his *destiny*; she can't."

Marquis scowled. "Kristina *shot* me," he reminded them pointedly.

Kagen chuckled then, more out of sympathy than humor. "This is true, but then she was not your true *destiny*, was she?"

Marquis shrugged his agreement. "So, we give Deanna every opportunity to know Nachari…as best she can. What if he doesn't awaken in time to convert her? In time to…" His voice trailed off. Clearly, the words *impregnate her* seemed harsh and even crude under the circumstances.

Kagen walked slowly back to his chair and sat down on the edge, looking down at the floor. He slowly raised his eyes. "There's not much we can do about the latter," he conceded. "If Nachari is not back in time to…foster that relationship, then all may very well be lost."

Silence echoed throughout the room as the words drifted amongst each of the males, none of them willing to comment on their gravity.

"And the other?" Nathaniel asked. "The conversion?"

Kagen nodded slowly. "I've been giving that a lot of thought, and actually, I think it can be done medically."

"Medically?" Marquis furrowed his brow.

Kagen turned toward the Ancient Master Warrior and held his gaze. "Yes, medically." He shifted restlessly in his chair. "The conversion is done with venom, right? And the venom is pumped through the veins beneath our incisors. I believe a catheter could be inserted into Nachari's veins, another into Deanna's carotid artery, and our brother's venom could be pumped steadily through her body until the conversion is complete. She *is* his rightful *destiny*. I see no reason why his venom would not convert her successfully."

Nathaniel frowned. "And the pain? The fear? The need to restrain her?" He stared pointedly at Kagen, his face a mask of uncertainty. "Conversion is a horribly traumatic event…even when you hold your *destiny* in your arms. We cannot put our women under because, in essence, they are dying and being reborn—it's too dangerous. And the concentration it requires to pump the venom restricts even the smallest telepathic communication at first. How then does Deanna endure such a thing? She will surely fight for all she is worth...and bolt."

Kagen felt the full weight of Nathaniel's words. Unlike Nathaniel and Marquis, he had not met his *destiny* yet; consequently, he had never had to endure the profound suffering of a woman he loved more than anything in the world before. But he had heard enough war stories to understand the breadth of the event. And he was a Healer. He understood, probably more than they did, what exactly had to happen physiologically for every cell in the human body to die and be reborn through the infusion of vampire venom. "I know," he finally said, speaking quietly. "It is not a good scenario by any stretch, but I'm just saying, if we have to do it, I think we can." He looked back and forth between Nathaniel and Marquis. "And yes, she would have to be restrained."

Nathaniel nearly blanched. "With straps? To a table?" He grimaced, appalled. "She would hate him...*and us*...and the whole free world," he added. "And rightfully so!"

"Agreed," Kagen said. "I think one of us would need to...be there with her. Go through it with her."

Marquis shrugged his shoulders then. "Human women have coaches other than their husbands in childbirth," he supplied. "Perhaps one of the women—Ciopori or Jocelyn, or maybe both—could attend to her as well."

It painted a gruesome picture, and no one spoke for a moment.

Finally, Kagen waved his hand in dismissal. "Hopefully, it won't come to that."

Marquis frowned. Being analytical as he always was, he stated, "It may come sooner than you think."

Both Kagen and Nathaniel stared at him expectantly, waiting for an explanation.

He glanced absently at his nails before continuing: "I agree.

BLOOD SHADOWS

It is unpleasant. I would not choose it for our new sister, but"—he planted both hands palms-down on his knees and leaned forward—"Nachari's life takes precedence for me. I am sorry, but that is simply the truth. If the presence of the woman as his *destiny* does not draw him out of his slumber, then perhaps a conversion will. If they share the same DNA, the same breath of life as it were, she may be able to reach him, perhaps literally affect his physical health, following conversion. If it comes down to it, I will make the call...pleasant or not."

Kagen didn't respond right away. Rather, he thought about the night Marquis had converted Kristina in a rage: The fiery redhead had been revealed as Marquis's *destiny* through a trick of black magic, a deception created by Salvatore Nistor with the blessing of the Dark Lord Ocard to ultimately bring about Marquis's demise. Unbeknownst to the Master Warrior, Marquis had believed Kristina to be his true mate; and in an angry act of domination—granted, she had blasted him with a shotgun, twice—Marquis had thrown Kristina over his lap, sunk his fangs into her neck, and converted her right then and there on his front porch, in plain view. It had been a hideous and painful time for everyone; but the point was—Kagen had no doubt that Marquis would make the call if he felt he needed to. And as the eldest Silivasi brother, the de facto head of their family following the death of their father, Keitaro, it was ultimately Marquis's call to make.

"We will obey you in all things, of course," Kagen responded, not wanting to argue at this point. "I am simply saying that I hope it doesn't come to that."

"As do I," Nathaniel agreed.

Marquis appeared genuinely contemplative as he regarded both brothers. "Of course," he said evenly. "I hope Nachari returns to us before it comes to that as well." He hung his head then, just barely, before raising his angular jaw once again in his typical, proud posture. "I am not the monster you would make of me, Kagen."

Kagen's heart constricted in his chest. "Marquis, I do not—"

He waved his hand. "It is of no consequence. I have long ago made peace with my station in this family...and my responsibilities."

"That may be," Kagen said sternly, "but if my brother thinks I see him as a monster, then that is not okay with me." He squared his shoulders to Marquis. "I do not."

Marquis shrugged. "Very well."

"No," Kagen argued. "Not *very* well." He stood, crossed the room, and placed a hand on Marquis's shoulder. "Do you not know how much you are respected...and loved...brother?"

Marquis squirmed uncomfortably and frowned. "I think you need a woman, brother."

Kagen laughed softly. "That may be true, as well. But did you hear me?"

Marquis growled. "Whatever."

Kagen backed away then, satisfied. "Yes...*whatever*," he parroted.

Nathaniel leaned forward and winked at the aggravated Master Warrior. "I love you, too, big guy."

Marquis shot to his feet. "Dear gods, I have pansies for brothers."

They both laughed.

"And yet, here you are," Nathaniel drawled, "ready to start a war between heaven and hell over a green-eyed wizard. I think thou dost protest too much." He smiled congenially.

Marquis rolled his eyes. "Very well, have your fun." He turned to Kagen. "Where is Deanna now? Is she still sleeping?"

"Yes," Kagen answered, "and I think she's going to be extremely exasperated, not to mention ticked off, when we awaken her...yet again."

Marquis nodded. "It couldn't be helped." He sat back down. "I think it is time to explain to our new sister just who she is, the world she has now become a part of, and the damnable Curse that rules us all. I will ask Ciopori to go through Nachari's things—try to find some important mementos, photo albums, and such. We should schedule visits with the women, perhaps even Napolean if that's not too intimidating."

"If?" Nathaniel said. "Jocelyn still goes out of her way to avoid him."

Marquis shrugged. "Okay, well, maybe not Napolean. The women will be less frightening anyhow. Just the same, it is time to begin her education, to bring her into our world." He stared at Kagen then. "I hope you are right, Healer, about her connection to our little brother. Because it is time for Deanna Dubois to get to know her vampire husband…as best she can. And pretty as he is, even sleeping, she had better love him."

Nathaniel lowered his gaze, hiding a smirk.

"As you wish," Kagen replied formally. He stood up, indicating that the meeting was over.

Marquis followed suit. He turned to march out of the room, stopped at the door, and growled. And then he turned back around. Without preamble, he strode across the floor, pulled Kagen into a harsh, one-armed embrace, and beat on his back two times with a fist before shoving him away. As Kagen stumbled backward, trying to catch his balance, the huge vampire took a step toward Nathaniel. He stopped, stared at the expectant warrior as if considering another embarrassing hug, took note of the sly, self-satisfied smirk on Nathaniel's face, and then apparently thought better of it. Tapping Nathaniel none too lightly on the side of the head in what could only be described as an affectionate ear-cuff, he snorted, "You're all right, too."

Nathaniel batted his eyes playfully and held out his arms wistfully. "What? No hug for your remaining warrior brother?"

Marquis stared at his open arms, each one in turn, hissed an answering growl, and strolled out of the room.

"Guess not," Nathaniel said. He turned toward Kagen, laughing. "What was that?"

Kagen glanced at the empty doorway and smiled. "I think our big brother just told us he loves us."

nine

They said she was his *destiny*.

And he was a vampire…

Bound by an ancient curse.

They said he had made an unbelievable sacrifice for their noble king, agreeing to die—allow his otherwise immortal body to flatline—in order to save the king from a horrible enemy who wanted to destroy the "sons of Jadon." Nachari had acted with honor, and he had made the ultimate sacrifice. And his brothers were terrified that they might lose him…forever.

Deanna blinked back tears of confusion and shock, unable to process such fantastic information. She sat forward in the comfortable armchair beside the bed—beside *Nachari's* bed—and stared at his chiseled face. "Are you real?" she whispered absently, following the line of his strong cheeks, sculpted nose, and handsome mouth with her gaze. She turned her attention to his hair, that impossible mound of thick raven locks that fell to his shoulders in such perfect, subtle waves that they resembled a halo surrounding him in slumber, and she slowly reached out to touch it.

It was strong.

Soft.

Every bit as silky as it appeared.

She drew back her hand as if she had just touched fire, feeling suddenly self-conscious. "I'm sorry," she muttered, "I…I had no right to touch you." He looked so serene and unconcerned, yet that couldn't be the truth. Not if what his brothers had told her was real. She swallowed her fear and raised her wrist, rotating it so she could study the pattern etched into her skin. It was beautiful, really. And more than a little surreal—the way it had just appeared. And still remained. *Perseus*. Nachari's reigning Blood Moon.

She shook her head, sat back in the chair, and hugged her arms to her chest, deliberately dismissing the thought. It was too much to take in right now. All of it.

It was all just too much.

The fact that the man in her drawings was real. The fact that vampires actually existed. The fact that she had been inexplicably drawn to this place and this male—and there was no denying anymore that *something* powerful had brought her here on purpose—or the fact that her life had already changed beyond her comprehension. She knew it in her bones as well as her soul. Nachari's brothers were not about to let her walk away, and somewhere deep down inside, where she didn't dare to go (not yet, anyway), there was a part of her that wasn't capable of leaving his side.

And then all at once, a strange peace began to settle over her, not unlike the ghostly fog just outside the window, descending upon the forest canopy. Without reason, it drew her inward, beckoned her forward, engulfed her in a tangible, discernible presence.

His presence.

Nachari's.

And in that suspended moment, it was as if she knew him intimately—his humor, his values, his unwavering confidence…his playful, ingratiating nature.

His magnificent, powerful soul.

Deanna glanced around the room and shivered. It was as if he were there—conscious, awake, and standing behind her. The feeling was so real that she half expected him to reach out and touch her on the shoulder. When nothing happened, she opened her mouth to speak…and then she closed it, feeling incredibly foolish.

It was just her mind playing tricks on her: the stress, the confusion.

Deanna turned back toward the bed, closed her eyes, and allowed several slow, deep breaths to calm her. She would take this one day at a time. One moment at a time. She would learn all there was to learn about this mysterious male, and she would—

The hair on the back of her neck stood up again.

She sat up straight and glanced over her shoulder. "What?" she whispered. "I'm here." She briefly closed her eyes. "I feel you."

Just then, a large raven passed by the open window, and the frenetic flutter of its wings caused Deanna to jolt in her chair. She spun around abruptly and stared wide-eyed and open-mouthed as the bird took perch on the windowsill and simply stared at her...with piercing, dark green eyes.

Ravens did *not* have dark green eyes.

And then the Panasonic receiver on the corner table across the room began to illuminate: One by one, blue and red LED lights softly lit up; a pair of small Bose speakers began to hum; and a faint but clear tune began to play—the sound instantly permeating the room: "Oh, my love, my darling; I've hungered for your touch, a long lonely time..."

The Righteous Brothers singing 'Unchained Melody.'

Deanna sat in stunned silence listening to every word, feeling every faint vibration within her body as if the notes played against her skin. She deliberately resisted the urge to jump up and run.

"And time goes by so slowly, and time can do so much. Are you still mine?"

Her mouth went dry.

Did he know?

How could he know?

That this used to be her father's favorite song before he passed away. That her father had listened to it day and night on an old forty-five, spun on an old, rickety turntable. That the album and the turntable remained her two most cherished possessions, even to this day.

"I need your love; I need your love. God speed your love to me..."

The song continued to play like a haunting melody, reaching

deep into Deanna's soul and stirring it in a way that nothing else could.

While her first impression was to view the strange occurrence as a message from her father—some sort of sign sent from the world beyond—she knew that it was not. "Unchained Melody" had a very special meaning to her as well: Following a terrible breakup with a lover she had once believed she would marry, Deanna had stayed up late into the night for two straight weeks, drawing on her sketch pad and listening to the words again and again. She had prayed that her heart would heal, and she had taken comfort in knowing that somewhere, someday, the right person would come along. And when he did, he would have the kind of love for her the Righteous Brothers sang about in their famous song—the kind that could never be separated by time, distance, or petty disputes.

"Lonely rivers flow to the sea, to the sea, to the open arms of the sea. Lonely rivers sigh wait for me, wait for me; I'll be coming home, wait for me."

And then just like that, the raven flew away, and the receiver shut down. The lights turned off, the speakers fell silent, and the melody ceased.

But the words still lingered...

"I'll be coming home, wait for me."

Deanna's body literally shook.

They said she was his *destiny*.

And she was.

ten

Saber Alexiares checked his watch and smiled. It was six PM on Tuesday, forty-five minutes after sunset. *Perfect.* The silly kid—what was his name? Braden something or other—would be heading to the clinic to sit by Nachari's bedside, or whatever the kid did when he was visiting the unlucky bastard; and the redheaded girl would be pulling into the driveway at any moment, back from her monthly hair appointment. He absently wondered how Salvatore Nistor knew all this shit—probably that ridiculous cube or something—but then he realized that he really didn't care.

He was grateful, however, that the female was living at the wizard's brownstone with the kid for a while, as opposed to staying at her permanent condo on the top floor of the Dark Moon Lodge. Trying to get next to her anywhere near that place would have been pointless at best. Too risky. Far too many sons of Jadon coming and going at all hours of the day and night.

Saber sneered, thinking about his natural enemy and the way they hovered over their females like bees around a honeycomb: hyper-protective, disgustingly macho, and just all-around annoying.

The sound of tires spinning over gravel caught his attention, and he turned to face the approaching vehicle: a flashy pink Corvette, quite the contrast to the traditional 1920s-style, brick-faced brownstone that the flashy car approached. He rolled his head on his shoulders, popped his neck, and tried to stretch his back while he waited for the ditzy girl to pull into the drive…and notice him. Even though the body he was wearing, so to speak, wasn't real—it was more or less a mirage, a convincing illusion created and held by Salvatore Nistor's Black Magic—it still felt a little odd. Ramsey Olaru was one huge, six-foot-five, muscled-up vamp; and while Saber was accustomed to carrying a lot of hard, tight muscle himself, it felt like he was wearing an extra fifty pounds, standing about five inches taller. The world just looked a little different from this vantage point.

No matter.

He sauntered across the front porch to a neat, bricked-in planter, crossed his arms in front of his chest, and copped a lean, waiting for the girl to pull up.

She was driving far too fast on her approach, but he figured that didn't matter, either. She had an immortal body now and was living life to the fullest. He could almost respect that.

About five more seconds passed—the female absently bopping her head to the music and singing up a storm—before she finally glanced in his direction and instantly hit the brakes, bringing the car to a screeching halt. She did a double-take, and Saber chuckled. He immediately registered the minor fluctuations in her body rhythms—an increased pulse, notable shallow breathing, and the distinct scent of raised pheromones. *Looks like our Kristina finds the dark-blond, hazel-eyed Olaru brother both intimidating and handsome*, he thought. *This is going to be interesting.*

She inched the car forward, pulling as far to the left as she could, before bringing it to a halt, all the while craning her neck to keep him in sight. She stepped out slowly, and he cracked his neck one more time.

Time to get in character.

As she shut the driver's side door, rounded the hood, and ambled toward the porch, he frowned. "You don't park in the garage?" Since Ramsey Olaru was one of three sentinels sworn to protect the citizens of Dark Moon Vale, Saber figured Ramsey's first concern would be the girl's safety—might as well make the performance believable.

"What?" she called back, her voice reflecting the potential for a gallon-sized attitude in a pint-sized body.

"Your car," he repeated, inclining his head in the Corvette's direction. "You should park it in the garage."

Kristina looked back at the car for a moment and shrugged.

"Oh, yeah, I guess...I mean, if you really think it matters."

Saber nodded. "I do."

"Fine," she said, not seeming to care one way or the other. "I'll do it next time." She stopped about three feet in front of him. "So...what are you doing here?" She looked over his shoulder, then out at the yard, as if she expected to see someone else standing there. "It's Rocky, right?"

He laughed out loud. "Ramsey."

She blushed and shifted her weight nervously back and forth between her feet. "Oh...damn...sorry." She forced a smile. "So, what are you doing here, *Ramsey*?" She wrung her hands together and then deliberately stopped fidgeting. "You're one of Napolean's dudes, right?"

He bit his lip. *Dudes?* This had to be the most ridiculous thing the Dark Council had ever asked him to do. "I was looking for you," he answered, cutting to the chase. Despite her brass exterior, the female was known to be insecure; and taking advantage of both characteristics would be Saber's best weapon.

"Me?" she asked. "Why? Is something wrong?" Her forehead creased with concern. "Has something changed with Nachari? Did something happen to Braden?" She immediately stepped toward the door and reached for the knob.

Saber reached out and placed a strong arm in front of her, blocking her path. "Slow down, girl—everything's fine."

She took a nervous step backward, retreating from the contact. "Okay...so then, what's up?"

He shrugged his shoulders with an easy swagger. "Don't know yet. I was hoping we might figure that out...together."

Kristina drew back. "Excuse me?"

He smiled then, slow and sexy. "You heard me."

She started fidgeting again. "Um, I'm pretty sure I don't know what you're talking about."

He raised his arm above his head, resting it against the door frame, and leaned in closer. His posture was both inviting and intimidating. "Oh, I think you do."

She looked almost irritated then—clearly defensive and

definitely off-guard.

Good. He preferred to remain in control. He smiled. "Should I spell it out?"

She raised her auburn eyebrows. "Spell what out?"

"You. And me. Male and female. Both in the house of Jadon. Both unattached." He chuckled low in his throat and moved back a bit, giving her a little room to breathe. A moment to let his words sink in. "I bet you can fill in the blanks," he added.

Kristina swallowed convulsively and held out her hand as if to push him away. "Um, I'm pretty sure my brothers aren't havin' any of that. And neither is Napolean."

Saber shrugged again. "Why not?" Before she could answer, he added, "And do you always do what Nathaniel, Marquis, and Kagen tell you to do?" He cocked his head to the side and stared at her, perplexed. "I didn't take you for a yes-girl."

She looked clearly bothered—if not directly insulted—but that was precisely what he wanted, to appeal to her pride. Being an incredible judge of character, Saber immediately saw Kristina as a ship without a harbor, a female who had been tossed even further out to sea by the recent turn of events: Her newfound family focused all their attention on Nachari and their mates, and she was left with a fifteen-year-old boy for companionship and nowhere to turn for attention. Under the circumstances, Saber didn't need to be charming or even convincing—all he needed to do was stand in the gap.

"The way I see it," he drawled, "there aren't that many single people in the house of Jadon. Especially women like you—who were turned under unusual circumstances." He reached out and boldly caught a lock of her curly red hair, letting it fall through his fingers slowly as he inhaled the scent of her shampoo. "You're not still thinking about spending time with human men, are you?"

She looked positively stunned. "I don't know!" She put her hands on her hips. "That's none of your business, really. And don't you have a *destiny* somewhere to be concerned about?"

"Whoa," he said, holding up both hands as if to surrender. "Back it up, sweetheart. No offense intended." He used Ramsey's striking hazel eyes and model good looks to their fullest advantage, holding Kristina's surprised gaze while offering a sheepish—if not devilish—grin. "I will have a mate to think of someday; that's true…" He reached out and brushed her chin briefly with the back of his finger. "As will you, I imagine. But not today." He paused. "Maybe not for decades to come."

She frowned and looked away. "And so you thought you could just materialize on my doorstep and what? Get the only unattached female vamp in the house of Jadon to give you some?"

Saber suppressed a chuckle. "Sweetie…" He spoke in a pacifying tone. "It's not all about sex—why I'm here." He tilted her chin upward with his hand. "Sometimes it's just nice to have someone to talk to…to be with…to help pass the time." He raised his eyebrows. "Are you going to stand there and pretend your heart isn't racing, your palms aren't sweating, and your breath isn't catching in your throat?" He leaned over to whisper in her ear. "I know it is."

She took two steps back, pressed flush against the front door, and wrapped her arms around her waist in a self-protective gesture. "Damn, Ramsey—are you always so direct?" She looked away. "So…I'm human. That doesn't make me a fool. Or easy."

He shook his head and laughed. "First of all, you're not human, baby girl. And if I thought you were easy, I wouldn't be here." He took a step back then. "Believe it or not, I'm not all that easy myself."

Now that got her attention.

Her eyes opened a little wider, and she appeared to be listening.

Thinking.

Perhaps even considering.

"Listen," he said. He raised his arm to his mouth, scored his wrist with the tips of his fangs, and held it up to her as blood trickled down his arm. "Forget about all that other stuff for now.

You're hungry; I can sense it. Accept this offer of friendship…and feed."

Kristina's hand flew up to cover her mouth. She tried to back further away but had nowhere to go. "No!" she protested vehemently. "I can't."

"You can't feed?" he asked.

"*No*…I mean, I can't…with you. My brothers…" Her voice trailed off.

"Ah," he nodded, feigning understanding. "The obedient little sister again." He released his incisors, dripped healing venom over the gash to close it, and withdrew his arm. "I got it."

Kristina frowned.

"That's okay," Saber quipped. "No worries. So I misjudged—no harm, no foul, right?"

Kristina seemed to be holding her breath, searching for a response. "Misjudged what?"

He didn't hesitate in his blunt appraisal: "You. Where you're at. What might be possible…between us." He backed away, stepped down from the porch onto the first of five steps, and shrugged. "If feeding…and friendship…are not even possible, then there's not a whole lot more to be said. My mistake." He turned and took another step, knowing he was taking a calculated risk: She might just let him go—which would place him right back at square one as far as his mission was concerned—but he was betting she would stop him before it went that far. Theirs was likely the only meaningful contact she'd had with an adult—other than Braden or her family—in months; and it was more than likely the only offer she'd had from any male in the honorable house of Jadon, period. There wouldn't be another one coming along any time soon.

He restrained a chuckle.

Kristina would be hard-pressed to let *Ramsey* go. Any needy female would.

He let the silence between them linger for a moment, and then he cleared two more steps. "I'm sorry if I offended—or frightened—you, Kristina. That was never my intention." With that, he took the remaining step in a casual leap and began to stroll down the walk.

"Wait," she whispered.

Her voice was barely audible, but Saber heard her loud and clear. He stopped dead in his tracks and stifled a smile. Slowly turning around, he met her tentative gaze. "What's up?"

She sighed in exasperation. "I'm not trying to say...anything...one way or the other. It's just that I don't know what—*hell*, I didn't even know your name ten minutes ago. I haven't had time to think."

He smiled regretfully. "A vampire shouldn't have to think to feed, Kristina. It should just come natural." He held up both hands. "Hey, it's cool. Truly. Your conversion was how long ago? Just over four months? So you're not ready yet—there's no shame in that, baby girl." He inclined his head toward the front door. "You take care, okay?" He turned around again, but not before he saw her eyes flash momentarily red.

"Fine," she snapped. "Since you know so much about everything, just go then."

He bit his lip to keep from smiling. *He had her.* Hesitating, he looked down at the ground and pretended to grapple with some internal frustration. When he finally turned around to face her, his expression was one of confused anticipation: "I'm having a hard time reading your signals here, Kristina. Do you want me to go, or do you want me to stay?"

She opened her mouth to speak and then faltered, unable to give him a clear yes or no answer, and he knew he had pushed her as far as she was able to go. In the space of a heartbeat, he scored his wrist a second time, materialized in front of her, and held the offering out a second time. "Feed, sweetheart." A blood exchange would do more to foster intimacy than sex ever could; besides, she would be dead long before she acquired enough skill to track him. So there was really no risk in feeding her.

She reached up hesitantly and took his arm in her hands. While her approach was as awkward as it was inexperienced—he was accustomed to soldiers who struck the jugular with force—

she managed to sink her fangs deep enough to take a healthy, drugging pull. And then she sighed with relief. As the full potency of his blood flowed into her, her eyes fell half shut, and she almost moaned from the pleasure of it.

"That's it, baby girl," he whispered. "Take what you need."

He waited silently as she drank her fill, all the while considering the situation: If his mission had been only to seduce her—or simpler yet, to take her by force and dispatch her—he could have pulled that off easily; but as it stood, Oskar and Salvatore had instructed him to get close to her, gain enough of her trust to discover her secrets, get inside of her head—which was something he had never had to do before—so, in a way, both of them were selling their souls in the encounter.

Before he could contemplate any further, Kristina withdrew her fangs, clumsily sealed the wound, and released her hold on his arm. Wiping her mouth with the back of her hand, she looked away, embarrassed. "Thanks," she mumbled.

He was about to ask her to invite him in—at the least, get the invitation out of her so he could come and go as he pleased, if needed—but then he thought better of it. The girl was uncomfortable now, almost as if they'd just had meaningless sex. "You all right?" he asked.

She nodded, insincerely. "Yeah…I'm cool."

He gently grasped her chin in his hand and tilted her head up to force her gaze. "Are you sure?"

She looked away but nodded. "Yeah…I'm sure."

Turning her head back with his hand, he bent over leisurely and pressed his mouth to hers. Careful to keep the kiss both gentle and short, he pulled away ever so slowly and whispered, "Friendship is a good thing, Kristina. *Relax*." And then he took her keys, placed the largest one in the lock, turned it, and pushed the door open. His skin began to burn as it crossed the threshold absent of an invitation, but he ignored the sensation and quickly tucked his hand behind his back before she could notice. "Go inside," he suggested. "I'll see you another time."

She looked surprised.

Relieved.

More than a little confused…

But she stepped inside the brownstone.

"Sleep well, baby girl," he called after her.

She cleared her throat. "Yeah, okay…you, too." And with that, she shut the door behind her.

Saber smiled, letting out a slow, deep breath. *Damn, that had been like pulling teeth.* But worth it, he figured. As far he was concerned, it might be a little touch and go going forward, yet she was more or less putty in his hands. He waited a moment before dematerializing. In truth, he couldn't wait to shed Ramsey's unfamiliar skin and get back to the colony, to his own kind, but he didn't want to seem too rushed in case she was peeking through the peephole.

All in all, he thought, Salvatore had done a pretty good job of maintaining Ramsey's persona for him—cloaking his own physical appearance for such an extended period of time. Just the same, his soul was reeling from the experience.

Killing—he understood.

Preying on the weak—nothing more than an automatic reflex, as easy as passing time.

But talking, flirting, and sidling up to a female—all easy, nice, and respectful?

That bullshit was for the birds.

Kristina shut the door behind her and fell back against it, trying to catch her breath: Ramsey Olaru? One of Napolean's sentinels?

Was she dreaming?

Never, in all her life, had a man that fine or that important wanted her…for anything. Even Marquis had only picked her because he had no choice. And before that, it had been Dirk— for years—a confusing mix of love, abuse, and way too much need.

Kristina could hardly believe what had just happened, and a wistful smile softened her mouth as she held her hand over her fluttering heart and laughed out loud. She could still taste the intoxicating flavor of his blood. It was like drinking pure energy, unfiltered power. Sure, Marquis's blood had been amazing. And Nathaniel's? *Damn*—just...damn! But this was unlike anything she had ever imagined before. There was something dark, dangerous, and sexy as hell about Ramsey Olaru.

And he wanted *her*.

Kristina told herself to get a grip—keep in mind that the male wasn't really available, and he would walk away the moment his *destiny* showed up—but so what. He was here now. She twirled around in delight. Very few girls got the chance to spend time with a male like that, not even for a day, let alone what could turn into years. *And he had chosen her.* Sure—she would probably get mated someday. More than likely, her brothers would choose some boring justice or healer for her, some widower who wasn't half as hot and edgy as Ramsey; but in the meantime, she would have her fun.

And her fine-as-hell man.

Baby girl.

Sweetheart.

He had called her both...

Oh...my...God.

Kristina shut her eyes and let the reality of it all sink in.

She concentrated on the feel of Ramsey's blood in her veins and tried to imagine where he was now—what he was doing. When nothing came to her, she shrugged: It really didn't matter.

Just so long as nothing and no one stopped him, he would be back.

She was sure of it.

The thought brought her up short. *Oh shit*, she really had to be careful with this one. Marquis, Nathaniel, and Kagen would have a cow. Even Braden would strut around trying to be all warrior-like and fatherly, or run off as fast as he could to tell

Napolean.

And wouldn't that just be the end of it all.

Kristina shuddered, thinking of how quickly this new affair might come to an end if the wrong people found out about it. No, that wasn't going to happen.

She wouldn't let it.

This was one secret Kristina Riley-Silivasi planned to take all the way to the grave.

eleven

Deanna stepped onto the stony River Walk, a meandering path that followed the banks of the Snake Creek River for at least a mile, following the beautiful woman with mysterious eyes who had married Nachari's brother, Nathaniel.

Jocelyn turned around and waited for her to catch up. "You sure you're all done shopping for the day?"

Deanna chuckled. "Yes. I don't think I could walk into another souvenir or specialty shop if my life depended on it."

Jocelyn nodded her agreement. The two had spent the day exploring the small, quaint towns surrounding the national forest at Kagen's bequest: The healer had insisted that Deanna get out of the clinic for a few hours, take in some fresh air, and stretch her legs. Just so long as they were back before sundown, there didn't seem to be any danger in the outing. And as far as running away or escaping was concerned, even Deanna understood how futile an attempt that would be: She was no match against a family of vampires.

Period.

Besides, the outing would give her a chance to talk with another woman—one who at least understood part of her predicament—without the males hovering around like hungry vultures; and Jocelyn Levi-Silivasi had seemed more than happy to escort Deanna on the excursion. Not to mention—truthfully—Deanna needed the break.

She was on information overload.

And then some.

After the bizarre experience in Nachari's room two days earlier, Deanna had questioned everyone she could about Nachari, the Vampyr, the Blood Curse, and anything else she could think of: She had been hungry for all the information she could consume.

"So," she said, falling into step beside Jocelyn and allowing the soothing rhythm of the creek to calm her frayed nerves, "you've adjusted well to this life already, then?"

Jocelyn smiled. "Yeah, I have." She shrugged. "It helps when you're madly in love with your husband and you have such a terrific son."

"Storm, is it?" Deanna asked.

"Yep," Jocelyn answered, "my little tornado."

Deanna tried to laugh, but it sounded as insincere as it felt. Out of absolutely nowhere, her laughter turned to tears, and she stopped, leaned against the rustic-wood railing, and covered her face in her hands. "I'm sorry," she whispered. "Just give me a moment."

Jocelyn turned around, her voice heavy with concern. "Not at all. Take all the time you need." She stood directly in front of Deanna for a while and then gently pried her hands from her face. "You know, you don't have to hide, Deanna. Not from me, anyway. I understand at least a little of what you're going through. This is far more than most humans will ever be asked to deal with in a lifetime."

Deanna nodded appreciatively, trying to control her emotions. "I know...I know...I'm just...damn, this is all so hard, so...unbelievable, so...unfair."

Jocelyn turned around and leaned against the railing, looking out at the river. "Yeah, well, that's one way of putting it. No argument here." She turned to face Deanna. "Do you feel like telling me what, precisely, it is that you're thinking about right now?"

Deanna wiped her eyes and looked out at the water, along with the other woman. The stream was so beautiful, so peaceful, so seemingly unconcerned. "Oh, man...where to begin."

"Anywhere you like," Jocelyn said. "I'm a good listener."

Deanna did manage to laugh a bit then. "You mean unlike your—" She stopped short.

"My mate?" Jocelyn said, smiling without offense. "Or my brother-in-law?"

Tessa Dawn

"Marquis," Deanna whispered, nearly shuddering. "Does he ever get less…intense?"

"No," Jocelyn said without hesitation. "You just learn how to deal with him—or you run and hide behind Ciopori."

Deanna did laugh then, thinking about the beautiful, raven-haired princess and how effortlessly she handled the six-foot-two overwhelming male.

"They do mean well," Jocelyn admitted. "All of them. They truly love Nachari…and each other."

Deanna felt her tears well up again. She sighed and took a deep breath. "Damn. Why can't I stop this?"

"I don't know," Jocelyn said. "Why do you think it is?"

Deanna turned around, pushed off from the rail, and stared up at the sky, placing a firm hand over her heart. "Because ever since that day…in his room…when I swear Nachari spoke to me through that radio—and trust me, I know how ridiculous that sounds—I can just…feel him or something. In my heart. It's like I know who he is, but I don't know him. And that really freaks me out."

Jocelyn didn't speak. She just looked at Deanna with infinite compassion in her eyes. Finally, she ventured: "Nachari is special, Deanna—even among the Vampyr."

Deanna drew to attention. "How so? I mean, what is it that you see in him that makes you say that?" She sighed then. "Please…oh please, don't lie to me—I don't think I could take it."

Jocelyn smiled kindly and held out her little finger. "Pinky swear."

Deanna hooked her pinky around Jocelyn's and nodded. "Okay."

"So, let's see," Jocelyn began. "What makes Nachari so unique?" She looked down into the water, as if picturing Nachari in the river's reflection. "Well, I would have to say that despite the obvious—his stunning good looks and swag personality—there's just something about his soul. Something quiet. Something deep. Something so good and pure that it precedes

101

him." She looked deeper into the stream while collecting her thoughts. "I think Nachari sees things that no one else does." Her vivid eyes sparkled with amusement. "Well, of course he does—he's a wizard—but I'm not just talking about the magic and second-sight. He sees people's souls, their intentions; he knows if a heart is good or bad, hurting or healing. He knows what people say versus what they mean…what they ask for versus what they need." She shook her head. "It's hard to explain, but it's like his relationship with the boy—"

"Braden?" Deanna interrupted.

"Yes, Braden. Nachari loves that kid almost unconditionally, and he just knows when to push, when to back off, how to bring him along." She chuckled wistfully. "You know, when I was first…how do I say this?" She smiled. "When I was first *ushered* into Dark Moon Vale, I had a couple of run-ins with Marquis that were unpleasant to say the least."

"Like what?" Deanna asked, sounding truly appalled.

"Mmm, like being accidentally tossed across Nathaniel's deck by the warrior and later locked up in a holding cell."

Deanna cringed. "Tell me you're kidding."

Jocelyn raised her eyebrows. "Do I look like I'm kidding?"

"Shit," Deanna whispered. "How did Nathaniel handle that?"

Jocelyn cleared her throat for effect. "Nathaniel was in his own hell about that time—definitely as keyed up as any male could be in the throes of his Blood Moon."

"And Kagen?"

"Well, Kagen was pretty much the way you see him now— mostly chilled out. Not one to go around making waves." She shrugged. "Nope, I'd have to say that Nachari was the one who really saw things from my point of view and showed it. His little…interventions…well, let's just say they weren't little at all. His kindness…his concern…it was how I knew things were going to be okay…ultimately. He brought sanity into an insane time."

"With humor?" Deanna asked. "I've heard he has a great

102

sense of humor."

"Yes," Jocelyn agreed. "That he does. He knows his brothers, and he can make light of their antics." She paused then. "But he also has compassion and gentleness. And wisdom—a lot of wisdom."

"No demons then?" Deanna asked, hopeful.

Jocelyn tilted her head from side to side as if weighing the question. "I wouldn't say that: Nachari also carries some pretty heavy weights of his own. The loss of his parents...and his twin."

Deanna nodded, understanding. "You mean Shelby?"

Jocelyn looked away, giving the impression that this was a subject she'd rather gloss over than elaborate on. "Yeah. Most definitely."

Deanna let the subject go. After all, who was she to push it or provide insight? She was a stranger amongst them all. And perhaps more confused than anyone. "I don't know what to do," she whispered, almost inaudibly, more thinking aloud than talking.

"About?" Jocelyn said.

Deanna shrugged. "All of this." She winced. "Kagen spoke to me about the possibility of *medical conversion*"—she made air quotes around the words—"based on the eventuality that Nachari might return one day." She stiffened. "Jocelyn, how in the world do I make a decision like that? Commit to someone I've never met? Irreversibly change my life—hell, my species— based upon the mere possibility that some guy I've never met might come back some day and claim me." Despite the evenness in her tone, she cringed at the words.

Jocelyn shook her head. "I don't know how to answer that, Deanna. I really don't. I wish I could tell you that it's the right thing to do—but I can't. Even though I already know, without question, that Nachari and you are right for each other, more than right, really...you're beyond right...you're perfect for each other—he will be everything you've ever dreamed of and more: I've just seen too much to doubt it—but you will have to find that out on your own. And I can't tell you the right or wrong way to get there."

"But how?" Deanna argued. "How do I find that out…when he's not even here?" She sounded as discouraged as she felt. "Through photo albums and walks down memory lane with people who knew him?" She caught herself. "I mean, people who *know* him."

Jocelyn stared at her then, her eccentric eyes shifting between subtle shades of green and brown, reflecting clearly why her mate so often called her tiger-eyes. "You know what I think?"

Deanna held her gaze. "What?"

"I think you're scared shitless, exactly as you claim, but not of Nachari, or conversion, or the Blood Curse—at least not primarily: I think you're absolutely terrified that he won't come back to you…that it might *not* ever happen." She averted her eyes. "I think that's why you came here, Deanna. Why you were the one who picked up so much information that it ended up in your drawings. I think you and Nachari are already…together."

Deanna stood in thoughtful silence, simply allowing Jocelyn's words to wash over her. The truth of them was almost too much to bear. She bit her bottom lip. "I'm not sure if I'll survive if he doesn't." She laughed a hollow laugh. "Don't get me wrong: If he did show up—say, on this bridge, right now—I would definitely take off running in the opposite direction; but yes, a part of me wants that so much it hurts, Jocelyn. I can't explain it; I just have to know. I have to at least…meet him."

Jocelyn reached out to place a gentle hand on her shoulder, and in the absence of resistance, gave her a bear hug. "It's going to be okay, Deanna," she whispered in her ear. "I really do believe that." Giving her one last squeeze, she pulled away. "It's only my opinion, but I think the key to the whole thing is not to try and figure it all out at once. Don't try to wrap your arms around so much at once…not at first. Just take it one day at a time…one piece of information at a time." She sighed. "And for whatever it's worth: If I were you, knowing what I know now, knowing Nachari the way I know him, I would fight like hell for that male—to know everything about him, to get him back, to create some kind of bridge of love that was strong enough to pull him out of the Spirit World, wherever he is. And if he showed up and I hated him, then oh well—you can cross that bridge when you come to it. But if you find out that he's the missing piece of your heart—the other half of your soul—you're going to want to know that there's nothing you didn't do to try and save him."

Deanna tucked her hair behind her ear and stared at the pretty woman next to her. A woman who was now a vampire. She was searching for seeds of truth, measuring Jocelyn's conviction, and it was all there, in her eyes, in her voice. She meant every word she said, and she certainly didn't come across as a fruitcake. Not to mention, everything she said was something Deanna had already thought of before. Needing a break from the intensity of the conversation, she walked further down the path, stopped to turn around, and called, "You coming?"

"Right behind you," Jocelyn said, hurrying to catch up.

Waiting, Deanna thought about the stern warning Nachari's brothers had given her earlier that day: "Do not play around when it comes to the time—be back before the sun goes down, or we'll send someone to get you." She shuddered, knowing full well who that someone would be.

Marquis Silivasi.

No, thank you.

Just then, Deanna glanced up at the sky, noticed grayish mottled clouds turning this way and that, and thought absently that a storm was coming: Maybe they should start to head back, after all. "Do you see those clouds?" she asked Jocelyn.

Jocelyn followed her gaze. "Yeah, I do."

"Maybe we should—"

"Turn back," Jocelyn supplied.

Deanna nodded and tried not to overanalyze the symbolism of those words: Whether or not the sky opened up and poured down rain was irrelevant. The truth was, a storm was definitely coming…

And the only question was whether or not Deanna would be ready when it arrived.

twelve

The Valley of Death and Shadows

Nachari Silivasi sat up on the old, rusted, iron bed in the dark chamber behind Ademordna's throne room and rustled his chains. The minions must have carried him back to his room after his last torture session, and he must have fallen asleep. How long ago had that been? he wondered. And how soon would they be coming back for him?

Since there were no windows in the damp, confined room, he had no natural way of judging time: not that there was any sun or moon to measure outside of the room anyhow.

He closed his eyes and tried to empty his mind, picturing the body of the Raven. The sleek black feathers came immediately into focus, cool and smooth against a rounded breast. He imagined the sharp beak, the hard edges and angled peak, the curved talons and the subtle ridges along the plumage; and he slowly allowed his consciousness to slip away. To become...other than he was. "Black as night, dark as coal; into flight, release my soul."

The transition got easier each time he did it—faster.

As the full form of the Raven emerged, not simply in his mind, but in his *being*—as his point of focus shifted from the green eyes of a vampire to the emerald stare of the Raven—the slip from one form of consciousness into another became seamless.

Without hesitation, Nachari spread his wings and flew beyond the confines of his prison—not far, mind you. That day in the clinic, when he had managed to separate not only from his body but from the Abyss, to see and hear Deanna in his room at the clinic, a lot of things had lined up perfectly to make that happen—not the least of which was the depth of Deanna's despair and confusion. The strength of her longing. Nachari had tried to return to her several times since that day without any luck—whatever providence had pierced the veil between worlds seemed closed to him now. Now…he could only use the eyes of his feathered friend to move around the Valley of Death and Shadows.

But it was better than nothing.

Spreading his raven's wings to their full four-foot span, he soared outside the fortress and took in his surroundings. Unlike the earth, where the sun's position in the sky suggested the time of day, where shadows fell at different degrees as the great ball of fire traveled across the horizon, the Valley of Death and Shadows was an empty cavern absent of true light. The unnatural atmosphere was one of relentless heat and dense fog that emanated from the energy of the souls within it: a projection of their essence. Just the same, Nachari had long since learned to distinguish the subtle shades of darkness, to differentiate the varied gradations of black and gray in order to discern the time, at least within an hour.

Confident that it was two or three in the afternoon, he released the form of the Raven and descended back into his body. Good. He had at least one to two more hours before Ademordna came to get him, before he would be taken back into the throne room for the evening's festivities—gatherings based entirely upon his perpetual torture.

He twisted around in an effort to bring motion to his tired body, stretched his rigid muscles, and regarded the bloodstained sheets. Disgusting, he thought, wishing his captors would at least change them now and then.

As if that was going to happen.

He reached for a flat, dingy pillow and placed it over a particularly troubling stain, one that had been caused by a head wound no doubt, and tried to concentrate on more important matters.

Getting home to his *destiny*.

What he could do to make that happen.

Tessa Dawn

So far, he knew three important things: First, he could take the form of the Raven at will—at least in so far as it meant traveling about the underworld; second, he had managed to leave his carnal form in the Abyss and penetrate the earth once—which meant if it were possible, he could do it again. And third, he had no allies or friends among his captors, save the misguided attentions of one being.

The dark demoness, Noiro.

The demented freak of nature thought she was in love with him. At least, she believed his DNA held enough promise and his wizardry was so advanced that it would be worthwhile to try and reproduce with him. Perhaps if his power were combined with hers, there would be enough energy to propel him home. All of him. If only he could get hold of four transformational elements from the four directions of the underworld: a frog from the east to symbolize the leap he must make from one realm to the next; the toxin of a southern scorpion to help pierce the veil between worlds; a spider from the west to help weave a spell powerful enough to propel him home; and a snake from the north to help him shed his metaphorical skin, thereby allowing him to slither between the worlds undetected. In truth, the dimensions were not that far from one another. The issue he had to contend with was one of vibration—the higher moving vibrations of the earth, and ultimately the Celestial realms, that were fueled by light, joy, and justice versus the slower moving vibrations of the underworld, which were restricted by darkness, evil, and fear. His fear for Napolean—his uncertainty about the process of dying—his desperation to save the king had created enough of a vibratory dissonance to make him vulnerable to Ademordna the day he had been snatched into the Abyss. He would have to recreate that same vibration—only much, *much* stronger—in order to force that portal open once again. And then he would have to trust in the overwhelming vibration of light and love—from his brothers and his *destiny*...and his king—to guide him home.

With the proper spell and the proper elements, he might just have a chance—one chance—to return.

But the demoness would have to help.

She would have to retrieve the elements for him. She might even have to join him on his journey through the realms—just as Ademordna had joined him on his way to the underworld to begin with. For surely the darkness would reject his light upon initial contact—the two energies would just be too discordant.

No, Noiro's presence would be a necessary evil, no pun intended.

Nachari sighed. So, how did he make that happen?

After all, demons remained in their own domain: The Valley of Death and Shadows. They did not travel back and forth between worlds unless they were summoned—as Ademordna had been by Salvatore and his dark brothers for the purpose of exacting revenge against Napolean. If Noiro traveled to the earth without the proper summoning, without the blood sacrifice required to pay her way, so to speak, she would become mortal—unprotected—capable of being killed.

And didn't that just cement the plan in his head.

He reclined on the bed and crossed his legs, resting his head on his folded arms while ignoring the heavy chains that abraded his chest. He had to get Norio to trust him. To want him so badly that she would follow him all the way to the earth—no, that she would willingly join him as they traveled between the realms. He had to create a wedge between her and Ademordna.

He had to dominate her will.

Reaching into the repository of knowledge he had stored from his time at the Romanian University, he began to search for an ancient spell, one that went beyond love or desire: one that bordered on obsession.

"Ancient fires, burning deep:
Come forth, alight, infuse with heat;
Unseen elements, which dormant lie,
Come forth to serve; submit, draw nigh.
Like clay beneath this potter's hand,
I bend your will to my command.

Yield her breast, her tongue, her mind,
Lay waste to reason; twist the vine...
"Obsession, ashes, mystic coals:
Draw void of reason; charred of soul,
and yield beneath this wizard's tongue,
my breath; her will—
combine as one."

The stony walls of the archaic room began to sway back and forth from the energy of Nachari's incantation. Red and blue flames licked along the mortar before intensifying into a blaze.

Nachari nodded, satisfied. And then he closed his eyes and pictured the evil twin of Orion—his dark, shadowed sister who had so tortured him since his arrival in the underworld. "Noiro," he whispered in his mind, envisioning the words as arrows shooting forth—straight and true—into the female's heart. "Come to me, now."

He held his breath and waited.

But not out of speculation or curiosity.

He already knew she would come; he could feel her twisted heart beating as if it were a second pulse beneath his own.

He could taste her every emotion on his tongue.

The universe had bent to his will.

Very well, then, he thought, *there's no time like the present.*

Noiro set down her heavy brush and sat up straight in front of her dressing table. Once again, she could not get the green-eyed vampire out of her mind. *Why, by all that was unholy, did the captive wizard get to her like that?*

She stood up in her bedchamber and began to pace the floor.

Ademordna would not be pleased if he knew the true extent of her obsession, if he understood just how much of her waking thoughts the vampire consumed. And it was growing stronger by the minute. *Cursed darkness*—it was growing *stronger!*

She frowned then, growing even more annoyed.

She was supposed to be the Beta Ruler of the Northern territory—a demoness of high stature and esteem in the Valley of Death and Shadows—yet here she remained, for ten more years, metaphorically chained to Ademordna's side in the Center Kingdom.

The Valley of Death and Shadows was divided into five provinces or quadrants, as it were, based upon the unique landscape of the underworld: It was created in the shape of a cross, with the top and bottom spikes being the Northern and Southern Provinces and the arms of the cross consisting of the Eastern and Western Provinces. Each province was ruled by a Prime Dark Lord, and within each province, there were four subordinate regions—north, south, east, and west—which were ruled by regional sub-lords: alpha, beta, gamma, and delta rulers. Each sub-ruler served their province Lord, and each province Lord served the Supreme Ruler in the Middle Kingdom, which was located in the precise center of the cross.

For as long as Noiro could remember, Ademordna, as the twin dark energy of the most powerful light god in the Celestial world, had reigned over the Middle Kingdom and thus, stood as ruler of the entire underworld. She stomped her foot against the floor, thinking how unfair the whole hierarchy was: Females were never allowed to rule provinces like they surely did in the Valley of Spirit and Light. No, down in the bowels of the Abyss, where might meant right, they were constantly subjugated by their more powerful counterparts, the male demon lords. Noiro had been one of only a handful of females to earn her way up the ladder to the subordinate position of Beta Ruler over the Northern Province, and she had held the position for fifty years until Lord Ademordna had called her into service in the Middle Kingdom...for an indefinite period of time. Which really meant, until he grew tired of her.

And what did that service amount to anyhow? "Yes, my liege. No, my liege. What can I fetch for you today, my liege?

Would it please you to use my body, my liege? Or would you rather offer it to another? However may I please you, oh Great Ademordna?" She spat on the floor, the green goo turning to acid and burning away as it hit the stony surface. It wasn't like each Prime Lord—including Lord Ademordna—didn't have an army of servants, male and female minions, in their province to wait on their beck and call already.

Her body began to shake, and she made a concerted effort to calm down. Should Ademordna sense her energy, there was no telling what demonic—and possibly delightful in its own horrific way—things he might do to her. Besides, she had a plan: to do the one thing no male could rival, regardless of his station.

Noiro had a plan to give birth to the greatest king the underworld had ever seen—a powerful ruler in his own right who would one day usurp the mighty Ademordna and rule the entire Abyss, himself. Well, of course, with the help of his mother.

The thought was practically orgasmic. Oh, the being she would create with the green-eyed wizard, a son of unparalleled beauty, power, and sorcery. Yes, she was precisely where she needed to be…in the Middle Kingdom with Ademordna.

And Nachari Silivasi.

Holding fast to her resolve, Noiro waved her arm in front of her body in order to create a flowing crimson gown of tattered silk and ash. *Beautiful*, she thought, staring at herself in the opaque oval mirror across from her dressing table. Now then, what would the arrogant vampire prefer today? By all that was unholy, she had tried everything to please him so far—what the hell did he want?

A sly smile creased the corners of her mouth as she began to envision a tall, buxom blonde. As long yellow locks began to fall down her shoulders and vivid blue eyes emerged in her sallow sockets, she licked her full lips and drew in a deep breath.

Today would be the day.

Surely, Nachari would take her now.

Careful to remain hidden from Ademordna's other minions,

she flew through the dark, misty halls of the Middle Kingdom's Fortress until, at last, she stood outside the heavy, wooden dungeon doors: Nachari's private chamber behind the king's throne room. Easy access was the name of the game.

She started to knock and then rolled her eyes. The male was still a *captive*, and despite his many talents—and oh, were they many—he was still her inferior, a being of both light and goodness who lived according to a ridiculous code of honor, family, and loyalty. He was nothing compared to her, and she would not show him respect.

Not even to seduce him.

She threw open the door and flew into the room like a gust of wind, surrounded by a dozen red bats, diving and circling wildly around her. "Good afternoon, dear wizard," she crooned, sashaying up to him with her hips swaying, her long legs flexing in six-inch heels. "Did you miss me?" Her laughter resounded like fingernails against a chalkboard.

The wizard sat up on the bed, turned toward her, and…smiled.

Smiled?

His perfect teeth gleamed white as ivory beneath full, inviting lips; and his sculpted cheekbones seemed somehow more prominent beneath the devastating light of his smile. "I did," he whispered.

Noiro took a measured step back and turned to look behind her. Was there someone else in the room? When she saw no one, she turned back to regard the striking male on the bed. "You did?"

He reached his hand out to her, lugging a heavy chain with him. "Come closer."

Noiro swallowed hard and turned her head to the side, glaring at him with her peripheral vision. *What gives*, she thought, growing instantly wary.

He chuckled then, a pure, resonant sound, both seductive and hypnotic. And then he placed a smooth, straight finger over his mouth and shook his head. "Hmm."

"Hmm, what?" Noiro demanded.

He shrugged, appearing far too nonchalant. "I am the captive," he drawled, "yet you are afraid...of me. Why is that?"

She stuck out her bottom lip in a pout. "I don't fear you, Nachari!" She punctuated the words with a sudden lunge at the wizard; and with a harsh swipe from her hand, she left a trail of blood on his upper lip in the wake of a sharp talon.

Nachari closed his eyes, licked the blood from his lips, and chuckled. "Is that supposed to intimidate me?"

Her mouth fell open.

"Sit down," he commanded, motioning to the mattress beside him.

Still stunned, Noiro took a step toward the bed and sat down—at the foot—where she could watch him guardedly in case he was up to something.

He looked her up and down and shook his head with disappointment. "This will never do."

Noiro stomped her foot in frustration. "What do you mean?"

"This," he repeated, gesturing toward her dress and shoes. He reached up to grab a lock of her blond hair, and she almost fell from the bed in surprise. "Touchy, are we?" he rasped.

"No, and how dare you insult my—"

"I don't like it," he said softly, cutting her off in midsentence. "This fake look. All these different appearances. One day, you're a redhead, the next a brunette, the next a bleached blonde. To whom do you think you are engaging?"

Noiro stood up then.

She walked to the other side of the room and stared at him, incredulous. She would rip those raven locks from his scalp and shove them down his arrogant throat; she would choke him while she disemboweled him, and then she would detach his manhood from his body just to see him scream...before he grew it back. To whom did he think *he* was engaging?

"What do you know about Vampiric conception?" he asked, ignoring what had to be a feral look in her eyes.

"What!" she demanded.

"Conceiving—*a child*—with a vampire. What do you know about it?"

Noiro huffed her indignation. "I know how to debase you...and torture you...like a little—"

He waved his hand in dismissal.

He was dismissing *her*?

"So you know about speaking a pregnancy into being and focused intention, I assume?" Before she could respond, he continued: "The fact that a male vampire must *command* a pregnancy in a female?" He paused, possibly for effect. "The fact that his seed will never take root unless he wills it to do so? *Tells* it to do so?" He sat back on the bed and regarded her curiously. "You can torture me, I suppose. You can debase me like a little—what is it? *Bitch*?" He laughed then. "You can even dismember me for fun—isn't that what you were thinking, my dear demoness?—but what you can never do is conceive my child...without my consent."

For the first time since Nachari had come to the Valley of Death and Shadows, Noiro was speechless. She hadn't considered this information. In fact, it hadn't even occurred to her before that she actually needed him to *want* to get her pregnant.

And by all the demon lords, it changed everything.

Shit.

Shit!

"Now then," he whispered, ignoring the look of bewilderment on her face. "The way I see it, perhaps we can assist each other."

Noiro narrowed her gaze. She didn't trust this wizard...at all. "Why would I help you—and risk Ademordna's wrath?" She sneered. "If you think I would ever help you to escape this place, or do anything to undermine my king—then you're as stupid as you are handsome." She squawked in defiance. "Never, Wizard. *Never.*"

He sat quietly on the bed, just staring at her. After an

extended period of time had passed, he sighed. "Way too much drama, Noiro: Males don't really care for that. Are you finished?"

Noiro felt her face flush with heat.

"*Now then*...you will bring me four simple things in exchange for my favors: In exchange for a kiss, you will bring me a frog from the marsh and seas of the Eastern Province; in exchange for my touch, you will bring me a scorpion from the desert region of the Southern Province; you will provide a spider from the West, the mountain territory, in exchange for my embrace; and a snake from the North, the expansive jungles, will suffice for my...consent to a pregnancy."

Noiro blanched. "Are you insane, Wizard? And just what type of magic will you employ with such powerful elements—from all four directions? Representing all four regions, no less?" She scowled in derision. "The soul of the underworld itself would be at your command. Such an act would be treason."

"No," he argued. "For one such as you, Noiro—a woman of your talent and ambition—such an act will be child's play. If I'm going to give you a son, and you're going to make him a king, you will need my magic to succeed. I suppose you haven't considered that, either."

Noiro considered his words...very carefully. Was it really possible—would he help her to achieve her aim? And how did he know what she wanted—well, outside of the fact that she was always trying to get him to take off his clothes and join her in bed.

Why not, she wondered.

What else did the wizard have on his plate?

It wasn't like he had something else to do, somewhere else to go... "Even if I could—"

"I'm not finished," he barked in a harsh, clipped tone.

Noiro stood motionless, waiting to hear him out—and whatever he had to say had better be good, or she would kill him for his insolence. Wondering which it would be, she whispered, "What else?"

"I will need to trust you, just as you trust me. To know that we are—how should I say it?—in this together."

She laughed, mocking him. *As if he would ever truly be on her side.* Not unless she had some kind of control over him, some way to keep him submissive and weak.

"You will share a secret with me—any secret—I don't care what it is, but it must be important, something I would never otherwise discover ." He lowered his voice. "Something that Ademordna would never want me to know."

"Why?" she asked.

"So that we are both...beholden...to each other. Less likely to betray one another."

Noiro shook her head. The male was insane. Torture had taken his good sense as well as his reason. He was trying to get them both permanently...dead. "Why would I place myself in your—"

"And you will do it all in twenty-five days."

This habit of interrupting was really getting old. "Twenty-five days? Fine, dear wizard, I'll bite: *Why?*"

He lay back on the bed, folded his arms behind his head—chains and all—and crossed his legs at the ankles. "Because you, my sweet, are not the only female in the underworld that has approached me...for a child. You are not the only demoness that wants my offspring. In other words—you're not my only option. If you choose to be the one who bears my son, that's fine. If not, that's fine, too. However, whatever you decide, it will be done within twenty-five days, or I swear on my brothers' souls that I will do everything within my power to plant a son in someone else's womb."

That was it. Noiro had finally heard enough.

The vampire was beyond insane.

He was insolent, indefensibly arrogant, and just plain delusional. And she would not put up with it a moment longer. Launching herself across the room, she shed her buxom blond persona, released her fangs, and dove at his neck, talons ready to rip him to shreds.

As she descended upon his prone body, he twisted to the right. Huge, black-and-emerald wings shot forth from his back as arms of molten steel locked around her back, and she instantly found herself beneath him, rather than above him, rotated and pressed into the mattress.

As the air left her lungs, a powerful thigh shot between her legs and pinned her to the bed.

Where was this sudden strength coming from?

He was in the Valley of Death and Shadows.

Her domain.

Her world.

The laws of physics favored her dominance and strength—not his—so why then was he manhandling her so easily?

Noiro felt the not-so-subtle taint of magic permeate the air, and she knew he had invoked some sort of spell. Dear Dark Lords, what kind of power did this male possess?

She wriggled and writhed beneath him, bucking like a wild animal, prepared to scream for Lord Ademordna; but before she could cry out, he placed his forearm against her larynx and thrust it deep into her throat, cutting off her airway. It felt like a thousand pounds of pressure grinding against her throat as he rendered her defenseless. And then he did the most unexpected thing possible: He rotated his hips in a slow, exaggerated grind against her core; and he growled the words: "Be still."

Noiro froze, caught between rage, terror, and spiraling desire. She simply lay beneath the arousing wizard and waited to see what he would say or do next.

He was glaring down at her now, and his eyes were like two radiating jewels heated with fire. They were burning holes through her reason, and Hades help her, she knew in that moment that she would trade her soul, if not her immortality, to have this male inside her. She would commit treason for this inferior being, whose very gaze wielded more power than all the inhabitants of hell.

And then, she also realized that she had dropped her persona, that the female staring back at him was not a beautiful blonde but a hideous demon with distorted features and beady yellow eyes. She started to correct it, but he let up on her throat and slowly shook his head. "No," he insisted. "Do not."

Noiro froze. "But, you...you are from another realm...where males prefer—"

"What?" He scowled. "You know *nothing* about me. Or my preferences." With that, he slowly lowered his head, pressed his lips to hers, and *kissed* her, passionate and hard.

His lips teased her senses, his tongue threatened her sanity, and his breath infused her debased soul with a living, breathing power unlike anything she had ever felt before. Her body was literally humming beneath him.

When at last he pulled away, she felt abandoned and empty, like a corpse reaching out to reclaim its soul. *So that's what a being of light is infused with.* The very idea left her reeling with both disgust and intrigue...confusion. She hated what he was, yet the taste of him was beyond enticing. It was animating. Intoxicating.

Life-giving.

Sustaining.

"Nachari." She breathed out his name in a breathless whisper.

He rolled off her then, propped his weight on one arm, and looked down into her eyes. "If I am to feel anything for you, Noiro—and in order to sire a child with you, I must feel *something*—then I need to see your true face, know the real demoness. No false appearances."

Noiro hissed her confusion until, at last, all the air drained out of her body. Her forked tongue lolled out of her mouth and draped to the side as she struggled for breath.

He didn't blink.

He didn't even flinch at the sight.

He just continued to stare into her eyes—which had to appear as twin balls of fire—and waited for her acquiescence.

Noiro stretched her neck up to kiss him again, and he backed away.

"Four gifts," he whispered, "and one secret. The deadline is twenty-five days. That is my price."

She held his gaze and nodded. "You swear…" She licked her bottom lip. "If I bring you these things, and it will take a tremendous amount of risk and time to get them, you will—"

"Twenty-five days," he reiterated. "And I swear to you, I will give you…all that you are asking for." He sat up abruptly then and motioned toward the door.

"What is it?" she asked, her voice sounding frantic, distressed.

"Ademordna comes early…for my torture."

She jumped up and smoothed herself out—afraid that somehow the Dark Lord would know what they'd been up to.

"You will not participate in my torture today, understood?" he warned her. "*That* I will not abide."

She nodded. "A frog from the East, a scorpion from the desert, a spider from the mountains, and a snake from the North. This is what you ask?"

"And a secret…from your soul."

Noiro hissed and drew back, not sure if she should oblige him, kill him, or report him. "Anything else?" she asked sarcastically, feeling all at once insubstantial and resentful.

Nachari smiled. "Yes, my love." His voice was scarcely audible.

She leaned forward and tilted her head, literally offering an ear. "What?"

"Get out of my room."

Deanna Dubois toweled off from her recent shower, put on a pair of warm, hip-hugging pajamas, and gathered a basket of her belongings. As she padded down the stairs and through the hall to Nachari's room, she made a mental note of the basket's contents, all things she had purchased earlier that day with Jocelyn: There were healing massage oils—not that she would actually have the courage to massage a sleeping vampire—but the scents were known to be therapeutic in their own right; she had soft, soothing music—Native flute, Celtic guitar, and Gregorian chants; and she had a copy of Nachari's favorite work of fiction, according to his brother Kagen, *A Tale of Two Cities* by Charles Dickens.

She entered the room quietly, not wanting to disturb the tranquility, and immediately turned her attention to the monitors before approaching the male on the bed. She had become accustomed to doing just that: checking for a heart rhythm, verifying that everything was all right before taking another step in Nachari's direction.

The ritual was more for her than him.

"Hello," she whispered in a soothing voice, realizing that it was ten o'clock at night and others in the clinic might be sleeping. *Well,* she thought, *probably not—being that they're vampires.* She quickly dismissed the thought, not wanting to go there, again—not right now, anyhow. "How are you?" she asked, pulling a nearby chair closer to the bed.

She stared at him then.

Really stared.

Trying to imagine what he might look like with his eyes open: twin emeralds staring back at her. According to all the other women, one glance from the confident wizard was enough to make a girl go weak in the knees. Judging by his stunning good looks—even sound asleep—she had no doubt that it was true. "I'd love to see that sometime," she said, setting her supplies down on the floor beside her. "I brought you some things." She took a deep breath. Her heart was racing, and she wasn't sure why. It wasn't like he was going to levitate off the bed any moment soon and bite her.

Yikes.

She shuddered.

"Hey," she said, leaning toward him, "if you do come back—*when* you do come back—maybe you could do it kind of slow and peaceful like, you know? Subtle. Quiet. Just stir a bit and then open your eyes." She sat back in her chair. "Because anything else is going to scare the breath out of me, understood?" She watched for any sign of cognition. When nothing happened, she reached down into the basket and pulled out a handful of CDs. "So what's your flavor tonight? Native American?" She watched for any change on his face at all, the slightest movement of his body. "Celtic music? I know it's kind of weird, but I love it. It's so transcendental, kind of haunting, you know. I think you'll like it." When, still, nothing happened, she continued: "Or Gregorian chants? Kind of feels like you're in a monastery—not that I know what it's like to be in a monastery, but you might. I mean, from your time at the university." She took a deep breath and rolled her eyes. *Yeah, that sounded really intelligent, Deanna. Probably a good thing he's not conscious—idiot.*

His Crest Ring, the one on his fourth finger bearing the crest from the house of Jadon on it, caught her eye; and she reached down to touch it. "This is so beautiful. Are there any special markings? Something engraved specifically for a wizard versus a healer or a justice? Do warriors have a particular ornament?" She stood in the silence, listening to the echo of her own words, and forced a smile. "Okay, well then, I guess...Celtic it is." She opened the Celtic guitar CD, walked across the room, and placed it carefully in the Panasonic CD player—who knew what a receiver like that cost, but she didn't want to be the one to break it. Snatching a throw-blanket from a pile of linens Kagen had placed on the counter by the sink, she crawled back into the chair beside Nachari's bed, reached down for the book, and tucked her knees up to her chest, covering the majority of her body with the coverlet.

She turned on the reading lamp beside the bed, opened the first page, and hesitated: The light was shining just so across Nachari's face, and it made his complexion appear almost luminescent. His skin was absolutely flawless. His features were so refined yet masculine—strong. She bent over and traced the back of her fingers across his cheek and closed her eyes. "Come back to me, Nachari," she whispered. "For whatever it's worth, I'm here, and I'm not going to run away." She chuckled then. "Okay, well, I'm not going to promise that I won't run at first…or scream…or just generally freak the hell out the moment I see you, but I won't go far. I'm your *destiny*, right?" *And I'm praying that you're mine.*

She sat back in the chair once more, turned her attention to the book, and opened it to Chapter One: *All right then, here goes nothing…*

"It was the best of times, it was the worst of times, it was the age of wisdom, it was the age of foolishness, it was the epoch of belief, it was the epoch of incredulity, it was the season of Light, it was the season of Darkness, it was the spring of hope, it was the winter of despair, we had everything before us, we had nothing before us…"

thirteen

Kristina Riley-Silivasi sat back in the plush leather seats of her pink Corvette beneath the high shade-bearing branches of a large oak tree outside Napolean's manse. It was Thursday, around six PM—two days since Ramsey Olaru had come by to visit at the brownstone—and she hoped she might catch a glimpse of him leaving Napolean's following a routine briefing.

The six-foot-five, heavily muscled warrior had not come by or called since Tuesday, and although it really wasn't that long of a time to wait, Kristina was getting curious. She'd had a lot of time to think about his words—and his actions—that night on the front porch; and she was more than just a little eager for a replay, especially considering all of the stressful events going on in her life at the time: Nachari's illness; her choice to stay with Braden at the brownstone; and constantly trying to adapt to her new life...and family.

She sighed, and then she perked up as she heard male voices in the courtyard saying their good-byes. She quickly rolled up her tinted windows, hoping to remain hidden, and watched as Ramsey rounded the corner and headed toward a parked black Escalade.

Shoot. He was going to climb in his SUV and drive away before she had a chance to—

What?

Watch him.

Stalk him?

What did she expect him to do—dance around the yard for her amusement? Stop and say wassup to the squirrels? Kristina frowned. She might as well just get out of the car and confront him—go say hi. After all, he was the one who had initiated their...situation; and he had seemed more than eager the other night: Why would tonight be any different?

She tucked her pink purse beneath the seat, pulled the keys out of the ignition, and stepped out of the car. A cool breeze washed over her as she strolled confidently across the grass toward Ramsey. She had no idea what she was going to say, but she figured she could make it up as they went along. Surely, he would take the lead.

The huge warrior heard the pile of leaves beneath her feet crush, and he spun around with perfect stealth and grace, all alert, ready…and yummy as hell.

Kristina smiled. "Hey!" She was still a short distance away.

He just stood there, staring at her like a bump on a log.

Okay. Let's try this again.

"Hey, Ramsey: Wait up." She hurried her steps to his car, and then she hesitated, taken aback by the completely inhospitable look on his face. His gorgeous eyes were narrowed and more than a little cautious; his sculpted biceps were taut, like he was ready to jump at a moment's notice; and his model-good looks were offset by a subtle but obvious expression that said, *Run, little mouse—before I eat you in one bite.*

Kristina took a step back. "Ramsey?"

He raised his eyebrows.

She cleared her throat. "Okay…hi…how are you?"

"What are you doing here?" he asked, ignoring all attempts at congeniality. "Are you here to see Napolean? Has something happened?"

Kristina smiled then, figuring of course he would think like a sentinel first. "Oh, yeah…uh, no, I mean—not at all. I'm kind of here to see you." She turned to point at her car. "Well, not here for that reason exactly, but I was driving by and well, yeah, I saw you and decided to stop." She paused, trying to force her mouth to close and stay closed—to just shut up. It didn't work. "So, what's up?"

He frowned and shook his head like she was a major nuisance or something, a fly or a gnat buzzing around his head. "You tell me," he said brusquely.

Kristina felt her heart drop into the pit of her stomach. *What the hell?* So, this was how he was going to play it? Like he didn't even know her? What was all this keep-your-distance-in-public crap? "You know, that's really not cool, Ramsey. I mean, I get the whole discretion thing, but you're being a bit of a...butthead."

The warrior's top lip twitched and a barely audible growl emanated from his throat. "What the hell are you talking about?" He looked her up and down derisively. "Kristin, right? Marquis's convert?"

Kristina's mouth fell open at the insult: *Marquis's convert?* Not Marquis's ex-*destiny?* Granted, the whole thing had been a mistake perpetrated by Salvatore Nistor and the Dark Ones— still, it had been very real to her and Marquis at the time. Ramsey could have at least referred to her as Marquis's sister or the newest Silivasi; but no, he had called her Marquis's convert, like she was some cult follower or something. "What's your problem," she demanded, her voice betraying her irritation.

He shook his head like it was full of cobwebs. "What do you want, Kristin?"

She was mad enough to spit now. "Kristin? It's *Kristina*, and you damn well know it!" She clenched her fists at her sides. "And what do I want?" She shrugged, bristling. "I don't know— I guess for some stupid reason I thought I wanted *you*, but I'm quickly changing my mind."

He was the one who stepped back this time. "Girl, what are you talking about...wanting me?"

Kristina felt hot tears well up in her eyes, and she quickly pushed them back. She would not cry in front of him. She would not give him the satisfaction of humiliating her like this—playing head games with her for sport, just because he could. She sidled up to him, striding more like a prostitute than a female vampire, and licked her lips. "Oh, you know the deal: I'm single; you're single; there aren't that many of us in the house of Jadon...maybe we could hook up and kill some time together... *That kind* of wanting you, *asshole*."

Ramsey cocked his head to the side and spat on the ground.

When he turned back to look at her, his eyes were a faint shade of red, and there was a subtle almost indiscernible twitch in his lower jaw. He crossed his arms in front of him. "Didn't your mother ever teach you not to play with fire, little girl?" He flicked his wrist like he was shooing away a bug. "You need to go home."

That was it.

The straw that broke the camel's back.

Enraged, Kristina extended her arm to slap his face, throwing everything she had into the lightning-quick strike. In an instant she was standing with her back to him, completely caught off guard.

The sentinel had caught her arm, spun her around, and linked both of her wrists together in a firm hold, all with the palm of one hand. He bent over her and breathed into her ear, a harsh, guttural sound that was more animalistic than human. "I don't know who you think you are, or what you're trying to accomplish, but you need to go home...go back to your brothers...and get a grip. I'm not some male you want to toy with, *Kristina*." He pressed his hard chest against her back. "Believe me; you don't want to turn me on—or piss me off. Succeed at either one, and you're gonna have a whole lot of vampire you can't handle to deal with, you hear me?" He pushed her away. Actually shoved her—however gently—causing her to stumble.

She spun around, incensed. "You are a total dog, Ramsey Olaru!"

He shrugged. "Perhaps." He inclined his head toward her car then. "Go home."

A sharply edged lock of his hair, the portion in front that he kept a little longer than the back, fell forward as she stared at him, incredulous. And then she sneered, "I really doubt you have anything I couldn't handle." She spoke with as much venom as she could project in her voice; and then she took a cautious step back, just in case he really was the Rottweiler others made him out to be. *Why hadn't she seen this in him the other night?* "I tell you what," she added as she slowly backed away, "I'll go home, and you—you just go *to hell.*" She focused her attack then: "Or better yet; why don't you go find that cursed, unlucky woman who's gonna be your *destiny* someday. See if she likes canines any better than I do. Maybe you can lift your leg and pee on her."

Ramsey whistled low beneath his breath, and then he stood stalk still.

Not a single muscle flexed.

Not a single hair on his head rustled in the wind.

He just stared at her—like a tall, intimidating, GQ predator: gorgeous…mean…and deadly. As if they were total strangers, and *she* was the one out of her mind.

Kristina turned around and jogged to her car, tears of outrage and disbelief clouding her vision. She jumped behind the wheel, turned over the engine, and slammed on the gas—unable to get out of there fast enough: Who the hell did he think he was? Toying with her like that? She had half a mind to run to Marquis and tell him everything. See how well Ramsey liked it when the one standing across from him was another ticked-off warrior.

She wondered then: Would Marquis even fight to defend her honor? Would any of her brothers? Or would they simply read her the riot act for flirting with the sentinel to begin with, for being so gullible?

She felt so stupid.

So ridiculous.

Gods in the Celestial heavens, why was she always such an easy target for men? Wiping her nose with the back of her hand, she turned onto the main street leading away from Napolean's mansion: As far as she was concerned, none of it ever happened. Ramsey really could just go to hell.

So long as the monster stayed away from her, she would never tell a soul.

BLOOD SHADOWS

It was late when Kristina pulled into the driveway. She had driven around Dark Moon Vale for hours, blowing off steam, stopping to pick up a quart of ice cream she had no intentions of eating, and even trying out a few local bars where they were rumored to sell stiff drinks: To hell with what the Silivasis said alcohol could do to a vampire's body. The whole situation was whack! This place, the people—no, the vampires—and their whole effed-up world was just...whack.

To hell with them all.

She stumbled out of her car and headed toward the front porch, concentrating on placing one foot in front of the other as she ascended the steps. "Doggie, dog-dog," she mumbled, swaying. "Woof, woof!"

A strong arm reached out to steady her. "Hey, there, baby girl." He paused. "Are you just now making it home?"

Kristina recoiled as if she'd been prodded by a red-hot poker.

Ramsey.

The jerk actually had the nerve to come back to the brownstone! Was he crazy? "What the hell are you doing here?" she shouted, suddenly losing her balance.

The hazel-eyed warrior caught her before stepping back to regard her with caution. "Are you...drunk?"

"Drunk, schmunk!" she shot back. "Who gives a rat's ass! What the hell are you doing on my porch, you...jerk head. And why does everyone call me *girl?*" She pointed at his face, wagging her finger back and forth in an exaggerated motion. "I'm not a girl. I mean I'm a female, but I'm not a...little female." She slurred her words. "I'm almost twenty-none...twenty-nie...nine."

Ramsey looked confused. "I thought you were almost thirty."

"Well," she shouted, feeling suddenly confused, "I am. But, I'm almost thirty."

"Whoa," he said. "Okay. Why don't you invite me in? We need to get you inside."

Kristina tried to wedge her keys between her fingers in order to stab him in the eye. "Never. *Ever.* You will not come inside my home...ever. Ever! I hate you, Ramsey Olaru...ooo...oooo. Do you hear me?"

He backed up then and stared at her, wide-eyed with disbelief. "Since when?" He reached out to place his hand beneath her chin to tilt her head up, and she tried to bite him. And then she began screaming. "Get away! Get away from me! I hate you." She turned toward the street and began to scream. "Someone, help me! Get him away from me, please!"

He shoved his hand over her mouth. "What the hell is your problem, Kristina?"

And then all at once she felt him enter her mind like a physical invasion, burrowing in forcefully like a worm into a hole. Her hands went up to cover her ears, and she tried to push him out.

What was he doing?

What was he reaching for?

It almost felt as if he was reading her thoughts, scanning her most recent memories. *Whoa, she had really had too much to drink.* "You get out of my head this instant, you bastard," she growled. "You know damn well what happened earlier at—"

He waved his hand in front of her face, and just like that, she lost her train of thought. It simply disappeared. The words drifted into the cosmos as if they had taken wings and flown away. But it was more than just her words and thoughts that vanished; it was her...anger. Her insistence. Her conviction.

What had she been so mad about anyway?

And why did she want Ramsey to leave?

He was her friend, wasn't he—her possible, would-be-lover? The last time she had seen him, they had stood on this very porch and kissed. She looked down at the keys in her hand; why was she about to stab this gorgeous male in the eye? "Ramsey?"

He looked at her cautiously, as if he was trying to gauge something, measure her stability. As if he was holding his breath. "Yeah?"

131

"When did you get here?"

"Just a few minutes ago," he answered. "Where were you earlier? Why did you go get so drunk?"

Kristina frowned and scratched her head. "I...I don't know," she answered honestly. "I went...I was...you know, in town...Dark Moon Vale..." Dang, she suddenly had a splitting headache. She reached for the information, but it just wasn't there: *Why had she gone into Dark Moon Vale?* She massaged her temples and shrugged. "I don't remember, Ramsey. I guess I just...got drunk." The moment she quit searching for the answer, her headache went away. She looked up at the sky then: It was very dark, and the heavens were littered with stars. "Holy cow—where has all the time gone?"

Ramsey nodded as if he was satisfied with her answer—which, of course, was strange, considering she hadn't been able to answer anything. "Invite me in," he whispered.

The alcohol surged in her bloodstream, and the universe began to spin around in topsy-turvy circles. She giggled like a schoolgirl. "Ramsey...oh Ramsey...please...." She forgot what she was about to say.

"Please what?" He tried to urge her on.

"Please?"

He frowned. "You said, 'Ramsey...oh Ramsey...please.' *Please, what?*"

She looked him straight in the eyes. "Please...let my people go!" She fell to the side in laughter, and he caught her by the arm.

"Kristina..."

She tapped him lightly on the tip of his nose. "I'm sorry." She giggled some more. "Truly, I'm very sorry...*Ramsey*. Hey, were you in that Ten Commandments movie?" Trying to give her best impression of a burning bush, she stood up tall and belted, "Moses....Mooo...ses. Take off your shoes, Moses; you're standing on—my porch." She threw back her head and howled.

Ramsey looked more than just a little irritated.

"Oh gosh, I'm sorry," she repeated. "Okay, okay...Ramsey Olaru, would you please come inside and—"

"What the heck is going on out here?" The front door flew open and Braden Bratianu, decked out in a whole lot of oversized combat gear, stood in the doorway with his fists braced on his hips. "Kristina, why are you making so much noise?"

Kristina spun around and smiled. "Bray! Wasssssssup!" She started to throw her arms around him to give him a hug, but he took one whiff of her breath and stepped back, blocking her with one arm extended outward. "What the hay, Kristina?"

She patted him on the head. "That's good, Bray—no cursing. *No cursing.* Nachari would be proud of you."

The kid stepped back. "Oh my gosh, Kristina, you're drunk, aren't you? What did you do?" He looked around the porch. "Who were you talking to?"

She spun around to point at Ramsey and jerked when she saw nothing but air. "Hey, where'd he go?" She tilted her head to the side. "He was just here."

"Who?" Braden asked, his voice beginning to register his alarm. "Who was here?"

She threw up her hands. "Ramsey."

"Who?" he repeated.

"*Ramsey!*"

"Olaru?" Braden asked. "You mean one of the sentinels?" He stepped further out on the porch and began to look around. "There's no one here but you, Kristina."

Kristina thought about that and frowned.

Okay.

She scrunched up her face. "Yeah, well...maybe he flew away." She reached out to grasp both of Braden's hands in her own. "Hey, that's an idea. We should fly, Braden. We should try flying."

Braden's eyes grew big, and he shook his head back and forth vigorously. "No way," he insisted. "I promised Nachari, no more trying out new skills without a master around to help me the first time." He paused and looked at her sideways. "Besides, you can barely walk."

Kristina stuck her lip out. "You are no fun, Braden Bratianu."

The kid visibly wilted. "That's not true."

Kristina smiled then. "I know…I know…I'm just"—she pinched the bridge of her nose and took a couple of seconds to collect herself, to concentrate on breathing—"pretty wasted, actually. Now I know why they tell us not to drink too much alcohol. Holy cow, I feel…help me inside, Bray. Please?"

The fifteen-year-old, once-human-turned-vampire puffed out his chest and reached out his arm to steady it against her waist. He pulled her into him, gingerly at first, as if testing her weight against his; and then he smiled, taking all of her weight at once. "Come on, silly," he said, leading her toward the door. He shoved it open, slowly walked her up the stairs to the guest bedroom, and dropped her on the bed. "Should I call Nathaniel or Marquis?" he asked, leaning over the bed to stare at her.

"No," she moaned, placing the back of her hand against her forehead. "Oh, God, I feel sick…get me a washcloth, Bray—please?"

The boy dashed out of the room, ducked into a nearby bathroom, and came back with a cool, wet cloth. "Here you go." He watched while she put in on her head. "Nachari says that vampires get really drunk really fast because the alcohol is absorbed almost instantly. But he also says that our bodies will push it out very quickly—we treat it like poison or something—so you should be good soon, as long as you quit drinking for a while."

Kristina nodded slowly. She closed her eyes and concentrated on the refreshing feel of the cool washcloth. Never in her life had she been that drunk, and that was really saying something, considering her past.

Rolling onto her side, she thought about Ramsey and the way he had disappeared the moment Braden showed up. He probably thought she was some immature ditz. Sighing, she put it out of her mind: There was nothing she could do to repair the damage tonight. She just hoped she hadn't ruined her chances with him by acting so stupid. The real question, however, was why she had done it. Why in the world had she gone to Dark Moon Vale and gotten drunk? And why couldn't she remember anything?

She felt the effects of the alcohol begin to lift as her body reached for sleep. Ah, yes—finally. Scooting up the bed to place her head on the soft down pillow, she decided to write it all off as a lesson learned: Do not drink too much alcohol. Not only did it deliver a sucker punch, but it wiped out your memories at the same time. Not a good combination.

Not a good combination at all.

Braden Bratianu watched as the skinny redhead nestled into her pillow and finally drifted off to sleep. *Whoa, had she gotten drunk*, he thought. He stared at her slight body, still clothed in a black mini, six-inch pumps, and a tank top covered in pink-and-red roses and thought about what she had said.

In her mind.

Whether she knew it or not, Kristina had been broadcasting her thoughts out loud on a common bandwidth, for anyone standing near enough to hear. She hadn't projected them far enough away to reach her brothers, but she hadn't shielded them very well, either.

He frowned, leaning back against the wall.

For some reason, she really believed Ramsey Olaru had been outside with her—that he had disappeared the moment Braden opened the door—but why would Ramsey do that? He shook his head, trying to figure it out: Ramsey, Saxson, and Santos—the three sentinels of Dark Moon Vale—were some pretty intense characters, and they took their job very seriously. They didn't hang out with kids—not that Kristina was a kid, but as far as Braden knew, they didn't *hang out* period. At the least, they didn't leave drunk females alone on porches at night, not even with a young vampire there to help.

No, that one definitely didn't make any sense.

Ramsey would have injected Kristina with blood or something, maybe drained out the alcohol. Who knew, but he would have done something other than just disappear.

And why was Kristina going into Dark Moon Vale to get drunk all of a sudden? She had been really cool lately, like really helpful to everyone in the family; this just didn't make any sense. It was bad enough that she was drinking and driving—Marquis would fling her car off the edge of some cliff if he found out, and get her a bus pass and a bodyguard, instead—but worrying about her *chances* with Ramsey: What the heck was that all about?

If it was anything like it sounded, then...*eww*...that was just...*yuck*.

Not to mention impossible.

Braden could not see that mean, husky warrior spending time with anything other than an AK-47—or maybe a tactical knife, peeling off pieces of flesh one by one from an enemy's corpse in order to chew it like bubble gum or something. Definitely not messing around with Kristina.

Nah, sorry—not Ramsey Olaru.

He tiptoed slowly out of the room and shut the door behind him. Maybe he would go up on the roof or something and look at the stars, like a wizard would do, and try to figure out his next move. He was a powerful seer now—Nachari had said so—which meant he just needed to go commune with the stars, maybe face north for a while...because...well, it was as good a direction as any.

Braden sighed.

Hell, he didn't know exactly what to do with all this...information.

Maybe he should go talk to Kagen and see what the Healer thought about it all. After all, Kagen was really, *really* smart. And he was pretty chill, too. He wouldn't just fly all off the handle like Marquis, or get all panther-ish and intimidating like Nathaniel. Kagen might even talk to Braden man-to-man. And wasn't that really the bottom line?

Braden was a male in the house of Jadon now, and protecting the females always came first.

Always.

Besides, Kristina really was a pretty girl, and when she wasn't all confused and acting out like a crazy woman, she could be cool as hell. Cool as heck.

Yep, that's what he would do.

He would go talk to Kagen.

fourteen

The next morning

Braden Bratianu took the clinic stairs two at a time, threw open the front doors with gusto, and strode down the hall with a clear purpose.

And then he froze in his tracks.

Standing directly in front of him, just outside of Nachari's room, was the most beautiful woman he had ever laid eyes on. She was just a little bit taller than he was—but that would change soon, anyhow—and she had the most incredible head of golden-brown hair that he had ever seen, all wavy and thick like braided ropes that had just been untied.

Her eyes were the color of glass marbles, kind of bluish-gray and more narrow than wide. Her cheekbones were high like a model's, set in a perfectly proportioned face, and her lips—well, dang—they were just kissable fine. She smiled, and her sleek, slightly arched eyebrows raised just a smidgeon, causing the air to leave his body in a whoosh. She was like some Egyptian princess and high-fashioned runway model all wrapped up into one.

"Hi," she called to him.

Braden looked over his shoulder to see if someone else was standing behind him, and then he squared his shoulders, stuck out his chest, and cleared his throat, prepared to speak in his deepest voice: "Hello." It sounded weird, and he cringed.

But she didn't seem to notice. "Are you here to see Nachari?"

"Huh," he answered, trying not to stare at her lean but curvy body. "Uh…yeah, yeah…I'm Nachari's wizard. I mean, son. I mean, I'm like a son 'cause he watches me…'cause he was told to…by the wizards."

The girl laughed, and it sounded like music. "You must be Braden, then?" She took a step in his direction and held out her hand. "Hi, I'm Deanna."

Braden extended his hand, drew it back, and wiped the sweat on his jeans. He extended it again. "Hi. I'm Braden Bratianu, adopted son of *Dario* Bratianu, chosen by the god Moniceros, the Unicorn; I'm going to be a warrior—or a Seer-Wizard—or maybe both." He looked down at the ground. *Damn, why had he said all that?*

Her eyes lit up with appreciation. "Well, that is quite…impressive, Braden Bratianu. In case you haven't heard, I'm Nachari's *destiny*, and I have no idea what I'm going to be this time tomorrow, let alone in the future, but it's nice to meet you."

The air left Braden's body like a deflated balloon. Of course, this was her—the one he'd heard so much about—*Nachari's* female.

For some unknown reason, he felt like…crying. He should have known the gods would give the finest woman on the whole planet to Nachari. The moment he thought it, he felt guilty. Of course Nachari deserved this woman. And if the gods would just let him come back to his family, Braden would never feel jealous again. He frowned. "So, what are you doing?" The moment the stupid question left his lips, he wanted to turn around and go back home: What an idiot he was.

"Well," she said, in a very sweet voice, "I have been getting to know a lot of people the last few days, spending some time in Nachari's room—hopefully it will make a difference—and trying to learn as much about him as I can for now. What about you, did you come to see him?"

"Um, yeah," he whispered, wanting to sound important and helpful. "Sure. I do every day. I'm surprised I haven't seen you."

"I think we've just missed each other, that's all." She gestured toward a small grouping of chairs just on the other side of the hall. "I don't suppose you would mind spending a little time with me before you go in to see Nachari?" She placed her

Tessa Dawn

hand lightly on his arm. "Don't get me wrong; I don't want to take away your time with him—I know how important that is to everyone—I just think there's probably no one who knows him as well as you do, who's as close to him as you are, and I would love to hear more about him...from you."

Braden's heart soared. Of course, Nachari needed him to help his *destiny* make the adjustment. This was something he could do really well. And besides, what if the worst thing possible happened—and Nachari didn't make it back in time? Deanna would need strong warriors to look after her and help her make it through. To take care of her. He straightened his back. Yes, he would do this for Nachari. "After you," he said, sounding very grown-up in his own mind.

"Why, thank you, Mr. Bratianu," she replied.

Braden positively swelled with pride as he followed Deanna to the small sitting area and took a seat across from her. He sat back with his legs out in front of him, placed one arm around the back of the chair, and then, feeling a bit awkward, sat back up and folded his hands in his lap.

That didn't feel very comfortable, either. Definitely not cool.

He thought about Marquis—how would the Ancient Master Warrior sit?—and he leaned forward, resting both elbows on his knees, his chin resting on his folded hands. Yes, this probably looked very contemplative or something. He cleared his throat again. "So, what is it you would like to know?"

Deanna smiled as she shook her head, her long, fluid hair swaying in response to the motion. "Whatever you want to tell me. Who is Nachari to you? What makes him so important in your life?"

Braden felt a sudden wave of emotion sweep over him. The last thing he wanted to do was cry in front of Nachari's female, so he swallowed hard and waited until he felt like he could talk. "Well, Nachari's kind of like a big brother and a father to me. He looks out for me and teaches me things. He's like...really funny and cool to hang around 'cause sometimes"—he looked away embarrassed then—"sometimes, I kind of, like, get

141

into…not trouble…but messes. I just don't always think things through, ya know?"

Deanna nodded sympathetically. "I do the same thing sometimes."

"You do?" He sat back up, straight in his chair, forgetting where to place his hands.

"Oh, yeah…I think everyone does, sometimes."

He frowned. "Oh…well, not quite like I do."

"But Nachari is helpful?" she prompted.

He brightened. "Oh, yeah. Really helpful. He just, like, figures things out and helps me do better the next time. But more important, he kind of sees things in me that I don't always see in myself."

Deanna smiled appreciatively. "Like what?"

He shrugged. "I don't know, like I have the ability to see things in my mind—or just kind of know things, and because Nachari is a wizard, he gets that and thinks I have a lot of talent." He turned to face her more squarely. "Did anyone tell you how powerful he is? Nachari, I mean?"

Deanna raised her eyebrows.

"Oh my god…I mean, gosh. He's like Batman, Superman, and Spiderman all wrapped up into one. I don't think there's anything Nachari can't do. And he's not even, like, stuck-up about it." He sat back in the chair, really enjoying the conversation now. "Well, okay, so not *stuck-up*, but he's kind of, like, really sure of himself. He has serious swag, if you know what I mean." He laughed then. "The ladies are just like bees buzzin' around honey whenever he's around; they just fall all over themselves and drool and stuff. And he's real cool about it, doesn't take advantage of anyone or show that he knows how magnetic he is, but then—" He stopped suddenly, all at once realizing how stupid that was. Deanna wouldn't want to hear about Nachari and other women. "Oh, snap," he said, waving his hand in front of him. "I didn't mean that—about other women or anything—he's not like a player or a dog. I mean, he bites the ladies instead of feeding off men because they just fall into his hands, so I guess it's easy, but he doesn't do…well…I mean…I don't think he does, but even if he has, he won't now…" His voice trailed off. "Sorry."

Deanna gave him a smug appraisal. "Okay…well, that's good to know." She nodded slowly. "I will have to make sure he finds a more…appropriate feeding source in the future." She winked at him then. "Don't worry—it's our secret. He'll never know I heard it from you."

Braden laughed apprehensively. "I hope I didn't get him in trouble."

Something conspiratorial gleamed in her eyes. "Not at all."

Just then, the cell phone in his jeans vibrated, and he reached into his back pocket to pull it out. He glanced at the screen; it was Blade Rynich from school. "Just one of my boys from the academy," he told Deanna, feeling emboldened by the call. "They're always blowin' up my phone." He turned it off, flipped it over, and laid it in his lap—a smooth move, if he dared say so himself. "I'll hit 'em back later."

Deanna nodded. "Cool." She paused for a moment. "I imagine the young ladies tend to swarm around you as well…"

He positively beamed on the inside, and then he reached up and absently stroked his chin a couple of times. "Yeah…yeah…you know how it is…"

Deanna sparkled with amusement. "Yes, I do; and I imagine it will get worse as you get older. Nachari will definitely have his hands full someday."

Braden blushed. "I guess…we'll see…"

Deanna paused for a moment before changing the subject. "Tell me about your parents." Her eyes held genuine interest.

Braden shrugged. "I dunno. I guess there's not that much to tell, really." He thought about their story. "My mom met Dario in Hawaii about ten years ago, when I was five. That's where we lived back then." He shifted in his seat. "After Dario claimed her, they had my little brother, Conrad, and then Dario met with Napolean to figure out how to convert me, too—so I wouldn't still be human."

Deanna drew a quick inhale of breath. "That sounds like quite the story to me."

Braden smiled broadly. "Yeah, well, I guess it is." He paused. "Maybe I'm just used to it all now."

Deanna nodded. "I see. So, how did you come to live with Nachari?"

Braden leaned forward with excitement. "Well, after my conversion, Dario and my mom decided to take me and Conrad on a one-year vacation around the world with them—I guess he wanted to show my mom a lot of cool things—like how the places had changed over time and stuff, maybe share his history with her." He cleared his throat. "Of course, he really wanted to start in Romania, so that's where we all went." He lost his train of thought and had to pause for a moment to remember what he was saying. "Anyhow, we spent about three months in Romania...at the University...when I guess the council of wizards decided that Nachari should spend more time with me." He gave her his best sly wink and sat up straight in his chair. "I think they thought I could help him or something."

Her eyes sparkled, and she seemed to be smiling inwardly, as if she knew something he didn't. "So, that's when Nachari brought you back to Dark Moon Vale?"

"Yep," Braden said.

"And since then?"

"Since then, my parents have been all over the world with Conrad—and I've stayed here." Before she could draw a bad conclusion about his family, he quickly added: "It feels like it's been a really long time, but it hasn't. Maybe six months or so." He sighed. "After my first month here with Nachari, my parents really wanted me back, but I begged them to let me stay—and Napolean and Nachari helped me, too." He tried to think of a way to explain it. "I have a lot of friends at the academy, and I'm learning a lot by staying here...you know, important things, like warrior and wizard things. If I were with them, I'd just be homeschooling and traveling from one place to the next, so I guess they finally agreed to let me stay...at least until their vacation is over, which should be in another four months or so."

"And what then?" Deanna asked.

Braden shook his head, suddenly feeling lost—*what if Nachari didn't return?* He didn't even want to think about it. That simply couldn't happen. "And then, they're going to settle back in Hawaii...for good. Hopefully, they'll agree to let me keep living here, at least until I graduate the Academy. I dunno. I miss them and everything, but I don't really want to go back to Hawaii—or to have to learn the Human Studies at home with my mom. Hopefully, I can just go back and forth on breaks."

Deanna grew quiet for a moment, clearly contemplating his words; and then she seemed to gather herself and move on. She pointed to his phone. "Do you have any pictures in there? Of you and Nachari?"

Braden swooped up the phone and smiled. "Oh, yeah, definitely." He turned the device back on, hit a few buttons on the screen, and began to scroll down through a series of photos. He leaned forward, turning the phone so she could see the display. "This is me and Nachari on the roof, using the telescopes. Kristina took the picture."

Deanna studied it very carefully, and Braden could tell by the look on her face that she was a little overwhelmed when she looked at him—just like most women were.

"And this is Nachari at the horse farm, training a stallion. He's like one with the horses when he rides, and you wouldn't think with all his swag that he would have the whole cowboy thing goin' on, but like I said, he can pretty much do anything."

Deanna reached for the phone. "May I?"

"Sure," he said, handing it to her.

She touched the screen to enlarge the picture and just stared at it.

Braden had no idea what she was thinking at that moment, but her eyes kind of misted over, and he knew that she already had some very real feelings for Nachari. That was good. She handed the phone back, and he scrolled to the next picture. "And this is Nachari with his cars." He emphasized the last word with pride. "He collects vintage Mustangs." He pointed to a 1970 Calypso Coral beauty. "This is his favorite—the one he drives all the time. It has a V-8 engine, and he keeps it polished. Nachari loves his cars."

Deanna smiled with appreciation. "Wow...I can see that." He flipped to the next screen, and she laughed out loud before he could scroll beyond it. "What was that?"

"Oh," Braden said, sounding embarrassed. "That was just...that was Nachari slapping me upside my head for trying to stand on the hood."

Deanna laughed. "That didn't go over too well?"

Braden shook his head slowly from side to side in an exaggerated motion. "You have no idea."

"Hey, Braden." A deep, smooth voice interrupted their conversation, and Braden looked up to see Kagen Silivasi standing in front of them in a pair of stone-washed Levi's and a blue muscle-tee.

"Oh, hey, Kagen," Braden called back. "Wassup?"

"Not much. When did you get here?"

"Just about ten minutes ago." He gestured toward Nachari's *destiny*. "I was talking to Deanna, telling her lots of important stuff about Nachari and showing her some pictures."

"Is that right?" Kagen said, bending over to look at the phone. Seeing the last photo on the screen, he laughed out loud. "Katia said you called ahead—you wanted to talk to me about something—what is it?"

Braden looked back and forth between Kagen and Deanna. He hadn't felt that good in a long time—having all of Deanna's attention to himself kind of made him feel special, like he was somehow closer to Nachari. Telling on Kristina wouldn't really make a difference in the world right now, but helping Deanna, that was as cool as it got. "Aw, nothing," he said. "It can wait for another day. Just man things, you know."

Kagen glanced back and forth between Braden and Deanna. "I see." His eyes grew narrow, and he furrowed his brow. "You sure about that, buddy?"

Braden waved his hand through the air coolly. "Yeah, I'm sure. It's all good."

"All right then," Kagen said. "I have a few things I need to take care of around here, so if you need me, I'll be available a little later tonight." He turned toward Deanna and brightened. "I'm glad you finally got to meet this one; he's extremely important to my brother."

Deanna regarded Braden pointedly. "I can see why," she said. "Sometimes, just knowing who a person loves gives you a good idea of who they are. I think I've learned a lot today."

"Good," Kagen said. "I know it isn't easy."

Deanna smiled and nodded, but Braden hardly noticed: *Just knowing who a person loves.*

That's what she had said.

Whatever the Silivasis had told Deanna about him, she knew Nachari loved him, that he was one of the most important people in Nachari's life; and for whatever reason, she was treating him really, really special. His heart filled with pride and joy; and he sat back in his chair.

Yeah, this was definitely the right decision. Getting to know Deanna was way more important than squealing on Kristina. In fact, it was turning out to be one of the best days he'd had in a long while.

In the privacy of his dungeon, Nachari rocked back and forth on his knees, trying to quell the nausea in his stomach. His blood dripped down from his mouth and nose onto the stone floor and pooled beneath him, but he didn't give it too much thought. He'd been there a thousand times before, trying to reorient his body as it struggled to regenerate following a particularly brutal beating.

Ademordna had kept him in the throne room longer than usual that day, giving several of his minions a turn with the lash.

BLOOD SHADOWS

After spiking his wrists and ankles to the stone, they had even spread some sort of animal grease over his naked body, just to make sure the spiked lash glided easily through his skin. He took a deep breath and tried to control his trembling; he could have sworn a few of those spikes nicked internal organs this time. *Gods, what he wouldn't give for some fresh human blood right now*—for his body to have something other than Ademordna's slaves to feed on.

He felt the bile rise in his throat, and he pushed it back down.

He felt the familiar pang of despair swell in his heart, and he fought against it.

Where was Deanna now? he wondered. What was she doing? And what would it be like to finally meet her? He had to concentrate on the future, because the present was simply too unbearable.

The click-click-click of spiked heels clattering on top of stone caught his attention, and he tried to turn his head to the side. The world began to spin around him, and he immediately held it back down.

"Ah, lover of mine; you don't look so good today."

Noiro.

Of course.

"Do you want something?" he bit out. He was so not in the mood for her antics.

"Oh, yes," she purred seductively, "but you don't appear in any shape to give it to me." She paused to chew on a painted fingernail. "Shall I bring you another slave to feed upon? You really look…awful."

"Why are you here, Noiro?" he growled.

She tossed something green to the floor beneath him. "Look, wizard—and you tell me."

Nachari blinked a trickle of blood out of his eyes and struggled to bring his vision back into focus. The rich, deep croak of a toad gave away the object's identity before his eyes recognized what they were seeing. He blinked several more times. "From the east?"

Noiro practically hummed with self-satisfaction. "From the marshlands in the center of the eastern province itself." She pursed her lips. "And trust me, my Adonis, it was hard as hell to get it!"

Nachari reached out and stroked the toad's back—testing for the corrosive energy. The vibration itself would tell him whether or not Noiro spoke the truth.

He felt the vaporous potency and almost smiled.

Almost.

He pried a stone free from the floor, a slab he had loosened earlier in anticipation of the four talismans, and placed the frog in the narrow hole beneath the opening. *Be still and sleep until I awaken you,* he commanded, watching as the reptile instantly complied. He turned to Noiro. "Help me up...please." He hated having to ask her for her assistance, but going forward with his plan was more important than his pride. And one day—yes, one day soon—there would be a reckoning unlike anything the demoness had ever seen. *Oh yes, her day would come.*

Noiro sidled up to him, ran her long, bony hand along his skin from his ankles to his shoulders, lingering at his buttock, and groaned. "Soon," she whispered, clearly lost in carnal thoughts of her own. She grabbed him by the arm and tugged. "Tell me then, did I do good, lover?"

"Well," he said derisively. "Did I do *well?* And yes, you did fine...for now. But you still owe me a secret." He leaned against her as she helped him to the bed and then dropped him carelessly, causing him to fall in a battered heap on top of the already soiled blankets. He quickly rolled off his back, biting down on his tongue to keep from crying out. "My clothes." He pointed toward the tattered rags crumpled in the corner.

"Oh, pooh!" she whined. "Do you have to get dressed?" She stepped forward, curled her hand around his manhood, and slowly stroked it up and down. "I can't wait to see this marvelous instrument in all its magnificence; won't you make it hard for me, Nachari? Please...at least give me a taste of what's to come."

"*My clothes*," he repeated.

Rolling her eyes, she huffed her annoyance and retrieved his clothes. "Here."

He took them and grimaced through the pain as he dressed. "Now then," he groaned, leaning back onto the bed—he didn't care that he fell in an awkward position; it was too much work to correct it—"there is still the small matter of trust...and a secret."

Noiro sat heavily on the bed, jostled his aching body callously, and snorted. "Fine, fine. We may as well get it out of the way." She shrugged nonchalantly. "Now then, let's see...a secret." Her devious eyes lit up. "Your brother Shelby was a very pure soul. I hear he is well respected in the Valley of Spirit and Light."

Nachari sighed, trying to gather his patience. "The deal, Noiro, was a *secret*: something I don't already know and can't easily find out. Something that would place you in jeopardy if anyone knew you told me." He frowned. "Try again." He shut his eyes and recited a short Latin incantation beneath his breath so the demoness couldn't hear. The spell was not strong enough to force her compliance, but it was definitely sufficient to confuse her mind—push her further in the direction of doing his will.

She threw back her head and shook out her hair as if the unruly mane was an erotic crown of glory. "Fine," she snapped, sounding both irritated and bored. "*Fine.*"

He waited quietly.

"The boy," she began.

Nachari sat up, alert.

"What boy?"

She turned up her nose in disgust. "The sniveling little accident-waiting-to-happen. You know, the one that follows you around like a lost puppy dog."

Nachari frowned. "Give me a name."

"Ha, ha," she mocked. "As if you don't know. Braden. Braden Bratianu. Satisfied?"

"Go on," Nachari urged, suddenly feeling afraid for his young protégé: What could Noiro possibly know about Braden that he didn't?

"The young acolyte Braden will never have a *destiny*. He is not born of the Curse. He was made. And while he may have been protected by the god Pegasus at the behest of his stepfather Dario, the Blood neither cursed him nor chose him."

Nachari sat very still for a moment, contemplating all he was hearing. Could the demoness possibly be right? And if so, what did this mean for Braden? "Elaborate..."

Noiro stood up and began pacing around the clammy room. "What more do you need to hear? Shall I spell it out?"

Nachari bit back a curse. "Please do."

She wheeled around on him. "The boy is a vampire because Dario turned him; however, he is not a product of the Curse! He was not born to a cursed male, nor is he a descendant of one of the original cursed males. Therefore, the gods have not chosen a mate for him—the Curse simply does not apply in his case."

Nachari inhaled sharply as a dozen questions raced through his mind. "Can he mate with—or marry—a human female, then? And if he does, will he have twin sons? Is he immune from the required sacrifice?"

She shrugged, clearly indifferent. "He can try. No. And yes."

"What do you mean?" Nachari pressed.

"I mean he can try to mate a human female if he wishes. However, I think we both know how badly such a thing would turn out. After all, he is a vampire—that much is a fact."

"And the required sacrifice? His twin sons?"

Noiro smiled then, not so much with joy as cunning, the antics of a woman who had the power to shock and unsettle a Master Wizard. "No Curse—no sacrifice."

Nachari let the information settle as he tossed it around in his head. Of course, if he ever made it back to Dark Moon Vale, he would have to gather his fellow wizards and Napolean and fact-check the information with the light gods, as it were. Even he was not foolish enough to trust a demon with a matter this important, but what if…what if Noiro was telling the truth? Then that would mean—

"Ah, yes…you are finally catching up with me," Noiro crooned, an eerie self-indulgence in her voice. "Braden Bratianu can sire female children." She laughed riotously then. "Pity he'll never have anyone to sire them with."

Nachari swallowed hard, his mind barely able to weigh the implications. "How do you know this?"

She looked away wistfully. "A brief tryst I had with the dark lord S'usagep—the twin energy of your revered Pegasus." Her lips turned up in a wry smile. "Mmm, that was quite the…aerobic…affair."

"And?" Nachari prompted, not at all interested in hearing about Noiro's demented sex life, past or present.

"And," she continued, "haven't you ever wondered why so many of your *destinies* come from broken homes or tragic pasts? Why they're orphaned or without much to speak of in the way of friends and family? It's certainly not by accident." She reached out to stroke his chin, and he had to force himself not to withdraw from her touch in disgust. "In this one matter, preparing a female human for her vampire husband, I'm afraid our twin energies interfere a great deal."

"So, you're saying that S'usagep interfered with Dario Bratianu and Lily, then?"

She laughed out loud. "Oh yes. As much and as often as he could." She stuck her lip out in a pout. "Poor S'usagep did everything he could to steer Lily away from her destined path: She was never intended to marry a human prior to meeting Dario, and she was certainly never intended to bear a human child with a human man. But S'usagep worked tirelessly at hooking her up with anyone he could—anyone but Dario."

"And that's how Braden was born?"

"Quite the accident—that kid," she said.

Nachari frowned, wishing he didn't have to wait to tear the evil deity's head off her shoulders. "I'm afraid I have to disagree," he argued. "Braden is turning out to be quite the miracle: Perhaps you dark lords should stick to what you're good at—scheming against one another in the underworld." After all, Lily had divorced her first husband and ultimately married Dario Bratianu anyway—just as the Celestial gods had destined. So Dario had been forced to convert little Braden under the protection of Pegasus, even though he wasn't his natural-born son, so what? The child had come through the conversion just fine, the first human turned vampire outside of the Curse; he was a blessing to everyone who knew him. Especially to Nachari.

Noiro's cruel eyes narrowed even further in anger, if that was even possible. "Watch your tongue, boy. You are still a prisoner in my domain, and I can still have you skinned alive!"

Nachari shrugged, suppressing a shudder. "Been there, done that. And frankly, I'm not impressed. Besides, my skin would just grow back, and it would waste a lot of time..." He glanced at her speculatively. "Your biological clock is ticking rather loudly, isn't it, Noiro?" He laughed, his own chiding pointed and derisive. "As are the clocks of many other female demons down here, I might point out: Perhaps I've chosen the wrong female."

Noiro gasped with indignation. "You promised!" she shouted.

"Shh," Nachari warned. "Lower your tone. Do you want to draw Ademordna's attention to our conversation?" For a moment, he thought about the high-stakes game he was playing with the wicked demoness: What if, for some ungodly reason, his plan didn't work? What if he crafted his spell, took advantage of Noiro in order to escape the Valley of Death and Shadows, and it didn't happen? He would be forced to remain in the underworld indefinitely, and Noiro would definitely hold him to his false promises.

The thought turned his stomach.

He would rather die a thousand deaths—spend a dozen eternities in hell—than father an aberration of nature with the vile female demon. In fact, he would rather enter Ademordna's throne room every day and night until the end of time than enter Noiro's malevolent body even once. He shook off the thought.

His plan would work.

It had to work.

She was staring at him with a combined look of both rage and terror in her eyes, and her hair began to sway about her shoulders, not in a beautiful, lustrous way but like a bundle of snakes wriggling about her misshapen head. "Shh," he whispered again, reaching out to cup her slimy chin in his hand. Ever since he had scolded her about changing her appearance so often, she had come to him wearing her true face and persona: a serpent-looking atrocity with wide nostrils and a forked tongue. While it was almost unbearable to look upon her, it was necessary in convincing the desperate creature that he had truly come to want her—exactly as she was.

All part of the mind game, the web he was weaving, to get home to Deanna.

He ran his finger gently along the line of her jaw, leaned in slowly, and placed a chaste kiss on her lips, lingering just long enough to make her want for more. "A kiss for the first talisman. I said I would give you what you need, and I will."

She looked surprised then. Pleased, if not wary.

"But," he added quickly, "not until I have what I need."

She slowly licked her lips, and her narrow, forked tongue almost made him heave, but he suppressed the urge without revealing his disgust. "And what is it that you need, sweet wizard?" She ran her hand suggestively along his inner thigh, first the back of her fingers and then the pads.

Nachari used an ardor spell to force his manhood to respond. It wasn't arousal, simply a biologic redirection of blood flow. When she drew back in utter delight and laughed, he lowered his voice to a soothing, seductive tone. "I need you…" He lifted his hand to trace the outline of a jutting nipple, erect at the apex of a heaving breast, and stopped just short of making contact. He brushed her hair behind her shoulder instead. "To give me…" He ran his hand along her shoulder, down her spindly arm to her waist, and pressed it firmly against her lower belly.

"Yes," she whispered, breathlessly.

He sat back on the bed, resting on his elbows. "...the remaining three talismans I asked for: a snake, a scorpion, and a spider from the remaining three provinces." He licked his lips slowly and smiled that infamous Silivasi smile—a gift rarely bestowed upon the wicked hag. "The timing of all of this is really up to you."

Noiro shook her head vigorously, as if coming out of a trance, and if truth be told, she was coming out of a spell of sorts. Despite the errant, uncooperative energy of the Abyss— the contrary laws of physics that rendered Nachari's magic too ineffective to control the barbaric machinations of his eager tormentors while he was under their constraint—his powers had grown astonishingly strong during his horrific stay in hell. The demon lords had managed to do more than the entire council of wizards at the Romanian University during Nachari's 400 years of study: They had forced him to retreat within; challenged him to create powerful alchemy using inferior elements; taught him the very patience, focus, and creativity that only came with centuries of practice. They had allowed him to channel pain into power.

They had turned him into an even greater, more powerful wizard.

Noiro was a deity.

An immortal lord of the underworld, wholly evil and without conscience, yet she bent to his will like putty beneath his hands. Despite all the years of being told of his incomparable beauty, his devastating effect on women, Nachari Silivasi knew that there was only one thing responsible for the successful manipulation he had achieved with Noiro.

Magick.

Deep. Powerful. And growing.

His.

"You will bring me these soon?" he whispered.

Norio shut her eyes and swayed back and forth, his words washing over her like molten liquid in a golden stream. "Should my lover wish it, I would bring you the head of our Supreme Ruler, Ademordna himself."

Nachari stared into Noiro's eyes, reading her sincerity, not daring to look away or break the connection.

If only it were that easy.

If only Noiro possessed the power to challenge the King of the Middle Kingdom of the Valley of Death and Shadows, his tormentor and relentless captor, to destroy his greatest enemy—

But she didn't.

Not by a long shot.

Still, there was no point in telling her that now. She would need such bold arrogance to complete the tasks he had given her. And there was no time like the present.

"I'll let you know if it comes to that, sweet love," he whispered. "But for now, bring what I've asked."

fifteen

Dark Moon Vale ~ Two weeks later

Deanna looked into Kagen's bottomless dark brown eyes, each shimmering with reflections of silver light, and searched for reassurance. While his handsome, kind features were shadowed with both concern and compassion, he simply couldn't give her the guarantee she needed: that she would come through the conversion just fine and everything would be all right in the end.

She looked at the sterile hospital gurney and the taut leather straps where her ankles, thighs, wrists, and forearms would be bound and felt her body begin to tremble. "Are you really sure those are necessary?"

Kagen glanced at his brother Nathaniel, who quickly looked away. And didn't that just tell her all she needed to know. "Unless you allow me to...hold you, they are." His voice was tender but matter-of-fact.

Deanna nodded then. Kagen had offered to take Nachari's place, in a manner of speaking, to position his body behind hers with his arms and legs wrapped firmly around her in order to provide the necessary restraint for the conversion, but she had refused the offer.

It wasn't that she didn't want the assistance.

Hell, it wasn't that she didn't need the constant contact, the comfort.

But it just didn't feel right.

It would just be too intimate, and she felt like she owed more...devotion to Nachari. "No, that's okay. We'll try it this way," she said.

Nathaniel whistled low beneath his breath and then looked at her apologetically: He obviously hadn't meant to make the sound. "If it gets...too rough...Deanna, then either myself or

Kagen will release the bindings and hold you, instead." He paused as if searching for an adequate explanation. "You can't expect us just to watch…without helping in whatever way we can."

Her smile was faint. "Yeah, okay." She glanced at the clinic door then. "Where is Jocelyn?" She looked at her watch—for the tenth time. "She said she'd be here."

By the look on Nathaniel's face, it was obvious that he was speaking to his *destiny* telepathically. After a short pause, he said, "Looks like she got held up in her self-defense class, but she's on her way." He paused, listening. "She says she'll be here in five minutes."

Deanna swallowed hard and looked at the hospital bed—at the magnificent male who was lying so serenely beneath the crisp white sheets—and took a deep breath.

She couldn't believe this was happening.

That the actual conversion was about to take place.

That she had committed her life, her future, and even her species—changing from human to Vampyr—into a beautiful stranger's hands, when she hadn't even met him.

She swallowed convulsively, bearing down on her resolve. The decision to go through with it had been primarily hers. While Marquis would have forced the issue earlier—all of Nachari's brothers believed the transition would make a difference; if nothing else, the sharing of DNA might provide Deanna with critical information about Nachari: where he was and what was happening to him, what was still keeping him away—the Ancient Master Warrior had backed off at the request of his younger siblings. They all wanted Deanna to come to Nachari of her own free will.

And she had.

Or at least, she was about to do just that.

She turned away as Kagen checked the connections on the intricate medical apparatus a final time. The seamless appearance of two razor-sharp incisors elongating beneath the Master Wizard's upper lip, following an injection of some sort of stimulant, had already unsettled Deanna enough. It wasn't like she hadn't seen fangs on Kagen, Nathaniel, and Marquis a time or two during her stay in Dark Moon Vale, but seeing them on Nachari—well, that was an entirely different matter.

It just brought it all home.

Made it all too real.

Nachari Silivasi *was* a vampire.

And gods willing, by the end of this procedure, she would be a vampire too—converted by this mysterious male, whom she'd never even met, with the help of his brother, the vampire Healer.

The catheters that protruded from beneath the extended fangs were equipped with a tiny pump, intended to extract venom directly from Nachari's glands, carry it along a short, narrow tube, and infuse it into a small port that led to Deanna's internal jugular vein for however long the conversion took.

Anxious tears threatened Deanna's eyes. *Oh, God, please don't let me panic*, she thought, staring once more at the clinic door. Weighing one last time whether to stay or run.

"Deanna." Kagen's soft voice interrupted her thoughts.

"Huh?" she asked, turning around to face him. He had the necessary tubing in his hands. "Why don't we go ahead and prepare the central line while we wait for Jocelyn."

Deanna looked at the intimidating apparatus and swallowed a lump in her throat. "Yeah, uh, okay."

Nathaniel practically glided across the floor in that sinewy, cat-like way that he always had, and placed a steadying hand on her shoulder. "Sister, *breathe*." She felt a powerful influx of relaxing energy flow through her as a result of Nathaniel's touch, and it allowed her body to relax for the first time. "This part will be painless—I will see to it," he reassured her.

Deanna nodded gratefully, wishing she was a little less squeamish around needles and blood...

Not to mention fangs...and vampires.

As Nathaniel promised, the procedure was utterly painless—and not because Kagen was such a great Healer, although according to everyone she had met, he was. The procedure was painless because Nathaniel was absorbing all of the sensations into his own body for her, the Vampyr method for blocking pain.

She watched in apt fascination as the Ancient Master Warrior stood perfectly still and relaxed, showing no sign whatsoever of the pain he was absorbing on her behalf.

Somehow, the gesture gave her courage: If he could do it, maybe so could she.

The door to the room flew open, and Jocelyn rushed in with a look of flushed apology on her face. "Hey, Deanna." She dropped her purse on a nearby chair and rushed across the room to give her a hug, careful to avoid the newly appointed apparatus. "I'm so sorry I'm late. It couldn't be avoided." She drew back and held both of Deanna's shoulders in a firm but gentle grip. "How are you holding up?"

Deanna frowned. "Kind of like a prisoner about to face the gallows. I'm a mess."

Jocelyn looked up at Nathaniel with an inquisitive look on her face.

"We're doing all we can, my love," he assured her. He turned to Deanna then. "We will do all we can until the procedure is complete."

Jocelyn turned back to Deanna and raised an eyebrow. "Marquis?"

Deanna grimaced, feeling a little guilty. "Kagen asked him to wait outside the room—at my request." She shrugged apologetically while glancing from one brother to the next. "I am sorry about that; he's just…so intense, you know?"

Nathaniel chuckled lightheartedly. "No worries, little sister. We will all be more relaxed without Marquis's…loving scrutiny."

Kagen chuckled himself then. "Well put."

A strange vibration swept through the room, and Deanna somehow knew that the brothers were answering for their recent comments telepathically; Marquis might not be physically in the room, but one could best believe, he wasn't far away in his mind.

Kagen stepped away from the gurney and dimmed the lights.

As if on cue, Nathaniel strode to the far side of the room and sat down in a comfortable armchair—one Kagen had brought into the exam room for just this purpose. There was also an empty chair beside Nathaniel for Jocelyn, in case she needed a break at some point, and Kagen? Well, he was not about to leave his baby brother's side until the last drop of venom had passed into his *destiny*—a commitment Deanna was completely grateful for.

Jocelyn gave her hand a gentle squeeze. "I'm right here," she whispered. Somehow, her voice was not as steady as before.

Before Deanna could respond, Kagen rounded the foot of Nachari's bed, where Deanna was sitting, stopped, and knelt in front of her. "Sister," he whispered, almost reverently.

She looked him in the eyes; they were practically glowing. "Yes?"

He whispered something beautiful yet foreign in an ancient language, and then he took both of her hands in his and repeated it in English. "You are Nachari's *blood destiny*," he said in a ceremonious voice, "the other half of his soul. You are the love he has waited a lifetime to find. The gift he will, gods willing, spend a lifetime trying to become worthy of. Your heart was revealed beneath the Blood Moon, your spirit chosen by the god Perseus, the Victorious Hero, to be honored, cherished, and favored by him—above and beyond all others—for all eternity. Do you accept this as your true destiny?"

Deanna was blown away by the beauty of the words, the ancient Vampiric vow between mates that preceded conversion. "Yes...I do believe that now."

Kagen smiled, and his face lit up like the noonday sun. "Deanna Dubois, do you come to Nachari now of your own free will?"

Deanna nodded.

He waited.

"Yes...*Yes*."

"Will you relinquish your heart, your life, and your body into his care—into our care—to be transformed, remade, and reborn? This night, unto forever, to be made immortal?"

BLOOD SHADOWS

Deanna knew that Kagen had added the words *into our care* as a concession. A promise. Nachari's brothers were promising to care for her always should the unthinkable happen—should Nachari not return. She summoned all the courage she had in her soul, and more than just a little faith, and nodded. "I will."

Kagen kissed the back of her hand and gently helped her off the bed onto the gurney, where he meticulously strapped her in, careful to place thick cloths between the straps and her delicate skin. He connected the loose end of the tubing to the catheter in her neck, looked her in the eyes, waiting for her nod of approval, and then gently flipped the switch on the pump.

Deanna held her breath.

Waiting.

She watched as the venom slowly made its way down and around the tube traveling toward her neck.

At first it felt like a bee sting, painful but not unbearable, as miraculously, Nachari's venom began to flow into her veins. She tried to breathe deeply...relax. And then the venom thickened. Not a single bee sting but several.

Ten.

Fifty.

One hundred.

She began to shift uncomfortably on the gurney, wondering what the hell she had gotten herself into. The venom began to heat up then, like liquid fire or molten lava flowing from a volcano, and her eyes opened wide with fright. "Is it supposed to feel like this?" she asked, her voice revealing her panic.

Jocelyn took her hand and squeezed it. "Yes, sweetie. Try to breathe as deeply as possible; don't hold your breath."

Deanna squirmed beneath the restraints. It had been less than five minutes since the procedure began, and the venom was burning her from the inside out like acid, tearing away at her skin. She moaned as the horrific sensation intensified.

And then she screamed aloud. Whatever the substance was, it was invading her bloodstream, traveling quickly toward her heart, and her very bones rebelled. She felt herself pull against

162

the restraints, realizing all at once that she couldn't do this.

She could never do this.

It was too unbearable.

"Untie me," she demanded, turning to Kagen. "I can't." A sudden surge of panic hit her, and she screamed again. "Untie me!" She turned to Jocelyn then. "Jocelyn—I can't do this." Her body began to shake violently from the pain, and she fought not to vomit.

Jocelyn reached for an EmBag and held Deanna's head. "If you need to throw up, do it in this."

Deanna's voice grew hoarse with desperation. "No…no! Untie me. Unplug it. Stop this."

Jocelyn's exquisite eyes filled with tears, and she stroked Deanna's cheek, which only felt like needles piercing her skin. "We can't, sweetie; you know that. Try to focus on something…an object across the room. Just breathe."

"To hell with that!" Deanna shouted.

If her body had been inflicted with a thousand wounds, and the Silivasis had dunked her in a tub of alcohol, the sensation of burning could not have been more intense. It was as if her internal organs were rebelling, collapsing, twisting into little knots. The venom was unlike anything she had ever experienced before: a dozen snakes biting her at once, her skin on fire, her organs under attack—her nerves imploding with agony.

Deanna Dubois threw back her head and shouted an ungodly, inhuman sound. She bucked against the restraints and wished to God she could bite into her hands, chop off her limbs—hell, slit her wrists—just to escape the potency of the pain.

What was it they had told her? She would die to be reborn? And all for this male she had never met? All because of a series of drawings that had compelled her to come to this place?

Helpless tears of anguish and frustration rolled down her cheeks as she moaned, groaned, and screamed in desperation. Delirious from her suffering, her mind splintered into a thousand pieces, and she turned her head to the side to regard the male who lay so still on the bed beside her.

How could he do this to her?

Didn't he understand the sacrifice, the leap of faith, the devotion she had shown to him—a total stranger? Was she insane, desperate, or just stupid? *I hate you!* she thought, needing desperately to lash out in some direction...any direction. *I wish I'd never heard of you. Stop this! Please...oh God, please...don't do this to me!*

A surge of venom passed through her heart and began to travel into her lower organs: her liver, pancreas, and kidneys. Like the sudden downpour of hail from a thunderous cloud, unspeakable agony began to rain down upon her, pounding her reason into dust, obliterating her will, rendering her speechless—and thoughtless—from the force of its unrelenting attack.

Deanna felt the gurney rock and tip.

She saw Kagen move with unearthly speed and set it right again.

She heard Jocelyn's voice, and thought she saw tears streaming down the beautiful woman's face, but she couldn't make anything out. Everything was fuzzy.

And inconsequential.

She watched as Nathaniel rose from his chair, released his incisors, and began to drip venom on...what? Her ankles?

Ah yes, she had torn through the cloth in her struggles, and her ankles were bleeding from the abrasion of the straps. He was healing the wounds as she made them.

She would have laughed, if laughter was something she had access to—compared to the siege taking place in her body, bloody wrists and ankles didn't even register on the pain odometer. Hell, childbirth would probably be a walk in the park compared to this.

Angry, forlorn, and utterly...insane, Deanna took a deep breath, held it in her sweltering lungs as long as she could, opened her mouth, and screamed all the way to the heavens and back.

Like the raining agony, she would never...ever...stop.

Tessa Dawn

From the midst of a torturous cauldron of boiling water, Nachari Silivasi sat up straight and ceased his cries of agony. It was a cruel bedtime routine that Ademordna reserved for those rare occasions when he entertained a host of minions and neighboring demons in his palatial court: He would fill a bath with boiling water, have Nachari submerged in the scorching liquid, and read bedtime stories to the wizard as his skin peeled back from his bones and floated around in the tub, cruel tales of life on earth, his brothers and their *destinies*, the world Nachari would never see again.

It was a torture unlike any other, and despite his best attempts to escape his body and the unbearable agony, Nachari could do nothing more than endure the vile brutality.

But tonight, something had jolted him out of his own misery.

Deanna.

He felt her—her own agony—and his heart skipped a beat in his chest, assuming it was even still attached at this juncture.

He struggled to focus.

Dear gods and goddesses in the Celestial heavens...

No.

Please tell me she cannot feel my pain! he prayed absently, addressing the petition to no one in particular.

In the midst of his torture, he reached for the body of the raven—just as he had done unsuccessfully a thousand times before. "Black as night, dark as coal; into flight, release my soul!"

In an instant, he catapulted out of his body, swept up into the form of the great bird, and soared through the netherworld, circling between dimensions.

Searching.

Great Pegasus, what had happened? How had he transitioned successfully this time? So quickly? So seamlessly?

BLOOD SHADOWS

He looked down at the body thrashing in the bath below him, still crying out in agony, and dismissed it. Something so much more powerful was calling to him, summoning him away from the throne room. Tugging. Beckoning. Insisting that he come...

Now.

Nachari followed the faint vibration, drawn to it like a moth to a flame, and as the raven soared higher...and higher...farther and farther away from his grim existence in hell, he began to discern small clues.

Deanna's voice.

Deanna's cries.

Deanna's reality.

He stopped in midflight: They were converting his destiny!

His brothers.

Using Kagen's medical skills—and Nachari's venom—in a procedure that had never been done before. And by all the gods in heaven, she was suffering immeasurably.

Without thought or reason, unaware of his current realm—or the next—Nachari drew the four winds into his body to give the raven more rapid flight. He aligned his unconscious mind with the collective, creative energy of the universe around him—all that had ever been created, and all that was yet to come—and he harnessed it in his breath. He became fire. He became water. He became the molecules that manifested the earth, and he became raw, unrestrained power, infinite potential awaiting a focused intention.

And then he flew like a rocket through a small, rectangular window.

With wings outstretched to the east and west, with talons curved and reaching for something nameless yet so important, with a curved beak extended to the sky, open, and screeching its rage, he landed on the far end of a hospital gurney and stared straight ahead...at the most beautiful, and tortured, woman he had ever seen.

The wizard inside him coalesced into a pillar of such

intensity that it manifested as a swirl of fire—red, orange, and blue energy blazing in an unnatural conflagration—enveloping the makeshift bed, surrounding the woman and her cries, reaching...piercing...demanding her very soul in that moment.

No male in the house of Jadon had ever escaped the cruelty of the Blood Curse: No *destiny* had ever escaped a moment of the agony that accompanied conversion. While some human women were converted in mere hours—and others suffered for days— none could be released from the slow, agonizing annihilation of their human bodies in order to find even a moment's reprieve.

But the Blood of the Slain itself could not deny the harnessed power of the Universe, coalescing in that one serendipitous moment...

In Nachari Silivasi.

The power of heaven reached down to sustain him; the brute force of hell rose up to surround him; and the power of all the dimensions between fused in his being—all submitted like soldiers to his command.

"Deanna!" he called out, compelling her attention.

Deanna felt a force like a whirlwind sweep through the room. It drew her briefly from her unrelenting hell, and turned her head to the side, drawing her full attention to the open window adjacent to Nachari's bed. The most enormous, magnificent bird she had ever seen flew through the window in a radiance of light, squawked in defiance, and fell like an anchor at the foot of the gurney. Its wings were like onyx silk, its eyes a luminescent, emerald green, as it stared beyond her. Through her. Inside of her.

Like an archangel sent from heaven, it called to her: "Deanna! Open your eyes. Come to me, now!"

While her eyes were already open, she somehow knew that this was not what the raven meant—what the being was commanding of her. He was asking for her spiritual sight, the eyes of her soul that saw beyond the physical.

As she stared ahead at the manifestation, a cascading fire burst forth from the center of the raven's chest, flowed swiftly around the gurney, and engulfed her body in a protective circle—yet nothing the fire touched burned. Kagen and Nathaniel rushed around feverishly, trying to determine the source of the phenomenon—trying to protect her from the flames—but Deanna knew she needed no protection from the wizard.

As long as she stared into the center of the flames, just below the space where emerald eyes had so recently stared back at her, there was no sensation.

No pain.

No reality.

There was nothing but peace.

And overwhelming, unadulterated power.

"Nachari," Deanna whispered, her mouth softly parted in wonder. She didn't know how she knew—she just did. He had come for her. He had come to help her...

He had come from the bowels of hell.

Her eyes swelled with tears as she stared at the miraculous apparition before her. *Holy mother of God, what kind of wizard was he?*

"Deanna. *Deanna!*" Kagen kept calling her name, demanding her attention, but she wasn't about to look away from the raven.

"I hear you, Kagen," she whispered.

"Are you okay?"

"What's happening?" Nathaniel asked.

Deanna stared straight ahead. "Nachari's here," she whispered.

The room fell silent.

"Can you see him?" Jocelyn finally asked, her voice filled with awe.

Deanna shook her head. "No. But I have the answers we've been searching for." The restraints fell away from her body, and she sat up slowly, still staring, dumbfounded, at the source of power before her. "He is neither alive nor dead. His corporeal body is bound to the earth because Kagen is keeping him alive; while his ethereal body, which has taken on a substance of its own, exists in the underworld—in the Valley of Death and Shadows." She drew a deep breath. "He's Ademordna's prisoner, kept in a cell, some kind of dark chamber behind a throne room in the...Middle Kingdom." She winced. "He's been tortured day and night for the amusement of demons, but he is...sentient...aware. And he is fighting"—she swallowed back her tears as the meaning of the words that flowed through her truly sank in—"he is fighting to come home." Deanna cleared her throat in an attempt to steady her voice. "There is one...I'm not sure...another presence, a female, a demoness. Very dark and dangerous. But she is collecting...something...no, several things for him...and when he finally has them all, he will try to create a rift between worlds, craft a spell to return home. His success is not guaranteed. It's a very difficult and risky—"

The stream of information disappeared as swiftly as it had come, and Deanna understood...

She knew that there would be no more words—no more visions.

No more psychic revelations.

The raven—Nachari—needed to focus all the energy he had on protecting her, not sending her a stream of psychic information: The wizard had harnessed an enormous amount of energy in order to communicate with her, and his power was swiftly waning. He had defied all the laws of the universe to be there, and what little he had left would be used to ease her suffering. There would be no argument. No other consideration. Protecting Deanna meant more to Nachari than revealing his own circumstances—than seeking his own salvation.

Deanna relaxed. For the first time since she had learned of the Vampyr, she understood just what kind of bond existed between a vampire male and his chosen *destiny*. She understood what Jocelyn and Ciopori had tried so hard to explain: The connection was beyond primordial; it was ingrained.

And it transcended a world larger than heaven and earth.

Or hell.

Deanna lay back on the gurney and stared at the light before her, knowing it would soon be gone. As desperate as she was to see Nachari in the flesh, animated and alive; as badly as she wished she could speak to him—with him—she knew she could not.

As peace and comfort enveloped her, she waited for her conversion to come to an end. Soon, she would be Vampyr—and forever bound to Nachari Silivasi—if only in spirit and memory. Regardless, what was happening in her body was a miracle, and the fact that she could no longer feel the pain was a rare and precious gift from a rare and unspeakably powerful wizard. It was an event that had never occurred before—and would likely never occur again.

Whether or not Nachari returned to earth, whether or not he could line up all the pieces he needed in order to make that happen, he had done the one thing he could for her: make it so that her entrance into his world did not command a price beyond what she had already paid.

Make it so that she would always know that he had cared for her.

Cherished her.

Honored both her courage…and her faith.

No matter what, Deanna would always know that, for at least one moment, Nachari had *loved her*.

sixteen

Kristina Riley-Silivasi rearranged the pillows on Nachari's stylish leather couch for the fifth or sixth time, not at all sure why she was going to so much trouble.

Ramsey had sent her a text earlier that evening asking if he could come by around nine. She checked the contemporary Asian clock hanging above the fireplace mantel: It was nine-fifteen. So where was he then? Braden had been staying late at the clinic a lot—ever since he had met Nachari's *destiny* two weeks ago—and Kristina knew that he would stay as long as he could tonight. After all, they were converting Nachari's *destiny*—using some weird medical procedure to pump his venom into her neck for him, as if that wasn't the creepiest damn thing she had ever heard of.

Kristina shivered. She knew she should have been there with her family. Waiting with the others. Maybe praying—or at least sending up some good thoughts—for her newest sister-in-law; but hell, they just didn't understand: Kristina couldn't be anywhere near a conversion. Maybe she had PTSD or something—who knew—but the very thought of another woman going through the torturous ordeal—and in such a horrific, impersonal way—was more than she could handle. It brought back too many memories of her own conversion. Of the night Marquis Silivasi had flung her across his lap like a weightless rag doll, held her down with his iron strength, and sunk those vicious fangs into her neck, converting her against her will, not caring one iota if she wanted it or not...if it was excruciating or not.

She shrugged.

Okay, so that was only part of the story...

True, she had tried to kill him. In fact, she had shot him with his own rifle...*twice*, and she had done it in defense of an ex-boyfriend who had just tried to kill her. A male who had directly challenged Marquis. And yes, of course, Marquis had just saved her life before it all happened. But still…what could she say?

It was a bad time for all of them.

Kristina and Marquis had been tricked by the Dark Ones into believing she was his true *destiny*, even though the two of them had about as much in common as oil and water; and considering where Kristina's head was at the time, the messed-up state of her life, she had acted with total belligerence and disrespect, not something that went over too well with the 1,500-year-old Ancient Master Wizard.

It had been an experience to remember, to say the least.

Kristina made a concentrated effort to dismiss the memory. It was in the past. A lot had happened—a lot had changed for the better—since then, and she couldn't stand to look back. Maybe that was why she couldn't be at the clinic tonight with the rest of her family; it was all just too difficult, still way too raw. She had said a prayer to the god of Nachari's Blood Moon for both Nachari and Deanna earlier, and Braden would definitely represent both of them—that was the best she could do. For now, what she really needed was a distraction.

She checked the clock again: nine-twenty. If Ramsey didn't get there soon, they might have to reschedule, and for some unknown reason, Kristina was really looking forward to having some sizable alone time with the scary-as-hell warrior in order to see where their friendship might go—

Okay, so maybe she was hoping for a little more than friendship, which was so incredibly wrong, on so many unmentionable levels—wasn't it?

But what did the world expect of her?

To give up her life, her past, the ex-boyfriend she had shared so many memories with, albeit many of them tragic, before Marquis had made such easy sport of him—and just skip down the path of life humming a happy tune because she was now a Silivasi?

She was grateful to all of them. And she had to admit, she

was much, much better off—not just financially, but in terms of everything—security, comfort, family...belonging. She had come to love a whole new circle of people, and if the truth be told, it was the first time in her life when an entire circle of people actually cared for her, too.

Genuinely.

But she was still human—well, vampire. *Damn, she had to stop doing that.* And she was still a woman.

She was still extremely...lonely.

She looked at the clock for a third time, a little bit annoyed now. She should have guessed the arrogant warrior would be late.

But what if he wasn't coming?

Dismissing the thought on its face, she ducked into the hall powder room and checked her appearance in the large mahogany mirror above the travertine pedestal sink. Her shoulder-length hair was hanging in its usual mass of untamed S-curls, but she had managed to pull the front back off her forehead with a pin, and the contrast sort of highlighted her bright blue eyes, made them look a bit more striking and even a little bit exotic. The subtle smoky gray eye shadow she had applied, just barely above and below a thin gray pencil line, didn't hurt, either, if she did say so herself.

She reapplied a light coating of rose lip gloss, one she had chosen for dramatic effect, puckered her lips, and then rubbed them together, evenly distributing the color. She stepped back and studied her reflection. Her teal miniskirt was soft suede, form-fitting along her hips and rear, and the silk black spaghetti-strap top hung enticingly over her firm breasts, all accentuated by a pair of wicked, spiked black heels.

Too much? she wondered.

She frowned. *Not at all.*

She was who she was, after all; and becoming the only *sister* in the house of Jadon hadn't changed that, overbearing vampire brothers or not.

She left the bathroom and checked the clock again. She was

just about to text Ramsey when she heard a light rap on the door. *Finally!* she thought. Taking her time, she meandered to the door, not wanting to seem too anxious, and peeked through the small security peep-hole. Her heart skipped a beat.

Ramsey was all ripped chest and arms on top of dangerously powerful thighs leading up to a hard, flat stomach. And all that dangerous male was wrapped up like a Christmas present in sexy black denim and a loose white silk shirt, the top few buttons conspicuously open, as if she needed any further suggestion as to what lay beneath. Kristina took a calming breath and opened the door. *Do not mention the time*, she told herself. *Act like you didn't even notice.* "Hey," she said, immediately wishing she'd had the patience to let him speak first. *Oh well...*

"Hey to you, too." He smiled like a lazy jungle cat, one that had just finished feasting on an innocent bird. And damn, were his teeth really that perfect? His eyes lit up with mischief. "Did you miss me?"

"No," she said, lying. "Last time I saw you, we were standing on the porch, and then—poof! Someone pulled the world's fastest disappearing act. What was up with that, anyway?"

He chuckled deep in his throat, an erotic sound that lingered in the air. "Are you always this contrary, Miss Riley-Silivasi? Can't you just say, *Hi, Ramsey?*"

Kristina smiled and shrugged. "Yep...and nope. Is that a problem?"

He leaned back in the doorway, crossed his sculpted arms in front of his chest, and considered her thoughtfully.

Kristina had to resist the urge to lick her lips.

"Not at all," he drawled. "I enjoy a challenge as much as the next guy—*sometimes.*" He winked at her, playfully. "May I come in?"

She rolled her eyes then. "I thought I gave you an official invite last time."

"I remember," he countered, "and that's why I said *may* I come in—as opposed to *can* I come in."

"Ah..." She was flirting. "And why does one of the three

sentinels of Dark Moon Vale need an invitation to enter someone's house, anyhow? Don't you guys have...blanket clearance...or something?"

Ignoring the specifics of her question, Ramsey said, "Maybe I'm a gentleman, and I simply wanted the lady's permission."

Kristina laughed out loud then. "Yeah, right. Somehow, I'm not really buying that one."

He laughed with her and gestured toward the front room. "So, are we going inside, or would you rather spend the entire evening in the doorway?" He looked over his shoulders several times then, as if he was somehow worried that someone might drive by and see them.

As if.

Nachari Silivasi lived in a stunning but isolated brownstone at the end of a dirt road, situated at the northern face of the forest cliffs.

Not wanting to make any waves, Kristina stepped back graciously and gestured toward the entrance. "Come in," she said, hoping she sounded more confident than she felt. He was just so damn intimidating. His presence was like...King Kong trying to condense himself into a James Bond vampire suit. Raw brutality in a silk package.

What if the package ripped?

Ramsey followed her into the entry, then up the short flight of stairs to the first level of the four-story brownstone, where the cozy, if not a bit too picturesque, living room awaited them. Kristina sat down in a single armchair by herself, needing a little distance to calm her nerves, and Ramsey chuckled, immediately taking notice.

Taking his own seat on the opposite couch, he tsk-tsked her. "I would say *don't worry, I don't bite.* But then, I'm a vampire, so we both know better." He laughed, and she shivered.

"Yeah, well, maybe if you're really good tonight, I'll bite, too." She couldn't believe she had said it out loud, and his answering smile told her she had just pushed the one thing she had hoped to take slow.

BLOOD SHADOWS

The attraction between them.

In an instant, Ramsey rematerialized directly in front of her. No longer on the couch, he knelt on the floor, his stomach pressed against her legs, and leaned into her. "Define *good*, baby girl," he purred in her ear. And then he leaned closer and ran the tips of his fangs from her collarbone, up the column of her neck, to just behind the lobe of her ear, and growled—literally growled. "I promise you, I can be very...very good."

Kristina's arms shot out in front of her instinctively, the palms of her hands making contact with his chest to push him away. It wasn't that she didn't want him—hell, what living, breathing female could resist?—but he was just...well, King Kong. And she felt like the maiden sacrifice tied to a pair of pillars in a foreign, foreboding jungle. "Can we slow down?" she whispered.

He tilted his head slowly to the side. "What's wrong?"

She shook her head adamantly. "Nothing. I mean, it's just that...you just got here."

"So?" he said.

"So—"

"So, you're still afraid of me, aren't you?" He reached for her hand, lifted the palm to his mouth, and pressed a gentle kiss right in the center. And then he slowly trailed his lips down her wrist, nicked her vein with his fangs, and swirled his tongue over the trickle of blood, sighing in pleasure. "We're not fragile humans. We don't have to do this carefully...or slowly."

Kristina pulled back her hand. "I know." Her mind raced for a way out—well, not so much out, but for a pause. "It's just—"

He began to sink his fangs into her flesh, startling her with the intentional pain he was allowing her to feel. Then just as quickly, the sensation vanished and turned to pleasure. Kristina groaned and squirmed in her chair. "Ramsey...Ramsey! Stop."

He withdrew his bite and rocked back on his heels. "Where is your bedroom?"

Kristina swallowed. "Ramsey, hey...look." She reached down and boldly grasped his face by the jaw, tilting it upward.

He didn't release her wrist. "Look at me," she demanded.

His vivid hazel eyes met hers, and she knew she was in trouble if she didn't think of something fast. "Tonight is just...I'm not completely here...my head is somewhere else."

Then let me take care of that. He spoke to her telepathically. And why not? He was a male in the house of Jadon, right? Of course he would have access to the common, central bandwidth. But then again, it didn't feel like a common bandwidth—it felt more intimate—like something he had forged just between the two of them...

By taking her blood.

Oh shit, she thought. She was letting him in—in ways she wasn't even remotely prepared to handle—without even knowing it; and he was controlling everything that happened between them with some really smooth moves, almost like it was deliberate.

Calculated.

But why?

Ramsey didn't need to take advantage of her innocence as a vampire—or even her ignorance of some of their ways. She was a willing participant, at a reasonable pace, that is. Right there with him. Clearly interested.

"Ramsey," she breathed out, almost sounding desperate. "I'm...it's...the clinic, you know? Everything going on with Nachari tonight. I just can't relax."

Now this brought him up short. His fangs receded, he pulled back to make unbroken eye contact, and his countenance all at once became serious. "The clinic? Everything going on with Nachari?"

She frowned then, confused. "Of course...I mean; you have to know what's happening tonight."

He froze for a moment, just the slightest hesitation, and then he immediately relaxed again. "Yeah, of course, but I'm...surprised you are so deeply affected."

Kristina drew back in surprise. "Why wouldn't I be?" She felt almost offended. "Nachari means a lot to me, and his *destiny* could die tonight." She stiffened. "And if something happens to Deanna, then Nachari is lost forever, too. So yeah, of course I'm *deeply affected.*"

Ramsey's brow furrowed, and he slowly licked his lips, only this time it was more contemplative than seductive. "I'm sorry," he whispered, sounding genuinely remorseful. "I've been a real...asshole."

He stood up, walked to the couch, and sat back down. And then he extended his hand to her. "Come sit with me, Kristina." When she hesitated, he frowned. "So we can talk—just talk."

Kristina eyed him warily. He seemed very sincere, and she was genuinely relieved. She got up slowly and took a seat next to him, still watching him attentively. "Thanks," she whispered.

"How long have you known about Nachari's *dest*—Deanna?"

Kristina shrugged. "I don't know. Kagen called all of us together to talk about a week ago—not long after my brothers found out." She thought about whether or not to share this next bit of information. "But you know, I actually met her before then—I ran into her the day she arrived in Dark Moon Vale, but my brothers don't know that." She sighed. "It's not like I knew who she was—I didn't—but I did know that something weird was up because she had some really weird connection to Nachari."

He cleared his throat. "Really? And...why...what makes you think so?"

She tilted her head to the side warily. "You're not gonna tell Marquis, are you?"

Ramsey shook his head with annoyance. "No. Of course not." He looked beyond her for a second before bringing his eyes back to meet hers. "Nothing we say is ever between anyone but us. What made you think this girl was connected to Nachari?"

Kristina sat up straight then, remembering that day in the meadow. "Because she went straight to the spot where Nachari had died—where he flatlined trying to save Napolean—and she was like rocking back and forth in the dirt, rubbing her hands in it and stuff, crying like her life had just ended...like she'd lost her best friend or something. It was really weird." She decided to leave out the part about her confronting Deanna and threatening the poor girl—thinking she might be connected to the Dark Ones.

Ramsey appeared stunned—far more than he should have been. So she had kept a secret? It wasn't like Ramsey wasn't keeping a few of his own right now...with her. "Does that make you angry?" she asked, a bit surprised by his reaction.

He grumbled, "No...no. I'm just—" He brought his hand up to his face and rubbed his jaw. "Um...I'm...trying to remember the date: You know, when we all found out that she was actually his *destiny*."

"Oh," Kristina replied. "You mean Nachari's Blood Moon? The night my brothers practically surrounded Deanna and corralled her like a horse—damn, I feel sorry for that girl. I mean, not 'cause she's with Nachari, but that had to be some crazy it-shay."

If a ghost had entered the room, stood before them, and asked Ramsey to share a spot of tea, the seasoned warrior could not have looked more stunned. Silence filled the room for nearly sixty seconds before he finally came back to his original question. "Right...right, but I don't know why the date is eluding me."

Kristina shrugged. "I don't know—it was the twenty-fifth, like nineteen or twenty days ago. I know because my brothers are keeping very close track of the Blood Moon, you know, Nachari's thirty days."

Ramsey started to speak, and he actually stuttered.
Stuttered.

He tried again. "You know, I'm not always privy to all the fine details—things that don't really matter much in terms of security—like what exactly makes Deanna's conversion so risky..."

Kristina was the one stunned this time. She had always thought of Ramsey Olaru—all the sentinels, really—as incredibly smart, capable men. Ramsey was acting almost clueless. And that just did not make sense. "Well, it's never been done before," she said. "So, of course—"

"Conversion of a male's *destiny* has never been done before?" he interrupted, sounding dubious.

Kristina felt like she was talking to a Martian.

"*Medical* conversion," she emphasized. "Doing it when the male is unconscious and unable to help out or do it himself."

"So, he's still...he hasn't woken up, then?"

Kristina frowned. She was positively stumped. "Are you okay?"

He face tightened with irritation. "I'm just saying that anything can happen, any moment, you know." He sat back in an obvious attempt to collect himself. "That's what we've all been praying for, anyhow. Being Nachari's family, you would probably hear—even before Napolean."

"Yeah," Kristina said, "I guess so." And then she frowned. "But I imagine Kagen would inform you and Napolean telepathically, like...the instant it happened. If Nachari woke up, that is."

Ramsey grew quiet. It was almost like he was afraid to open his mouth and say anything else ridiculous. He shifted nervously in his seat, and for the first time since the self-assured sentinel had arrived, he seemed completely off balance. No longer in control.

Absolutely shut down.

And really, for Napolean's second in command, *what...the...hell?*

Saber knew he must have sounded like an idiot, but he just didn't care. He had asked every question he could think of without directly arousing the girl's suspicion, and if he thought he could have gotten away with it, he would have pierced her mind for further information and scrubbed her memories afterward. But in his current state of agitation, he might just leave a trace of the invasion in his wake—a kernel of the darkness he wasn't able to control or contain behind. And the moment the Silivasis saw Kristina next, they would pick up on the errant energy.

Since killing her, at least right now, was not an option, Saber had to be careful: Not only did he need both Salvatore and Oskar's permission to snuff the girl out for good, but it appeared as if they might just need her in the future to feed them more information about Nachari and his *destiny*—to keep them informed.

Informed…

The word sounded like a joke.

They hadn't been informed at all!

Nachari Silivasi's *destiny* had waltzed into Dark Moon Vale, been revealed beneath a Perseus Blood Moon—and just why in the hell hadn't any of his dark brothers seen that damn sky or the moon, anyhow?—and claimed by his older brothers before the sons of Jaegar had even the slightest chance to get to her.

And now they were performing a conversion? Medically? In Kagen's clinic?

What in the hell was going on—this changed everything! If she died, the Silivasi brothers—not to mention Napolean—might be provoked to seek vengeance; and he and his brothers would be caught completely unaware. If she lived, Nachari might somehow find a way back to her. Saber knew that the pull between a male from the house of Jadon and his *destiny* was beyond powerful. It defied all the laws of the universe—including common sense and reason.

Son of a bitch.

Just how incompetent was Salvatore?

And as for that damn, bizarre, divining Cube of his—someone needed to blast the thing into oblivion, plant one end of a stick of dynamite in the cube and another up Salvatore's ass. Because both were utterly worthless!

Saber stirred in his seat, trying to think of a plausible way to get out of there—to get back to the colony and inform his brothers as to what the hell was really going on above the surface. He turned toward Kristina, who looked a bit confounded, not caring if he came across abrupt or abrasive. "Baby girl," he said, lacking his normal finesse, "I absolutely hate to do this, but something's come up—and I've gotta go."

Kristina rose from the couch as if she couldn't get far enough away from him fast enough. "Really? Like what?" Her voice was harsh and staccato.

"Something," he said.

"Oh...I see. So, I can tell you everything, but—"

"Business is business, Kristina. Don't go there." He hesitated. "Please...I'll be back."

She laughed sarcastically then. "Yep, and if Braden shows up, you'll disappear. And if something comes up, you'll just walk out. So, I guess you say when, you say where, and you say how long—and I just jump when called?"

Saber stood up. He didn't have time for this shit. "Girl, you're bringing too much drama into all of this—this is supposed to be fun, nothing more, remember?" He sauntered over to her, bent down, and kissed her on the cheek. "I'll be back, Red." He fingered her hair and smiled. "Besides, you knew the deal from the beginning, right? Responsibilities come first."

Kristina slapped his hand away. "Whatever, Ramsey. Just go."

It was meant sarcastically, but Saber could play dumb as well as the next guy. "Thanks, sweetie," he murmured.

And then he simply disappeared.

Kristina flipped off the empty space where Ramsey had just stood.

She marched up to her room, threw herself on the bed, and

pounded the pillow as tears of frustration she could hardly explain rolled down her cheeks. Everything she knew about the males in the house of Jadon—about Napolean's revered sentinels—told her that they were males of honor and character, that they respected women, fought for their people, and could be trusted...to the nth degree. But some subtle voice inside of her—something she couldn't even pinpoint or explain—told her the exact opposite about Ramsey Olaru: He was the devil incarnate, and as much as he acted like he liked her, he didn't. He didn't respect her or even care about her. She didn't know how she knew, or why she thought such a thing, when, after all, he was just acting like a horny male who probably hadn't had sex in a decade or so—no blame in that—but the idea continued to niggle at her.

In fact, if she didn't know better, she might conclude that the harsh, selfish warrior reminded her somehow of Dirk—her first real love and boyfriend—the one who had beat her senseless for so many years before Marquis finally put an end to it.

The thought bothered her.

A lot.

Ramsey couldn't be anything like Dirk...*could he?*

Maybe she was just out of practice. Maybe she was just being paranoid. Maybe she was just frustrated because Ramsey kept leaving every time they got together, and she hadn't had a chance to get to know him yet.

Maybe she just wished she were woman enough to handle him.

"Kristina?" Braden Bratianu's soft voice interrupted her thoughts.

Kristina turned around, surprised. She hadn't heard him open the door, let alone enter the house and climb the stairs. Great vampire she was. "Oh, hey, Bray. How are you? When did you get home?"

The kid smiled, but he looked tired. "Just a couple minutes ago."

"Is the conversion over?"

He shook his head sadly. "Nah, but I didn't want to hang around anymore. Didn't think I should leave you here alone."

Kristina winced. If only he knew. "No worries. Hey, how's Deanna? Was it...awful?"

Braden shrugged, then made a sympathetic gesture with his hands. "At first, it was pretty bad. I mean, we could hear her screaming all the way out in the hall, but then it got quiet. A little later, that is. And Kagen told me something important had happened—that Deanna was okay and he would give me the details later—but the important thing was, she wasn't suffering anymore, and it looked like she would come through the conversion...eventually."

Kristina looked surprised, but not just at the news: "And you came all the way home...just for me?"

He looked down at the floor and shifted his feet nervously. "Yeah, you know...I can't explain it. Just a weird feeling. Like...I wanted to make sure you were all right."

Kristina flashed her best smile then. "Ah, Bray, you're a good guy, you know that? I'm cool. But thanks."

Braden frowned then, and his Adam's apple bobbed up and down. "Then why have you been crying?"

Kristina drew back. How did he know? "It's nothing."

"*Kristina.*"

The kid hated being treated, well, like a kid, and Kristina knew enough by now to realize that, young or not, Braden Bratianu had some amazing psychic powers. Maybe it was better to give him at least a watered-down version of the truth. "It's just girl stuff, Braden. You know, every now and then we get a little down on ourselves, that's all."

Braden frowned with disapproval. "And you felt that way tonight?"

"Yeah...a little."

"Why?"

Kristina sighed. "I don't know. It's complicated."

Braden rubbed his jaw, considering. "So...try me."

She shrugged. "Maybe it's a lot of things: Nachari and Deanna, Nathaniel and Jocelyn, Marquis and Ciopori... Don't get me wrong, though, I'm definitely glad about Nachari and Deanna; it's just that sometimes I wonder if anyone decent will ever want me like that, ya know?" She sighed. "I mean, even if I wasn't in such a horrible circumstance—you know, the only lioness in a den of lions, all of whom already have their own mates—there still wouldn't be much of a future for me. I've just never had any luck with men."

Braden shook his head. "I don't think that's true. Besides, you're really pretty, I think."

Kristina's heart warmed. "Yeah, well, thank you, Bray; but there's a lot you still have to learn about relationships. Sometimes being pretty doesn't matter when you have horrible taste in men, and none of the good ones want you anyway." She looked away. "I'm beginning to think that maybe no one ever will."

Braden shook his head emphatically as if dismissing her argument on its face. "That will never happen to you, Kristina; you just have to have faith."

She smiled then, genuinely appreciating the kid's kindness. "Yeah, well—maybe you're right: Someday my big strong lion will come prowling through the door, and we'll all live happily forever...like in Pride Rock."

Braden shifted his weight from foot to foot and angled his body toward hers. "Exactly. You should definitely keep hope." He shrugged his tense shoulders, and then his burnt sienna eyes lit up with a spark. "Besides, it's not all up to fate. I'm going to be very big and strong one day—like a lion—and I would want you. So, if no one comes along, then, yeah; I'll mate you."

Kristina opened her mouth to speak. She shut it, then opened it again, completely stunned. "I...uh...I..." She sat up on the bed and just stared at the clueless, but admittedly handsome, teenager, dumbfounded.

Where in the world had that come from?

Did Braden pity her that much?

BLOOD SHADOWS

Looking into his eyes she saw a lot of things—wisdom maybe, staunch determination, even conviction—but not pity.

He actually meant what he was saying.

At least right now, at fifteen years old.

"And what about your chosen *destiny*?" she finally asked.

The boy shrugged. "I dunno…I guess when she comes along, I can mate her, too." He stood up very straight then. "But you would always be first."

Kristina laughed out loud. "Wow, Braden, you do know how to charm a lady…and comfort a friend." She rose from the bed, crossed the room, and gave him a big hug. "Thank you, Bray," she whispered in his ear. "I believe that may be the sweetest thing anyone ever said to me. However polygamist and unappealing."

"Cool," he replied casually. And then the kid exhaled, as if his entire body had just relaxed, and he nonchalantly left the room.

seventeen

Deanna Dubois accepted Kagen's hand, gripped it shakily, and rose from the gurney.

How are you feeling? he asked her telepathically, using the common Silivasi-family bandwidth—he had long since taken a small amount of her blood in order to track her in the event that she got lost...or something worse happened.

She concentrated on her tired, worn-out, but magnificently enhanced body and nodded. "I'm fine." She spoke out loud, then chuckled. "Not quite sure how to do that ESP thing yet."

Kagen exhaled with tremendous relief. "It'll come in time," he reassured her. He took her vital signs for the second time and nodded in satisfaction. "How is your hearing? Your sense of smell?"

Deanna took a few steps around the clinic-room, gingerly testing her legs, and then she stopped to test her ears: She could hear voices—conversations—occurring in the waiting room, and more, so much more: squirrels chattering in nearby trees, a gentle breeze rustling through the leaves, a car's wheels spinning over dry gravel...at least one mile away. She started. "Whoa—is it always this overwhelming?"

Nathaniel rose from his chair and glided across the room. "You will learn to turn it down; it really is as simple as focus. Place your attention elsewhere."

She tried, with no luck.

Nathaniel smiled warmly. "Use a visual aid for now: Imagine the things you are hearing, then place them inside of a small box. Open the lid in increments, then close the lid in increments. In your mind, allow only as much as you want to hear to escape."

Deanna practiced the exercise several times and practically laughed with excitement when it worked. "And smells?" she asked. "Can I use the same trick for smells?" Right now, the

187

overwhelming scent of pine, juniper, and fir was practically assailing her nostrils.

"Indeed," Nathaniel answered.

Kagen gathered up the medical supplies, stacked them on the gurney, and began to wheel it out of the room. "I can't say that was an enjoyable experience for anyone," he muttered, "but I am so glad it is over…and that it worked!" He turned to Deanna then and smiled warmly. "I imagine you would like some time alone…with Nachari."

Everyone turned their attention to the peaceful-looking male still lying in the hospital bed; the one who had converted his *destiny* without even knowing it.

Well, that wasn't entirely true, now was it?

Nachari had been there for the entire eight-hour ordeal, not only lending his support in the only way he could, but crossing astral barriers in order to shield Deanna from the agony she had been experiencing, a feat that Kagen insisted had never been done in the entire history of the house of Jadon.

Deanna nodded solemnly. "Yes. I would like to clean up…and spend some time alone."

Nathaniel declined his head respectfully. "Welcome to the family, Deanna." As his body slowly shimmered out of view, he added, "Be well, sister."

Kagen nodded in agreement with Nathaniel's lingering words. The Healer looked exhausted, depleted, and basically spent. Clearly, he had nothing left to say: It was four AM, and even though he was a vampire and, most likely, accustomed to keeping late night hours, Deanna had no doubt that he would retire to his private quarters and sleep. Soundly.

"Thank you," she whispered, knowing that he understood.

He sighed. "We are always close by if you need us, and I have a data feed linked to Nachari's monitors in my private quarters. Still, don't hesitate to call me—or any of your brothers—should you need us for any reason."

"I won't," Deanna said.

"Then I will do my best to stay away for a couple of hours."

He chuckled because they both knew that he never went more than a short period of time without checking on Nachari, no matter how hard he tried.

"I appreciate it," Deanna said. And then she watched as he silently left the room.

Reaching both arms to the ceiling, she arched her back and stretched her shoulders; and then she bent down to touch her toes and stretch her legs. She padded to the open window and stared out at the picturesque night, noticing how vivid the stars appeared in the sky, how deeply blue the canvass reflected above her. She felt alive. Changed. Humbled.

As if something so much more transformative than the conversion of her body had occurred that night. Not that changing one's species from human to vampire was not transformative enough, but what had happened in that room had defied all the limitations of her imagination, belief, and experience: She had lain in the presence of pure magic, unrestrained power... unyielding protection.

And it had come from *him*.

She turned around to stare at Nachari. How odd it seemed that so much took place around him—because of him—and yet, she had yet to meet him or hear his voice. She had never seen him smile. Or carried on a conversation with him. Or even had a formal introduction.

Yet, here she was...

Eternally bound to him by blood, DNA, and an ancient, unmistakable connection.

Sometimes she wondered; would she love him instantly? Would he love her beyond the common, universal love that a wizard innately felt for all living beings, beyond the inherent, programmed loved that flowed through his DNA? Would he *know* her? See her for who she truly was? Would he want her—not because he had to—but because he did?

And would she do the same?

She strolled across the room, marveling in the fluid, easy movement of her muscles, the graceful glide in her step that had not been there before—feeling almost invincible—and stopped at the side of his bed.

"Hi," she whispered softly. It was always how she began her one-sided conversations with him—she didn't know how else to begin. "Well, this was a hell of night, wasn't it?" To her utter surprise, her eyes welled up with tears, and she tried to remember what Kagen had taught her about a vampire's intrinsic connection to the earth, the effect strong emotion could have on the weather and other natural patterns around them. She didn't know if it would happen that soon, or if she was even that strong of a vampire, but she closed her eyes, wiped the tears away, and waited until she could go on without crying.

"I did it," she whispered. "I can't believe the insanity that has become my life these last weeks—but I did it." She reached down and tentatively took his hand in her own, wondering at how soft yet strong it was, how smooth and warm his skin felt against hers, how perfectly his fingers, nails, and bones were structured. His hands could have been used as a prototype for a clay praying statuette: Even now, she could picture them in perfect bronze. Or a golden inlay.

She could picture them in the flesh, so to speak, reaching out for her, touching her hair, her cheek, her waist...

Making love to her with all the grace and power that was embodied in his flawless form.

She shivered and started to release his hand—to step away—but she stopped herself.

No. She could not keep her distance forever.

She could not continue to see him as a stranger when they were practically married—more than married really—connected at the very chains of their DNA. He lived inside of her now, even if he couldn't stir from the bed.

Deanna swallowed her fear and sat down next to him, her hip brushing against his. She took a deep breath and turned to gaze at his face, looking closer than she had ever looked before. She reached out courageously and brushed a thick lock of hair behind his ear and smiled. "It's not fair, you know—why men always get the best hair." She imagined him smiling the way Jocelyn, Ciopori, and even Braden had described, a nearly stellar event that rivaled the moon and the stars in its brilliance…and beauty.

She imagined his green eyes lighting up, using the memory of what she had seen reflected in the Raven as her guide. "I guess I should say thank you," she whispered, "for what you did tonight…for helping me through this." She considered the event and sighed. "It was weird to say the least, going through that with your brothers, but I have to admit, I'm glad you weren't here…I mean, in the flesh. I don't think I would want you to experience me that way."

She shuddered and released his hand. "Oh, god." She shook her head in frustration. "I don't know how to do this! The truth is: You scare the good sense out of me!" She laughed nervously. "I mean, honestly, does it get any more intimidating than a six-foot-tall vampire wizard who everyone describes as this wonderful, magnificent soul who just happens to be gorgeous enough to challenge the gods for attention?" She swept her own hair behind her shoulder. "Not that I'm insecure…because I'm not." She leaned in closer then, as if to whisper conspiratorially. "Just between us? I've heard the words *arrogant* and *proud* tossed around a lot when people talk about you—not the cocky *I'm better than everyone around me* arrogance that really comes from insecurity, but that solid, self-assured knowing that says, *I know my place in this world, and I'm not going to pretend that I don't. I'm not better than anyone else, but I'm certainly not worse.*" She smiled. "That's always been my motto, too, so—I have no problem with your infamous…pride."

She boldly stroked his cheek. "In fact, I rather prefer it in men. But still…" She sat back and just stared in silence for a minute. "You scare the hell out of me, Nachari Silivasi: You really do."

As a wave of exhaustion rolled over her—and why wouldn't it? She had been up all night dying in order to be reborn—she got a crazy idea, an overwhelming impulse, and fought not to dismiss it. She got up from the bed, grabbed the thick brown throw she had come to favor, and returned to Nachari's side with her own pillow. Fluffing it, she placed it gently beside his head, careful not to move or disturb him in any way, and then, with an effusion of resolve, she slowly lay down beside him and draped the throw around her body.

As the bed was too small to accommodate them both lying on their backs, she eventually shimmied into a feasible position on her side, her leg resting over his with a bent knee, her arm lying gently across his belly, her head resting partially on his arm. Using her newly enhanced sense of hearing, she tuned in to the chirping of the monitors—to the very electricity pulsing through the wires—listening for even the smallest fluctuation, wanting to be sure that her presence, her weight, did not jeopardize him in any way. After several seconds passed, during which she nearly held her breath, she finally relaxed against him.

"Good night, Wizard," she whispered.

And then she closed her eyes and drifted off to sleep.

Nachari Silivasi lay awake in his prison chamber, staring up at the damp ceiling, replaying the night's events in his mind, over and over: He had come through the night's torture in Ademordna's throne room with no memory of the event, and *Deanna had come through the conversion without harm.* He said a silent prayer to the god Perseus for giving him the strength and the power to take flight in the Raven's form—to be there when Deanna had needed him most.

His brothers had been stunned by what they had seen.

Even Marquis had broken his promise to stay away; eventually, even he had entered the room in order to glimpse the phenomenon taking place—the fire surrounding the bed Deanna lay on. No doubt, each of the Silivasi brothers had hoped to see their youngest sibling emerge from the flames, to hear him talk and reveal his presence once again for the first time in months—but Nachari had not been...himself.

He had been something other. Something more. His own essence combined with the Universe around him. The substance of his ruling moon united with his burgeoning magic. He had been pure will and intention with only one goal: to see Deanna through the arduous conversion she had submitted to.

And what a sacrifice she had made for a male she had never met!

Nachari stirred restlessly, wondering more about her: Who was this exotic, beautiful woman who had so much courage, determination, and grit? What manner of power had brought her to Dark Moon Vale in the first place? And what supernatural talents did she possess—what had made her aware enough to follow the impulse and trust her instincts?

Deanna Dubois had to be an incredible judge of character. She knew enough to ultimately trust Nachari's brothers, as well as her own inner voice—her soul: Why else would she accept the truth of the Blood Curse, of her and Nachari's fate? How else could she have known that their bond was true, that their connection was right—know enough to submit to it in spite of never meeting him? Of never falling in love?

She was there.

In Kagen's clinic.

Surrounded by an entire community of strangers.

Yet she wasn't wilting like a delicate flower or fleeing in spite of what had to be a healthy amount of fear. She was surviving one moment at a time, existing in the *now*—where all true creative power lay—and trusting her heart and decisions, one after another, to carry her forward, without needing to know the ultimate outcome.

For the first time in ages, Nachari Silivasi smiled.

Genuinely smiled.

This was the right mate for a Master Wizard. Whether Deanna had any formal training or not, her soul was wise...and evolved. Without even knowing it, she had mastered a basic foundational tenet of simplicity, embraced an elusive truth which millions of beings who touted complicated theologies never got hold of: Trust your inner voice...above all others.

Acknowledge your fears, but never, *ever* let them guide your decisions.

And walk forward in faith by embracing your now, even if you are blind to the path in front of you.

Nachari shook his head in wonderment. He could not wait to meet Deanna Dubois, and now that he had channeled his power in such a spectacular way, he was beginning to believe, more and more, that it *would* happen.

It *had* to happen.

And soon, for that matter.

There were ten days left in his Blood Moon, only eight days left in which he could still impregnate his mate...or forever forfeit his future.

The sound of an iron key turning in an ancient, rusted lock brought his attention back to the room and his immediate circumstances. Was it Noiro coming with another gift? What time was it, he wondered. He closed his eyes and concentrated on the elements around him, sensing their position and passage through space: It had to be at least four or four-thirty in the morning. Who else would be visiting him now?

He sat up on the edge of the bed and waited, hoping like hell it wasn't Ademordna seeking another round of torture-play simply because the demon couldn't sleep. As a shadowed form slunk through the doorway and into his room, Nachari blinked several times. He recognized her—or so he thought he did—from one of his many torture sessions: the demoness Suirauqa—the twin energy of Aquarius.

The female was as odd-looking as she was distasteful: evil, with green skin and strangely pale eyes that were deeply set in a sunken skull, her narrow face surrounded by thinning white hair and crooked teeth.

"Suirauqa?" he said hesitantly, not waiting for a formal introduction.

She smiled chillingly. "Ah…Wizard. You are better, then? Recovered from your recent bath?"

Nachari frowned. "Why are you here?" Ademordna was very possessive and clear about his trophy prisoner: No one was to look or touch without his invitation.

Without warning, the female demoness sprouted wings and flew across the room, diving directly at him. Nachari reflexively swung his fist, connecting solidly with the center of her face just before she could bite him. The female recoiled, flew backward, and slammed into the rock wall, knocking several stones loose. She hissed a sound mixed with fury and desire at the same time.

What the hell?

Nachari leapt to his feet as the demoness cartwheeled off the ceiling, landed on her toes, and began to circle him slowly. "I've been watching you," she screeched in a high, devilish voice. "Day after day in Lord Ademordna's throne room, and I've come to exact my own pound of flesh."

Nachari blanched and tried to summon a protective ring of fire around him, but the dense quality of the Valley of Death and Shadows prevented the ring from forming a solid barrier.

"You are in my domain, Wizard!" she shouted. "And I am the Gamma ruler of the eastern realm, the providence of the marsh and sea. Your Celestial Magick will not work in my presence." She sent a flaming bolt of fire from her fingers to his groin, and he instantly felt his organ swell. "But other things will." She laughed almost hysterically. "It is this flesh that I seek to pound." Screeching once more, she leaped at him again, only this time, she moved so fast that she was on top of him before he could react. Normally, on earth, he could match, and even surpass, such acrobatics—his heightened vampire abilities made it effortless—but here, everything was backward.

Nachari strained his neck to the side to avoid her kiss and grimaced as her protruding teeth sank deep into his throat. He pressed his hands to her chest to push her away, even as he felt his own clothes dissolve along with hers. Two enormous thighs straddled his hips.

BLOOD SHADOWS

Great Celestial gods, he thought. *Not even in hell!*

As he struggled to dislodge her—a feat that should have been easy as pie for a 500-year-old vampire who could lift a truck as easily as a stone—he was shocked by the total immobility of her mass. It was as if she were an extension of his own body: immense and immovable. He recoiled as he felt a slippery heat begin to attach itself to his manhood, and then he made an instantaneous decision that could very well cost him his life.

He would have to kill her before she joined their bodies—slam a fist through her chest and extract her heart before she could fully mount him.

He was just about to release his deadly talons, draw back his fist, and plunge forward at the speed of light, for all he was worth, when a violent explosion of bone and flesh began to rain down upon him from above.

Noiro had appeared out of nowhere, spinning about like an enraged contortionist, clawing, scratching, and gouging out pieces of the demon temptress's body. She twisted Suirauqa's head until it hung from a thread of dangling tendon, gouged her eyes from their sockets, and dug at her internal organs with a swollen, bloodied fist, screaming and screeching in in a wild display of unleashed fury.

Nachari pressed his lips tightly together, trying to keep bits of flying carcass from entering his mouth. He turned his head to the side to avoid taking any errant pieces in the eyes, and he watched in stunned silence as Noiro grinded the other demoness into nothing more than a pile of otherworldly burger beside him…and then kept right on pounding it.

"Noiro," he said sternly, trying to get her attention. "Stop."

The crazed demoness kept right on screeching and pounding. "He's mine! He's mine!"

"Noiro," Nachari repeated with a shout.

She didn't look down. *"He's mine!"*

A deep, resounding voice rang out like thunder as Ademordna stormed into the room and backhanded Noiro off the bed—off the pile of meat. "No, bitch! I believe he is mine." He threw his head back and roared like an angry lion. "What the hell is going on in here?" His face was a twisted mask of unrestrained fury and disbelief.

Noiro cowered against the wall, finally coming to her senses, and began to stutter. "My liege…I…I…I found Suirauqa trying to—"

Ademordna hurdled the bed in one graceful leap and snatched Noiro up by the throat. As his clawed fist closed around her windpipe, he shouted, "Are you insane!" He shook her like a rag doll. "So what if Suirauqa—or a thousand other demons—want to mount the wizard until the end of time! That is my concern. My issue to deal with. The vampire is *my* property—not yours!"

Noiro struggled against Ademordna's grasp, trying to wrench his hands free from her throat, to no avail.

Oh gods in heaven, Nachari thought. *Please don't let him kill her.* He did not have a plan B; and time was running short.

Ademordna held Noiro high in the air above him by one arm, tilted back his head, and screamed until the very foundations of the fortress shook, and then his eyes turned a ghostly white, he opened his mouth, and he began to inhale.

The essence of Noiro's soul.

It poured out like black fog, streaming out of her eyes, ears, nose, and mouth, funneling down Ademordna's throat in a swirling vortex.

Nachari stilled his mind and began to chant inwardly, weaving a web like a black widow spider, an incantation designed to catch another's rage in the interwoven threads and spin it into a silken ball.

Slowly, reluctantly, Ademordna's fury began to cool until he finally stopped sucking Noiro's life force and dropped her to the floor, limp and barely breathing. He bent over, his back a horrible, twisted arc of disgust. "If you live, you will never, *ever* kill a demon for a vampire. You will never, ever turn on your own kind again!"

Noiro lay flat against the cold stone floor, too close to death to even tremble or respond.

Ademordna kicked her hard in the side, breaking several ribs as well as her back. "From this day forward, you will stay away from the wizard; do you hear me? You are not to attend his torture sessions—you are not even to speak his name!"

Noiro tried to nod her head but was too weak to do it.

Turning to glare at Nachari, Ademordna paused for a moment, and the wizard wondered if he hadn't just inhaled his own last breath. And then, the demon pointed at the pile of meat that used to be Suirauqa and spat in the center of the pile. "And that's what you get, Witch, for touching what was mine." Regarding Noiro one last time, he hissed, "Clean up this mess, then get out of my captive's room. And don't ever come back!"

The door shook on its hinges as Ademordna stormed out of the chamber.

Waiting just long enough to ensure that the demon lord was not coming back, Nachari rose from the bed, walked slowly toward the broken demoness on the floor, and crouched in front of her. "My lover," he whispered, pouring every ounce of contrived compassion he could muster into his voice, "are you okay?" He knew his next action would cost him dearly, spiritually, but it had to be done.

Times were desperate.

He bent to her mouth, parted his lips, and exhaled his own pure essence into her mouth.

As she took what he offered, their breath mixed, and it assailed him like maggots and worms, crawling up his airway into his nostrils, before squirming inside of his brain. When at last Noiro had enough essence to maintain consciousness, she pulled herself into a sitting position. "You give me your pure soul, Wizard?"

"Shh." Nachari placed his finger over her lips to silence her. "Listen to me carefully, Noiro. Ademordna will never allow you to carry the child you wish to create…with me. He would never have allowed it before today." He braced her body with his arm and began to rub gentle circles along her broken back, willing it to heal. "But you were right all along: Our son will be more powerful than even the Supreme Ruler of the Middle Kingdom himself. He will have the powers of darkness and light. He will have the speed and cunning of the Vampyr and the sorcery and skill of the Demon. He will weave spells like a wizard and rule souls like a deity. He will have my beauty and your…savvy. You must not allow Ademordna to stop us now."

Noiro looked at him with shocked incredulity. "Why do you say this now, Wizard?" She clearly distrusted his words.

Nachari shook his head. "Come on, Noiro. You are smarter than this. Do you think I don't hunger for retribution—thirst for revenge? Do you think I have endured all these lashings and beatings, baths in boiling water, without imagining my own rise to power someday? Wanting to dole out my own form of torture to those who have injured me?" As a demon, she would have to believe this to be his true motivation—as a being of pure carnal darkness, she couldn't conceive that there might be anything in the world worth living for that was greater than hate, power, or vengeance. "Our son can give me the retribution that I seek"—he paused, choosing his next words very carefully—"but like a bastard son banished from his father's homeland only to return many years later in victory, our child cannot be sired or raised in the Abyss. We must find our own place…on earth…to give life to this dream, to this hunger—so that we may also return one day when we are strong and ready to take back what is ours. The moment you come to me with the remaining talisman, you will have disobeyed Ademordna, and your life will be worthless to him. Just as it is worthless now." He bent slowly to her ear. "Ademordna did not spare your life, Noiro: *I* saved you with my Magick. And now, you, too, have a secret that could destroy me."

Noiro blinked several times, her eyes growing wide with disbelief. She thought about his words for a moment, no doubt trying to decipher the different ebbs and flows of energy to discern the truth. And then her expression softened. "You're telling the truth."

Nachari smiled. "Yes, Noiro...I am."

She licked her lips. "Then...then you are asking—"

"You know exactly what I'm asking: Go to the Southern province and find a scorpion; travel to the West and bring me a spider; complete your tour in the North and provide me with a snake, and don't come back until you are ready to leave this realm. You only have eight days, Noiro"—he thought of a plausible lie—"eight days before the moon and the sun and the elements of my planet render me too weak to pierce the barrier between our worlds; but if you do this thing before then, I promise, I will open up the portal between this world and the next and take you with me in order to bear a son. You have seen a glimpse of my power; you know I can make it happen. On all that is holy, I swear this to you."

It was true.

Gods willing, he would open up the portal to the next world, and he would take her with him, and his purpose would indeed be to bear a son...

With Deanna.

Noiro studied his face for a frozen moment. When she finally spoke, she whispered, "Swear it on the name of your god—every word—and offer your immortal soul in exchange for the truth of your words."

Without hesitation, Nachari grasped her by both shoulders and looked deep in her eyes. "I swear to you on the name of the great god of Celestial light, Perseus, the Victorious Hero, the ruling lord of my birth, my life, and my death: I will open a portal between our worlds and take you with me, Noiro, so that I might sire a son. And if the words I speak are untrue, then I forfeit my immortal soul to the very god whose name I swear by. May he strike me down without mercy for my desecration."

Noiro stared at him suspiciously—and thank the Celestial lords, she was too beaten, confused, and desperate to really decipher his words.

She finally relented. "If what you say is true, Wizard, then prove it: mate with me now."

Nachari didn't cringe…or blink.

Everything he had ever wanted—his life on earth, Braden and his brothers, meeting and claiming his *destiny*—was on the line. Still, he could never betray Deanna in such a way. To one day place his body inside of Deanna's after being somewhere so vile…so corrupt…first.

It was unthinkable.

Unfathomable.

But what he could do, he would.

Nachari would enter Noiro's mind, change and erase her perceptions, and implant memories of his own choosing. For the first time since he had arrived in the Valley of Death and Shadows, he had the energetic advantage: Noiro was weak, pliant, and at his mercy. And he was the one with the power.

Thanks to Ademordna's rage.

Would wonders never cease?

He bent to her mouth, ignoring the spiked teeth and forked tongue that distended to greet him, and pressed his lips to hers, kissing the demon witch like his life depended upon it…because it did.

As he gathered the energy from the magic web he had already spun, he couldn't help but think, *Oh yes, he would penetrate the hideous demoness all right,* but it wouldn't be his seed that filled her. He would empty the seeds of Ademordna's hatred, vengeance, and unyielding rage deep inside of her being—the intention he had captured in a spider's web during the evil one's murderous fury—and he would turn every last ounce against the Supreme ruler of the Middle Kingdom himself.

Noiro would not stray from Nachari's plan—no matter the cost.

She would burn with a pregnant hatred, blister with the need to destroy, up until the very moment the two of them took flight from the evil realm…

Together.

Ademordna had guaranteed it with his rage.

eighteen

The Next Day

Saber knocked on the heavy wooden door just outside Salvatore Nistor's private lair. When the large, medieval-looking hatch flew open on its own, he strolled in casually. "What's up, Salvatore," he said, glancing around the room. While adorned with large antique furnishings, a massive chandelier, and an equally ostentatious iron bed, the lair still reflected its ancient, underground roots: Stalactites hung from the ceiling in naturally occurring formations, and stalagmites sprung forth from the earthen, clay floor, peeking out from beneath dark, random crevices.

"Ah, Saber, so nice to see you." Salvatore bowed infinitesimally from the waist. "Thank you for coming."

"Yeah, yeah," Saber replied, stopping a few feet in front of the aged sorcerer and crossing his arms in front of his chest. "I assume Oskar filled you in on the details—what I learned from the redhead during my last visit—so why don't we cut through the niceties and get straight to the point."

Salvatore shrugged slowly and smiled languidly, still taking his time. "I rarely rush anything, Saber—it's just not my style."

Saber shifted his weight impatiently. "Yeah, well, every second we stand here is another second Nachari Silivasi may be growing stronger—another second his *destiny* is running around Dark Moon Vale, healthy and alive."

Salvatore declined his head in an understanding gesture. "Indeed," he drawled. He swept his arm out, gesturing toward a large red sectional, discreetly appointed toward the back of the room in front of a giant flat-screen TV. "Nonetheless, allow me to at least act like a gracious host. Have a seat."

Saber sauntered over to the large davenport, sat down, and

bent his left leg over his right, leaning back into the plush, expensive fabric. From his new vantage point, he could see Salvatore's enormous iron bed, perched atop a large raised platform, and the bizarre divining cube that sat like a crude relic on the nightstand beside it. The thing gave him the willies; it was glowing like the Northern lights—for all the good it had done them. "Why do you keep that thing, anyways?" Saber asked, unable to help himself.

Salvatore cringed as if the very words spoken aloud might offend the ridiculous object. "Watch yourself, my friend—*darkness* hears...very well."

Saber raised one eyebrow, watched the cube for any sign of sentience, and shook his head. "Ah'ight—whatever." He slowly rolled his shoulders. "So, back to Kristina then—or more importantly, our brothers who walk in the sun. What's next?" Before Salvatore could answer, he leaned forward and added, "Because I have to tell you, I've had just about enough of all this *the spy who loved me* crap. Not getting us anywhere in my opinion."

Salvatore took a seat opposite Saber in a high-backed armchair and sighed. "Agreed. It is definitely time to change tactics."

Saber's ears perked up. *Finally.* "And?"

"And you are right, my impatient subject—Nachari and his newly arrived *destiny* are a much more pressing issue."

Saber nodded, liking where the conversation was going. Well, everything except the part where Salvatore referred to him as his subject—impatient or not. As far as he was concerned, he served the house of Jaegar because it was his home—and the males were his brethren, so to speak—but last he'd checked, he wasn't anybody's subject. And never would be. "So, what's the plan?"

Salvatore folded his hands in his lap and looked off into the distance, considering; and then a wickedly conniving smile curved the corners of his mouth. "No more dilly-dallying around. You will use your connection to Kristina to strike at Deanna." He met Saber's eyes and practically purred his next words: "Get Nachari's *destiny* away from the Silivasis and kill her." He smiled broadly then. "Is that clear and direct enough for you, Mr. Alexiares?"

Saber licked his bottom lip and chuckled. "Yep. That does it for me."

"Good." Salvatore nodded, pleased. "Now then"—he inclined his head toward Saber's hip pocket, indicating the untraceable cell phone they had programmed for his ongoing dalliance with the redheaded ditz, and raised his shoulders— "there's no time like the present, correct?"

Saber chuckled, thinking of a plan. "Couldn't agree more," he said, removing the cell from his pocket. He pressed a finger to his lips, warning Salvatore to remain quiet, while he retrieved Kristina's number and hit the dial button.

The phone rang three times before she picked up.

"Hey, baby girl," he drawled into the phone. "It's Ramsey— miss me?"

She said something less than ladylike and threatened to hang up.

Saber laughed quietly, careful to keep his voice low and soothing. "Ah now, c'mon, Red, don't treat me like that—you're breaking my heart. I told you I would get back to you as soon as I could." Sensing that the female had probably had enough of his games, he quickly shifted his approach before she could respond adversely—or become angry. "Look, Kristina. I thought about the last time I saw you, and you're right. I'm an ass. No excuses. I come and go as I please, as if I could care less how things affect you, but you have to know that couldn't be further from the truth. I'm just rusty, you know? I don't know how the hell to be with a beautiful woman...so maybe I'm still a little rough around the edges, but it's got nothin' to do with you— everything to do with me. And I just need you to be a little patient."

That seemed to get her attention as she *mmm-hmm'd* him with only a minimal amount of sarcasm and waited to hear what else he had to say.

"So, on that note, I've been thinking of a way I could make it up to you—and honestly, about something I think might be meaningful to you."

"What's that?" she asked him, her interest finally piqued.

"I want to take you somewhere peaceful...relaxing...to the hot springs by the southern lake, but more than that, I want to help you branch out a little, make some new friends—because, really, isn't that what's behind some of the tension that keeps popping up between us? The fact that I can't be there as often as you deserve...but you still have the need for company?"

The phone went silent, and for a moment, Saber thought she might have hung up. "Baby girl?"

Nothing.

"You still with me?"

She cleared her throat. "Yeah, I'm here. What the hell are you talking about, Ramsey?"

He drew in a deep breath and deliberately slowed his speech. No point in rushing it. "I was thinking you should invite Nachari's new lady to join us—just the three of us, you know? The two of you get to know each other better in an easy setting...where I can kind of act like a buffer."

Kristina started laughing then. Actually laughing. "Yeah, because you're such a social giant, Ramsey. Why would I need you to help me make a friend?"

He went straight to the heart of the matter, hoping to rattle her into submission. "Because we both know that you're basically a loner." He softened his voice. "Yeah, you have your new family—the Silivasis and their mates—but whether you believe it or not, I have learned a few things about the spicy redhead who seems to monopolize my attention both day and night anymore: She's fiercely independent and has a mind of her own. She doesn't like obligatory relationships or being told what to do. She needs some kind of space—or life—of her own that's not under anyone else's control, least of all her new, overbearing brothers." He chuckled then. "Or her new overbearing love interest."

"Love interest?" Kristina parroted sarcastically.

Saber placed his hand over his heart deliberately, hoping to add drama to his voice. "Ah, baby—you don't love me yet? I'm wounded. Why are you so cruel?"

She huffed her annoyance, but he could hear a note of playfulness emerging in her voice. "Is that a trick question?"

"Yeah, yeah…okay. I'm not that lovable, I concede; but the point is, baby girl, you are. And I think a new friendship—one of your own making and choosing—would be good for you. Besides, there's actually a little more to it than that—let's just say it's a gesture of sorts."

"A gesture?" she asked curiously. "What kind of gesture?"

Saber spoke gently. "A gesture of good faith from me to you. You think I'm just trying to use you—that I want to sneak in, in the middle of the night, and leave before anyone sees…because I'm ashamed…or you're not good enough to take in public." He was reaching now, and he knew it. She had never actually said those words to him, but he was close to the underlying feelings—her ever constant insecurity—just the same. "And it isn't that, Kristina—it really isn't."

When she remained deathly quiet, he took it as a sign to continue: "Like you, I want something separate from my everyday life—something that has nothing to do with the king or the other warriors, my own private space…and relationship." He held his breath for a heartbeat and then dove in with both feet: The argument would either work…or it wouldn't. "And I'm hoping that by taking both you and Deanna to the hot springs, you will at least come to see that I'm not ashamed of you; I'm not afraid of being seen in public with you; and that I care about more than just…getting next to you." He went straight for the ego and sense of belonging. "Besides, if nothing else, Deanna will see us together, and she'll know that you have someone who really digs you." He stopped then, waiting to feel her out, to gauge her response.

"And what if Deanna comes to the conclusion that you're nothing but a dog playing hound games, and I should step?"

Saber smiled—*damn, but this girl was feisty.* "Then I brought that shit on myself, right? Fair is fair."

Kristina's hesitation indicated she was mulling it over...seriously. "So, you would actually hang out with me—and Nachari's *destiny*—at the hot springs for an entire evening—"

"Night," he interjected. Unbeknownst to her, Saber had to make damn sure the sun had gone down before he *hung out* with anyone. "For as long as you like, baby girl."

"Hmm," she said. "So when do you want to do this?"

Saber sighed, not realizing that he had practically been holding his breath.

"Let's meet up Sunday," he answered. "Just the three of us. You pick up Deanna and bring her to the hot springs around nine o'clock. I'll meet you both there...with bells on."

Kristina giggled then. "Only bells?" she teased.

He growled low and wicked. "I will if you will."

Kristina's delight sparkled in the tone of her voice. "Fine," she finally agreed, "I'll give Deanna a call and invite her. But, Ramsey," she interjected seriously, "I swear, if you stand me up or bail out in front of Deanna, that's it. You don't ever come by again or call back. I mean it. It's over."

Saber swallowed his retort, satisfied. If Kristina Silivasi could get Nachari's *destiny* to the hot springs alone, it would indeed be over. For both of them. He nearly shuddered with anticipation. "Fair enough," he drawled. "I'll see you tomorrow then? Nine o'clock? Just the three of us—our secret."

Kristina feigned indifference. "Yeah...*yeah*...it'll be fun, I guess."

"Oh," Saber insisted, "you can count on it, baby girl."

"Fine," she said, "see you then."

"See you then, Red."

He hung up the phone, tucked it back into his pocket, and turned to face Salvatore, who was grinning from ear to ear while shaking his head in amusement.

"You will kill them both, then?" Salvatore asked.

Saber raised his shoulders and stared at the diabolical

sorcerer, trying to read his resolve. "Do I have the council's permission?"

Salvatore shrugged nonchalantly, appearing surprisingly indifferent. "I must admit, we had hoped to use the redhead much longer; she is such an easy, convenient source of information." He exhaled slowly. "However, one must adapt to circumstances, no?"

Saber held up his hands. "The best laid plans of mice and vampires…"

Salvatore chuckled heartily. "Indeed." And then he leaned forward in his chair, rested his elbows on his knees, and dropped his voice to a fine, icy purr. "Do not dally with Nachari's girl, Saber. If there's information you can garner from her, then fine—get it. But don't take unnecessary chances. We want her dead. *I* want her dead." He took a deep breath and lightened his voice. "And as for the other one—do whatever you want with her, however you like, if time permits—but yes, in the end, kill her, too."

Saber rose from the stiff davenport, wondering absently why the wealthy sorcerer would keep something so uncomfortable in his lair. No matter. Soon, he would be done with this frivolous assignment and his far too frequent association with the Dark Council, and he could get back to living his own life. "As you wish, councilman. Your will—their graves."

With that, he sauntered out of the room.

Braden Bratianu watched curiously as Kristina checked the caller ID on her cell phone, covered the mouthpiece with her hand as she answered it, and quickly shuffled out to the deck, closing the patio door behind her in order to keep Braden from listening in on the call.

As if he couldn't just use his superior vampire hearing to eavesdrop if he chose.

He rolled his eyes, feeling more than a little annoyed and, frankly, put out. Since when did Kristina keep secrets from him? From her family? Since when had she started acting so weird? He wondered if it had anything to do with Ramsey, and he almost had half a mind to get up and follow her onto the deck—demand to know exactly who she was talking to and why. Just like Marquis would.

But then he noticed the small spiral notebook she had left behind on the couch, the one with the painted pink dragon on the front, the one she often used as some kind of journal or diary. Everything in him told him it was wrong to snoop, that even Marquis and Nathaniel would be disappointed in him for doing something so disrespectful and immature, but he just couldn't help it.

It was right there.

Lying upside down on Nachari's couch, the pages already open.

And what if Kristina really was in trouble? Then Nachari would expect him to act like a true male from the house of Jadon—duty before self.

He looked through the large pane of floor-to-ceiling glass on the second level of the brownstone, wondering how he would get away with it, but Kristina was quickly walking toward the far end of the deck with her back turned to him, putting as much distance between them as possible—so she could sneak behind his back. All obvious and everything.

Well, fine—two could play that game.

Using the stealthy glide of his enhanced Vampyr body, he slinked noiselessly across the room and picked up the diary. He glanced out the window again—from this vantage point, he could no longer see Kristina's full body. The only thing that remained in his line of sight was a lock of Kristina's wild red curls; and if he couldn't see her fully, then she couldn't see him, either. Gazing down at the well-worn page beneath him—it was practically covered in illegible blue ink—he began to scan the uneven lines, reading as many words as he could, skipping randomly through the paragraphs as quickly as possible:

I'm just so torn. I don't know if Ramsey cares at all or if he just wants to use me for sex...

I know he'll leave me when his destiny comes, but he still wants to have a good time...

I hate how he disappears the minute somebody shows up or leaves the minute anything comes up. Like everything always has to be this huge secret, but I guess he has to do whatever Napolean tells him. Still, it sucks to be in this position...

God, I can't believe I could think he's as cruel as Dirk. Sometimes I even wonder if he'd hit me. Or force me? There really is something so dark and dangerous about him. But it's sexy as hell, too...

Shit, my brothers would kill me. I don't even want to think about it. No, they are never gonna know. No matter what happens. Never!

So, I guess the jury is still out for now, but I do have to decide something soon...

Ramsey is not a little boy playing games, and he's so forceful. It's gonna happen one way or the other if I don't get rid of him...

Damn, he is so fine, though. I really do kind of want him...

I don't know what to do.

This totally sucks!

Braden grimaced as the words sank in, tossed the diary back on the couch, and quickly arranged it the way he had found it. And then he scrunched up his face and took a step back, staring out the window at Kristina's back.

What in the world had he just read?

Kristina and Ramsey? *Eww.*

He shook his head as if it were full of cotton candy. Why would Ramsey try to do *that* with Kristina? He was way too...something. Big. Old. Mean?

Braden ambled across the room and sat back down in his chair just staring off into space. He couldn't understand it, but he was angry.

Really angry.

He sat there tapping his foot against the ground, trying to think of what in the world he should do, and waiting for Kristina to come back inside.

His head hurt.

And that made no sense for a vampire.

When the patio doors finally slid open and Kristina waltzed back inside, he could tell by the look on her face that she must have been talking to Ramsey.

Dang, he was so mad!

"Who was that?" he demanded, jumping to his feet. His hands went immediately to his hips.

Kristina drew back in surprise. Quickly recovering her composure, she stepped into the room and placed her phone on an end table. "Excuse me?"

Braden puffed out his chest. He could feel his heart begin to race. "You heard me. Who was that! On the phone?"

Kristina glanced absently at her diary lying on the couch, blanched for a second as if realizing that she had left it within his reach, and then squared her shoulders in defiance, obviously confident that the book hadn't been touched.

And he wasn't going to tell her he'd read it, either. At least not now. He wanted to know if she would keep lying to him.

"Frankly, Braden, that's none of your business."

Braden felt a funny tingle in his mouth, like his gums were retracting, and there was a strange, swirling energy flowing up and down his arms that made him feel almost like he was shifting inside of his own body. Really, really weird. He swallowed some extra saliva and made a concentrated effort to pitch his voice low—like the Silivasi brothers always did when they were being stern. "Woman," he barked, doing his best Marquis imitation, "I'm not playing games with you. Tell me who was on the phone." The sound reverberated through the room like a heavy globe ricocheting through a pinball machine, and Braden could hardly believe it had come from his mouth. A subtle growl punctuated the end of his sentence, the sound equally surprising.

Kristina looked positively stunned.

And none too happy.

"Are you crazy?" she asked, raising her voice. "You better chill out, Bray. What is your problem?"

The boy's feet felt like shifting pillars against the ground, quaking and rising beneath him, and for a moment, he started to feel afraid of what was happening. "My problem? What's your problem?" His voice wavered, betraying his underlying insecurity. "Why won't you talk to me? Why are you being so…sneaky?"

Kristina frowned then. "It's not sneaky, Braden. It's called *privacy*. And I have a right to it. Damn, why don't you just…go find a crossword puzzle or something?"

Braden widened his stance, planting both feet approximately a shoulder's length apart and bending his knees. He was trying to appear threatening and had instinctively fallen into an attack stance. "Who was on the phone," he repeated, sounding more predatory than he had ever sounded before—the guttural tone of the words rolled out on a snarl.

Kristina took a step back, for the first time appearing unsure. "It was just a friend—some girl I used to know from the casino, okay?" She walked over to the couch, picked up her diary, turned on her heels, and started to leave the room. "I'll talk to you later, Bray, maybe after you've calmed down."

Braden felt hot tears sting his eyes, and he hated feeling so weak in the face of a potentially serious situation. "Stop!" he yelled, sounding more desperate than commanding.

Kristin spun on her heels angrily, squaring off to face him, and by the heated look in her bright blue eyes, she was no longer playing around. "Don't tell me what to do," she snapped. She pointed her finger at him and waved it as she spoke. "You might be my friend, but you ain't got it like that. Comprende?"

Braden felt like the room was spinning around in circles now. "I'll do what I want," he argued, knowing he sounded crazy. "And you better start listening."

Kristina shook her head, incredulous. "Whatever!" She waved her hand in a brisk dismissal and turned to leave the room again.

To Braden's utter surprise, he shot across the space at lightning speed, not at all sure if he had flown or dematerialized to get there that fast, stopped directly in front of her, and squared his ever expanding adolescent shoulders, creating a wide barrier to block her path. "You're not going anywhere, Kristina!"

"Excuse me?"

"Not until you answer my questions first."

"Get out of my way, Braden. I mean it."

"I can take the answers from your mind if you won't give them to me," he threatened.

"Cannot," Kristina snapped, sarcastically.

"Can too!" he argued.

"Can. Not." She punctuated each word separately.

"*Can. Too.* I can do whatever I want! I've dug into people's minds before."

Kristina smiled then, but there was nothing lighthearted or congenial about it. "Oh, what are we talking about now? Katie Bell? The little girl who you almost *lobotomized* while trying to play wizard? The mess that Nachari had to clean up for you?" She leaned toward him, her hands planted firmly on her hips. "You mess with my head in any way, Braden, and Marquis will have your hide." Her voice rose proportionately as she continued to counter his threat. "Not only is it forbidden, but I highly doubt you're even capable of it. More than likely, you'd just…accidentally kill me. Is that what you want?"

Braden felt like he was going to cry. And why was that, anyhow? He was a male in the house of Jadon, a warrior in the making, a vampire with the burgeoning skills to one day be a great wizard, besides—why was he letting her get to him like this? "Don't you talk to me like that," he barked defiantly, unable to think of a better comeback. "I want to know who you were talking to, and I want to know *now.*"

Kristina shook her head in disbelief. "*Braden…*" She lowered her voice. "I don't know what's going on with you, but I'm not going to stand here and argue: It's none of your business, and that's the end of it."

Braden felt himself shaking. "It is, too, my business." He cleared his throat, searching for a better argument. "If I'm going to mate you one day, then you're damn right, it's my business."

Kristina laughed then, and Braden was surprised at how much the derisive sound hurt. "Oh my God, Braden," she snickered. "Are you serious?" She rolled her eyes, as if whatever he was thinking wasn't even worth the time it took him to think it. "You are not going to mate me one day, Braden. That was just...you trying to be nice because I happened to be feeling down." She took a step back and looked at him distrustfully. "Seriously: Are you okay? Do I need to call Marquis or something?"

Now that was just insulting.

Braden looked down at the ground. When he finally raised his head again to meet her gaze, he felt heat envelop his body, and his senses heightened—his eyes narrowed their focus, and his hearing grew more acute. "Why have you been lying to me?" he asked, speaking almost too softly to be heard.

Kristina took a step toward him. "Wow...okay, this conversation really is over." She gestured toward the hallway, making it crystal clear that she wanted him to step aside so she could leave the room. "Move. *Please.*"

"I asked why you've been lying to me," he whispered.

She stared at him for a minute and then squared her jaw. "Move, Braden."

He stood his ground.

She brought both hands up, placed her palms squarely on his chest, and shoved him—hard. "Move!"

Braden dug in his heels, surprised that his body didn't budge. "Just tell me why—"

"It's none of your business!" To his absolute shock, she kicked him in the shin with the spike of one heel and elbowed him in the gut, shouting, "I said *move!*" Her face flushed red. "I'm not playing with you anymore, Braden. You're acting crazy—like an asshole—and I've had enough. Get out of my way!"

BLOOD SHADOWS

He stared at her in shock. He couldn't believe that Kristina was actually being this mean to him—especially when *she* was the one who was lying.

Furious, she glared at him and grinded her teeth. "You know what? You're trying way too hard to act like Marquis these days—you're not my boss, and you're not my mate, and you're never going to be!" Her voice continued to rise with anger. "And in fact, contrary to what you might believe, you're not a warrior or a wizard yet, either!" She stomped her foot and leaned toward him. "You're just a fifteen-year-old boy who's about to get slapped if he doesn't get out of my way. *Now, move!*" She was just about to shove him again when all at once he whirled around like an angry lion, a supernatural hunter outmaneuvering its prey.

He locked his right arm tightly around her waist, pressed his chest hard against her back, and gripped her chin with the fingers of his left hand, instinctively tilting her head to the side to expose her jugular. Before she could move or even protest, he released his fangs and pressed them hard against her vein, the sharp tips piercing her skin deeply enough to draw a trickle of blood, and then he growled deep in his throat, issuing a clear, feral warning: "I may be a kid, but I'm still a male." As power surged through him, he spoke in a harsh, heavily accented voice. "And I *am* Vampyr." He bit down ever so slightly while inhaling her scent before slowly adjusting his fangs. "And you *will* yield."

Braden heard his own voice as if it belonged to someone else.

Someone older. Someone wiser. Someone far, far more powerful...

As the words drifted around in some ancient, unknown memory, his canines continued to throb with a growing, almost inexplicable need. There was something he wanted. Something he couldn't name. Or even understand.

Not blood.

Not power—well, not really...

Dominance.

Absolute, unyielding control.

Tessa Dawn

Braden Bratianu wanted to break Kristina's will and impose his own; he *needed* to etch his identity into her very DNA for all time so she would never challenge him again. He could not—*he would not*—have his manhood tested by this female or any other. The very idea of it made him want to drink her blood until she grew weak and limp beneath him, cowering at his superior strength.

The idea of being emasculated by her went against his very evolution.

He may very well be a boy—just fifteen years old—and he may very well be known for all of his mistakes, mishaps, and messes, but he was still a male...and a vampire...and a member of the house of Jadon, and he would not kowtow to the defiant whims of an obstinate woman like a sniveling idiot.

Not now. Not ever.

He tightened his grip, daring her to move or resist.

After what seemed an eternity, Kristina finally swallowed and wet her lips, preparing to speak. "Bray?" Her voice was shaky and unsure.

He closed his eyes and tried to find himself again. To lose the haze.

"Braden?" she repeated his name. "Please...let go."

At last, her body yielded like a limp noodle. There was no resistance left, whatsoever, and the contrasting reaction from a woman who had just moments ago been so spirited and defiant left him feeling confused and unsure.

He relaxed his arm. "I'm sorry," he whispered hoarsely.

"It's okay." Her voice was hesitant. "Just...just let me go." She wrenched her neck free from his teeth.

When he finally pulled away and stepped back—and glanced down at his body just to make sure it was really his—he could have heard a pin drop in the room. Kristina was staring at him like he was an alien; and honestly, he kind of felt like one.

What in the world had come over him?

"I'm sorry, Kristina," he repeated, appalled. "Did I hurt you?"

217

She smoothed her clothes and shook her head. "No...no...I'm cool."

"Are you sure?" He felt like the world's greatest bully.

"Yeah...yeah, that was just—wow." She forced an insincere smile. "You're a trip, you know that? There's way too much going on with you, I swear."

Braden nodded. It was true. Every time he turned around, something strange and unexpected popped out; and he didn't know if it meant that he was becoming more of a vampire—finally growing into the species he had been converted to—or just more of a mess. But jumping all over Kristina? Now that was just crazy. Wrong. And he needed to figure it out before he said or did anything else that might make him act even crazier.

Hanging his head in both shame and bewilderment, he whispered, "You're not mad at me, are you?"

Kristina shook her head slowly, still staring at him like he had mud on his face...and maybe with a little newfound respect. "No...not really...I mean..." Her voice trailed off, and she reached up to rub her neck. When she brought her hand back down, her fingers were coated with a light film of blood.

Braden's stomach did a strange, queasy flip. "Do you need some venom?" he asked, reaching up to awkwardly feel the edge of an incisor. He wasn't entirely sure if he could make one come down.

Kristina shook her head. "No...that's cool, but thanks, I've got it." She turned her head to the side, as if a bit embarrassed, released one of her own incisors, and dripped some venom onto a finger. Then she dabbed the small puncture wounds at her neck and shrugged. "See? All better."

Braden nodded, and then he looked away, unable to face her. He had never felt so awful in his life. How could he have attacked Kristina? Okay, so *attack* was too strong a word, but still—despite their differences, and her obvious head-trip over Ramsey, they were supposed to be friends. And with Nachari gone, with the other brothers so busy with their mates or at the clinic, Kristina was really all he had for now.

"I really am sorry," he said.

Kristina shrugged her shoulders. She stepped forward, approaching tentatively, and slowly wrapped her arms around his shoulders in a gentle hug. "It's okay, Bray—really. It's not like we both aren't still trying to figure out this whole vampire thing, right? The only oddballs converted for reasons other than the Blood Curse." She released him, stepped back, and smiled. "Besides, in a way it was pretty cool—that you can get all predatory, wild, and stuff like that. Just don't do it to me again, okay?"

Braden nodded vigorously. "I won't! I swear it."

"Cool," she said, "and drop the third degree? Please?"

Braden frowned. He still had a lot of questions—and he still felt like he deserved honest answers—but he could hardly press her now. After what he'd just done, he would be lucky to keep her friendship. Reluctantly, he nodded. "Yeah, okay."

"Braden?"

"Yeah, *yeah.*" He swallowed his pride in an effort to let it go. "I promise I'll leave you alone."

"Then you'll drop it?"

He frowned, feeling defeated. "Yeah…I'll drop it."

For now.

nineteen

Valley of Death and Shadows ~ Sunday

Nachari Silivasi jolted awake in his stiff, uncomfortable bed, disturbed by the sound of an iron key jiggling in the lock of his heavy prison door. He rubbed his sleep-filled eyes, struggled to catch his bearings, and immediately leapt from his horizontal position on the dingy mattress to the other side of the room, perched low and ready in the corner.

Ever since Suirauqa's visit—and the mayhem that had rapidly ensued—he kept a much more watchful eye. Yes, he was still a prisoner at the mercy of his captives, but he was also a vampire on a mission to make it home. Alive.

As the door slowly creaked open, he rocked back on his heels, ready to strike if necessary and face Ademordna's wrath later. Of course, that depended upon who it was. If it did happen to be the Supreme Ruler of the Middle Kingdom—Ademordna himself—then he would just have to take his medicine as he always did, comforted by the knowledge that there were only nine days left in his Blood Moon—seven before the deadline he had given Noiro would come to pass.

Gods and goddesses, be faithful—please let the crazy demoness succeed in her mission.

As a spattering of unnatural light shone through the broadening crack in the door, his lethal eyes fixed on a stumpy, diminutive form shuffling into the room; and Nachari had to shake his head to clear his vision. The demon, minion—whatever it was—that entered the cell could not have been more than three and one-half feet tall, more like a child than a man. However, his gruff manner and obvious masculine features made it crystal clear that it was indeed an adult, a fully mature demon.

221

Nachari watched as the male's thin lips drew back in a sneer, and rotten, jagged teeth shone beneath the hollow spaces. Sharp, reptilian scales rose from the back of his spine, and his clawed feet hooked into the stony floor as he came forward with supreme confidence.

"Wizard!" the short demon called. "Where are you?" He spun around in all directions, instantly locking eyes with Nachari before smiling a putrid grin full of malicious intent. "Ah, there you are." He held a medium-sized, ornate box in his tiny hands, the cover appearing heavy as if made of granite. "I come bearing gifts."

Nachari stood up to his full height, not exactly afraid of the little weasel but definitely wary; after all, he wasn't a fool. He knew where he was and what kind of souls surrounded him. "Gifts from whom?" he asked suspiciously.

The little demon snickered. "If I tell you, I'll have to kill you." He cackled like he had really said something funny.

Nachari stifled the urge to roll his eyes. Unfortunately, he recognized the high-pitched whistle in the demon's voice now, the insidious and frankly downright irritating drone of his laughter; and he knew this character all too well. The demon had religiously attended each and every one of Nachari's throne room torture sessions, usually taking a seat in the front row, if not shuffling to the floor right in front of the action, in order to get a closer look. If he could have sat on Nachari's back while avoiding the lash, or submerged himself in the boiling water without feeling the pain, he would have. The troll was a sadist—which, of course, most demons were—but he took inordinate pleasure in watching every drop of blood spill, in savoring every cry wrenched from the suffering wizard's throat. On more than one occasion, Nachari had wished he could break free from his bonds and snap the little bastard's neck.

He turned his attention to the box in the demon's scaly hands, now doubly concerned about the contents. "What's in the box?" he asked pointedly.

The little demon slid forward one foot at a time as if trying to engage Nachari in a two-step, playfully rubbing his hand over the lid. "Wouldn't you like to know," he hissed.

"Couldn't be why I asked," Nachari mumbled, his irritation growing.

The demon threw back his head and puffed out his chest, causing two rather pathetic wings to shoot forth from his back in a pitiful attempt at dominance—or at least what the little fool believed to be a show of dominance. To Nachari, it looked more like a wounded bat trying to scare off a velociraptor—not all that intimidating.

As wisps of smoke curled at the apex of the wings, plumes shooting out from the apparent attempt at rousing fire, Nachari whistled in mock appreciation and took an exaggerated step back. Holding both hands up in front of him, he pretended to be impressed. "Whoa, now—I'm just trying to ask a question. No need to get angry." It took every ounce of self-restraint he had not to call down a fire-and-brimstone spell and show the irritating freak what real magic looked like.

The demon seemed pleased. "Just so you know who you're dealing with," he snarled.

Nachari shook his head graciously. "I can see that." He waited while the demon strutted around in an oblong circle before pressing the issue once again. "So, here's the thing: I assume you came here for a reason, and I'm just very curious to know what it is."

The demon puffed out his chest again. "Are you afraid?"

Nachari bit his lower lip. "Trembling in my boots."

"Perhaps I have a medieval torturing implement in the box, vampire—perhaps I'm here to put on my own show."

Now that gave Nachari pause. Not so much because he feared a one-to-one standoff with the monster, but because it would create a lot of political problems for him and Noiro. He wasn't feeling particularly inclined to submit to a one-to-one torture session at the moment, and especially not with a clearly inferior halfwit, although he had to give him some credit: *Implement* was a fairly impressive, three-syllable word. Just the same, now was not the time to antagonize Ademordna by sending one of his servants back in a dozen or more pieces, and as satisfying as it would be to finally vent his full rage on the little idiot, he had to play it smart.

Nachari waited silently, allowing the overblown demon to have his moment in the sun, as it were, while he contemplated the possible outcomes.

Finally, when it seemed like the little booger would never speak, the demon inclined his head in a gesture of condescension. "Very well, vampire," he crooned, "today just might be your lucky day."

Nachari suppressed a smile. "Thank you." What else did the fool expect him to say?

With all the aplomb of a magician on stage, hoping to captivate a watchful audience, the demon waddled to the mattress, set the box down right in the center, and tapped the lid. And then he leaned over conspiratorially and whispered, "It's a gift from a lady friend."

Nachari held his breath.

"Noiro," the demon added.

Nachari swallowed hard. How in the world had Noiro pulled this off—convinced the short demon to assist her with her plan, a plan that amounted to no less than treason against Lord Ademordna?

The demon laughed heartily then. "A snake from the northern territory." He practically danced in place. "Noiro assures me that the reptile has been charmed—programmed to bite you again and again and again. To fill your miserable veins with excruciating poison as you sleep so your flesh will rot from the inside out, even when you aren't being formally tortured." He cackled like a lunatic, literally jumping up and down in place. If the Valley of Death and Shadows had a Land of Oz, this little freak would be headed down the yellow brick road in uncommon, idiotic style.

Ah, so that's how Noiro pulled it off, Nachari thought, by convincing the foolish monster that transporting the gift was actually an act of torture. Still, that didn't address the primary concern regarding Ademordna—the Supreme Ruler of the Middle Kingdom would not be so easily fooled...or forgiving. "And the Supreme Lord?" Nachari asked. "He has given you permission to do this?"

The demon spun around angrily. He raised his chin high in defiance. "What makes you think I need permission, vampire! This is my realm—not yours."

Yeah, yeah—if *ifs* and *buts* were candy and nuts what a Merry Christmas it'd be...

But they weren't.

Nachari eyed him carefully. *Hmm.* No one—but no one— came near Ademordna's pet vampire without Ademordna's express consent, which meant that Noiro must have really gone out of her way to fool the little cretin.

"Besides," the demon added defensively, "Noiro assures me that the orders to capture and bring the snake come straight from our lord himself. That I will win his favor by delivering the beast and announcing my part in the process at court this evening." He reached into his pocket and pulled out a crumpled missive. "A formal invitation to your own torture," he explained, practically giddy. "Noiro felt it would be a fitting touch to invite you—as if you have a choice—in your ancient Romanian tongue." He stared at the missive like it was a golden tablet, turning the calligraphic letters this way and that in an attempt to read the words—which he obviously couldn't do. Perhaps the little fool was illiterate, or perhaps he just couldn't speak Romanian. Either way, he had no idea what the missive actually said, and that gave Nachari a clear advantage.

"May I?" Nachari asked, holding out his hand.

The demon squealed with glee. "Yessss....yessss," he hissed, ecstatic that Nachari was apparently going along with their diabolical plan to inflict more pain and suffering upon him. "Read it aloud, vampire. I want to hear you speak in your native tongue. It's soooo ssssexy."

Nachari raised an eyebrow, trying to shake off the ick factor, and then he stepped forward gingerly, hoping to appear more compliant than threatening. "As you wish," he said, waiting for the demon to place the missive in his hand.

The demon moaned as the missive exchanged hands. "Read it. Read it. Read it."

Nachari stared at him, incredulous. Did these things have mothers? Or fathers? Siblings, perhaps? If so, then there might actually be a handful of beings in hell who were suffering worse than he was: No doubt, spending eons with the likes of this idiot would be a fate worse than death. Turning the missive over, Nachari began to read aloud, his deep melodic voice filling the room with the splendor of his native words: "Ucide mesagerul sau infrunta-ti propriul decis." He spoke each word slowly and deliberately, all the while fighting to suppress a growing smile. The missive translated into a very simple but direct statement: *Kill the messenger, or face your own demise.*

It was a message to Nachari from Noiro.

The demoness had done the best she could to get the second talisman into Nachari's hands, but she could not account for the messenger—that was Nachari's problem. And if he let the little bastard go, their plan was over. Ademordna would find out, and they would both be—

Well, it was better not to think about that.

The problem at hand was more than enough of a challenge all by itself—how in the world did Nachari kill the messenger without alerting Ademordna? And what in the world did he do with the body?

"What did it say? What did it say?" the swarthy demon asked, interrupting Nachari's thoughts. He was practically chomping at the bit to know the meaning.

Nachari frowned and thought up an appropriate lie. "It said my torture will be endless now—there will be no escape day or night."

A gleeful smile crossed the demon's face, and he snickered with satisfaction. "Take the snake out of the box, now," he commanded, trying to throw some bass into his voice. "I want to watch him strike you. I want to watch the full power of the northern territory seep into your blood and bring you to your knees...in agony."

Oh, now this was the fellow Nachari knew and recognized from the throne room. Of course, he would want to watch. And cheer. And cackle like a hyena.

Very well.

Nachari walked slowly to the bed, his head hung low like he was dreading what was to come, as he carefully approached the heavy box. All the while, he gathered the errant energy of the Abyss to him with his words and his intention. With his Magick. As quickly as he could, he built a conflagration of kinetic energy in order to fuel the spell he would need to achieve his goal. His head rolled back on his shoulders as his body protested the vile energy that swirled like a dense, beguiling fog all around him, dipping and diving inside of him, stroking and claiming his soul.

Black as night, stealth and might;
be swift; be sure—embrace this fight.
My heart, my soul, my vengeance due;
I humbly call and yield to you.

Knowing that he could use the transformative venom of the snake to complete the spell—that he would *need* to use the venom in order to command the laws of physics in a place of such low, resistant density—Nachari gingerly lifted the lid from the box, scooped the hissing reptile up in one hand, and brought it to his face, meeting the serpent's gaze, eye to eye.

Brother of darkness,
Serpent's tongue...
Strike now; strike swiftly
Make our venom one.

The snake uncoiled in his hand, wrapped its smooth, deadly body around Nachari's arm, and slithered up his wrist to his forearm where it perched on his shoulder. With slow, delicious delight it dipped its head and unlocked its massive jaw, prepared to strike at the wizard's jugular. And then, with slow, measured precision, it sank its twin fangs deep into Nachari's vein and began to inject the poison of hell.

Nachari fought to relax his muscles, to still his heart, even as the obnoxious demon began to clap his hands in delight. He welcomed the poison and the pain, gave himself over to the transformative Magick—however black and repulsive.

And then his bones began to transform, to soften and break.

To change.

He gasped at the intensity of the pain even as he welcomed it with a compliant heart.

His spine twisted and popped; his skin grew thin and pliable; and his jaw expanded and released at the joints. As the blackness filled him from within, it began to transform him from without. Sleek, tawny fur coated his limbs and crowned his skull, until the fully matured body of a gigantic male panther at last emerged in his place.

Nachari spun around in the body of the panther, prowling in a tight, revolving circle. His pain gave way to unbridled power, and the snake slithered away to cower in the corner, a tight ball of fear and submission, even as the little cheering demon began to quake in his boots.

Nachari growled low in his throat, reveling in the sound— the vibration—the rapture of pure, unadulterated supremacy. He stretched his sinewy limbs with stealth and grace. He drew back his lips and snarled, meeting the trembling demon's eyes with eyes the color of flames. The little monster tried to release his own pathetic wings and shoot fire from his mouth, but he was no match for the stealth and speed of the puma. In one ferocious leap, Nachari was upon him, wide jaws locking firmly around the demon's neck, huge canines sinking deep into fetid flesh, a raspy tongue taking its first taste of rancid blood.

Nachari shook the demon furiously, giving into the cat's need to play with its prey. He swiped large, lethal paws along the demon's face and chest; he serrated the demon's thighs and groin; and he toyed with him for several minutes, slowly...insidiously, before finally going in for the kill. With one powerful clamp of his jaws, he snapped the demon's neck. No more laughing, clapping, or watching for this one.

As the broken, bloodied body of the demon fell to the floor in a pile of useless flesh and bone, Nachari sank back on his haunches. His jaw twitched several times as he surveyed the awful mess before him and steadied his resolve: There was only one way to insure that Ademordna never found the demon's body—that Norio's treachery remained undetected, and his plan to escape remained viable.

And that was to destroy the evidence.

Purring with lazy canine satisfaction, Nachari Silivasi licked his lips and lowered his head to the demon's torso. He sank even lower on his haunches, dug into the entrails, and began to feast in earnest—

He had fifty pounds of demon to eat before someone came to his door and discovered his rebellion.

twenty

Dark Moon Vale ~ Sunday

Kristina Riley-Silivasi walked through the front doors of the Dark Moon Vale Clinic with one solitary mission: to get Deanna out of there as quickly as possible before Kagen Silivasi began asking questions. She was relieved to see the beautiful, bluish-gray-eyed woman waiting for her in the foyer with an oversized tote bag and beach towel in hand, clearly ready to go.

"Hi, Dee," she called in her cheeriest voice. While they really didn't know each other that well, Kristina always shortened people's names and figured Nachari's *destiny* would be fine with it, unless she was unnaturally uptight.

Deanna smiled graciously. "Hi, Kristina."

"You ready?"

Deanna held up the tote bag and nodded. "Think so. I have my suit, my cell phone, a large bottle of water, and a towel. Was there anything else I needed?"

Kristina opened the front doors and stood in the doorway, motioning Deanna forward. "Nope. That should do it." She reached out, took the towel from Deanna's hand, and quickly stuffed it down in her tote. When Deanna appeared slightly taken aback at the impulsive behavior, she shrugged her thin shoulders. "Easier to carry that way."

Deanna opened her mouth to reply, then apparently thought better of it and nodded, letting the odd behavior go. She followed Kristina to the door, and they had almost cleared the doorway when Kagen's deep, resounding voice rang out from down the hall.

"Hold it," he called, picking up the pace to catch up with them.

Kristina watched the purposeful way he walked, impressed

231

as always with the sleek, animalistic stride that defined his gait: *Damn, but she had some fine brothers.* She sighed, hoping to conceal her nervousness, and plastered a huge smile on her face. "What's up, bro? How are you?"

Kagen smiled warmly. "I'm well, and you?"

"Peachy," Kristina answered, leaning against the door to prop it open. "Looking forward to an exciting night at the blackjack tables."

Deanna eyed her sideways, frowning. "I thought—"

"Well, we might try our hand at a little Texas Hold-Em and the slots, too, but I am a total sucker for the blackjack tables." She winked at Deanna conspiratorially and prayed her newfound cohort would not give them away before the night had even begun. If the Silivasis knew they were headed to the secluded hot springs, even with one of Napolean's sentinels as escort, they would insist on coming along. However, if they thought they were at the casino, they would leave them be. After all, the casino was run by none other than Marquis Silivasi; it was loaded with security cameras and kick-ass personnel; and there were enough vampires—sons of Jadon—going in and out of the place on any given night to cast a Dracula film. It was probably the safest place in Dark Moon Vale. She grabbed Deanna by the wrist and gave her a gentle squeeze of reassurance. "We shouldn't be out that late—maybe midnight, one o'clock." Kagen eyed her suspiciously then, and she danced from side to side on her toes impatiently.

"Where is Ramsey?" he finally asked, peeking over her shoulder.

Kristina turned her head to look out toward the car, careful to remain centered in the doorway in order to block Kagen's view. "He's out in the car, waiting—didn't want to come in." She felt a sudden stir in the air around them, and knew that Kagen was about to reach out telepathically to the steadfast sentinel in order to verify her statement. "Kagen!" she exclaimed impatiently, "*damn*—are you ever going to let up? Can I at least plan my own girl's night out with Deanna, or do you plan on micromanaging that, too?" She glanced at Deanna and frowned. "I swear they think females are nothing but weak and incompetent." And then she glared back at Kagen. "And it gets *very* old...very fast."

Kagen redirected his attention toward Kristina, releasing the telepathic bandwidth—*thank god*. "Not a minute past twelve-thirty," he said in an authoritarian voice.

"See?" Kristina said, rolling her eyes. "You would think we were twelve years old." She pointed at Kagen. "And *he* was our father instead of our brother."

Deanna chuckled, apparently finding the whole situation amusing. She held both hands up in a gesture of surrender. "Hey, my dog's not in this fight. You two figure out what you want to do; I'm just along for the ride."

Kristina smoothed her skirt. "No fight; it's all good—right, Kagen?"

Kagen looked back and forth between the two women. "Not that Ramsey needs to be told, but make sure he stays with you the entire night...direct line of sight, got it?"

Kristina nodded in agreement. "Of course." She did feel a bit guilty for lying about where they were going, not to mention the fact that Ramsey wasn't actually in the car—he was meeting them at the hot springs—but all in all, it really wasn't *that* dishonest. Ramsey Olaru *was* one of Napolean Mondragon's bad-ass sentinels, and he *would* be with them all night—*direct line of sight*. Kristina might be rebellious, and even a bit too independent, but she would never take an unnecessary risk with her safety...or Deanna's. She knew what was up. She had been through a Blood Moon from start to finish, and she knew quite well who the Dark Ones were—and the kind of shit they liked to pull. So, she didn't care to have her first real evening out with Ramsey and Deanna spoiled by Nathaniel's inquisitive eyes and Marquis's inexcusable rudeness. Sue her.

They were safe.

And that was all that really mattered.

She turned to Kagen and grinned. "So, what's the word, bro?

Do we have a hall pass or not?"

Kagen ignored the familiar sarcasm and turned to Deanna instead. "You have my number programmed in your phone?"

Deanna nodded. "Yes, I do."

"And Marquis's and Nathaniel's as well? Jocelyn's?"

Deanna laughed. "Everyone's, I think."

Kristina couldn't help but chime in then. "And it's not like she can't just call you guys telepathically if she needs you...right?"

Kagen flashed a gentle smile and placed his hand lovingly on Deanna's arm. "These things take time to learn, Kristina. You know that."

"Yeah," Kristina replied sarcastically, "and it's not like I'm going to be right there with her or anything." She rolled her eyes in an exaggerated manner. "Can we go now, Daddy?" She added a note of pleading to her voice: "Before Ramsey gets out of the car and comes in here to get us?"

That seemed to put Kagen at ease. "Okay," he said reluctantly. "Just be back by curfew...*daughter.*" He chuckled then. Turning to glance at Deanna, he added, "And you call if you need anything, okay? *Anything.*"

Deanna nodded. "Will do." As she followed Kristina out the door, she slung her bag over her shoulder, raised her eyebrows, and whispered, "You sure that was wise? Lying to him like that?"

As the door slammed shut behind them, Kristina snickered and blew out a long breath. "I'm surprised I got away with it." Gesturing with her hands, she added, "All he had to do was dip into my mind, or worse—step out the door and look inside the car."

"Look inside the car?" Deanna's frown betrayed her confusion.

"Oh, yeah," Kristina said. "Ramsey isn't actually riding with us; he's meeting us at the hot springs."

Deanna stopped dead in her tracks and squared her shoulders to Kristina. "And what else aren't you telling me?"

Kristina reached out for Deanna's arm and gave it a firm tug, urging her forward. Laughing, she whispered, "Okay, so it's like this: Ramsey and I are kind of *seeing each other*, if you know what I mean." Her next words were rushed. "Well, we haven't been hanging out that long, but we're kind of trying it out, and I just don't need a bunch of overprotective brothers giving him—or me—the third degree right now; feel me?"

"Ohhh," Deanna sighed, her eyes alighting with sudden understanding. "So, then, why did you invite me on this...date? Won't I be a third wheel?"

Kristina shook her head adamantly. "No! Not at all. I really want to get to know you. In fact, I'm hoping we can be friends, and I know you could really use a break from all the intensity. Besides, I think it would be good to spend some social time with Ramsey—you know, not always just the two of us alone—I just don't want to do it with the Silivasi clan. So in a way, you're doing me a huge favor by coming."

Deanna looked as if she had a dozen questions, each one just dying to leap off her tongue, but to her credit, she held them back and shrugged. "Well," she said, "it's your world, and I'm just the new girl—so I'll have to trust your judgment. Just so long as it's safe."

Kristina couldn't believe how cool Deanna was; maybe they really would become good friends. She gestured toward her pink Corvette and smiled. "No worries, Dee—we're gonna have a great time. And trust me, we're perfectly safe."

Braden Bratianu stood outside Napolean's manse pacing back and forth on the lawn, mulling the problem—and his dilemma—over for the umpteenth time: To tell or not to tell. That was the question.

To risk Kristina's anger—or see to her safety?

To risk Marquis's disappointment or provoke his wrath?

To betray a friend or honor the house of Jadon?

BLOOD SHADOWS

He stared at the front door and steadied his resolve: He *had* to say something. He just had to. What he had read in that diary was wrong, and Napolean needed to know about it. He was just about to approach the front door when he felt the distinct presence of another vampire's energy close by; and by the size and intensity of the vibration, he knew it was someone fairly formidable.

Spinning around on his heels, he found himself face-to-face with Ramsey Olaru. The warrior was standing less than two feet away, clad in a pair of dark blue jeans and a hunter-green shirt, with a characteristic scowl on his GQ face and a thin reed of grass protruding from his teeth. Braden had never even heard him approach. "Oh...uh," he stuttered, "Ramsey...I didn't hear you—"

"You got some business with Napolean?" Ramsey asked, his penetrating hazel eyes taking the kid's measure in the space of a second.

"Yeah, well...sort of." He tried to stand tall and puff out his chest. "I guess I kind of have some business with you."

Ramsey's perfectly arched brows shot up in curiosity. "With me?"

"Yeah," Braden mumbled in a shaky voice. He took a deep breath and tried again. "Yeah—with you."

Ramsey shrugged, seemingly indifferent. "All right."

"I wanna know what's going on," he said, practically forcing the words out of his mouth. Ramsey Olaru was nobody's punk—the guy could swallow you whole and spit you out just as easily as look at you. He was notorious for being both ruthless and cruel—just for the hell of it—and no one, but no one, took him on unless they had to. Or questioned him. Yet here Braden was, a fifteen-year-old, once-human-turned-vampire kid, squaring off with the legendary warrior over a silly redheaded girl who was being played like a fiddle by the much older, much more experienced sentinel. Braden drew courage from the knowledge that Kristina was in jeopardy, Ramsey was simply wrong in what he was doing, and Napolean was *hopefully* not that far away. "With Kristina Riley," he added.

Ramsey spit the reed out of his mouth and took a lazy step backward, crossing his massive arms over his iron chest. He looked the kid over but said nothing.

Okay. What now? Braden wondered. "Well?"

"Well, what?" Ramsey said, his gravelly voice growing short with impatience.

Braden sighed. "Well, what the hell is going on with you and Kristina?" The moment the curse word left his mouth, he regretted it; but it was too late to take it back now. Shaking a bit in his boots, he struggled to maintain eye contact.

The corner of Ramsey's sarcastic mouth turned up in a parody of a smile. "I think you better watch your tone, boy."

Braden squared his jaw. "And I think you better watch who you're effin' around with." He gulped at his own audacity.

Ramsey ran a huge hand through his hair, causing Braden to flinch in response to the sudden motion. He chuckled at the kid's reaction. "Little nervous?"

Braden shook his head defiantly. "No. Are you?"

"Not in the least," Ramsey drawled lazily.

Braden took a bold step forward. "Well, maybe you should be."

At that, Ramsey laughed.

Laughed.

"What's so funny?" Braden demanded.

Ramsey shrugged and swept his hand in a gentle arc. "This. You. What the heck's going on, kid?"

Braden felt his eyes dampen with moisture, and more than anything, that made him even angrier. Bolder. "You know damn well what's going on." His hands shot to his hips and he leaned forward in a threatening manner, unable to stop his smaller body from moving. "And you better start talking!" As if possessed by someone else, he felt his arm raise, his index finger extend, and his hand move toward the massive giant's chest. To his utter horror, he poked Ramsey Olaru squarely in the bread-basket. "*Now,*" he growled. Apparently, his voice had been hijacked as well.

Ramsey Olaru didn't flinch. And to Braden's great relief, he didn't eat the kid in one bite, either. He simply stared down his nose at the finger affixed to his chest and frowned. And then he sent Braden a clear, unmistakable warning. It happened so quickly it was barely discernible, but his eyes flashed red, and a deep, menacing growl rumbled beneath the pad of Braden's finger before Ramsey's calm, cool demeanor settled back upon him. "Move your finger," he whispered.

Braden tried to withdraw the digit, but it wouldn't budge. "No." His wayward mouth was at it again.

Ramsey cocked his head to the side in a gesture of both amusement and surprise, and then he smiled. "How long have you been Vampyr?" Before Braden could answer, Ramsey continued, "I've been Nosferatu for seven hundred years; and unlike you, I put in four hundred years at the University to become a Master Warrior." His pectoral muscles flexed, pushing back against the small finger still resting upon them. "I'm your elder and your sentinel, and that means you're going to show me some respect." His last words lingered in the air. "Move your finger."

"Fine," Braden yielded, at last withdrawing his wayward hand, "I'll move my finger. But I won't show you any respect— because you don't deserve any."

Ramsey's brow curved into a deep frown as if to say *what the hell*, and he slowly licked his lips. "Boy, have you lost your mind?" He measured him sideways. "What's this about? A girl? That silly redheaded female? Marquis's progeny?"

Now that really ticked Braden off. "Watch your mouth."

At that, Ramsey threw his hands up in the air, turned around, and began to walk away.

"I'm not through!" Braden shouted, his voice cracking a bit.

Ramsey glanced over his shoulder and sneered. "I am."

Braden stood there stunned, watching the Master Warrior retreat as if nothing he had to say was of any consequence, as if he was as easily dismissed as a fly at a picnic. He might not be a warrior yet—or a 700-year-old sentinel—but he wasn't...*nothing*. And frankly, Ramsey was just full of it.

Scanning the ground beneath him, Braden reached down, picked up a good-sized rock, and hurled it at the warrior's back, putting all the speed and agility he had as a vampire into the throw.

His back still turned to the younger vampire, Ramsey sidestepped so fast that the motion appeared blurry, and as the stone missed him by a country mile, he turned on his heels and began prowling back toward Braden, his eyes locked fiercely on the young boy's gaze. "You want to play games, kid?"

Braden tapped both hands hard against his own chest, not unlike a dominant ape demonstrating power to an underling, and held his ground: He figured there was no getting away at this point—and he could at least put on a good show before he died. Try to go out like a man, defending Kristina's honor. "I'm not scared of you," he snarled, forcing his feet to stay in place, his legs not to turn tail and run. "Bring it, then."

Ramsey took another step toward him, his eyes fixed narrowly on his prey like a dangerous assassin. "Bring what, boy?"

Braden made two fists and held them out in front of him. "*It*," he snapped, knowing he sounded as stupid as he felt. For a moment, he thought about calling out to Marquis to save him, and then he remembered what the Master Warrior had taught him: *When a confrontation is imminent, always fight to win. Strike first, and try to take your enemy down with the first blow before he has a chance to harm you.* As Ramsey took another step forward, Braden released his fangs, rotated from the balls of his feet to his toes, and sprang at the sentinel's neck. A vicious snarl emanated from his throat as he prepared to latch onto the sentinel's jugular.

Ramsey swatted him away like a mosquito, sending him sprawling across the front yard in a series of violent rolls, but Braden sprang to his feet and faced him again. Crouching low toward the ground, he released his talons and prepared to swipe at anything that came his way.

Ramsey shook his head in bewilderment. "Calm down, Braden," he cautioned. "You need to stop before you get hurt."

Braden snarled low and deep, impressed by the feral sound that came out of his throat. "And you need to stop trying to get into Kristina Riley's pants!"

Ramsey crinkled his brow and shook his head. "What the hell are you talking about?"

"I'm talking about this bullshit game you're playing with Kristina's head! Sneaking around with her behind everyone's back, trying to get her to give you some just because she's the only female vampire in the house of Jadon. You think you can use her like a widow, without having to mate her, and it's wrong! I'm talking about you pressuring her. Nearly *forcing* her. Taking advantage of her when you know damn well that you have a *destiny* somewhere out there. You've totally messed up her head; she's completely afraid of you; and you're still trying to screw her anyways!" His voice cracked from the force of his emotion. "That shit is so wrong, Ramsey." He slammed his fist against his palm. "And I'm not gonna let you do it anymore. I'm not!" With that, he sprang at the powerful warrior again.

This time, Ramsey caught Braden in midair, twisted his body around until his back was arched forward beneath Ramsey's broad chest, and forced him to the ground on his knees. "Be still," he commanded. He locked his arms around Braden's chest to restrain him.

Braden struggled valiantly. "Let me go! Let me go!"

"Be quiet," Ramsey snarled. "Be quiet...and *listen*."

Braden's ears perked up. Was Ramsey going to respond to his accusations at last? Was he finally going to explain himself? Apologize? Promise to stop using Kristina?

"Boy, I haven't touched that girl," he said plainly. "Are you insane?" He lowered his voice to a deep, soothing tone. "She came onto me, *once*, right here at Napolean's, and I sent her home. I have no idea what you're talking about, but rest assured, I would never dishonor or hurt any female in the house of Jadon. And if I was looking for a woman just to...screw, as you so crudely put it, I would pick someone other than Marquis's ward."

Braden struggled to understand the words he had just heard. "But...but...that's not true." He relaxed his shoulders, and Ramsey loosened his hold.

"It is true," the sentinel assured him.

Braden shook his head adamantly. "But I saw it...in her diary. Everything you've been doing to her."

Ramsey let go of him, settled on one knee in the grass in front of him, and looked off into the distance. "You saw this in her diary?"

"Yes," Braden snorted.

"And you're sure it was me—my name in the book?"

"Yes," Braden repeated. "Plus, I know something's going on because she sneaks around on the phone and hides things. I've caught her crying, and she's all confused in the head now." He took a deep breath, embarrassed at sharing Kristina's secrets, but... "In her diary, she said that you were trying to force her, and she was thinking about giving in, even though she knew you were just using her."

Ramsey scowled, his face a mixture of disbelief and disgust. "What the hell..." He looked away, and then all at once, a light came on in his eyes. "Oh, damn," he murmured.

"What?" Braden asked.

Ramsey grabbed the kid by the arm and sprang to his feet, lugging Braden's body up, along with his own, effortlessly. "We need to take this to Napolean."

Now it was Braden's turn to be surprised. "Why?"

"If Kristina truly believes it's me, then that means the male must look like me, talk like me, act like me...and that has sorcery written all over it."

Braden blanched as understanding dawned on him. "The Dark Ones?"

"Precisely."

"Then why haven't they killed her," he asked, his stomach turning over at the thought. *Oh gods, had he failed to protect her?*

"What do you think they want?"

Ramsey shrugged as he headed for Napolean's front door, practically dragging the kid behind him. "And isn't that just the million-dollar question."

twenty~one

Kagen Silivasi paced nervously around the foyer, stopping to glance at Ramsey and Braden in turn as the two quickly filled him in on the details of what they had discovered. The angry males had rushed through the clinic doors like Wyatt Earp rounding the corner at the OK Corral, full of steam, vinegar, and deadly intention, and Kagen had not been able to get a word in edgewise as Ramsey quickly and succinctly brought him up to speed. He turned to glance at Braden, who had a sickly look on his face, his skin growing paler by the minute. "And you're positive the diary had *Ramsey's* name in it?" Kagen asked.

"Oh yeah," Braden said, sounding out of breath. "Absolutely."

"I don't think there's any doubt," Ramsey chimed in. "By the way she came onto me that day outside of Napolean's…" He paused, looking both remorseful and infuriated. "*Damn*, I just…I just didn't think much of it. From everything Marquis has ever said, Kristina tends to act flighty at times. Impulsive. It never occurred to me that there was something more serious going on."

Kagen nodded impatiently. Few things slipped by the insightful sentinel's recognition, and no doubt, Ramsey was feeling horrible at having missed all the signs of danger, the Dark Ones' plotting…*yet again*. Kagen's blood heated in his veins, and he knew his eyes were changing color involuntarily as the obvious suddenly occurred to him: He had been so taken aback by the two males rushing into the clinic that he had failed to ask the most important question first: "Oh, shit! Ramsey?" His voice was unusually harsh. "Were you with Kristina and Deanna a half hour ago?"

Ramsey raised his eyebrows. "No…why?"

"You weren't outside, waiting in the car to escort them to

243

the casino?"

"No, Healer," he repeated, "I was with Braden trying to figure out what the heck was going on. What's up?"

Kagen swallowed his fear. Reaching out telepathically on a community bandwidth so both Braden and Ramsey could hear, he immediately called to his brothers: *Marquis! Nathaniel! It's urgent!*

It took less than a second for the Master Warriors to respond.

Kagen, what is it? Marquis's voice was brusque with concern, his demeanor fully alert.

I'm here, Nathaniel chimed in. *Speak, brother...*

Kagen drew in a deep breath, not wanting to make the situation even worse than it was by sending both of his brothers into an instant rage—they all needed to be calm and cool in the face of danger. *We have a situation,* he began, *a very serious situation.*

Neither one responded. They weren't willing to waste even a second with unnecessary words.

As you know, Kagen explained, *Kristina invited Deanna to spend time with her tonight—they were headed to the casino with Ramsey riding escort.* He paused for only a scant second, his psychic voice revealing his anxiety. *Only Ramsey is standing right here in the clinic next to me. He never went with them.*

He felt Marquis push against his mind, as if the Master Warrior was about to reach in and extract all the pertinent information faster than Kagen could relay it, but to the warrior's credit, he remained silent and waited.

Nathaniel's energy was growing darker by the moment, the lethal vampire's own patience being tested to the limit. *Two sentences or less, Kagen: bottom-line assessment and immediate course of action.*

Kagen sighed with relief: They could catch up with details later. *Bottom-line assessment: We believe one of the Dark Ones has been impersonating Ramsey and spending time with Kristina...romantically. We think he's with them now. Immediate course of action—*

Nathaniel! Have Saxson and Santos meet you at the casino, Marquis commanded, instinctively taking over. *Ramsey, meet us there, and conceal your weapons—we don't want to alarm any humans unnecessarily. Kagen, alert Napolean.*

I've already spoken to Napolean, Ramsey cut in. *And my brothers*—he was referring to the other two sentinels of Dark Moon Vale, Saxson and Santos Olaru—*are already on standby, armed and ready to mobilize.*

Good, Marquis said. *Kagen, have you tried reaching out to Kristina or Deanna telepathically in order to warn them?*

Haven't had a chance yet, brother; I called you and Nathaniel first.

Do it now! Marquis ordered. *As for the rest of us, let's move, warriors. Now.* With that, the telepathic link was broken.

As usual, Marquis Silivasi was not wasting time.

Deanna sank deep into the large, bubbling hot springs, letting the soft mineral water sweep over her body and wash all her cares away—if only for a moment.

The bath felt heavenly.

The rising steam caressed her skin, soaked her hair, and dampened her forehead, even as the natural currents soothed her tired muscles. For the first time since she had arrived in Dark Moon Vale, she almost felt at peace.

Opening her right lid lazily, she glanced out the corner of her eye at Kristina, who was sinking deep into the bath opposite her own position, perched on a smooth, natural stone. The fiery redhead's hair was tied up in a loose, messy bun, and she was trying her best to act relaxed while sneaking constant, worried glances at her cell phone in order to check the time. Ramsey was late. And while the skinny girl tried to play it off as no big deal, it was obvious to Deanna that Kristina was becoming more and more irritated—if not worried—with each passing moment.

A faint stirring rippled through Deanna's consciousness, almost like a soft cerebral wind playing notes against her forehead from the inside out, and Deanna reached up and brushed a trickle of sweat from her brow. *That was funny,* she thought, wondering if there wasn't some strange, if not supernatural, quality to the water, something ethereal about its composition that caused a funny tickling inside the body.

It happened again—only this time stronger.

Deanna sat up, more alert.

Kristina looked up at her then. "Is your head tingling?" she asked, seeming to know what was going on.

"Yes," Deanna responded curiously. "Is yours? It's really…weird. Do you think it's the water?"

Kristina rolled her eyes lazily. "No…I think it's Kagen Silivasi, trying to check up on you telepathically. He's doing it to me, too."

"Oh," Deanna said, puzzled. "What should I do? How do I answer him?"

"You don't," Kristina responded resolutely. "Give him an inch, and he'll take a mile." She laughed out loud then. "Unless you want your new brother—all of your new brothers—popping into your head every five minutes, it's best to set some boundaries now…early on." She lifted her cell phone from the stony ledge, where it sat precariously close to the water, and checked the time again. Sighing, she added, "I told Mr. Kagen we would check in every hour on the hour; we still have thirty minutes." She set the phone back down and sank back into the water. "He can hear from us then." Waving her arms back and forth as if gently treading water, she added, "Just imagine a chalkboard with writing on it—words that keeps appearing on the surface out of the blue—and erase it in your mind; it'll turn the volume down so Kagen's little intrusions don't tickle so much."

Deanna found her rebellious companion's advice rather odd—wouldn't it just be easier to answer Kagen now, let him know everything was all right, and just get on with their bath?—but she didn't feel like it was entirely her call to make. After all, she was the new kid on the block, a complete stranger to this odd, supernatural world, and Kristina had spent a lot more time in this strange valley with the vampires than she had: While Deanna Dubois wasn't one to succumb to peer pressure—or really give a rat's hind-end what other people thought as a rule—she also wasn't one to alienate folks unnecessarily. And...Kristina Silivasi was Nachari's little sister, if only by default. The main thing was—they were fine; they were safe; and thirty minutes wasn't that long to wait. Besides, she could always plead the fifth if Kagen got too paternal, claim ignorance of customs and protocols, blame it all on Kristina if it came down to it. "Okay," she agreed reluctantly, "if you say so; but if there's any fallout, it's all on you. Just so long as you know that."

Kristina smiled broadly. "Yeah...yeah. It always is. No prob."

Just then, the largest, meanest-looking, albeit sexiest male on the planet strolled up to the hot tub as if he hadn't a care in the world. He was dressed in a stunning black-and-tan bathing suit, which hung low on his flat, masculine hips and matched his spectacular hazel eyes perfectly. He winked at Deanna, placed a lone finger over his lush mouth in a gesture of *quiet*, and slowly tiptoed behind Kristina as silent as a mouse. "Hey, Red," he drawled in a lazy, far-too-confident voice. "Sorry I'm late."

Kristina jolted upright, startled by his voice. Frowning, she splashed a large surge of water on his chest. "I was about to give up on you!" she snapped, feigning irritation.

The side of his mouth curled up in a mischievous grin. "Ah, baby—that's harsh, don't you think?"

Deanna smiled, instantly taking notice of the strong attraction between them, and hoping she wouldn't be made to feel like the odd man out. Kristina was completely full of it, pretending to be angry; her entire being lit up in the man's presence. Deanna sank deeper into the water in an effort to mind her own business.

Seeming to notice Deanna's discomfort for the first time, Kristina gestured toward her. "Ramsey, I don't think you've actually met Nachari's *destiny* yet. This is Deanna...Dubois, right?"

Deanna nodded. "Yes."

Kristina turned back toward Ramsey, her eyes taking his measure appreciatively. "Deanna, this is Ramsey Olaru, one of the three sentinels who guard Dark Moon Vale."

"Hi," Deanna said in a polite yet distant voice. "Nice to meet you."

"Nice to meet you," Ramsey responded in kind. "How's the water?" He dipped a large hand into the pool.

"Heavenly," Deanna responded. She leaned back and closed her eyes in a gesture of retreat, wanting to offer the two lovebirds at least a semblance of privacy.

"Why don't you get in?" Kristina said, her voice brimming with eagerness.

"Love to, darlin'," he said in a deep, gravelly voice.

Deanna couldn't help it; she peeked beneath her hooded lids and watched as Ramsey slowly made his way into the deep pool, sat as close to Kristina as another body could get, and then propped his enormous, muscled arm behind her back. "Did you miss me, baby girl?" he whispered, as if Deanna couldn't hear him as clearly as day. Deanna shut her eyes a second time, shifted uncomfortably in her seat, and wished like hell that she had remembered to bring her iPod.

The water swished this way and that as Ramsey and Kristina evidently repositioned themselves in each other's arms and nestled closer for a kiss: one that was easily heard, even over rustling water, with enhanced vampiric hearing.

Deanna sighed low beneath her breath.

Oh hell, what had she gotten herself into?

Well, maybe the couple would just *say their hellos*, get it out of the way, and go back to soaking in the water like decent, rated-PG company.

No such luck.

The hushed gentle murmur of an adoring kiss—two lips meeting in an intimate greeting—quickly grew to something altogether different: a harsh, animalistic growl that reverberated against Deanna's eardrums like distant thunder rolling across the pool, rising to clash against her sensibilities.

Oh, God, please tell me you're kidding…

How much further were they going to take this?

They wouldn't dare…

The last thing Deanna wanted was to bear witness to some barbaric display of otherworldly, pre-mating behavior between the two passionate vampires; and it wasn't just about being a third wheel or having her peaceful repose disturbed: Deanna did not want to come face-to-face with the reality of her own impending *situation*, assuming, of course, that Nachari was able to make it back from the Valley of Death and Shadows in time. She did not need a reminder of what went on between vampires of the opposite sex—of what Nachari really was beneath the peaceful sleeping façade of a beautiful wizard and deeply beloved brother: a primal male who had as many primitive instincts as refined.

A male who snarled and growled…

And bit.

And drank blood.

Deanna shivered and clutched her arms to her body

It was all too overwhelming.

She opened her eyes abruptly, hoping to remind her companions that she was right there in their midst, close enough to witness their…passion.

As if sensing her unease, Ramsey withdrew from the kiss, turned to stare at the female sitting just across him in the pool, and smiled.

And then he winked—a slow, insidious smirk stamped on his face.

With crude alacrity, he released what appeared to be an enormous set of wicked-sharp fangs, tickled the tips with his tongue in a cruel display of dominance, and yanked on a handful of Kristina's bundled hair. Forcing her head awkwardly to the side, he bent to her neck and struck in one fluid, serpentine movement, sinking his fangs so deep that the redhead cried out in pain as he latched on and began to suck in earnest.

Kristina struggled to push him away, her tiny hands anchored against his massive chest in a death grip.

Deanna sat up straight and gaped, open-mouthed, at the two of them, utterly stunned and dismayed. If this was how vampires *mated*, then Deanna Dubois wanted no part of it.

Not ever.

Not even with Nachari.

If this was how males of the species treated their females, then she was headed out on the next train from Dark Moon Vale station.

This was beyond horrifying.

Or disturbing.

This was obscene.

Dark crimson blood rolled down Kristina's neck, funneling into the pool like a leaking jet, seeping from the loose seal Ramsey had made over the bite. Deanna cringed and tried to back away. She watched in dazed horror as Kristina's hands fell slowly from Ramsey's chest, slid down along the front of his muscled body, and plopped into the pool like weighted stones, finally coming to rest palms-down in the water. The redhead's body began to twitch violently then, jerking this way and that, completely haphazard, like a wild marionette on the end of a crazed puppeteer's strings.

Ramsey could not have cared less.

He placed his imposing hands on Kristina's shoulders to hold her steady; began to suck with even greater ferocity and purpose; and swallowed the blood in great, drugging pulls, appearing for all intents and purposes to be experiencing ecstasy.

It took a moment for Deanna to fully realize what she was seeing.

This wasn't a mating ritual or the behavior of two passionate animalistic beings. This was one predator destroying another.

Ramsey Olaru was draining Kristina Silivasi right in front of Deanna's eyes.

He was *killing* her.

250

Tessa Dawn

"Hey!" Deanna shouted. "Stop!" Her voice was surprisingly strong despite the rising fear that engulfed her. She wanted to jump from the hot springs and run as fast as she could...as far as she could go. Instead, she sat forward and glared at him, her eyes feeling heated and peculiar. "I said, *Stop!*" The end of the command was punctuated by a startling yet distinct growl.

Ramsey opened an eye—just one—and the narrow orb blazed red as he fixed her with a disturbing, malevolent gaze of his own.

Deanna gasped at the unnatural sight.

He looked like a demon!

Some kind of evil creature from hell.

And then, before she could scream, he began to mutate before her eyes—to simply transform his appearance as she watched. His straight, harshly tapered blond hair became a dense, inky black, extending in length until it fell just below his shoulders; and his stunning, natural snowy highlights became bands of coral red, intertwined in the now thick raven tresses, like bands encircling the body of a king cobra. The color of his skin changed, too. The hue became a deeper tan, and his physique grew more sinewy. While still very large and strong, he was no longer a hulk of a man with the bearing of a Roman gladiator; rather, he dropped four or five inches in height—from six-foot-five to an even six feet tall—and his rock-hard chest grew taut with definition. His high, model-like cheekbones softened in their angles and planes; and the effect was somewhat harsh, lending a cruel edge to a different set of handsome features.

His plush lips grew thinner, his wily smile...nastier.

Deanna could hardly comprehend what she was seeing.

This was not the same male.

This was a completely different being crouched low before her, and he was snarling with unrestrained fury as he lapped up what remained of Kristina's blood in a murderous frenzy.

To hell with bravery!

Deanna jumped up from her seat, desperate to climb out of

the pool. She had to get to her cell phone…to call Kagen…to get back to the clinic where her new brothers could protect her.

As she struggled to move through the water, the liquid mass resisting her weight with every push toward the edge, she fought not to stare at Kristina. The female was limp and pale, practically lifeless in the monster's clutches, and Deanna knew without question that despite her newfound strength and abilities, there was no way she could budge the creature beside her. Not on her best day—or on his worst.

As her fingers fought for purchase along the steep, stony edge of the pool, she curled her toes around a large smooth stone beneath her, desperate to push up without slipping as she climbed from the bath.

A searing pain shot through her ankle, and she spun around, shrieking, only to find Ramsey directly beneath her. He had tossed Kristina's body from the pool with a mere flick of his wrist—pitching her thin, frail frame across a large expanse of grass and trees as if she weighed no more than a tiny stone hurled from a slingshot—while he wrapped the claws of his free hand around Deanna's ankle and tugged. His eyes alighted with fury as he dug the talons in deeper and snarled. "Leaving so soon, love?"

Deanna kicked back against him, surprised at her own strength. "Let go!" she demanded.

He grunted as the kick connected with his jaw but resisted her easily. "Not today," he snarled. And then, with one brutal tug on her ankle, he flung her back into the pool.

Deanna's head, shoulders, and back hit the water parallel as if in a reverse belly flop. As the impact stung her skin, she sank deep beneath the surface, her neck hyper-extending backward. As she flailed her arms, trying to regain her bearings, her mouth flew open and she swallowed what felt like a gallon of water. Using all of her strength, she pulled her body upright and splashed wildly, desperate to break the surface and breathe.

Ramsey laughed like a sadist.

He held her under and twisted her body this way and that,

sinking brutal talons into her hips and waist in an effort to reposition her onto his lap. Finally, when Deanna had grown utterly desperate, convinced that she would drown, he wriggled his body beneath hers and allowed her to break the surface.

She came up coughing violently. Feeling like her lungs were on fire, she spit out large streams of water and gagged as the fluid left her windpipe in ferocious sputters. "*Help. Someone.*" She tried to scream, but it came out weak and muffled.

"Shh, love," he whispered in her ear, pulling her back against him and bracing her chest with his arms. His right fist was just below her left breast, the palm of his left hand planted firmly on her left thigh; and the dual sensations, along with her burning lungs, made her feel queasy. "Let me go, Ramsey," she panted between gasps for air.

"Be still," he bit out, showing her no quarter.

After what seemed like an eternity, she managed to draw in several clean breaths of air and stop struggling. Her heart was beating so hard it felt like it might come out of her chest as she fought to hold back tears and reason with the maniacal vampire. "Why are you doing this?" she managed to whisper.

He sighed as if it were all a game. "Why, indeed," he replied. "Perhaps the real question is not why...but who."

"Who?" she repeated, her voice betraying her confusion as well as her terror.

"Yes," he answered. "*Who.*"

He shifted his weight beneath her as if trying to get more comfortable, and she cringed. "I don't understand."

"Mmm," he groaned in her ear. "Perhaps you will—once we have formally met." He licked her earlobe, and she sat perfectly still. Waiting. Listening. Cringing. "Now then," he drawled lazily. "Allow me to introduce myself properly."

Deanna stared straight ahead, waiting in morbid anticipation and horror, her eyes fixed on nothing in particular.

He lifted his hand from her thigh and placed it over the back of her left hand as if in a reverse mockery of a handshake. "My name is not Ramsey Olaru—thank the Dark Lords." He spoke

253

in a slow, Eastern-European accent as if the situation suddenly called for formality. "It is Saber Alexiares, and I was born to the house of Jaegar." She could feel him smile against her jaw—actually *feel* the slow curvature of his lips against her skin just below her ear. "I am an enemy to all those who name themselves in the house of Jadon—which now includes you, sweet *destiny*." He gripped her chin with the fingers of his right hand and wrenched her head backward so she could see him as he spoke. Eyes flashing a deep crimson red, he added, "Mine will be the last face you will ever see."

Deanna's mind raced a mile a minute: processing his words, deciphering his claim, trying to make sense of all she had learned from the Silivasi brothers and their mates about the house of Jaegar and the descendants of the original, evil twin.

The Dark Ones.

They were the mortal enemies of the lighter vampires.

They were the monsters who had tried to kill the king—Napolean Mondragon—the ones who had hatched the plot that had ultimately wounded Nachari so deeply, the ones that Marquis warned her would surely want her dead and seek to kill her at every turn, if they were able.

She looked back at the soulless creature behind her, stared at what she now recognized as the signature coronet of the Dark Ones—his hair, the crown of the king cobra—and the full realization finally sank in.

Kristina had been duped.

Lied to.

Used.

They had both been lured into this animal's trap, *and they had lied to Kagen about where they were going.* They had refused to answer his telepathic calls when he'd tried to check up on them—

Oh god...

She eyed the heartless demon one last time as he slowly released his fangs and bent to her neck. She had come to Dark Moon Vale to find the man from her dreams...*of her dreams*...the tortured soul in her sketches.

In a sense, she had followed her destiny in order to become his.

And now they were both going to die.

twenty-two

Nathaniel Silivasi stormed out of the casino supply room closet and threw up his hands in frustration. Confusion nearly clouded his vision. They had searched every inch of the casino: the main floor lobby and gaming rooms as well as the second-floor offices. They had called in extra security, the sentinels, and other Master Warriors. They had utilized the hidden game-table cameras, the eye in the sky, their heightened sense of sight, sound, and smell; yet Kristina and Deanna continued to elude them.

They were simply nowhere to be found.

Marquis Silivasi strolled anxiously toward his brother, his face a mask of barely restrained fury and stark concern. "Nothing?"

"No...nothing," Nathaniel answered. "I don't get it."

Marquis turned to Saxson and Santos, who were approaching from the right. "Anything?"

"No," Saxon said, sounding equally perplexed. "If there's a Dark One somewhere on these premises, my name isn't Saxon." The agitated sentinel turned up his lip in a sneer.

"I concur," Santos said.

"Son of a bitch!" Marquis snarled. *Kagen, brother, they aren't here. No one is here.*

Kagen chimed in on the common telepathic bandwidth instantly. *You sure?* he asked. *And you've checked everywhere.*

Everywhere, Nathaniel assured him.

Did you try again to reach them telepathically? Marquis demanded.

Several times, Kagen said. *No answer.*

But you have taken her blood?

Yes, Kagen responded. *Hold on.* The Healer didn't need to be told what to do. What they were asking was obvious: Kagen was the only brother who had taken Deanna's blood, ingested a small

257

amount in order to keep track of her if necessary; he would be the only vampire capable of quickly tracking her whereabouts.

Nathaniel stood perfectly still, listening to the beat of his own heart, his nerves completely frayed, his body itching with the need to fight…to move…knowing that whatever he was experiencing, Marquis was feeling double as they waited for Kagen Silivasi to turn his high-powered senses inward. To grab hold of the unique strands of DNA that represented Deanna Dubois, strands that now flowed within the Ancient Master Healer's own blood, and follow them backward like a homing beacon until he could pinpoint her position in the casino.

Hurry, Marquis urged him, obviously knowing that such a thing wasn't possible. They were talking about deciphering information on a minute, quantum level.

Nathaniel tapped his foot nervously on the floor. If something happened to the girls before they got to them…if something happened to Deanna…

Dear gods…

He wasn't going to give life—or energy—to the thoughts.

After what seemed like hours, but could not have been more than several minutes, Kagen Silivasi chimed back in, his psychic voice ripe with fury. *They aren't at the casino, brothers.*

What? Marquis stormed. *How is that possible?*

Kristina lied to us? Nathaniel asked, speaking to no one in particular.

Holy mother of Auriga, Kagen muttered as the information became clear, *they went to the hot springs…and something is wrong.*

What? Marquis demanded, his voice betraying his disbelief.

The Dark Ones have already gotten to them.

"Go!" Marquis thundered, his penetrating eyes boring into his brother's—the command was implicit to the other sentinels as well.

Not one of the warriors answered Marquis's imperious command verbally. Each had already shimmered out of view.

258

Tessa Dawn

Deanna didn't know what was worse, the horrific, unbearable pain in her neck—the feeling that someone had driven a spiked railroad tie through her jugular and was killing her slowly with unmitigated agony—or the realization that as her life's blood ebbed out of her, so did Nachari's future...and his family's hope.

Her eyelids drifted down for the third time, growing increasingly heavy. If she had to die—if they all did—she wished Saber would just get it over with. The pain was more than she could bear.

She wanted to fight.

Wished she could fight.

But at this point, she didn't even know which way was up.

All that existed was pain. And weakness. A slow slide from consciousness into a gray murky void where, soon, all that she had known in her young, vibrant life would grow forever dark...and empty.

An abrupt jolt of energy startled her from her semiconscious state, bringing her suddenly to attention. Saber withdrew his fangs from her neck, spun around in the water like a living cyclone, and dropped low into a fighting stance, his powerful back turned to block her view. The air pulsed with energy. Streams of vibrating color gathered together at enormous speeds. And then, one by one, the harsh, angry faces of warriors—*males from the house of Jadon!*—appeared before her, surrounding the natural pool.

Deanna gasped at the terrifying sight of Marquis Silivasi: His eyes glowed feral red; his canines protruded from his upper lip like medieval daggers, sharp as a blade and deadly with purpose; and his left hand bore the extension of elongated claws while his right hand sported some sort of a crude, ancient implement—a spiked cestus, fisted and ready to strike.

Hope entered her heart for the first time.

"Marquis!" she exclaimed, her cry both desperate and pleading. In her peripheral vision, she could see two warriors bending over the slumped body of Kristina, lifting her gently off the ground, turning her over, and applying...something...maybe venom to her wound.

"Step back, Deanna!" Marquis ordered, his voice fierce with intensity. His eyes never left Saber's. "Go to Nathaniel!"

"Yes," Saber hissed haughtily, glancing over his shoulder, "run to your brothers like a coward. See if they can save your life. Or not."

Marquis growled in response, and the low, angry echo shook the sides of the pool, instantly raising the temperature of the water by a couple of degrees.

Deanna moaned at the heat, trying to force her heavy eyes to focus. *Nathaniel...where was Nathaniel?* She tried to turn her head, to look behind her shoulder, but the world spun around in dizzying circles. "Nathaniel," she called, "where are you?"

Two strong hands appeared out of nowhere, anchoring her beneath both armpits—*Was Nathaniel in the pool with her? Where had he come from?* As her mind struggled to orient her body in space and time, she felt herself lifted from the pool as easily as one might snatch a Raggedy Ann doll from a pillow, and she and Nathaniel flew backward together.

Saber spun around in a mad fury, taking flight in quick pursuit. In the space of a heartbeat, he lashed out at the two of them, swiping deftly at Deanna's stomach with a handful of murderous claws; no doubt, he intended to disembowel her before she could get away.

Deanna screamed in horror, but Nathaniel moved faster than the sound, slicing his right arm down in a graceful arc in order to take the full brunt of Saber's fury. When he drew back the limb, it was marred by a deep laceration and oozing flesh and blood.

"Not today, Dark One," Nathaniel hissed, appearing to ignore the pain. He bent his head slowly to the wound, lapped up the blood in one slow stroke of his tongue, and met the Dark One's eyes with a sinister smile on his face. "You fight like a girl," he chided, laughing. Setting Deanna aside, he pushed her gently behind him and took a confident step forward. "If it is blood sport that you want, then blood sport you shall have...but our games will remain between *men*." Glancing over his shoulder, he called out to Ramsey. "Attend to her," he said, focusing his full attention back on Saber.

Before Deanna could take another step back, the real Ramsey appeared at her side, wrapped one enormous arm around her waist, raised the other to his mouth, and tore open the vein at his wrist with his fangs. He placed the wound against her mouth. "Drink," he crooned in her ear. "You have lost too much blood." His voice was hypnotic, as if heavily laced with compulsion, and Deanna felt her body respond on its own accord.

At the first taste of the coppery substance, Deanna's stomach did a backflip, threatening to make her retch. She felt positively queasy. Whether from the idea of drinking blood so soon after her conversion, the overwhelming weakness in her own body that had her so close to death already, or the knowledge that it was Ramsey—as opposed to Nachari—that offered this strange new sustenance, she had no idea. She only knew that the act was abhorrent to her mind, and if it weren't for Ramsey's compulsion, she would never be able to get through it. Not this soon. Not in this type of setting.

As if the act of taking blood was not enough, she suddenly felt a sharp stab against her neck and instinctively knew that Ramsey was injecting her with venom even as she was feeding from his wrist: He was working to heal her injuries.

Deanna gathered her courage, summoned that all-pervasive innate will to live, and forced her body to relax, to continue to take—and receive—what Ramsey was giving her. All the while, she watched with rapt fascination, and more than a little fear, as her new brothers faced off with the Dark One who had tried to take her life.

BLOOD SHADOWS

Nathaniel faced Saber Alexiares head-on, even as Marquis flanked him from the rear, both appearing as if they could kill him with their eyes alone. Their bodies were primed, eyes focused, muscles twitching, each waiting for the enemy to make the first move.

Saber was as calm as a cucumber. "Haven't we met before?" he asked, his weight shifting to his back foot as if he were simply copping a leisurely lean. He smiled a grin of pure derision.

Marquis's eyes lit up with recognition and a frown creased his brow. "In the valley by the snake river...when the Lycans attacked outside the old cabin."

Saber shrugged then. "Ah, yes." He turned to eye Nathaniel. "I believe I met your wife." He snickered. "She stroked my hair and whispered sweet nothings in my ear before that blond animal tried to have his way with her. Pity I didn't have a chance to get to know her better."

Nathaniel didn't respond.

He didn't even move, not even a twitch.

He just stared blankly ahead, and the complete absence of emotion on his face was far more frightening than any overt display of rage could have ever been. It was like watching a calculated robot—something that contained neither reason nor emotion—like death on two feet, simply waiting to strike.

Deanna winced.

Saber turned to Marquis then. "And you—you mated an original princess. Hmm, interesting. We did enjoy her visit in the colony, by the way. I hear she spent a delicious amount of time in the chamber of snakes—offering her body to the cobras for Salvatore's amusement. If you ask me, the male is a couple cards shy of a full deck, but then, who am I to understand the mind of a sorcerer?" As he spoke, he very subtly rotated his body so that both of the Silivasi brothers were in his forward line of sight as opposed to surrounding him. His eyes took in his full surroundings—the placement of the other warriors, the carefully hidden weapons concealed in the warrior's cloaks—and Deanna got the distinct impression that Saber Alexiares was neither insane nor maniacal but very, *very* calculated and intelligent. *Why don't they just attack him?* she wondered.

Connected to her by physical touch as he was, Ramsey Olaru apparently heard her thoughts. *It's a very delicate dance,* he whispered in her mind. *Saber may be from the house of Jaegar, and thus, an inferior-trained warrior, but he is Vampyr, which makes him extremely dangerous. Not only can he render himself invisible, but if he moves faster than Marquis or Nathaniel, he could possibly dematerialize before they can anchor him with a diamond collar, get hold of a vital organ, or bleed him out to the point of weakness. It would be unheard of for a Dark One to retreat from a battle—regardless of the odds stacked against him. They are much too arrogant, but one never knows...*

Your brothers want only to fight. To kill. They are waiting for that chance.

Deanna shivered at the thought, wondering if Nachari was anything like his brothers. Before she could contemplate the question further, she saw the slightest of movement in Marquis's body—his left pectoral muscle twitched. "Do the cowards in the house of Jaegar always stand around and talk?" he asked, his voice thick with contempt. "Here in house of Jadon, we prefer to fight."

Saber smiled broadly then. "Yeah," he agreed, "hotheads one and all." And then he flicked his wrist outward, sending a searing bolt of fire from the tips of his fingertips directly at Marquis's chest.

As the Master Warrior deflected the flame with his hands, sending it back in Saber's direction, the Dark One flew into the air in a calculated backflip, missed the arc of the flame, and landed on his feet behind Marquis. His hand shot out in a targeted effort to puncture Marquis's chest from behind and grasp at his heart, but Marquis moved too quickly. He spun to the left, threw a lightning-quick punch with the spiked cestus, and landed it squarely against Saber's jaw before the enemy could move out of the way. Saber's jaw cracked audibly as he launched backward as a result of the punch. He shook his head furiously to diffuse the blow, and immediately flew back into the fray. Nathaniel met his approach with a sustained spray of silver-tipped bullets, emptying the clip in his AK-47.

Saber deflected each bullet with the ease of a camper swatting away a swarm of flies before they could land and do any damage. Nathaniel tossed the gun aside, launched into the air, and leapt on the Dark One's back, wrenching his neck in an unnatural position even as Marquis plunged a hidden dagger into the center of Saber's gut and began to twist the blade. Saber struck back with a fury, connecting a high, balanced kick with the Master Warrior's jaw and following it with an immediate strike to the groin. One, two, three lightning-quick strikes followed, all connecting with Marquis's manhood. As Marquis doubled over in pain, Saber grasped both of Nathaniel's hands by the small pinky fingers on the end, rotated his wrists outward to break both digits at the carpal ligaments, and freed himself from the choke hold. He immediately flipped Nathaniel over his shoulder, slammed his body hard into the ground, and pinned him down beneath iron, contracting thighs.

Nathaniel's eyes became two focused beams of light—red, lethal lasers boring a deep, horizontal incision into the Dark One's forehead, cauterizing toward his brain, but incredibly, Saber ignored the pain. Blood dripping into his eyes, he plunged a set of deadly claws into Nathaniel's chest, breaking several ribs upon entry, and tunneled toward the heart. Nathaniel grasped Saber's arm with both fists and wrenched in opposite directions, snapping the bone in half like a mere twig.

Saber grunted in pain as he withdrew his arm.

His hand hung limp at the end of his wrist, but he didn't stop fighting. Lunging forward, he dove at Nathaniel's jugular. As horrible fangs sank deep, he snarled in a crazed effort to tear Nathaniel's throat out.

Nathaniel's left fist slammed against the back of Saber's head, over and over in quick succession, like a jackhammer, even as he fought to gouge at the Dark One's eyes with his free thumb. While the two vampires struggled for advantage, Marquis crawled to a nearby mountain pine, ripped the tree out by the roots, and sprang to his feet, ignoring the pain in his groin. In the space of an instant, he brought it behind his shoulders like a baseball bat and swung. The resounding whack was deafening, stunning the Dark One stupid for a moment before he collapsed on Nathaniel's chest.

Slithering out from under his heavy body, Nathaniel crouched low on his feet and watched as the Dark One who had tried to kill Kristina and Deanna slowly slumped to the ground, landing on his side. Marquis kicked him over onto his back and squatted down beside Nathaniel. The dagger Marquis had stabbed Saber with was still protruding out of his stomach, and Marquis took the blade by the hilt and removed it. Reaching into his waistband, he tossed another matching dagger to Nathaniel and nodded. "You take the head, while I remove the heart."

Nathaniel removed the blade from the scabbard, the corner of his mouth turning up in a wide grin of anticipation. "My pleasure."

As the two warriors began to wield the sharpened blades in unison, the sky grew at once overcast, and a faint but discernible wind swept through the air. As Deanna looked up, she had to blink several times in order to understand what she was seeing.

Descending from the sky like a warring angel from heaven was a powerful, stately male with burnished skin, chiseled features, both handsome and fearsome at the same time, and long silver-and-black hair, which whipped about his face like a medieval halo.

"Wait."

One word.

The male spoke one word, and both Marquis and Nathaniel released their blades, bent to one knee, and bowed their heads.

Who was this guy?

The male strolled forward with the authority of one who owned the entire world—no, the entire universe—and held out what looked like several diamond-studded collars.

"Milord?" Nathaniel asked, looking at the collars skeptically.

"We will question him before we kill him," the male said in

an imperious voice. He wasn't asking. He was telling.

Marquis visibly wilted. He was clearly biting back his anger in an effort to show obedience. "Milord, this Dark One attacked our sisters...my first mate. The right of blood vengeance is ours."

The handsome vampire nodded his head, his eyes strong with compassion yet determined. "Indeed, Marquis," he responded in an almost lyrical voice, "but it is time that we make an example out of our enemy for all to see." He handed the diamond-studded bands to Marquis and glared at the vampire on the ground. "Bring him to the Chamber of Torture—The Blood is not the only power around here capable of exacting a pound of flesh. We will get whatever information we desire out of him, and then we will stake him to a post in the Red Canyon on the Sunday after this next and feed him to the sun, so that even those cowards hiding underground in the colony will hear his screams and know his agony."

Nodding his understanding, Marquis took the bands from the male's hand and began to affix them around Saber's throat, ankles, and wrists.

Nathaniel sat back and watched. "This is the male who saved Jocelyn that day in the shed. From the Lycans." He shook his head in disgust. "I told her he had no soul."

The vampire nodded and turned to eye his surroundings. "Kristina?" he asked.

A vampire with light, ash-colored hair stood up from his place about fifteen feet away, where he knelt beside the thin redhead's body. "She's still unconscious, but she will live," he said, answering the king.

"And she will be questioned," the king said.

"And throttled as soon as she gets better," Marquis grumbled.

The king placed a firm hand on Marquis's shoulder and gave it a slight squeeze. "Debriefed, Marquis—not throttled. She is young and new to our ways. And no match for the cunning of a Dark One. No doubt, she will feel tremendous shame and remorse."

He released Marquis's shoulder and took a step toward Deanna then. Instinctively, Deanna stepped back.

"Greetings, Ms. Dubois-Silivasi. I am Napolean."

He held out his hand as he approached even closer, and Deanna just stared at it. As ridiculous as it was to consider her appearance at this moment, she couldn't help but feel self-conscious—she was standing before the sovereign leader of the house of Jadon in a torn bikini, with puncture holes in her neck and bloodstains around her mouth; and her knees were literally knocking together.

She swallowed, pushed a clump of matted hair away from her eyes, and wiped her hand against her thigh to remove some dirt. "Hi." The word came out hoarse, so she tried again. "Hi. Nice to meet you."

Napolean held her hand for a second longer than customary and then gently released it, giving her the distinct impression that he had taken something from her mind. Perhaps her memories...or information about Nachari? "Thank you for your commitment to the Master Wizard, Nachari. What you have done—coming here to Dark Moon Vale of your own accord—took tremendous courage, and we are all praying that the gods will smile upon both of you for your kindness. I am sorry you had to go through such a horrible ordeal tonight."

Deanna nodded. Or at least she thought she did. The male was simply too intimidating, even for a confident woman like her. Jocelyn had previously mentioned that there was just something about Napolean Mondragon—something that made a person want to take off running in the opposite direction—and now, Deanna understood completely. "You're welcome," she managed to reply.

With that, Napolean seemed satisfied. Turning to face the sentinels, he said, "Saxson, you and Santos remove the prisoner and take him to the holding cell outside the Chamber of Sacrifice and Atonement. I want him carefully guarded at all times. Ramsey, take Kristina back to the clinic so Kagen can attend to her, and then gather the warriors in my conference room to discuss a defensive strategy. We must be prepared in the event that the Dark Ones attempt to come after their missing soldier. Marquis"—he turned to face the Ancient Master Warrior—"you and Nathaniel accompany Kristina and Deanna to the clinic and debrief everyone, including Braden, thoroughly. I want to know everything that has happened these last weeks, since the Dark One began impersonating Ramsey. If you must, view each person's memories firsthand—I want to know *exactly* what was going on inside of Kristina's head and why the Dark One chose her as a target. No one's *destiny* is to venture out without an escort until I say otherwise. Understood?"

"As you wish, milord," Nathaniel answered.

Marquis nodded his head. "Trust me; we'll get to the bottom of this."

As the vampire with the ash-colored hair, the one called Saxson, joined Ramsey and the other warriors, Deanna couldn't help but stare at the redheaded girl still lying limp in his arms. She took a long measured look at Kristina and all her many bruises, and winced. *Holy cow*, she thought. *Could we have come any closer to dying tonight?*

Suddenly, all of her certainty and conviction—deciding to come to Dark Moon Vale; trusting her instincts to go forward with the conversion; even waiting anxiously, if not somewhat fearfully, for Nachari to return—came into question. And she felt more alone than she had ever felt in her life.

More lost and confused.

What in the world had she gotten herself into?

And what in the world would happen next?

twenty~three

One Week Later

Deanna shut her eyes and poured all of her concentration into making her voice sound steady...even...unaffected. Kagen was knocking on the door for the third time in the last five minutes, and it was all she could do to hold it together. "I'm all right, Kagen," she called out, the vise around her heart tightening with every word of the lie. "I'll be out in a few. I just"—her voice began to quiver—"I just need a minute...alone." She hoped it was good enough.

Kagen paused for a moment, no doubt trying to find a way to collect his own emotions. "Okay," he murmured through the thick oak door, "but if you need us, we're..." His voice trailed off. "You don't have to be alone right now; that's all."

Deanna clutched the thick white bath towel wrapped around her slender body, her typically tan fingers turning blotchy red and white with the effort. "Thanks." The word came out as a whisper. It was the best she could do.

The moment she heard Kagen's footsteps recede from the door, she padded toward the shower like a robot, cold and unfeeling, and turned on the spray in an effort to create some white noise: to block out the world. Stepping away from the stall, she let the glass swing shut, and then she pressed her back against an adjacent wall and slowly slid down to the floor.

With her elbows on her knees, her face in her hands, she drew in a deep, unsteady breath and began to tremble as the tears finally broke free.

They were out of time.

All of them.

Nachari.

Her.

BLOOD SHADOWS

The Silivasis…

The day had begun like any other, with one exception: The heavy awareness of time had risen with each of Nachari's loved ones as they awoke from their slumber.

Day twenty-eight.

Fifty-seven hours until the end of the Blood Moon. A nine-hour window for Nachari to return. Even less time than that for Deanna and Nachari to conceive a son *in time*…

To avoid the ultimate penalty of the Blood Curse.

Deanna had been a nervous wreck all day, waiting on pins and needles for some miraculous event to take place: half expecting to see the Master Wizard levitate from the bed like a true vampire of old, rising from a coffin, and half expecting to see him stroll into the lobby as if nothing had ever happened, wearing that infamous smile so many of his friends and family had told her about. She had battled terrible fear—what if he actually showed up? What if he never did?—and the uncertainty had taken its toll. She had already taken three cold showers, hoping to shock her system into some sort of normalcy, to clear her mind; and she had jumped at every knock on the door, every creak of the building beneath the gusty wind.

What she wanted more than life itself, she feared more than death itself—for Nachari to return in time. And if he did, she would likely run the other way. And if he didn't…she would never be the same.

She wasn't even human anymore.

Dearest angels in heaven, what had she done?

As the seconds ticked by, minutes passing as slowly as hours, she battled both terror and relief, guilt and remorse. She soothed herself, forgave herself, and hated herself all at the same time.

Now, staring absently into the shower, she watched as the cold spray hit the mosaic tiles, met in a swirl at the center, and rapidly disappeared down the drain. A part of her wished she could blend her essence with the water and simply wash it all away. Wash *herself* away.

"Oh, God," she murmured, hugging her knees to her chest

and hiccupping a sob. "Help me." She shook her head, trying to clear the cobwebs, and glanced up at the solar clock for the millionth time: It was six-fifteen PM. The sun would be setting in thirty-seven minutes—and wasn't that just an appropriate end to a horrifying situation—and Nachari had simply not returned. There had been no miraculous resurrection, no peaceful rise from slumber, no trumpets sounding to herald his return.

Absolutely nothing had happened.

An inappropriate laugh escaped Deanna's throat, the sound a mixture of nervousness and incredulity: If she wasn't pregnant in the next forty-five minutes—*pregnant in the next forty-five minutes!*—Nachari was dead. And his brothers would be—

She slammed her hands over her ears and pressed hard. No. *No!* She couldn't think of their devastation, their grief...the funeral. Her body began to slowly rock back and forth as her mind clung to a very thin thread of sanity.

Get up. Get dressed, she told herself. *Yes, fix your hair and put on clothes. Don't think. Don't feel. Don't....don't....don't...*

Anything.

Nachari Silivasi ran both fingers through his thick, wavy hair and paced along the uneven stone floor, his heart pounding in his chest. *By all the gods, we are running out of time! Where the hell is Noiro?*

His mind was swimming with thoughts—recalculating his every move, questioning his every decision: Had he pushed Noiro hard enough? Had he emphasized the importance of the timing strongly enough? Had Ademordna found out? Was Noiro dead? Was it over?

Deanna.

What was she going through right now?

She had to be half mad with anxiety and dread, fearing his return yet dreading his loss.

BLOOD SHADOWS

Confused!

She had to be in a living hell all her own.

And his brothers—were they providing her comfort or coming unglued themselves?

He threw his head back and shouted his frustration. Tears stung his angry eyes, he grit his teeth, and he slowly exhaled. "Lord Perseus," he cried, knowing nothing else to do, "for the sake of all that's holy...for my brothers...for Shelby...for *me*. Please...I have yet to curse you; I have yet to ask you why; but now I am begging you—get me out of here!"

A key turned in the lock, and Nachari spun around swiftly, half expecting to see the Celestial god himself walk through the door.

When Noiro entered, dressed in a tight black mini dress and heels, her hair shimmering flame red, he felt a moment's disorientation. And then he quickly recovered. "Do you have them? The remaining talismans?" He closed the distance between them in two long strides.

Noiro smiled as if they had all the time in the world. At least she had replaced her customary jagged fangs with the illusion of straight white teeth. "So anxious, are we, lover?"

Nachari took a deep breath and nodded, staring down at the ornamental box in her hands. "We are committing treason," he reminded her.

"For love?" she asked whimsically.

There were only so many lies a being could tell before they no longer sounded believable. "For vengeance...and a child," he reminded her. "Perhaps love will come in time."

Noiro rolled her eyes. "You do realize, Wizard, that I may be banned from the underworld for all time—that I am trusting you with my eternal soul?" She frowned then. "Will you ever come to love me?"

For the gods' sakes, Nachari thought. The witch was a demon. "Taste my answer," he said convincingly. And with that, he encircled her waist with one strong hand, pulled her tight against him, and covered her mouth with his. He poured all of his longing, desperation, and desire to return home into the kiss, leaving the stunned demoness breathless. When at last he pulled away, she stumbled to regain her balance.

Nachari opened the rectangular box and sighed a deep exhale of relief as he stared down at the small scorpion and spider, both oozing darkness and lethal energy. "From the western and southern kingdoms?" he asked, just to be sure.

Noiro smoothed her dress. "Y…y…y…yes," she stuttered, "of course."

"Good." Nachari immediately spun around and crossed the floor to retrieve the other two talismans—the frog and the snake—and set them carefully on a makeshift stone altar he had constructed beside the bed. Kneeling before the aberration, he laid both hands across the stone, palms up, and began to chant an ancient incantation.

As the frog began to croak, the snake slithered over his wrist and bit him. As the scorpion stung him again and again, the spider pierced his skin and began to burrow beneath the outer layer. Yet Nachari held fast—chanting and praying and visualizing the way home.

Noiro crept up behind him and placed both hands on his shoulders. "I will be right behind you, lover. Do not forget your promise." Her words were as much a threat as a reminder.

In an instant, Noiro and Nachari were flying backward, speeding through a narrow tunnel at a pace that defied comprehension. Darkness swirled around them, endless gradations of gray, black, and divergent light. Shrieks, moans, and shrill cries of agony rang through the air like symbols clashing against one another. As they sped further and further away from the Abyss, the terrible sounds grew fainter and fainter.

Noiro kept her eyes focused on the wizard's back so she

wouldn't lose her way. His ever-increasing spirit of light acted as a lantern, guiding them both through the cavern from hell as a Magick more powerful than any she had ever seen conjured by an earthbound soul drew them earth-ward. She smiled inwardly, knowing the wizard's true plan—yet trusting her own implicitly.

Noiro, the twin dark energy of Orion, was not stupid.

She was as old as time, as dark as night, as cunning as a fox, and she knew what she wanted: to rule the Middle Kingdom of hell. And for that, she needed a son of unequaled power and strength. She wanted the prowess and stealth of the Vampyr, the Magick and authority of a Master Wizard, and the darkness and cunning of a demon to embody the child who would usher her rise into power.

And she wanted revenge on the dark lord Ademordna.

Of course, Nachari would seek to trick her. He would run into the arms of his *destiny* and the honor of his house; and through it all, his immortal soul would remain protected by his carefully crafted lies. But it wouldn't matter—in the least.

She was a demon, a dark deity, a goddess over their kind. He was no match for her, and he never would be.

Noiro shut her eyes—only for a second—in order to savor her soon-to-be victory: Nachari would enter the earth through the portal in which he left, the meadow by the cabins. She, however, would enter in Deanna's room. She would kill the *destiny*; rape the wizard; and return to hell impregnated before Ademordna even knew she was gone. Of course, she could blame the pregnancy on any number of sadistic rapists.

The point was—the vampire's escape would become legend in the underworld, no doubt talked about for eternity, and so would the name of her son.

twenty~four

Deanna sat down on the soft queen-sized bed in her private quarters; she just couldn't bear to wait another moment in Nachari's room. She avoided looking at the clock on purpose. There was really no point—she knew what time it was: six-thirty PM. In one-half hour, Nachari would be as good as dead, and they could all begin the process of making final arrangements, preparing his unconscious body for the Death Chamber—and just how the hell did something like that work anyway? Handing him over to the Blood for final retribution?

Deanna would not think about it a moment before she had to.

She would survive this—if she could survive this—by living one moment at a time, placing one foot in front of the other, allowing time to carry her through the inconceivable, one painful emotion and event at a time. She finger-brushed her hair to remove any remaining tangles, and tightened the knot on the heavy bathrobe—dressing had seemed an insurmountable exercise, after all. It had been all she could do to wash her face and dry her hair.

Turning to open the blinds on the window—perhaps she could watch the sunset and buy herself another five minutes of sanity—she felt a strange stirring in the room, and an inexplicable feeling of panic began to rise in her heart. The hair stood up on the back of her neck, and it felt as if she were suddenly in the presence of a very dense energy, a distinct vibration of evil.

Before she could identify the source of her unease, a swirl of dark colors began to illuminate in the room before her. She took a step back toward the window, watching in suspended dread as an extremely attractive, tall redhead simply shimmered into view. The woman was wearing a thin black dress, the hem just below the apex of her thighs, and extremely high, spiked black heels. Her hair was an unnatural color, like the center of a flame, and her eyes were beyond vacant. They were aberrations of nature—unnatural—two vacant coals lodged in a plastic face, peering out at Deanna from a world far beyond this one.

Deanna swallowed hard. "Who are you?"

The female sauntered forward and slowly licked her cherry-red lips. "My name is Noiro." She rolled her words with a heavy, seductive lilt. "I am the twin energy, if you will, of the Celestial deity Orion." She shrugged nonchalantly. "His demon sister, if you want it in plain English." Her voice turned icy cold. "And I am your rival for Nachari's affections."

Deanna frowned as she tried to process what the woman was saying. She had no doubt that this…thing…was a demon from hell, but if this Noiro knew Nachari—and she was here on the earth—then where was he? Could Nachari be—

"Shh," Noiro interrupted, wagging a long finger back and forth through the air. "Now is not the time to think; it is the time to *listen.*"

Deanna stared ahead at the demon, not daring to utter a word, even as she used her peripheral vision to take measure of the room, calculate what objects might be used as a weapon, and determine the most direct route of escape.

Growing up in the tough streets of New Orleans, Deanna was no stranger to conflict or street brawls. As a child, she had been forced to fight the bullies at school in order to keep her lunch money until she had finally grown into her full height. Unfortunately, after that, there had been a handful of altercations with jealous females, girls whose boyfriends had come on to Deanna, albeit without any encouragement on her part. Still, she had learned how to hold her own; and while she knew she was no match for a demon, she also had no intention of lying down and dying without a fight.

"I've never even met Nachari," Deanna said defiantly, trying to stall for time. *Kagen!* She would try the telepathic route; maybe she could call for help. *Marquis, help me!*

The demon threw back her head and laughed, flame-red hair swaying back and forth along her shoulders. "Your powers are no match for my own, silly woman. This room is locked. No energy gets in. No energy gets out." Her eyes narrowed, and the pupils transformed into vertical slits like a cat's, glowing in the center of the orbs. "I hate you," the demon whispered.

Deanna blanched.

Not that demons didn't pretty much hate everyone in general, but the focused rage was like a dagger being thrust at her heart. Why would this particular demon single her out? "You don't even know me," Deanna argued instinctively.

Noiro slowly shook her head and frowned. "Oh, I know you, all right. I know that the Master Wizard loves you, that he wants you, that he would move heaven and earth to get to you, when he could have me instead."

Deanna shrank inside. Unfortunately, she knew all too well where this was headed. Eyeing the narrow brass lamp on the nightstand, she measured how many steps it would take to reach it; the angle she would have to yank at to dislodge the cord, and the swing she would have to muster to connect with Noiro's skull. It would buy her all of two seconds to escape, and she would have to climb over the bed to get to the door. She thought about the window, which was closer, but the opening was too narrow and the drop was too high. So be it.

"Look. Nachari and I aren't really—"

"No, you look!" the demon screeched, her phony seductive voice suddenly turning monstrous and unbalanced. "You look into the face of death, and you know that I shall take his body, his soul, and his offspring before he dies!"

Deanna watched in growing horror as the woman's appearance began to change: Her straight white teeth morphed into a hideous set of crooked fangs and rotten gums; her tongue became forked and slithered in and out of her mouth as she spat in anger; and her beautiful doe eyes narrowed into tiny yellow slits.

As reason gave way to rage, the demoness crouched lower

and lower into a squat, preparing to pounce.

Deanna had seen enough.

Summoning all the strength and speed of the Vampyr, she flew toward the nightstand, grasped the base of the lamp with her right hand, and spun around swinging. The center connected with the demon's forehead just as she launched into the air; a stiff crack rang out, and Noiro catapulted backward.

Deanna leapt onto the bed. She led with her right foot, extending her left foot forward in an effort to hurdle the remaining expanse as she fled toward the door. She let out a high-pitched cry of pain as a pair of gnarled hands grasped her around the ankle and tugged. Deanna thrust her hands out in front of her to avoid banging her head against the tile as her body met the floor. Her head swung forward with momentum but barely scraped the tile. She twisted like a cat, amazed at her newfound agility, and used her strong abdominal muscles to pull herself up and onto the bed, all the while twisting out of the demon's grasp. She kicked hard at Noiro's face—if that was even what one could call it—putting everything she had into knocking out those horrendous teeth. "Get. Off. Me!" she bit out, her own anger rising.

Noiro began to levitate into the air then, rising like some ghostly apparition from a horror movie, her aura spreading out around her in thick, inky waves of darkness. Fire shot forth from her mouth, and her eyes glowed like the flames of hell, even as her laughter ricocheted off the walls. "You want to fight? *Me?*" The utterance that came out of her next could only be compared to a sound from the movie *The Exorcist*. It was a low, grotesque, demonic roar; and it sent waves of terror down Deanna's spine like nothing she had ever experienced before.

"Oh, God..." Deanna murmured, backpedaling on the bed.

She instinctively held her arms out in front of her, both to block Noiro's descent and to prepare to fight, but the demon simply laughed. And then, a dozen arms came out of nowhere, each one slithering like a vile snake, wrapping around Deanna's arms, legs, and torso. As Noiro tightened her grip, her body descended toward the bed, rolls of fat jiggling in undulating waves. Slimy scales of skin broke free from demon flesh and spiraled downward like snow, coating Deanna's quivering body.

A forked tongue shot out of Noiro's mouth and flicked back and forth in rapid waves…taunting. "Do you want to play for a while…or die quickly?" She spewed green vomit at the headboard behind Deanna's head, and a dozen little green maggots squirmed down the oak bedpost toward the bed.

Deanna clenched her mouth shut, knowing instinctively that the worms would enter her body through her mouth if they could. And then she watched in absolute horror as five claws from one of Noiro's hands merged together, becoming one round, serrated blade. The blade began to twist and turn in rapid succession like a bit at the end of a drill. Noiro held the aberrant hand over Deanna's forehead and raised her eyebrows in question.

Deanna squirmed and shook her head.

She moved it lower over Deanna's abdomen and shrugged her shoulders.

Deanna grimaced and started to whimper.

And then, with a wicked smile upon her face, she held it even lower, between Deanna's legs, and snickered.

"No!" Deanna protested, horrified at the thought. "No…please." A small green maggot leapt at her mouth, and she quickly shut it, catching the worm by the head before it could enter any further. She spat it out with revulsion.

"Then where?" Noiro asked, her voice dripping pure, malicious venom. She pressed the blade against Deanna's inner thigh, and Deanna screamed beneath a closed mouth, the sound coming out as a high-pitched hum.

"Ah, the stomach then?" Noiro hissed, raising the blade once again.

Deanna's eyes filled with helpless, horrified tears, and she shook her head in defeat. The stomach would be horrendous; it would take forever, and she may or may not die. "The head," she bit out between pursed lips.

Noiro smiled brightly. "A lobotomy then?"

Deanna bit back a sob and slowly nodded her head. As Noiro raised the spinning blade to her forehead, Deanna closed her eyes and said a quick prayer to her father: *I'll be home soon, Daddy—please be there to meet me.*

Nachari Silivasi struggled to regain a sense of time and space, to orient himself in his ever-changing reality as he sped through the endless tunnel. On several occasions, he could feel Noiro's presence close behind him as the colors, sounds, and smells assaulted his heightened senses; and he had to continuously remind himself to stay focused, prepare to act quickly, remember to think clearly, get ready to strike immediately upon emergence. Noiro would not be an easy opponent. She was a demon, after all, and it would require all of his cunning to defeat her swiftly. And time was definitely of the essence.

Now, as his astral body began to slow, adjusting to the slightly less dense conditions of the earth, he drew all of his strength and power inward, amassing it into a tight ball of focused power, preparing to strike the moment his spirit reentered his physical form. He could almost feel the glorious expanse of his shoulders, the burgeoning strength of his waiting arms, the familiar support of his powerful legs beneath him; and although he was aware that his body would be weakened and unsteady from months without use, he had no doubt that he could compensate for atomic deficiencies with mental focus. Yes, he could hardly wait to feel his heart beating beneath his chest once again.

And then it happened.

Emergence.

A transition so smooth and seamless that it was hardly even felt.

One moment he was spinning without end at speeds that

defied the laws of physics; the next, he was simply sentient, aware, and grounded on earth.

Slightly confused and off balance, Nachari ran his hands down his chest, expecting to feel his earthly, physical form beneath him, even as his eyes searched for the familiar sight of a hospital bed and white sheets, understanding that his brothers had kept him in the clinic, but…something was wrong.

Off.

Not as it should be.

As Nachari surveyed the scene around him, the impressions he got were not *sterile and white* but *earthen and brown*. The texture beneath him was not soft and smooth, but hard and uneven. His body had not emerged in a horizontal position but parallel to the ground. And there was no beating heart in his chest.

Nachari spun around in horror, his eyes taking in the familiar meadow around him. He scanned the trees, the cabins, and the grass. For a moment, he spied the exact spot where he had died, the place he had lain that fateful day when he had flatlined in order to go after Napolean, but his mind could not grasp hold of it.

There simply wasn't time.

All five of his senses acutely alert, he listened for a second presence. He scented the air for Noiro's distinct, identifying fragrance. He scanned high and low with his eyes for the faintest hint of movement, switching effortlessly to infrared detection in order to identify any unusual patterns of heat. He turned his palms upward and felt for microscopic disturbances in the air, movement from something larger than a squirrel or a rabbit. He detected a deer not too far off in the forest, and a mountain lion several miles away, but nothing human—or demon, as it were—in the meadow. He licked his bottom lip to test the presence of acidity in the air, searching for proof that the demoness was there.

But she simply wasn't anywhere to be found.

She simply wasn't there.

And then it hit him. Like a thousand pounds of bricks

crashing down on top of him: *Deanna.*

Noiro had gone to the clinic. And he had emerged in the meadow—without his earthly body.

Time stood still.

His breath caught in his throat.

Moving faster than he had ever moved before, Nachari raced against time, praying that he wasn't too late.

twenty~five

Kagen Silivasi sat at the end of Nachari's bed, staring at his youngest living brother with bitter hopelessness. He just couldn't believe this was it. All the days, the nights, the endless prayers and hopes—the countless smiles and memories from the past—they had all come down to this, a silent exit into final death.

Another brother lost.

He turned to look at Marquis and Nathaniel, each one perched silently in a chair beside Nachari's bed, and he had to turn away. There was nothing to be said or done; they were not even strong enough to comfort Deanna. Hell had visited the Silivasi family with a vengeance, and it was about to take the heart and soul of their clan…forever.

Kagen rotated his wrist to check his watch again, six thirty-five; and then, he shot up from the bed and backed away as a furious gust of wind swept through the room like a cyclone. All at once, a deafening roar shook the clinic walls, and a ball of blazing fire descended through the ceiling and tunneled into Nachari's body with the power of a freight train.

Marquis backpedaled so hard that the frame of his chair split into pieces and his body flew backward, slamming into the wall. "What the hell!"

Nathaniel's wings shot out of his back, and he swept up toward the ceiling in a feverish, defensive posture.

And then Nachari's once quiescent form shot up from the bed like lava spewing from a volcano. He braced his feet several feet apart; bent his knees; and blinked his stunning green eyes rapidly, several times, before settling back into a keen, alert focus. "Where is the demon!" he demanded, his voice far rougher and much more commanding than Kagen remembered.

"The…the…what?" Marquis asked, still lumbering to stand back up.

Nachari turned toward Kagen, and the intensity in his eyes almost backed the Master Healer up. "Deanna! Where is she?" The words came out in a harsh, no-nonsense shout, and Kagen had to collect himself in order to answer.

"It…she…second floor…guest rooms."

Just like that.

Nachari was gone.

Nachari did not need anyone to tell him which guest room to go to—he had spent far too much time with Noiro not to recognize her vile energy. Without hesitation, he plowed through the plaster, wood, and drywall, ready to face whatever he might find on the other side; and the sight that met him assaulted his eyes and seized his heart:

Deanna was lying prone on the bed. She was strapped to the mattress by a dozen or more demonic arms, and Noiro was lowering a singular blade made of vicious claws, collectively spinning like a high-powered drill bit, toward Deanna's skull.

His *destiny* looked terrified.

The demoness looked demented.

"Desino!" Too frightened to access his own native language, Nachari shouted in Latin, and the aberrant drill bit exploded into fragments in the air, several pieces flaking into the demon's eyes.

Noiro spun around in shocked fury. "No!" she shouted. And then she lunged at Deanna's throat with her mouth.

Nachari had seen this scene before—the murder of the demon Suirauqa, the one Noiro had turned into hamburger on his bed in hell—and he wasn't about to witness a replay. Fire shot from his fingers, enveloping Noiro's red hair, even as he lifted a small, round paperweight from the nightstand with his mind and hurled it into her mouth.

Several fragments of ruptured enamel flew out before the ball lodged in Noiro's throat, and she began to gag on the remaining teeth.

Nachari gave her no quarter.

He sprang toward the bed in a feline bound and grasped her by the shoulder, his talons sinking deep. With one strong flex of his arm, he pulled her from atop Deanna and flung her into the wall. Bones snapped as the plaster gave way, and Noiro struggled to get back to her feet. Somehow, she dislodged the ball and began to hiss.

"You traitor," she screeched. "I will strangle you with your own innards!"

Nachari leapt the distance between them, drew back his arm, and backhanded her across the face so hard that her neck twisted 180 degrees.

She screamed in agony and kicked at his groin. "You won't need this anymore!"

He blocked her kick, caught her ankle, and tightened his fist slowly—his heart seething as he crushed the flesh and bone beneath his hands.

Noiro spat then, sending searing green phlegm into his eyes, nose, and mouth, burning him with the full fury of hell. She stumbled onto one foot, threw her hands up in the air, and allowed her head to fall back. A violent wind extinguished the flames as the demoness howled, looking entirely unholy and profane. "Death and destruction, agony and pain; rain down on the wizard, destroy him again!"

Nachari felt the full fury of the spell slam into him like a cannonball. His breath caught, and he stumbled backward trying to brace himself against the instant pain that assailed his body. His mind spun from the dizzying sensation, the overwhelming agony, and he had to fight to remain conscious.

"From spirit to body, from death to life; destroy the flesh, and kill him twice!" Noiro shouted another refrain with wicked glee, and Nachari felt his soul turning inward. She had called upon Final Death, a curse against his immortal, vampiric flesh.

He could not survive this.

He could not fight such demonic power—not even to save

Deanna. Not as a vampire and not as a wizard. Certainly not as a…*man*.

Pushing against the pain and the closing hand of death, Nachari tapped into the poison that still flowed through his ethereal body: the snake from the Northern Province; the frog from the Eastern Province; the scorpion from the south; and the spider from the west. And he called forth a spell of his own.

"Scourge of darkness,
creatures of night…
from all four directions,
I beseech you to fight;
In my blood, merge your venom;
In my power, ignite!"

At once, he was surrounded by a white-hot ball of flame, and as his flesh gave way to the growing conflagration, several images morphed out of his own: A snake as dark as the black mamba slithered across the floor and wrapped itself around the demoness, squeezing with lethal force; a toad as poisonous as the South American dart frog leapt onto her back and began to ooze secretions against her skin; a scorpion the size of a cat crawled slowly up her trembling body and stung her through the chest in the heart; and finally, a small, seemingly insignificant spider—a black widow—crawled into her mouth. All the while, Nachari waited, unharmed, in the body of a black panther: Since the spell Noiro had conjured was against the flesh of a man, he was no longer a man.

Noiro's body began to seize as the hellish venom began to take effect. After several minutes had passed, the panther slowly padded forward in a sleek, circular approach, at last lying languidly at her side.

Reaching out to grasp his fur in a trembling hand, she panted, "You can't kill me, Wizard. I'm a demon."

The panther rose lazily to his feet, licked his chops as if he had just finished a man-sized meal, and then instantly morphed back into a male vampire with thick black hair and haunting green eyes. As Nachari rose up on one knee, he looked her dead in the eyes. "You weren't summoned here, demon. You're mortal."

Noiro's eyes widened with shock and surprise, and her mouth flew open. For whatever reason, it had never crossed her mind that a demon's jurisdiction on earth only existed in the heart of the tainted soul who sought her out through summoning. Noiro had come of her own free will, and the minute she had left her protected realm, she had made herself vulnerable; she was no longer invincible. Nachari had counted on this fact to be his saving grace, and he had never been more grateful that he had taken the time to read the stolen copy of the Blood Canon, the ancient book of Black Magic.

As the truth of his words finally sunk in, Noiro swiped a clawed hand at his face and screamed: "Noooooo!"

Nachari licked his lips and smiled. "Yes, love. *Yes*."

Her pitiful, hideous form morphed back into a beautiful redhead, and she looked up at him with pleading eyes. "I only did it because you're so...*so* beautiful. I love you." She reached out to brush the back of her fingers against his jaw, and he slapped her hand away.

"And you're so...*so* repulsive." He leaned down until his nose was almost touching hers, and in an act of gentleness, placed his full palm over her neck. "I never felt anything for you but contempt." And then he closed his fingers in a slow, deliberate motion, crushing her larynx as he did so. When she clenched her eyes shut in terror, he said, "Look at me. Open your eyes, and look at me."

Noiro slowly opened her eyes, and for the first time, they were not only dazed but uncertain. The demoness had been laid low. She had finally been humbled.

In a voice so faint only Noiro could hear, Nachari Silivasi whispered, "My beautiful face is the last thing you will ever see." With that, he broke her neck and waited until her heart beat no more.

twenty~six

Deanna Dubois scrambled from the bed as if her very life depended upon it. She scurried across the tile floor and ducked beneath a narrow writing desk in the corner of the guest room. Whether it was the four creepy-crawly, poisonous things; the sleek black panther that had just padded across the room toward the demon like he owned the entire stratosphere; or the focused fury that glistened in his stunning green eyes as he took the demon's last breath, she knew that she was out of her league. In way over her head.

Her very soul shook with terror.

This was not a happy-go-lucky, good-looking guy with a smile to rival the sun and a warm sense of humor. This was a force of nature that could cripple a demon, call down—or up, as it were—the forces of hell, and unleash his own day of reckoning.

She was tough.

She was strong.

She had faced some of the best and the worst life had to offer, but this was beyond her purview. This was beyond her comprehension!

Folding her body into a tight little ball, she grasped her knees to her chest and held her breath. *Invisible*, maybe she could somehow make herself invisible. And while it was true; they would all end up dying as a result of her selfishness, she simply couldn't help herself. Even his brothers were giving him a very wide berth. They had been standing in the doorway for the last five minutes watching with revulsion. And their faces had registered every bit as much shock and horror as hers.

Deanna shivered all the way down to her bones.

She could not go home with…him.

She could not live like…that.

With that.

She definitely couldn't let him touch her.

Every bone in her body wanted to retreat into a subatomic particle.

Nachari rose gracefully from the floor, almost as if he were still in the panther's body. He dusted off the loose black sweat pants and matching T-shirt Kagen had kept him clothed in and turned toward the bed. "Deanna?" His voice was a satin purr...like a whisper on the wind. When she didn't answer, his face grew taut, although only slightly. "*Deanna...*" He said her name again, this time with more authority, in an even deeper, smoother tone.

Deanna watched in horror as he looked around the room, and her heart sank like a lead weight when his indescribable eyes alighted with recognition as they swept beneath the desk. He crouched down and stared at her as if *she* was the strange one! "Sweetheart, what are you doing?"

The very vibration of his voice played over her skin like music, a skillful bow stroking a cello's strings, and she knew he had to be using magic. She covered her ears. He stood back up and turned toward his brothers. This was good. Wasn't it? Maybe he was going away.

"Is my brownstone empty?" he asked.

She couldn't tell which one he was addressing, so she peeked out from beneath the desk to see.

Nathaniel's brows were furrowed, and he looked more than a little uneasy. "You..." The word came out gruff, and he cleared his throat and tried again. "You do know us, right? I mean...we're good?" His palms were raised in a universal gesture of surrender. Holy shit; he was scared of Nachari.

Nachari smiled then and something in the air shifted; something in the room lifted. It wasn't enough to allay Deanna's fears, but it definitely added another dimension to an already unbearably handsome face. It was, in a word, spectacular. "Yes, brother, I know you." His eyes swept up to the clock on the wall, and the smile left him. It was six forty-five already. "But I

Tessa Dawn

don't have time for a reunion now; is my brownstone empty?"

Marquis spoke up for the first time, seeming to be testing his own voice for steadiness. "Uh...no...I think...Braden's there."

Nachari held out his hands in frustration. "What's empty?"

Kagen brushed a short lock of brown hair away from his eyes as if it might help him to focus if he could see more clearly. "Um...uh...Kristina's apartment."

Nachari nodded. "Thank you."

The three Silivasi brothers just stood in the doorway, staring open-mouthed, like they were watching a ghost.

Nachari's eyes flashed with urgency. "Leave us."

No one moved. They just continued to stare at him like three deer caught in headlights. Finally, after what seemed like forever but could not have been more than thirty seconds, Marquis cleared his throat. "You only have fourteen minutes."

If looks could kill, all three of them would have been laid out on the floor. "Really?" Nachari answered.

"Shit," Nathaniel finally said, whistling low beneath his breath. "We're out."

Nachari nodded. "Oh, and incinerate that body for me...just in case."

"Consider it done," Marquis responded. And then he booted Noiro's corpse several feet down the hall, out of the way.

"Welcome back, brother," Kagen said, shuffling quickly behind Marquis and trying to close what was left of the door behind him, as if there wasn't a gaping hole in the wall.

Letting out a measured, deep breath, Nachari turned around and slowly—in a very nonthreatening manner—strolled across the floor. Stopping a couple feet in front of the desk, he squatted, braced his elbows on his knees, and turned his full attention on Deanna.

Her breath caught in her throat.

Dear God, he was stunning!

Not even real.

It was almost painful to look at him, and she struggled to hold his gaze, however sheepishly, which was so not her!

291

"Sweetie," he whispered gently, letting out a sigh of understanding. He looked down at the floor and then back up into her eyes. "Oh, baby…we really don't have time for this."

Deanna blanched. The idea of it all…what he was thinking…referring to…was just…beyond…

Beyond the grasp of her mind.

She crossed her arms over her chest as if hiding her naked body, and checked the tie on her robe to make sure it was secure.

His eyes registered everything, and he quickly looked away out of respect. Rising to his full height, he walked across the room to the chest of drawers and picked up her portfolio. "This is yours?" he asked, holding it up. "Your drawings?"

Deanna frowned. How could he know that she was an artist? She nodded, and then realizing that his back was partially turned away from her, she relaxed a bit and forced herself to speak. "Yeah…yes it is."

He smiled faintly as he opened the portfolio and thumbed through several of the sketches.

Deanna cringed, knowing they were all of him: The ones in front depicted the scenes she had seen in her dreams back in New Orleans; but after that, the later sketches portrayed him in his hospital bed or replicated photos she had seen of him and his family—illustrated stories his friends had shared with her about his life. It looked like a stalker's collection, and she felt positively mortified.

"Thank you," he said, slowly closing the portfolio and setting it back on the dresser.

Deanna waited for him to elaborate. When he didn't, she asked, "For what?"

He turned around then and leaned back against the dresser as if they had all the time in the world. "For coming here…after me. For the drawings. For caring."

Deanna swallowed hard. *Oh hell*, she was really messing things up. She had come here to save a stranger, and now that she'd met him, she was about to kill him. "I'm sorry," she mumbled.

Nachari crossed the room again, his gait a little more purposeful this time. He squatted in front of her once more and drew in a deep breath. "Sorry for what?"

Her mouth fell open. He knew…for what.

"For being scared to death of demons and snakes and…panthers? For being scared to death of me?" He gently shrugged his shoulders. "That's okay."

She bit her bottom lip and nodded, surprised by the sudden onset of tears welling in her eyes.

Nachari sat down on the floor and glanced once again at the clock.

Deanna started to ask him what time it was but bit back the question in shame.

"Six forty-eight," he answered, as if reading her mind.

"Twelve minutes," she whispered, looking away.

"Twelve minutes," he echoed.

She cleared her throat. "I don't suppose…" She stopped and tried again. "I don't suppose that maybe…maybe you could just give me a few minutes…some time to collect myself."

Nachari smiled a devilish grin. "Seriously? I'm assuming that was a rhetorical question."

She swallowed a lump of anxiety and worried her bottom lip. "No, not seriously," she agreed. "It's just…" Her words trailed off.

"It's just," he prompted.

"It's just—you're really freaking me out."

He laughed then, completely unrestrained. "You're really freaking *me* out."

Her eyes lit up with mock indignation. "No, I'm not," she argued. "How can I be? Hell, I'm a grown woman hiding under a desk—how threatening can that be?"

He started to say something humorous and stopped himself. "Look, sweetie—"

"I wish you wouldn't call me that…yet." She immediately felt like the world's greatest jerk for saying it. What in the world was wrong with her? She was being positively…juvenile.

"Okay," he said softly. "Mrs. Silivasi?"

"Dubois," she retorted.

He blinked in surprise. "Oh." He looked at her curiously. "We aren't mated then? You didn't come through the conversion?"

She huffed, exasperated. "Yes. *Yes!* Of course, I did; it's just that…" She looked away, feeling foolish.

"You don't like my name then?" His voice revealed a playful charm.

"I don't know your name." She rushed the words, realizing immediately that they were utterly nonsensical.

He drew back in surprise. "You don't know *my name?*" He blanched. "Damn, my brothers really do suck."

"I know your name!" she exclaimed. "Oh, God." She scrubbed her face with her hands, wishing she could just disappear. "I meant I don't know *you*…yet."

He laughed softly, a pure hypnotic sound. "I'm sorry," he whispered sincerely. "I shouldn't tease you like that; I knew what you meant." Drawing her in with his smile, he continued: "So what are we to do then, Ms. Dubois? Because I have to be honest—right now, I find you positive *adorable*; and if we had more time, I think I could do this all night." He glanced at the clock. "Unfortunately, that doesn't seem to be the case."

Her eyes followed his, and she almost felt as if she might panic. She did not want to lose this man. "You hate me," she whispered, wholly surprised by her own statement.

His smile was positively radiant and more than just a little mischievous. "Um, that would be a *no*. I can most definitely assure you of one thing: I do not hate you. Quite the contrary."

She eyed him warily. "You don't even know me."

His face took on a serious expression, and he leaned toward her. "Angel, I'm a wizard; I know a lot of things I probably shouldn't know." He gestured toward the chest of drawers and the portfolio full of drawings he had just thumbed through. "And by the look of those sketches, I think you could say the same—about me." He held her gaze, unwilling to look away. "My heart knows you, Deanna. My soul knows yours intimately."

When she averted her eyes, he reached out and placed the warmest hand she had ever felt on her forearm and caressed her wrist just above her pulse with his thumb. "Look, *Deanna*, the way I see it is this: You are one of the bravest, most courageous women I've never met." He chuckled at the play on words, but his eyes remained deathly serious. "And not unlike me, you've also been to hell and back. And right now, we have to do something"—she shifted nervously, and he reached under the desk with his other hand to gently grasp her chin and guide her gaze back to his—"we have to *create* something...*together*...that neither one of us is comfortable with." He released her chin but continued to caress her wrist. "This is harder for you because you're a woman. And you have to take down a barrier—allow me to cross a boundary—that should never be crossed without first being earned. And I..." He shrugged his shoulders. "I have to conduct myself as the world's worst lover, which, I can assure you, I'm not. But either way, it's a horrible predicament."

Deanna gasped at the frankness of his words, and the sound elicited another chuckle from Nachari. "Ahh...she smiles at last," he teased.

Deanna grabbed the collar of her robe and clutched it in two tight fists. "I'm dying here," she said, not sure what had provoked the confession. As tears of anxiety filled her eyes, she wiped them away and shook out her hands, trying to shake off the emotion. "God, I swear; I'm not usually a fruitcake."

"No worries," he said, "I'm not usually a panther...or a demon killer, but when in Rome...or when in hell, as it were..." His voice trailed off, and she couldn't help but chuckle softly.

"You're kind of crazy, aren't you?" she said.

"So I've been told," he replied. And then in a serious tone of voice, he added, "I'm scared, too, Deanna. Terrified, actually."

Deanna looked up at him with surprise. He was way too handsome—way too powerful—to be afraid of anything. "Of what?" And then it dawned on her. "Of dying?"

He scoffed in earnest. "I've spent the last three months of my life in hell. Death doesn't have quite the influence it used to have over me. No, I'm afraid of somehow harming the most important person in the world to me." He released her wrist and took her hand in his, careful not to grip it too hard. "I'm afraid of dishonoring your bravery with selfishness; of taking something I have no right to claim. But most of all, I'm afraid that these few moments we share together might be the last we ever have—and that one day, the regret will haunt you when I'm no longer around to comfort you."

Deanna could hardly believe her ears.

Of course his *passing* would haunt her.

Devastate her.

For the first time, she truly understood that this male was not sitting on the floor trying to seduce her—this wasn't an effort to convince her to have sex with him—he was just *being there* the only way he knew how; and he would die before he would force her or use magic to coerce her. She felt her body tremble and wished she could make it stop. Among other things, the entire situation was humiliating. Glancing at the clock, she took a deep breath: *nine minutes left...*

"Okay," she whispered, nearly forcing the words from her mouth. "Okay...just do it."

Nachari pulled back in surprise. "By myself?"

Deanna smiled and shook her head. "Oh God, you're...impossible."

He smiled in return, and truly, the entire room lit up. "Listen," he said softly—his voice was positively magical, "there will come a time, when you are ready, that I will make love to you, and you will know all the way down to your soul that you are cherished beyond imagining. But the gods haven't given us enough time to make that happen today. However, what I can do, I will, if you will let me: I can use my powers to make this easier—to take you someplace easy...disconnected...less overwhelming. I just need you to—"

"Trust you?" she said.

Nachari shook his head emphatically. "No. I'm not asking that—you don't know me." He leaned in closer and squeezed her hand. "To trust yourself, Deanna. The same way you trusted your drawings and your dreams. The same way you trusted your instincts when it came time to undergo the conversion. To listen to that wise, authentic voice inside of you that has always guided you—the part of you that has always faced adversity with courage and has always come out ahead. I don't have to know you all that well to sense your strength or to feel your courage, to know that whatever is inside of you, whatever that spark is that makes you unique, you aren't about to give it up now...or lose it to the likes of me. You're too determined. Too aware. I'm asking you to listen to that voice, Deanna, and to trust it...for me. Because this"—he gestured at the desk and the obvious fact that she was hiding beneath it—"isn't you."

Deanna looked up at the oak desk above her and barely avoided knocking her head on the wood. Ducking, she smiled self-consciously. "You're right." Slowly...hesitantly...she allowed him to pull her out from underneath the desk. Standing to her full height, she stretched her back and blushed when he regarded her with obvious appreciation.

"You're tall," he said, appraising her height approvingly.

"So are you," she said, glancing away.

"You're beautiful," he whispered. "*Very* beautiful."

She bit her bottom lip like a teenager on a first date. "Yeah, well, from everything I've heard, you don't need to be told that."

He laughed then, the sound both unrestrained and welcoming. "Come here," he whispered, placing a light hand on her waist and tugging her forward.

Deanna squealed and jumped away, and then she struggled to regroup: "Oh...shit...sorry." She shook her hands out to quell her nerves and glanced once again at the clock: *eight minutes.* "Okay, okay..." She regained her composure as best as she could.

Nachari tried another approach then. He came up behind

297

her and bent toward her ear, and she immediately shuffled her feet like a nervous horse prancing in place.

"Would you be still?" he said.

She responded with a crisp, short nod. "Yep, I can do that. Okay. *Okay*. I'm still...still as a cucumber."

Once again, he bent slowly to her neck, and she squirmed like a worm, clutching her arms to her chest instinctively. Again, she mumbled, "I'm sorry...I'm sorry."

"I haven't even touched you."

She wrung her hands together. "I know...I know...okay. Try again."

He dropped his head forward and laughed. "Try again?"

She nodded, then shifted in place. "Mmm hmm."

"Do you drink a lot of coffee?" he asked.

"Ha, ha—very funny," she retorted. "Do you drink a lot of blood?"

"Not lately," he drawled. Then bending to kiss her neck, he added, "But I could be persuaded—"

She leapt at least six inches in the air, inadvertently slamming the back of her head into his jaw and causing him to smash his teeth together.

He took an involuntary step back.

"Oh, God," she said, truly mortified this time, "I can't believe I just did that—did I hurt you?"

"Only my feelings," he said, testing his bite playfully.

Too anxious to go along, she glanced at the clock again and practically came unglued: *seven minutes*.

He shook off the collision, reached around her waist, and anchored her arms at her sides, all the while trying not to laugh as she hopped from one foot to the next in place. "Deanna!" He put some authority in his voice this time. "*Stop*. Be still—or I *will* have to bite you."

"Don't you dare," she said, her voice rising in pitch.

He tightened his grip on her arms and pulled her back against him, waiting while she slowly relaxed into him; and then he nuzzled his strong, angular jaw between the space beneath her ear and her shoulder.

"What are you doing?" she whispered, realizing that for all intents and purposes she had inexplicably regressed to the maturity level of a two-year-old, and she was making a complete and utter fool of herself.

"I *am* preparing to bite you," he murmured in her ear.

She stiffened. "No you're not. I—"

"Shh," he whispered. "Hush."

"Don't tell me to hush," she retorted. "You—"

And just like that, he bit her.

Actually bit her.

Deanna froze, completely astonished, as her mind tried to process the dual sensations of pain and pleasure radiating in her neck. She immediately recognized the familiar imprint of Nachari's venom flowing through her veins and—

Nachari was pumping his venom into her veins?

Why?

Before she could protest more enthusiastically, the floor gave way; she felt a vortex open beneath her; and they were suddenly somewhere else, flying high above the earth's surface. An unbelievable feeling of freedom and well-being engulfed her, enrapturing her senses, and then they were all at once descending, gently, like mere feathers in the wind, drifting slowly together, their bodies entwined in a graceful dance, toward a beach filled with crystal white sand.

It was beyond surreal, yet it was heavenly.

His hands were warm and strong against her waist, feeling for the ties on her robe, yet it didn't seem frightening. It didn't seem strange. It was like...he belonged.

Like they belonged.

Her robe fell open, and something deep inside her told her she should protest—stop him somehow, for some reason—but she couldn't imagine what it was. The sensation of soft sand beneath her back, warm sunshine against her face, and clear water brushing over her heels was just too heavenly. Too inviting. How had he known that this was her ultimate fantasy?

BLOOD SHADOWS

The one place she would most desire to make love?

The thought of making love to Nachari Silivasi seemed outrageous, but it was somehow too far removed from her consciousness to grapple with. She was free…weightless…beautiful.

Desired.

His hands swept beneath her hips, and she felt her body strain in his direction, becoming more and more pliant beneath his somehow distant ministrations.

Was he touching her?

Looking at her?

Seeing her body…naked?

A cool breeze swept beneath her robe, and she knew in an instant that he was—that the welcoming sensation of a gentle breeze against her skin was somehow Nachari's mouth—his lips, his tongue, exploring her body languidly.

Languidly?

Her mind fought for a purchase on reality.

They had seven minutes—maybe less than that—how could he be exploring her body languidly; and how could she feel such sweet sensations yet remain so disconnected from the immediacy of what was happening? It was like a strange, erotic dream.

Heat, like that of a burgeoning flame, began to engulf her core, and she almost gasped at the intensity of it. The fire burned, but not like a hot iron…not like a scorching sensation— there was no pain or fear. It was more like a building conflagration within her soul, a mounting need, a desperate yearning for…something.

"Oh…God…" What was he doing now?

She felt the muscles in her stomach contract even as her panties seemed to magically disappear, and for the faintest of moments, she understood that this was foreplay—he was preparing her body to accept his—and she wished that she could actually feel what he was doing.

Her wish was his command.

Hot breath wafted over her cool, erect nipples; the dual

sensation both teasing and alarming her with its erotic force. Her womb clenched in reaction, and she moaned.

The sound was distant to her ears.

Nachari seemed to appreciate this because his tongue traced a circle around the straining peaks, first one and then the other, before he gently drew her into his mouth and suckled.

Deanna fisted the sand, shocked by the overwhelming pleasure the male was giving her. He teased her with his fangs, his lips, his tongue—tasting, suckling, tugging ever so gently, before biting and then appeasing the sting with his breath. Her eyes drifted shut, and she arched her back instinctively.

His kneading hands tightened beneath her, massaging every thought from her brain, embracing her in a gentle strength and peaceful security that had her longing for...forever. She writhed beneath him, and he responded in kind, his firm, narrow hips pressing into hers, revealing for the first time a powerful, straining erection, as stiff and hard as iron.

He was thick and long and impressive, and the idea of his size sent waves of heat into her core; yet still, he remained elusive. Like he was there, but not entirely. She felt him, and yet she felt separate—at ease—alone on the beach.

Perfectly at peace.

She released the sand beneath her fingers and reached up to touch him. She had to connect more fully, to know the male beneath the power—the heart beneath the talented hands and mouth. "Nachari," she whispered, her voice heavy with desperation. "I need you to be here."

He rose above her then, and when she opened her eyes, she saw him fully. His face was etched with indescribable pleasure; his eyes filled with something she could only describe as love—but how was that possible? She stared at his sculpted lips, noticing for the first time how perfectly balanced—how smooth, firm, and shapely—they really were. "Kiss me," she pleaded, needing something she could hardly name.

Nachari bent to her mouth slowly, and the visage of his eyes, his hair, his skin, the knowledge that someone so incredibly beautiful was giving himself to her, filled her with wonder. And then their lips met, and the earth stood still.

There were no beaches or oceans or skies.

There was no past or future.

No Blood Curse or required sacrifice.

There was only the pure sensuality of the male above her and the exquisite pressure of his lips. Deanna tasted as much of him as she could, reveling in the flavor, the texture, the utter perfection that was him. His tongue danced with hers, sweeping, teasing, exchanging passion on a level she had never known before.

She wanted.

With every fiber of her being.

She needed.

To feel, to capture, and to know…all of him.

As his lips left hers and began a slow, torturous descent along her neck, her collarbone, stopping to lave exquisite attention on her breasts, she ran her hands along his sculpted, bare back and marveled at the arch in his spine, the dip near his hips, the two muscular globes that made up a magnificent ass. And still, she wanted more.

That primal, integral part of him that made him male.

The very essence of his soul.

No wonder a demon had fallen in love with him; he was beyond resisting. What had she ever been thinking?

His mouth made contact with her core, and she nearly jackknifed off the beach. As her thighs fell further apart, he nestled between her legs, settling in as if he had all of eternity to spend in her service; and then he placed one hand firmly on her stomach to hold her in place, the other at the top of her mound.

She groaned with anticipation as he began to rub slow, tight circles against her cleft, all the while making love to her with his mouth, his tongue, his teeth—as if he knew every single sensation that she felt. And truth be told, maybe he did.

As a pair of expert fingers slid down from her mound and entered her core, she whimpered. There was no way to contain

Tessa Dawn

the pleasure, the mounting sensations; and tears of ecstasy spilled out of her eyes.

She reached down and grasped a thick handful of hair, hoping she wasn't hurting him but helpless to stop herself. Tugging upward, she pleaded, "Now. I need you now—inside of me." He rose above her like an angel of mercy; perfect in form, body, and spirit; and she allowed her legs to fully part, practically writhing beneath him.

As he found his place between her thighs, she lost her ability to wait and reached down to guide his erection. Her hand didn't fit around the width of him—not even close. As she grappled with the realization that her open fist surrounded less than half of his enormous shaft, a small twinge of fear enveloped her.

It was quickly washed away as his mouth descended upon her breasts once again, taking each one in turn, until she forgot her own name.

She raised her hips to meet him, and he didn't disappoint: He entered her in one powerful thrust and immediately sealed their mouths together in an effort to kiss away the shocking, stretching sensation. As her body molded around his, she quivered in pleasure.

His rhythm was impeccable.

Long, slow, even strokes in an easy circular grind.

Alternating short then deep thrusts, teasing her with mere inches before once again giving her the full length of his shaft in mind-numbing sequences—all as he arched his magnificent back.

"Look at me, Deanna," he whispered, punctuating his words with a soft kiss on her mouth.

Unable to resist anything he might desire, she opened her eyes and stared for the first time into the true face of her destiny. Not a stranger. Not a wizard. Not just a vampire—but her forever partner.

The other half of her soul.

He smiled that magnificent grin, and any remaining resistance melted away. How could she have ever considered

303

letting him die? Or walking away?

He stroked her cheek with the palm of his hand and stared into her eyes, even as he continued to thrust in and out of her; and the intensity was almost unbearable. "You are fully with me, Deanna—without any Magick." His breath caught on the last word as a storm of sensation rocked his graceful body.

Deanna frowned in confusion, and then suddenly looked around her. They were no longer on the beach, and there was no ocean. There was no sky above her, no sand beneath her. And it wasn't a dream. Rather, they were lying in a guest room, just adjacent to the one she had occupied in Kagen's clinic for what seemed like forever, and they were definitely making love. Together. Apparently, they had neither had the time nor the inclination to get to Kristina's apartment.

Her eyes sought out a clock: *eight thirty!*

They had been making love for an hour and a half?

She immediately glanced out the window and noticed the complete darkness outside. "Oh my god!" she exclaimed, panic finding a real place in her heart. "The time...Nachari...*no!*"

He pressed his fingers to her lips and shook his head. "Shh...it's okay." He smiled sheepishly then. "I did...*what was necessary*...in the first two minutes, and you've been pregnant ever sense." He slowed his pace to a slow grind and pressed his pubic bone against her clitoris. "This...is for you."

Deanna gasped at the pleasure and sighed with relief. "You've been making love to me"—her voice caught as her womb contracted in a pre-orgasmic spasm—"all this time?" He raised his eyebrows with self-appreciation, and for the first time, Deanna saw the confident—if not slightly arrogant—wizard many of her new friends and family had told her so much about.

She laughed with appreciation, and her heart leapt with joy. He was exactly who they had said he was.

And then, without warning, her body splintered into a million pieces as the *real,* intimate orgasm he had worked so patiently to give her erupted and sent her spiraling into the cosmos—and beyond.

Tessa Dawn

A moment later, she felt Nachari's back arch and stiffen. His muscles tightened in a powerful spasm; and his penis began to pulse in violent waves of pleasure as his seed poured into her...

And in that moment, she couldn't help but think that what held him to her was...love.

twenty-seven

Nachari stepped out of the shower, toweled off, and donned a pair of Kagen's extra scrubs. It was the best he could do under the circumstances. Strolling back into the room with his usual, confident swagger, he caught the eye of the beauty on the bed and quickly padded to her side. Tracing a slow circle around her belly button, he smiled mischievously. "Hi," he said, grinning for all he was worth, "I'm Nachari."

Deanna laughed and playfully slapped his hand away. "You, I'm starting to believe, are an idiot."

Nachari laughed, a rich, natural sound, and then he shook his head in earnest. "No. Not at all. In fact, I'm practically a sage."

Deanna rolled onto her side and brushed a long lock of hair away from her face. "Yeah? So what divine wisdom do you have to share with me now, my handsome sage?"

"Well," he said, frowning and looking away as if in serious contemplation. "Right now, I'm divining the close proximity of my brothers; they're waiting for me in Kagen's office." He pressed two fingers to his forehead as if tapping into some deep, hidden information. "And if I don't go to them in—oh, let's say about sixty seconds—all three of them are going to be in this room, in this bed, with us."

Deanna cringed and pulled up the covers. "Go," she said.

He smiled lovingly then. "Will you wait for me, pregnant woman?"

She covered her eyes with her hands. "Where else am I going to go?"

He shrugged his shoulders. He was about to say *to hell if you don't pray*, but the familiar refrain was no longer funny.

Not even a little bit.

He took a deep breath to clear his mind. "Seriously, though,

Deanna—I really don't want to leave you, not even for a minute, but I do need to see them."

Deanna reached up and stroked his face, albeit tentatively. "I understand. I do."

He smiled, pleased by her touch. "Things are going to happen very quickly from this point forward," he said. "The birth, the sacrifice, our marriage and naming ceremonies—the next forty-six hours of this pregnancy may be the only private time we have together for quite a while, and there is so much we need to talk about."

"I know." She nodded. "I have a dozen questions…and concerns."

Nachari regarded her with deep appreciation. He fingered a lock of her soft brown hair and smiled. "Things have happened so fast," he said quietly. "We have hardly had a chance to talk, to get to know each other, and there are so many things we need to discuss—things we have to deal with right away." He looked down at his hands and absently turned them over, as if studying them intently. "I'm so sorry about everything, Deanna—everything you've had to go through, the fact that I wasn't here to walk you through it…slowly. The fact that you're looking at a man you don't really know—one who wants nothing more in this entire world than to make you happy."

She studied his face thoughtfully, as if measuring his sincerity, and then she slowly smiled. "I know that. I do."

"Do you?" he asked, arching his brows.

She nodded. "I think so."

He took her hand in his, hoping to convey the depth of his sincerity. "I hope so," he said, "because it's very important to me that you know that *I get it*. That I understand."

She met his gaze with interest. "Get what?"

He squeezed her hand. "I get that your life has been turned upside down, and I do understand how many sacrifices you've made—are still making—for me. And I'd like to believe, at least to some extent, that I also *get* what kind of person you are."

Her gaze lingered on his mouth, and he bent down to kiss

her. When at last he pulled away, he sighed. "We *will* talk about everything, Deanna: Where we're going to live—whether my brownstone is something that will work for us or not—your art, your friends, your life back in New Orleans—I do assume you have a job—and how we're going to define our new life together going forward. I know that it has to reflect both of us equally: our choices, our needs, and desires." He released her hand, leaned back, and considered his words carefully. "You have to understand: From my perspective, both as a male and a vampire, you are unequivocally mine, and I would never let you go"—he made a concerted effort to soften his voice—"but I do understand that you bring your own perspective to this mating, and we will find common ground. On everything."

Deanna propped herself up on one elbow and turned toward him. "I'm glad that you see it that way." Her voice was uncharacteristically serious. "The fact that you...respect my individuality...will save us a lot of grief."

Nachari chuckled. "I wouldn't have it any other way." He glanced at the door, feeling the unrelenting pull of his brothers tugging at his heart. "Rest for a minute then; and when I return, we will talk." He hesitated for a moment, wondering if he should say anything else right now...or wait...

"What is it?" Deanna asked, seeming to sense his reluctance.

He held her gaze. "There is one thing that is too important to treat...democratically. And perhaps it would be best for you to think about it while I'm gone."

"Okay," she said, raising her eyebrows. "I'm listening."

"Sweetheart, we cut things very close last night, as you know. And that means I will have less than five minutes from the time the Dark Child is born to place him on the altar in the Chamber of Sacrifice and Atonement, to relinquish his body to the Blood—or I *will* be dead. There is no room for hesitation—or error—which means there is no time for processing, mine or yours. I *will* do what I have to do, no matter how it appears...or affects you: Do you understand?"

This time, it was Deanna who took his hand in hers. "I have

a fairly high IQ, Wizard," she said, meeting his intensity with a strength of her own. "And I do understand—I've already thought about it." She softened her tone and smiled sympathetically. "Do you always worry so much?"

Nachari exhaled with relief. "Actually, I rarely worry at all— just ask our king."

To his amusement, Deanna cringed. "Yeah, well, I'll get right on that—maybe next millennia." She chuckled lightheartedly. "In the meantime, go see your brothers."

Nachari wrapped a gentle arm around her and pulled her to him. Kissing the top of her head, he said, "You are loved, Deanna...desperately, madly, deeply...even if you think it's too soon."

She momentarily lost her composure, then quickly regained it. "Now you stop..." He raised his eyebrows in question, and she simply shook her head. "It's just...this is all so... overwhelming...that's all." Pushing against his chest, she added, "Go. Before they come in here. *Go.*"

Grateful beyond measure for her words and her kindness, Nachari rose from the bed and headed out the door.

Marquis, Nathaniel, and Kagen were waiting rather impatiently in Kagen's office when Nachari sauntered through the door like it had been only days since he last saw them. Each one stood at attention, their eyes fixed on his, and as much as he had told himself that his emotions would not get the best of him, they did.

His shoulders nearly shook from the realization that he was actually standing among his brothers again.

Kagen approached him first. He crossed the room in three long strides and wrapped his heavy arms around him. "Brother," he exhaled, as if he had been holding his breath for months, "I...I have no words."

Tessa Dawn

Nachari returned the embrace—it was not as if he could have broken the unyielding hold if he wanted to, which he didn't. "Kagen," Nachari whispered. "Thank you. I can only imagine what this time has been like for you."

And just like that, Kagen's floodgates broke loose. "You have no idea." The memories seemed to converge, one after the other, all the things Kagen couldn't express before now, all the burdens he had been forced to carry; and when he began to speak again, his words rolled off his tongue in an anxious, heartfelt litany: "I couldn't bring you back. I couldn't make it right. I couldn't fix whatever was wrong. I don't know...what I was doing...I didn't know...I'm...I'm so sorry!"

Nachari choked back his emotion. "You didn't do anything wrong, Kagen." He pushed away from his brother and gripped him by both shoulders. "Look at me." Kagen's eyes were distant and so full of remorse that it nearly broke Nachari's heart. "You didn't do anything wrong."

"You...you suffered?" Kagen posed it as a question, but it was really a statement.

Nachari looked away. "It's over."

"Is it?" Marquis broke in. He stepped away from the wall in order to join Kagen and Nachari in the center of the room. "Are you...are you handling it?"

Nachari shook his head and looked down. "Time heals..." His words trailed off.

"We have to know..." Nathaniel spoke with deep emotion and compassion. "Whatever those demons put you through, we have to help...somehow."

To his own dismay, Nachari started to shake. "Don't ask, Nathaniel. Just don't." He swallowed hard and glanced away. "I can't process it right now...maybe ever. It's...too much."

Marquis placed his hand on Nachari's shoulder. "We all failed you, myself most of all. I should have never let you—"

"*Stop!*" Nachari said. His voice was sharp with insistence, nearly bordering on anger. "Just stop." He threw his hands up in an unusual show of frustration. "My mind was made up, and you

311

know it. Besides, this is not about you." He stared at Marquis, Nathaniel, and Kagen, each brother in turn, in a rare demonstration of challenge. "It's not about any of you, so let's get one thing straight right now: We are not going to discuss who let me go; or who couldn't bring me back; or who supported my decision to go after Napolean. That is all ancient history." He knew that his words were uncharacteristically harsh and that he might even sound irrational, but there was so much his brothers just didn't understand: so much horror and trepidation still bottled up inside.

So much confusion about who he was, what he had endured, and what he had done—while stranded in the Valley of Death and Shadows.

Until this moment, he hadn't truly realized just how terrified he was that he might have sold his soul, become a monster.

Now, standing in the warm, accepting embrace of his brothers, it was like someone had held up a mirror, illuminated all of his own questions and confusion, and he simply wasn't ready to gaze into the looking glass. "For as long as I can remember," he said, "I've been the one that made it all okay— whatever *it* is—for the rest of us, the one that smoothed things over with a word or a joke, that offered an explanation, no matter how inane; but I can't fix this for you guys this time—not and maintain my own sanity. I can't really deal with your questions…" He turned to look at Marquis. "Or your regret…not right now." He shrugged, unashamed to let his confusion show. "I'm sorry."

Marquis looked utterly stunned and deeply troubled. "Nachari, we just want to know—"

"Know what?" he interrupted. "What do you want to know, brother?" He gave Marquis a halfhearted smile. "What they did to me? What I did while I was there?" He laughed, but the sound was completely devoid of humor. "No—you don't. Trust me on that one. *You don't.*" He wrapped his arms around his middle and stepped backward as if he could simply retreat from the conversation.

Tessa Dawn

"Sometimes, imagination is worse than reality," Nathaniel whispered thoughtfully. "Not knowing is a hell all its own."

Nachari frowned sardonically. "How easily we throw that word around, brothers—*hell*. Well, I can assure you that nothing we think of as hell even comes close." He let out a deep sigh, wishing his words would fall a little softer. "What do you want to hear, Nathaniel?" His tone was severe but still remained polite. "That I was brutalized, beaten, lashed, and even boiled? That I conjured spells from the Book of Black Magic, shared my essence with a demon to make her love me? That I *ate* the flesh of my enemy, or that I prayed for death...every day? Because I did, you know. *Every day*...until Deanna came. But the joke was on me—because death wouldn't come." He met his brothers' horror-stricken gazes. "It wouldn't come. And now that I'm back, all I can think about is the fact that there might be something so dark, so malignant, in my soul that I can't even fathom its potential to cause harm to others." He scrubbed his hands over his face, revealing his weariness. "How do you think I got out of there, Nathaniel? By telling jokes or making friends?" His head began to pound—which was unheard of for a vampire—and he slowly rubbed his temples in small, gentle circles. "I don't even know what I am anymore—Vampyr or animal, wizard or sorcerer, good or evil—or something in between." He sighed. "I don't know if I'll be able to adjust back to a life without agony and brutality as its staples—without evil as its core. And, honestly, what does that say about me?"

"It says that you're strong and resourceful," Marquis responded without hesitation. "It says that you're a powerful Master Wizard and a formidable enemy."

Nachari nodded, more in appreciation than agreement. "Perhaps, brother. Perhaps. All I know is that there is a woman down the hall who is carrying my son—a child that needs a healthy and stable father—and somehow, I have to try to figure this out, to grasp at proverbial straws if necessary, to make that happen....for her. For Deanna. So, please, don't ask me to make it happen for you, too. To connect the dots or smooth it

313

out…or make it okay. Because I can't; and it's not. And I'm just doing my best to breathe from one moment to the next." Truly feeling breathless, he stood before them feeling more naked and vulnerable than he had ever felt before, a part of him wishing he could just retreat inside of himself and live like a hermit for the rest of his days.

"You don't have to fix anything," Kagen said quietly. "But as to your questions about light and goodness…the purity of your soul. Grapple with them if you must, but don't expect us to join you. You and Shelby were born with two of the purest souls I've ever known."

Nathaniel stepped forward and placed a steadying hand on Nachari's shoulder. "Brother, you are not wicked—not in your soul. Such a thing could never even happen—like attracts like. Evil seeks after its own kind. The vibrations would never match. *You survived*. And that is all."

When Nachari inadvertently dropped his shoulder from beneath Nathaniel's hand and tried to step away, Nathaniel took a calculated step forward and blocked his path. "Where do you think you're going?"

Nachari shrugged, feeling slightly overwhelmed and more than a little trapped. His brothers meant well, but they truly didn't understand the depth of the turmoil inside of him.

Kagen chimed in stubbornly. "You're not alone, Nachari, not anymore. And we aren't going to let you retreat into yourself behind this."

Nachari didn't know if he should thank them or curse them, but one thing was for sure: They weren't backing off anytime soon.

"That woman down the hall let you into her life, her soul, her body—even after everything she witnessed with that demon," Kagen continued. "And do you know why? Because somewhere deep inside, she recognized your soul. She knows who you are. What you are. Just as we do. Forgive us if we sound dismissive or insensitive, but you don't get to dismiss her judgment—and ours—quite that easily."

Tessa Dawn

Marquis waved a glib hand through the air as if to say, *There will be no further debate on this matter.* "You will not bear this alone," he declared in his usual matter-of-fact style. "That is all there is to it." He paused to consider his next words. "We will suffer together, heal together, or go up in flames together. But you will not bear this alone."

Moved by the weight of all he was feeling—and hearing—Nachari sank to his knees. *Dear gods, where was all this emotion coming from?*

In an uncommon act of gentleness, Marquis knelt down before him, reached out to cup his head in a giant hand, and cradled it against his shoulder, much like he would a baby. "Give it time, Nachari. You just got back. We are with you. We believe in you more than you know." In a forced, lighthearted voice, he added, "Maybe you are the one who needs therapy now, yes?"

Shocked by the impropriety of the statement—not to mention the fact that Marquis had just tried to make a joke—Nachari couldn't help but smile. "Wow, Marquis. Really? That's your...comfort?"

"Is it working?" Marquis asked.

Nachari shrugged and chuckled, and Marquis finally let him go. Meeting the Ancient Master Warrior's eyes, Nachari said, "I'm sorry if I sounded disrespectful before; I've just been keeping so much bottled up inside. Sometimes I don't know whether to shout, break down, or just fly off the handle. And I'm trying so hard to be strong for Deanna."

Marquis snorted. "That's okay. You are just a wizard, after all." His eyes brightened with mischief. "Do you need me to let you kick my ass?"

Nachari smiled an arrogant grin then. "Haven't you been listening? Don't be so sure I couldn't do it all on my own now."

Marquis considered the statement, his face a mask of quiet contemplation. Finally, he raised his eyebrows and conceded. "Hmm, perhaps with the aid of Magick you could."

Kagen smirked. "Finally...someone who can take Marquis."

Nachari knew the comment was half tongue-in-cheek: In the

315

worst throes of a Mr. Hyde rage, Kagen Silivasi could take just about anyone. Perhaps even a demon. Still, he chuckled.

Nathaniel softened. "Nachari," he said, once again commanding his full attention. "I think the point is: It's all good now. Whatever it is. It's all good. You're home."

Nachari met Nathaniel's eyes with gratitude, and then, suddenly aware that someone was missing, he looked up at Kagen. "Where is Braden? Does he even know I'm back?"

"He knows," Kagen answered, "and he's waiting to see you at the naming ceremony—if he doesn't have a chance to meet up with you before then—which I know he would prefer."

"Good," Nachari said. "I can only imagine what this has been like for him."

"See," Marquis pointed out. "Now, are those the words of some half-cocked, half-evil nut job? You're not going to go all demon crazy on that kid or anyone else, Nachari. I'm not even worried." He looked away for a minute. "Well, unless you want to do something wicked to Kristina—that might be okay. Speaking of which, can you bring the panther back at will?"

"Marquis!" Kagen and Nathaniel chided in unison.

"Now is not the time, brother," Nathaniel explained.

"What?" Marquis retorted. "It was a reasonable question."

"What happened with Kristina?" Nachari asked, ignoring Marquis's antics.

"Later," Nathaniel said. "There is much we need to tell you to bring you up to speed, but it can all wait until later."

"She lost her ever-loving, redheaded mind; that's what happened," Marquis offered.

"*Marquis,*" Nathaniel barked at him. "Seriously, dude—chill!"

Marquis shrugged his shoulders. "Very well, but Nachari has to promise to call us if he has another mental breakdown so we can psychoanalyze the problem and fix it." He turned toward Nachari and frowned. "Promise me this, and you can go back to your woman." And then he winked.

Winked.

Marquis Silivasi was making fun of himself, and in that rare, unfamiliar moment, Nachari knew for the first time that things were really going to be okay.

twenty-eight

Deanna watched in utter fascination as Nachari wove an intricate pattern of designs in the air with his fingers. She immediately felt the energy stir all around her and became breathless with anticipation.

The companion that stood next to the Master Wizard was equally enthralled. His vivid, burnt-sienna eyes were wide with expectancy, and his mouth was practically hanging open; yet he stood so tall and proud, his back straight, his chest puffed outward. Clearly, Braden took his duties quite seriously.

Nachari had asked the young vampire to come to the clinic for the birth of their son. In a gesture meant more to appease the boy than assist with the event, he had told him, with all seriousness, that he would have to move very quickly to appease The Blood with the required sacrifice, and that meant Deanna would need a protector—someone to help with the baby—while Nachari was gone. The kid had been practically giddy with eagerness.

Deanna had to admit that she had shed more than one tear as she witnessed Braden and Nachari's reunion; the fact that the boy had been utterly lost without him—that Braden loved Nachari dearly with his whole heart and soul—could not have been missed by anyone. The fact that Nachari clearly felt the same might have been more of a revelation, one she looked forward to watching unfold over the years to come.

Now, staring up at the swirling rainbow of color surrounding her belly, Deanna held her breath as Nachari bowed his head gracefully and begin to recite an eloquent prayer in the ancient tongue. Although Deanna did not understand the words, the rhythm was hypnotic and beautiful, mystical in its simplicity and purity.

And then, just like that, Nachari commanded his unborn son

319

into the world, and the baby began to appear.

Beautiful, glistening light arced above Deanna's belly, and a whooshing sound, like water rushing through a rapid river, filled the air. The luminescent colors began to coalesce into a dim outline—into the form of an infant—and slivers like that of gold dust flaked off in its wake. Deanna's heartbeat increased as her eyes fixed intently on the miracle before her: Nachari reached out his strong hands, placed them just above her belly, palms open wide, and the child simply materialized inside of them.

Deanna gasped in wonder, struggling to sit up and see.

The infant was beautiful!

Beyond beautiful.

Perfect!

Stunning green eyes stared back at her, their hue a perfect match to Nachari's; and copper-tanned skin covered his wriggling arms and legs, a perfect match to the tone of her own. His hair was thick and downy, almost black, but there were clear highlights of brown throughout. He was truly a mixture of both of them. "Oh, Nachari," she breathed, unable to contain her adoration. "Let me hold him."

The Master Wizard blinked back a tear as he placed the child in Deanna's arms. "Sebastian Lucas Silivasi—meet your mother, Deanna."

Deana laughed aloud as she heard Nachari speak the baby's name for the first time; they had chosen to name him after her father, and thus, the Spanish origin of the name.

Braden Bratianu practically bounced up and down on his tippy toes—his eyes as wide as saucers now. "Can I see him? Can I see him?"

Nachari smiled in the gentle, fatherly way Deanna was already becoming familiar with. "Of course," he said. "But be gentle with him."

Braden gave Nachari a cross look and frowned. "I know how to handle babies. I look after Storm and Nikolai all the time."

Nachari held his hands up in apology, his voice contrite. "Of course you do. My bad."

Braden seemed to like this.

And then, Nachari brushed his fingers gently over the back of Deanna's hand. "Sweetheart, I have to call the unnamed one now. Would you rather look away?"

Deanna nodded. "Yes, I would." She turned her attention to the door and briefly closed her eyes. Both Jocelyn and Ciopori were waiting outside, should she need them. After all, the women had been with her through so much already—they had all waited together for Nachari to return from the Abyss—and Deanna hadn't known, until that very moment, whether or not she would take advantage of their offer to help her through the birth. But now, as the inevitable approached, she knew she would benefit from their presence. "Nachari, would you—"

"Call your new sisters?" he supplied.

"Yes." She nodded. "I'm sorry; I know this is supposed to be private"—she glanced at Braden and smiled—"*semi-private*, but I think—"

"No explanation needed," he said.

"Thank you." She turned her attention back to the child in her arms and waited while Nachari contacted the women telepathically. The door opened immediately, and Ciopori was the first to enter, her regal stride and unearthly beauty preceding her.

"Greetings, sister," she called in her usual formal manner.

"Hi, Ciopori," Deanna said, beaming as she gestured toward the firstborn infant.

Ciopori drew in a deep, bedazzled breath. "Oh my gods..." She hurried to the bed and sat down beside Deanna. "He is *magnificent*." She looked up at Nachari and nodded her approval.

Jocelyn entered more quietly, her mood a bit more somber. She took a place on the other side of the bed beside Deanna, and reached out to stroke the baby's cheek. "He is as handsome as his father," she said appreciatively; and then she lightly tousled Deanna's hair and smiled. "And how's the mom?"

Deanna shook her head in disbelief. "Mom? That's gonna

take some getting used to."

"Indeed," Ciopori offered.

Nachari cleared his throat, clearly a little uncomfortable with the audience. "I'm sorry, sisters, but time…" He glanced at the clock. "We don't have any."

Ciopori turned to face Deanna directly then, her eyes locked only with hers. "Do you wish to see?"

"No!" Deanna said, without hesitation.

"Very well." With a graceful arc of her hand, Ciopori wove an illusion much like a dense fog over the bed and waited while it coalesced between Deanna and her belly. "You will see only us, then."

Deanna had to constantly remind herself that Ciopori Demir-Silivasi was one of the original females—she was an ancient princess from a Celestial race—and consequently, she had access to a different kind of magic, a power no one else in Dark Moon Vale could rival. Grateful, she held Ciopori's gaze and nodded. "Thank you…I'm ready."

Without delay, Nachari called forth the second child, an evil hiss filled the air, and the room went deathly quiet. Even Braden looked away.

Deanna blanched. "Oh my God, what's wrong? Is he—"

"Evil," Jocelyn said. "Don't look, Deanna."

"But I thought they always came out acting and looking…beautiful…deceptive. Like that was also part of the Curse."

The women listened in stunned horror as the Dark Child growled and spat at his father before releasing a pair of rapidly flapping wings. It was obvious that there was some kind of struggle going on as Nachari immediately switched into wizard-mode and began chanting a verbal spell to control the unruly being in his arms.

"I've never heard of one coming out as a demon, evil both inside and out," Jocelyn whispered to Ciopori, immediately regretting her words. "Oh, Deanna—*I'm sorry*. I'm such an idiot."

Deanna shook her head. Her greatest concern right now was for Nachari. While he knew the second child was soul-less, cursed from birth, an evil apparition that only appeared human—or vampire as it were—in order to fool and torment his parents as part of the Curse, this moment could not be easy. Nachari Silivasi had been prepared all of his life for this situation, and he was doing an incredible job hiding his inner turmoil. Still, Deanna knew that there was a war raging inside her newfound mate: that Nachari was struggling with the light or darkness of his own soul. Ever since his return from hell, there had just been something…distant…something he either didn't care to talk about—or didn't want to face. The emergence of a clearly evil child had to be a blow of epic proportions.

"The child is not of your soul, nor of Nachari's," Ciopori stated emphatically, speaking loud enough for Nachari to hear. "He is the spawn of the Blood, the progeny of malice, hatred, and vengeance. No part of your soul is in his." It was almost like she knew what they were all thinking.

Deanna nodded, gathering strength for Nachari. In her mind's eye, she could still see her very first drawings—the images that had brought her to Dark Moon Vale in the first place—and she would never forget the tortured soul on the stone. Nachari had suffered more than enough; he did not need any more pain.

"Take him, and get it over with," Deanna said, her voice strong with conviction. "Then come back to me and Sebastian."

Nachari had finally managed to silence the Dark Child, no doubt using considerable magic to do so. "I'll be back as soon as I can." His voice was steady and even, but Deanna knew that there was a world of turmoil simmering beneath it.

"We'll be here," Deanna offered, wishing she could say more.

Nachari nodded. "Okay."

With that, Deanna reached up and gripped his forearm in a powerful grasp. "*Nachari…*"

His eyes locked with hers.

BLOOD SHADOWS

"We will be here."

His gorgeous mouth turned up in a faint smile, and his eyes registered understanding. "Thank you."

Nachari watched with calloused indifference as the ethereal hands of The Blood reached up with skeletal fingers, funneled through dense black smoke, and snatched the child from the altar, leaving the smooth granite basin empty once more on the large oval platform. He had offered the prayer of supplication with the same level of indifference and was beginning to wonder if he was even capable of feeling anymore.

The birth of Sebastian had been so amazing, yet the emergence of something so clearly evil, so obviously foul and unholy, had shaken him to his core.

Regardless of what Ciopori had said, he felt like his seed had created that monster: The child's eyes had even shone a deep emerald green before flashing demonic red.

Nachari sat back on his heels and waited patiently for the shrill cries and shrieks to end, for the inky darkness to recede, and for the just plain exaggerated antics that The Blood always put on during its hideous, vengeful rituals to come to a close— wishing it would just hurry-it-up.

As if.

Nachari had spent over four months in hell, living in the Middle Kingdom with the supreme lord of darkness himself. This sick, vengeful aberration of all things holy was hardly worth his attention. Deanna had been right: *Get it over with, already.* "Forgive me if I'm not impressed," he mumbled beneath his breath.

The Blood shrieked in angry defiance, but it was all smoke and mirrors. There was nothing it could do to him now...or ever again. He had fulfilled the demands of the Blood Curse, and he was, at last, free from it...forever.

When, finally, the macabre show had stopped, Nachari rose from the chamber and started to head home, to return to Deanna and his son, to begin building a new life with the woman who waited so devotedly for him.

And then he thought better of it.

Less than fifty feet away was another set of doors, a holding cell that sat adjacent to the Chamber of Sacrifice and Atonement. It was one of several large halls that made up Napolean's compound, the official complex behind his manse, which ultimately included the Death Chamber, and it was also the place where Shelby had lost his young life.

But Nachari had no interest in ever visiting that place again.

It was what stood beside it that held his interest: the cell where Napolean held Saber Alexiares until Sunday's upcoming execution.

He licked his bottom lip, wondering if he should just leave well enough alone. Over the past forty-six hours, he had learned all about Salvatore's insidious plot and Saber's role in pretending to be Ramsey Olaru in an effort to get to Kristina. And he had learned about the incident in the hot tub with Deanna. There was nothing good that could come from standing face-to-face with another evil being so soon. The last thing he needed was to eat Saber, too.

Still, something extremely territorial—something programmed deep into his primal, Vampyr DNA—would not let him walk away. Turning on his heel, he headed toward the holding cell, and the enemy of his kind.

twenty~nine

Once the decision had been made, Nachari didn't hesitate to stroll confidently into the rectangular holding cell where Saber Alexiares lay, chained with heavy manacles, to a narrow cot, his body revealing the evidence of recent, unhealed torture. And Saber's guards hadn't dared to try and stop him, although Ramsey had warned Nachari to leave the bastard alive.

Now, as Nachari stared at the enemy of his house—the monster that had attacked Deanna—he struggled to connect with his feelings.

Saber smiled like a lazy cat. "Wizard," he said, his voice full of contempt. "I was wondering when you would come to see me."

Nachari feigned indifference. "Well, good—then I don't disappoint."

"Come to exact your pound of flesh?" Saber asked.

Nachari shook his head. "Maybe. Maybe not."

"Ah," Saber drawled, "to chat then. Well, I would sit up and greet you properly, but as you can see, I'm a bit tied up at the moment."

Nachari scowled. "You're in an unusual state of good humor for a male who's about to be fed to the sun." He watched Saber closely for any sign of reaction, but the Dark One's face remained stoic. In that moment, Nachari knew that Saber Alexiares was truly a bad-ass in real life—he didn't just play one on TV. This wasn't just a front.

"Shit happens," Saber said.

"Indeed it does," Nachari retorted. He grabbed a metal chair, dragged it across the room, and straddled it backward directly in front of Saber's cot. The male looked at him warily, and his heartbeat sped up, if only infinitesimally. Apparently, Saber wasn't completely indifferent to pain and torture. How well

327

Nachari understood. "Do you have any idea how bad it's going to hurt? The sun, that is?" Nachari asked, actually just wondering.

Saber didn't smile then. "What's it to you?"

"Nothing," Nachari answered honestly. "For me, the sun's just a good source of vitamin D. Maybe a tan. But for you...ouch."

"That's why you came here, Wizard?" Saber said derisively. "To taunt me?"

"In a way," Nachari answered.

Saber gave him a cool, sideways glance, not quite able to figure him out.

"I came here for Deanna," Nachari said, his voice remaining eerily steady, "not that you would understand that kind of loyalty or devotion." He leaned forward in the chair and placed his folded arms against the back, elbows resting on the metal. "But I wasn't sure until now what I was going to say...or do."

"And now you've got some sudden sense of clarity?" Saber chuckled derisively. "Do tell."

Nachari snickered. The male was quite the smart-ass, but it didn't matter. "Do...tell..." he repeated. "Well, let's see—what I could I possibly have to tell you...about where you are going: The Valley of Death and Shadows."

Now this caught the Dark One's attention.

"I could tell you that there are five provinces, each one ruled by a different prime lord, and that each territory has a kingdom...servants...minions...and slaves...a wasteland that surrounds it. I could tell you that our kind, the Vampyr, are used as slaves for the purposes of entertainment by torture at the hands of the demons—kind of like a show they put on to amuse themselves." He shrugged. "They're very creative, the demons: They like to break bones, pierce our flesh and joints, whip us until our skin falls off, boil us in scalding baths...the list just goes on and on. As does the torture and their amusement." He pushed back from the chair and stood up then. "I can't actually say that I saw any of your brothers—males from the house of

Jaegar—during my enlightening stay, but I heard about them. And I knew that my fate with the dark lord Ademordna was their fate every day of eternity. That it's going to be yours."

Saber's face turned a sickly pallor, but the contempt never left his eyes.

"Yeah, I could tell you all about it in shocking detail," Nachari added. "Or I could just show you." With that, he took a step toward the bed, palmed the sides of Saber's head, and leveled a hate-filled gaze. "View my memories, Dark One, and know your future."

Nachari unleashed hell into Saber Alexiares's mind, pouring each memory, each agonizing second of the torture he had received in the Abyss, into Saber's consciousness as if by personal awareness: The defiant Dark One felt each act, each moment, as if he were experiencing it right then and there—as if time and space no longer existed and Nachari's hellish existence had become his own, and for the first time, the evil son of Jaegar lost his cool.

The Dark One bucked and screamed and showed true signs of insanity from the inescapable agony. His breath grew shallow. At times, his heart nearly stopped beating, and sweat poured from his brow as he grimaced and writhed on the cot, begging for absolution in languages Nachari didn't even recognize.

When at last there was nothing left to share, Nachari let him go and stepped away from the cot. The horror on Saber's face was beyond description.

Nachari checked his watch. "That was just ten minutes, Dark One," he said. "Imagine eternity."

He strolled toward the door and slowly turned around. "Oh, yeah, you don't have to imagine it. Soon enough, it will be your reality...forever." He winked at him then. "Sucks to be you, doesn't it?" Strolling out of the cell, Nachari rounded the corner with his usual poise and swagger, and then, the moment he was out of Saber's sight, he doubled over and reached for the wall.

Replaying those memories had taken a chunk out of his soul, and he felt like he was going to be sick.

"Are you all right, son?" A deep voice drew him from his misery.

Napolean.

"Milord." Nachari struggled to choke out the word.

Napolean rushed to his side, placed a hand on his back, and regarded him with concern. "Come, sit down."

Nachari shook his head. "No." He covered his mouth with his hand. "I just need a minute…"

Napolean nodded understanding. "Perhaps an eternity."

Nachari smiled faintly. Of course, the Great One knew. How could he not. "Yeah…perhaps." He took a long, measured breath and waited for his stomach to stop doing backflips.

When, at last, Nachari had regained his composure and his equilibrium, Napolean met his eyes with an unusually compassionate stare. "I was waiting to speak with you after the naming ceremony," the sovereign lord said, "but now is as good a time as any."

Nachari looked perplexed. "Milord?"

Napolean waved his hand and shook his head. "None of that…not from you."

None of that? Nachari thought. *What did that mean?* The sons of Jadon had always treated their king with the utmost respect and formality; it was both expected and proper. "I don't understand," Nachari said.

Napolean's gentle eyes assessed him warmly. "Don't you?"

Nachari shook his head and waited, and then he practically lost his balance when Napolean rested both hands firmly on his shoulders and held him in the embrace of equals…of brothers. "I am here because of you," Napolean said. "My *destiny* is here because of you. Our son—and your future king—*exists* because of you." Napolean narrowed his eyes. "What you did that day in the meadow; what you sacrificed and endured for our people…for our future…" His voice trailed off, and he had to clear his throat. "I can never express my gratitude—there simply are no words."

Nachari looked away, slightly embarrassed. "It was my duty,

milord."

"Yes," Napolean agreed, "and you paid a higher price than any soul should ever have to pay. If death is supposed to be the ultimate sacrifice, then what you gave—what you endured—is something altogether more."

Nachari blinked, embarrassed.

"And now," Napolean continued, his deep voice growing even deeper, "and now you fear some intangible blackness in your soul." It was simply laid out on the table like a noonday meal, displayed in plain sight for all the world to see; and Nachari didn't even bother asking how the king knew.

Napolean frowned then. "I cannot begin to know how deeply you were harmed in that place; what metaphorical, if not literal, demons you carry with you as a result of your sacrifice." He averted his eyes for a moment out of respect. "I can't know what it is like to reside inside of your mind right now, but I do know that you are no longer just a servant or a Master Wizard—not that you weren't always unique and gifted with potential—but now, you are my brother, Nachari. The one I never had." He thumped a solid fist over his chest to emphasize his next words. "You are my heart, Nachari Silivasi. You live here…in my soul."

Nachari swallowed his surprise and simply stared, dumbfounded, at Napolean, hoping his mouth wasn't gaping open. The wise, handsome king appeared wiser still, somehow changed, as intimidating as ever, but also accessible.

"And there is nothing I will not do," Napolean added, "to see that you are made whole again." He leaned over until his face was only inches away from Nachari's. "Even if it means taking your place…removing your memories by adopting them as my own."

Nachari stared back at him with stunned surprised. Vampires did not erase other vampires' memories; it was simply not done. But to take another's place—*in their memories*—was to literally trade time and reality between souls. To adopt one's past as if it were your own. To think their thoughts and remember their pain, not as theirs, but as yours, much like a male absorbed the pain of a female during a rapid pregnancy—but more. Napolean was offering to simply take it all away, and own it, live it, carry it himself...forever.

"I could never let you do that, milord," Nachari responded instinctively, still shocked by the very idea. "It is a very heavy weight I carry."

Napolean nodded. "I know this, son, and that's why I said *even if it means taking your place in your memories.* If I thought for one moment you would simply allow me to carry this weight for you, I would have already done it. If I could go into your mind, without your permission, it would already be so. But as it is, I can stand with you as a brother, watch over you as your king, and help you through this transition." He looked at him with an unbroken stare. "But know this: You are not the only practitioner of Magick in this valley. You are not the only one who is willing to break all customs, conjure contrary forces, and do whatever is necessary, in spite of the propriety of the deed. If the day comes when I determine that your mental or spiritual health is truly in jeopardy, I *will* take that which has not been given. I will not let you die for me twice, not in any sense of the word."

Nachari swallowed hard. He hadn't even thought about what it might be like to live without the knowledge of his time in the Abyss; to move forward without the repercussions, as if it never were. But to give the burden to Napolean?

Napolean held up his hand to halt Nachari's words before he could respond. "I'll be watching you, Nachari." And then he said something that Nachari never thought he would hear in a million years—not from the formidable, ancient leader of the house of Jadon. "I love you, brother."

Nachari opened his mouth to speak, shut it, and then opened it again—only to let it hang open and catch flies for a moment. "I think...I'm speechless."

Napolean rocked back on the balls of his feet then, apparently satisfied. "Am I that bad?" he teased.

"No!" Nachari said immediately before catching the joke.

"You're just…intimidating…and I've always secretly wondered when or if you were going to…kill me, actually."

Napolean laughed wholeheartedly. "Wizard, I'm going to have to reach into my grab bag of theatrical skills to even pretend to be angry with you from this day forward—and I know that you will do something eventually that requires my correction."

Nachari chuckled then. "Probably. Most likely."

Napolean shrugged. "I don't think you truly get it, but you will. In time. Our relationship has changed."

Nachari looked at him skeptically, and then, as if someone else had magically possessed his body, he threw a playful fist at the king's shoulder, socking him like he might have once done with Shelby, just to test his reaction.

Napolean rolled his eyes. "Oh, shit—what have I started?"

Nachari took a literal step back. "Did you say *shit?*"

Napolean shook his head. "No." And then he smiled.

Nachari grinned. "So, I can come play with your kid; drive your Land Cruiser; and TP your house on Halloween?"

Napolean chuckled deep and low in his throat, the reverberation giving Nachari pause. "You *will* come play with my kid—often; you will *never* get your hands on my Land Cruiser; and if you TP my house, then you had better watch your back." He paused for emphasis. "I said I was your brother, not a punk."

Nachari laughed loud and heartily then. *Wow.* Napolean Mondragon had a sense of humor.

Who knew?

Turning all at once serious, he crossed his arms in front of him. "There is something of importance I have to tell you, something I learned from the dark lords while I was away." He told Napolean about Braden and the secret Noiro had shared— the fact that the male was exempt from the Blood Curse and would never have a *destiny.* Since Braden was unquestionably Vampyr now, he could never mate with a human female, either. And the cruelest joke of all was the fact that Braden was probably the only male in the house of Jadon that could actually

BLOOD SHADOWS

sire female children.

After several minutes had passed, Napolean finally shook his head and grimaced—a strange reaction, indeed.

"What?" Nachari said, slightly taken aback.

"You know what this means?" Napolean asked.

"No, what?"

"He will have to be promised to Kristina."

Nachari stood stock-still, just allowing the information to settle in for a moment. Finally, he whispered, "Oh...shit."

"Indeed." Napolean laughed out loud.

thirty

Nachari stood outside on his rooftop terrace just gazing at the stars and contemplating how beautiful the sky was, how deeply he had missed the stars and the moon. He needed to unwind after his meeting with Saber, as well as his discussion with Napolean, and he wanted to make sure that his energy field was clear and his thoughts were focused before he turned his attention to Deanna.

Despite his best intentions, the door to the tranquil space opened, and Deanna walked out onto the roof, her long, model-esque frame taking his breath away at first glance.

"Hey, you," she called softly.

Her voice was a welcome sound. "Sebastian?" he asked instinctively.

"Sleeping," she answered, smiling. She sidled up behind him and wrapped her long, elegant arms around his waist, resting her head against his back. "How'd it go tonight?"

Nachari stroked her arm and sighed. "It went," he answered. "And I'm still in one piece."

Deanna took a deep, cleansing breath and looked up the stars, but she said nothing.

"I went to see Saber," he continued in a thoughtful voice, "and I spoke with Napolean."

To her credit, Deanna didn't react. "And the...Dark One...is he still alive?" Her voice was as soothing as it was direct.

"He is," Nachari answered. "At least until the sun comes up on Sunday."

Deanna shook her head rapidly as if dismissing the horrific thought. "Will you be there?"

Nachari lifted his arm and brought her closer, beneath his side. "It depends on what my *destiny* wants—if it's important to her, for closure, then it's important to me." He shifted his weight to bring her even closer. "It's not going to be a pretty scene, Deanna; death by sunlight is pretty…horrendous."

Deanna shrugged and nuzzled closer. "I don't really have a preference," she admitted. "I mean, the moment your brothers knocked him out, I had closure. I knew they would never let him get to me again."

Nachari couldn't help but think that she had no idea, whatsoever, how truly strong and unshakable she really was. Or what he would give to roll back the hands of time and be the one to confront Saber in that hot tub—to get there before Napolean.

"The main thing," she continued, "is what you need. Do you want to be there?"

Nachari considered her question carefully. "I guess it's a house of Jadon thing—code, honor, justice—it's the way I was raised, so yes, I do."

Deanna nodded in agreement. "Okay, then. We'll go."

She seemed to simply understand. She just got it. That he was as much a warrior as a wizard. That he was of a different species—Vampyr—which meant he didn't think or react like a human. But how she understood this so easily, he couldn't fathom.

Nachari shrugged then. "In all honesty, compared to where I've been the last four months, the entire execution will probably seem sterile." He frowned apologetically. "I'm sorry, Deanna. It must be *uncomfortable*, to say the least, to hear your mate making constant references to hell." He tried to smile, but he really wasn't feeling it.

Deanna ducked from beneath his side and took a step forward to face him. She leaned back against the terrace wall and thought about his words. Apparently, deciding to change the subject, she gestured toward the ground. "Did you know that I used to be terrified—and I mean scared out of my wits—of heights?"

"Used to be?" Nachari asked.

She shrugged. "Now that I'm Vampyr," she spoke the word halfheartedly, "and I have so many strong, capable brothers to catch me, there's little reason to fear much of anything."

Nachari growled possessively, surprised at his own base, territorial response.

Deanna ignored it, unaffected. "*And,*" she continued to elaborate, "just for the sake of general information, I was also afraid of spiders, really bugs of all kinds; that, and popping corn."

Now this made him laugh. "Popcorn?" he asked for clarification. "You mean the stuff made by humans like Orville Redenbacher?"

Deanna flushed and looked away. "Not the popcorn itself," she bantered, laughing. "The sound of it...the popping...it's a sensory thing, I guess."

"Hmm," Nachari teased, eyeing her warily. "And to think, I thought you were utterly perfect."

Deanna slapped him playfully. "What does that have to do with being perfect?" She raised her jaw. "I am!"

He smiled broadly then. "You are," he said, agreeing.

She rolled her eyes.

"What?" he asked, feigning innocence. "I said you are perfect."

"No," she corrected. "That's what you said with your mouth; what you said with your eyes was something entirely different."

Nachari chuckled. "Ah, so you can tell the difference already?"

"Yep," she answered, a look of self-satisfaction alighting her eyes, "I can." She looked away then. "And that's how I know you aren't being completely open and honest with me...yet. Even though you want me to be completely open and honest with you."

Now this concerned him. He lowered his head to better meet her gaze. "Deanna..." When she continued to look away, he reached for her chin and softly guided her eyes back to his. "Don't look away, sweetheart. What do you mean?"

She paused, fidgeted a moment with her hands, and then calmly placed them at her sides. "I'm the one who drew you in my sketches, remember? I'm the one who saw all those horrible images of the underworld...of the torture." She raised her hand, traced a soft finger along his jaw, and then placed it back by her side once more. "I saw the truth...with you...long before I met you. Do you really think that I see it any less, now that I actually know you?"

Nachari wanted to change the subject, to simply push it aside, reassure his *destiny* that everything was fine, and go on being lighthearted, but he didn't dare. The woman before him meant way too much to him already, and earning her friendship, gaining her respect, was way too important to their future. "What do you see, angel?"

Deanna looked deep into his eyes. "I see an incredibly handsome, absolutely spectacular—yet haunted—male." She tilted her head to the side. "I see you, Nachari."

He reached out and brushed the back of his hands against her stunning face, marveling at the smoky color of her eyes, the fullness of her lips, the high, gentle plains of her exotic cheekbones. Brushing a thick lock of dark golden-brown hair behind her shoulder, he said, "Does it bother you—what you see?"

Deanna shook her head emphatically. "No, Nachari...far from it." She stood silently while measuring her words. "What bothers me is that I don't know how to break through the invisible walls of the prison you're still living in, and I don't want to start our lives...going forward...looking from the outside in." She paused, as if still searching for the right words. "Nachari, I didn't know you before, so I can't give you any words of encouragement. I can't try to convince you that you're still the same person, and honestly, I know if I had gone through what you did, I wouldn't be the same. But I do know a kind heart when I see one. And character isn't something easily built...or destroyed." She studied his expression as if reading every nuance. "You are an honorable male, Nachari Silivasi, and as

338

impossible as it might seem, you are even more beautiful inside than out. This, I know for a fact. I just do."

Nachari's ageless heart warmed beneath the sweet caress of her words. He took both of her hands in his and kissed her knuckles, each one slowly in turn, before gently prying her fingers open in order to kiss the center of her palms. "And you are my entire world, now, Deanna—you and our son."

"And Braden," she teased, "and your brothers…and the honor of your house." She smiled broadly then. "I get it. And I'm fine with it."

He hesitated, looking away. "Okay, so you get it—but tell me this: Do you think, in time, you will actually come to love it?"

"To love *it*?" she repeated, chiding him playfully.

He dropped his head and laughed, knowing he'd been caught. And then he raised it and held her gaze with uncommon courage and intensity. "To love me."

Her breath caught in her throat, but she matched his courage ounce for ounce. "It's already starting to happen," she whispered, and then her face blushed a deep coral red.

"Come here," he growled deep in his throat. "Show me." With that, he hauled her forward and covered her mouth with his.

Deanna molded easily into Nachari's arms, his wondrous height making him the perfect fit for her softer, more pliant body. She reveled in the feeling of his lips over hers and sought his tongue in earnest.

He didn't hold back.

Giving her more of his passion.

More of his heart.

When his eyes began to burn red with intensity, she knew she had ignited a deep fire within him, and she had no intention of extinguishing the flame.

She reached up to cup his face in her hands and whispered, "Make love to me, Nachari. Here. Now."

He growled once more, grasped her by the waist, and began to kiss her more earnestly. Eyeing the door to the brownstone, he murmured, "Let me get a blanket."

Deanna shook her head, knowing that he was still being so very careful with her feelings, her body, her comfort. "No," she whispered. "You don't understand. I want you to make love to me...*now*."

Nachari's eyes darkened with fever, and a slow moan escaped his lips as his eyes met hers, almost as if searching for verification.

He got it.

Oh, did he ever get it.

Reaching for the tie to her robe, he pulled the opposite ends apart and slid it off her shoulders. As it fell to the ground, he ravished her neck, her shoulders, her breasts, dropping all the way down to his knees to taste her stomach...and her need. But feeling her urgency, he didn't stay there.

He tugged his shirt over his head with one hand, while deftly unzipping his jeans with the other; then he kicked off his pants and made quick work of his skin-tight boxers. His movement was almost feline in its grace and agility.

At a glance, there was no doubt that Nachari was ready for her—his arousal was positively magnificent in length, width, and virility. Stunning her with the swiftness of his movement, he grasped her by the waist, lifted her onto the terrace wall—glancing only momentarily at the perilous fall behind her—and parted her thighs. In an instant, he was inside of her, pressing all the way to her womb, and she gasped at the startling sensation.

And then her head fell back in ecstasy.

His body moved with restless urgency, plunging in steady, mind-numbing thrusts as a series of moans and groans escaped his lips, each one more primal than the last.

Deanna arched her back and concentrated on the heavenly feel of him—every inch, inside and out—the magnificent flesh that pressed against her soul, causing stronger and stronger friction to build in her core; the strong, muscular arms that held her aloft and intimately, possessively close; and the harshly beautiful face that grew taut with feral pleasure as his own passion mounted.

His fangs began to extend, and she couldn't help but stare, all the while grinding tightly against him. He was driving her out of her mind. Not knowing if she would love it or regret it, she pushed her long, layered tresses behind her shoulder and tilted her head to the side. He groaned with approval and need. "Oh, gods…Deanna."

And then he bit her. Not like a timid animal, either, but like some kind of ferocious beast. His canines sank deep into her artery, and his pelvis pressed hard against her mound as he took all that she offered him like a being who was dying of hunger and thirst.

Deanna nearly wept with the purity of it.

She shuddered beneath him as he continued to take long, drugging pulls from her artery, swallowing as much as he could in every gulp. And then, when it seemed as if he had actually taken too much, the earth beneath her spinning in rapid waves of vertigo, he scored his own wrist and pressed it to her mouth. "Take this."

Deanna drank like she had been born to the custom, her hands seeking the tight, round globes of his ass for purchase as she continued to grind her ever-more-desperate core against him.

He grit his teeth and snarled.

Deanna groaned beneath him as together their bodies rocked back and forth in spiraling passion. At last, they seemed to reach the peak together, hurtling over the edge without a moment's warning, each one equally caught off guard by the intensity of the orgasms that rocked them.

Deanna clung to his shoulders. She wasn't altogether certain, but she could have sworn she scored his back with her nails, and he responded by exploding all over again, his powerful member pumping stream after stream of seed deep into her core.

She held on until the climax stopped. Until their bodies ceased trembling, and they both came down from the heavens.

And in that perfect moment of peace—and clarity—she saw him more clearly than she had ever seen him before.

Not only his body, but his soul.

"Nachari," she whispered, running her hands through his hair. "I see you."

He chuckled, not quite understanding. In a deep, satiated voice, he murmured, "I see you, too."

"No," she argued, trying desperately to convey what she was really thinking. "I *see* you."

He drew back then, his glazed, hooded eyes meeting hers. The wizard inside of him somehow heard the importance of her words, even if he didn't fully comprehend. "Tell me what you see."

Deanna struggled to find the right words. Grasping his face in her hands, she murmured: "You don't need the four talismans—you never did."

His brow creased, and he stared at her fixedly, giving her his full attention.

She sighed in frustration. "The power is in *you*; it always has been."

Nachari shook his head. "I'm sorry; I…I don't understand, Deanna."

She shook her head and drew back her shoulders. "You are so focused on the trappings that surround you—the Book of Black Magic, the incantations you learned at the University; the spells used for centuries to conjure this or that—that you fail to recognize its source." She placed the palm of her hand over his heart. "It's right here…inside of you." She spoke more rapidly now, anxious to get it all out before she lost her train of thought. "You are more than just a wizard, and you could have killed Noiro with your own Magick—you didn't need the darkness."

Nachari ran his hands through his hair and considered her words. "What are you saying?"

Deanna stood even taller. "I'm saying that I felt it...just now. I felt all of you, and this darkness that you fear—this unnamed evil—isn't in you. What is inside of you is a resolute passion, unbridled power. It's the reason you survived the Abyss, the reason Noiro was so drawn to you that she betrayed her own kind. And *it*—not some mysterious darkness—is the reason you can command the raven and become the panther. You are the one who sent my dreams to me...all the way from hell. It has always been inside of you."

He leaned back on his heels and stared at her in rapt fascination.

"I think that there are scars—that there will always be repercussions from the torture and the close association with black Magick—but it isn't what you recognize inside of you. And it isn't what you fear. You fear the totality of what you are, the immeasurable power you haven't even begun to tap into." She smiled then, and her heart sped up in an excited rhythm. "The puma is a part of you, and it's no wonder he came out. You can embrace him anytime you want, and you don't need any spells to do it."

Nachari swallowed hard. "Where in the world is this insight coming from?"

Deanna shrugged. "I don't know." And then she sat forward. "But I know I'm right. I just need you to trust me."

Nachari felt the truth of Deanna's words as if from far away. And the moment he latched onto the roots, it was like a blooming seed, tugging at his soul. Blossoming toward freedom.

Not from his life or from her...or their son.

Not even from the horrible memories of all he had endured, but from the illusionary walls of confinement that had held him ever since his parents' death. The imaginary boundaries he had never been willing to cross, even in his quest to become a great and proficient wizard.

His soul stirred inside him, and his power began to coil...

To build.

Deanna smiled knowingly and nodded her head as if she felt it, too. "Go," she said, gesturing toward the other side of the wall. "Be all of who are you, and know that your son and I will be right here waiting...always waiting."

Inexplicable tears clouded his vision as her voice seemed to disappear into a tunnel, slowly fading away from his conscious awareness. *I love you, Deanna*, he tried to whisper, meaning it with every ounce of his being, but he didn't know if his words had been heard.

As the puma grew stronger inside of him, more insistent and demanding, he clutched his amulet for reassurance: Shelby—his twin—had been the most pure, untainted soul he had ever known. If he could produce such powerful Magick while connected to Shelby, he could be certain that the source of it was light.

Sleek, nimble legs began to extend gracefully beneath him— almost as if they had always been there—each one resting on a gigantic, level paw. Smooth, silken fur began to take the place of his skin, downy and black as the night, but absent of any taint of evil. And as his jaw extended forward, his mouth filling with sharp, carnivorous teeth, he finally understood what he couldn't comprehend from such a place of fear and uncertainty: The day he had eaten the demon, he had not absorbed a soul of evil.

The light had consumed the darkness.

He wasn't tainted.

He was victorious.

Just like his ruling lord, Perseus, the Victorious Hero—the one who had never left him, not even in his darkest hour.

As the panther supplanted the vampire—if only for a time— he threw back his feline head and roared at the heavens, a deafening sound of triumph. And then he turned to measure Deanna, hoping he hadn't scared her into hiding.

She was still standing on the terrace, naked and ravishing in all of her feminine splendor, with tears streaming down her alluring cheeks. Never had Nachari Silivasi seen anything more beautiful. Never had he felt more pride or gratitude in his heart.

She nodded her head in solidarity. "Yes, Nachari. *Yes.*"

And didn't that just say it all.

Yes, she would be there for all the days of his life. Yes, she would accept him exactly as he was, even as he became more. And yes, she was the perfect match of determination, strength, and wisdom to complement his immortal soul.

For this reward, he would spend a dozen lifetimes in hell.

As he bounded to the top of the terrace wall in one smooth leap, he looked back behind him one last time. There was the singular world he had known until then, and the plural world he would discover—with Deanna—going forward. And who wouldn't gladly make that leap?

Purring deep in his belly, a sound of rumbling satisfaction, the puma bounded over the wall and sprinted into the forest, eager to run and play and embrace the shadows, all the while being guided by the light of the moon and the stars.

Epilogue

Sunday — before sunrise

Damien Alexiares paced the floor in his underground lair, feeling the confinement of the colony more acutely than he had ever felt it before. His stomach literally hurt, and the helplessness that consumed him made him want to fly off in a rage and commit indiscriminate murder. The sun would rise at six thirty-five AM, and with its arrival, he would lose his eldest living son, Saber.

And there wasn't a damn thing he could do to stop it.

Even if they were willing to go to war, they could not survive the sunlight.

Leaning back against the cold stone wall of his underground lair, he stared at his remaining sons, Dane and Diablo, wondering if the waiting was killing them as much as it was killing him.

Dane bared his fangs and scowled. "Why can't we go get him—before the sun comes up?" He had already asked the same question at least a dozen times. For a 600-year-old male, he was sometimes a little slow to catch on.

"You and whose army?" Diablo said with a scowl, sarcastically.

"The sons of Jadon aren't gods!" Dane stormed, his face twisted with rage. "Why doesn't anyone believe we can take them?"

Damien sighed, determined to try once again to provide his youngest son with an explanation. "Male to male, one-to-one, of course we can. They have no powers we do not also possess—may the strongest soldier win—but as a group? Our colony against their army? It's a different matter entirely."

"Why?" Dane demanded.

BLOOD SHADOWS

"Because they have Napolean, and even under the cover of night, he can channel the power of the sun. We can't fight in the daylight, and we can't fight in the light of Napolean's being."

Dane laughed derisively. "The king has never supported an all-out war between our houses, and he won't support one now." He squared his jaw defiantly. "It was different when he came to rescue the princess; she was a valuable commodity, an irreplaceable relic in the house of Jadon, but outside of that one incident, when has Napolean Mondragon ever done anything other than break up the wars and keep both sides from destroying each other, and more important, from killing thousands in the human population? I'm telling you, one expedition will not become a war!"

Diablo pulled his hair in frustration. "It's not just that, Dane. Who in the house of Jaegar will die just to bring Saber back safely?"

"Lots of males will fight to the death for Saber!" Dane was practically incensed now, the veins in his forehead throbbing, his blood beginning to boil. "Saber has led hunting parties for decades, stood as a loyal and faithful servant to the house of Jaegar—hell, that's how he got caught, doing the council's dirty work—don't tell me there is no one who will fight for our brother!" He sprang from his chair, and Damien intercepted him before he could wrap his arms around his twin brother's neck.

"Your hatred is misplaced, Dane. I know this is killing you, but attacking Diablo isn't going to bring Saber back."

"Bring Saber back?" Dane echoed frenetically. "You act as if he's already dead."

Damien stiffened, stilling himself against the pain of Dane's words. It was just too much to bear. Stepping outside of the room for a fresh breath of air, he seriously considered petitioning the dark lords—or even the Celestial gods—whichever set of deities might be most inclined to save his son, for help.

And wasn't that just the dilemma of the past eight centuries—as well as the greatest lie he had ever told? The most seditious secret?

Which group of deities was he to petition?

Damien rubbed his palm against the cold, abrasive wall and then scratched a mysterious symbol into the stone with a hardened claw. Placing his palm over the pictogram to hide it, he hung his head in shame, remembering the night of Saber's birth. Recalling everything he had done.

Wishing like hell that he could just go back in time and have that moment to do over, he shook his head in confusion: Would he, though, do things any differently, that is?

Damien had brutalized the frail human woman for days, before viciously mounting her in order to sire his first set of twins—surely, there was nothing he would have done differently there. The female had been a small, diminutive woman of little consequence: In fact, he could hardly remember if her hair had been brown or blond. He did remember, however, that she had put up quite a struggle on the sacrificial stone as his twin sons clawed their way out of her fragile body, tearing through her innards, shattering her ribs, and forcing their way into the world. He had been forced to incinerate her corpse almost immediately in response to the horrific smell, and then he had turned his attention directly to his duty: to the requirement of the Blood Curse—sacrificing the firstborn son.

He moaned at the strength of the memory. He had turned his back on the second-born child, the one who would live, for only a second—*just one second*—while he had placed the firstborn child on the altar.

But that one second had been one too many. Far too long.

Why had he set the baby down?

The decision, as he thought back on it, was incomprehensible. Maybe he had wanted to keep his living child far, far away from the greedy clutches of The Blood, lest the vengeful spirit get confused and take them both. Or maybe he had just been so full of hubris, heady from the power of the rape and kill and the ensuing birth, that he had thought himself and his children invincible.

BLOOD SHADOWS

Damien Alexiares had been wrong.

Dead wrong.

And his remaining son had paid with his life when the human brother of the woman he had violated, a vampire-hunter on top of everything else, had stormed into the cavern and sprayed the child with diamond-tipped bullets, tossing him into the very fire that consumed his sister in his lust for revenge.

Damien had flown into a virulent rage. He had been utterly inconsolable. On one hand, the Blood had come for his firstborn son, taking him in an eternal cycle of vengeance that never ceased, even as, on the other hand, the brother of the worthless piece of trash he had used to incubate his children had put his second son to death.

He had been absolutely devastated—just as he was now.

Rendering himself invisible, Damien Alexiares had shredded that brazen vampire-hunter into a thousand pieces of so much trash, sending him to whatever afterlife his sister now inhabited. Yet even that had not been enough. He had stewed and paced and spat in a red haze of fury, until, in a rare moment of clarity, he had remembered the house of Jadon and the recent Blood Moon: that damnable, taunting sign that appeared in the heavens whenever a son of Jadon was given his *destiny*…and his own twin sons.

In the midst of his grief and rage, Damien had somehow recalled the fact that the sign had occurred exactly thirty days before: The Celestial god Serpens had showered his favor on one of the sons of Jadon, giving him thirty days to claim his *destiny*, bear twin sons of his own, and sacrifice the Dark One of the two progeny to the Blood.

It didn't require any divination to figure out who the chosen male was—or to obtain the name of his human *destiny*: Such things were common knowledge in the house of Jaegar, and whenever they could, the Dark Ones used that knowledge to strike out at their formidable enemies of light. Indeed, the male had been a Master Warrior, not yet an ancient, named Rafael Dzuna; and his destiny had been a human woman passing through the valley by the name of Lorna. A quick trip to the upper hall of annals, and Damien had garnered the name of their surviving son: Sabino Dzuna, born under the ruling moon of the god Serpens, child of light to a sacrificed twin of darkness.

Had Damien's own tragedy occurred only a couple of hours earlier, he might have had a chance to steal the Dark Twin, the child that was to be turned over to the Curse, but fate had not blessed him so that day.

Thinking of Saber now, how could he wish that? The dark lord of hell could not have given him a better son than the one he had taken on that fateful night.

Sabino.

Saber.

He smiled at the memory, even as his heart wept from the knowledge of his impending loss. Eight hundred years ago, the Light Vampyr had lived in hidden cliff dwellings as well as sparse stone lodgings that were much more spread apart. As attacks from Dark Ones were infrequent, they were generally carefree in their comings and goings.

Taking Sabino—Saber—from his crib had been as easy as taking blood from a human baby, hardly sport at all. But the moment he had looked into those dark eyes, he had known...this was his son for all time.

And so it came to pass: He had brought the light infant back to the colony and passed him off as the child he had lost, a son of his own blood, subject to the approval of the dark lord S'nepres—the twin energy of Serpens, residing in the abyss. When at last he bathed the child in his own blood, and S'nepres consecrated the babe by turning his hair a true crimson and black, like those of the males born to the house of Jaegar, Damien had known it was fate.

Providence.

Always meant to be.

For whatever reason, his true firstborn son had been lost, but Sabino Dzuna, inaugurated with the name Saber, had simply and divinely taken the lost child's place. And 200 years later, when Damien had decided to kidnap and violate another human woman in order to sire more sons, he had been allowed to keep both of the twins: Dane and Diablo.

His family had been complete.

Only now, he would lose one of his own, the most precious to his rotting soul.

Saber.

Damien stared at the symbol he had etched into the wall, the pictogram representing the Celestial deity Serpens, and quickly scratched it out, lest the dark lord S'nepres strike him dead where he stood. Would S'nepres answer his prayer now and save Saber? Demons rarely delighted in the giving of life—but if he prayed to Serpens, the true god of Saber's birth, would even Serpens care enough to help the child now?

He hung his head in despair and fury.

By all that was unholy, Saber was going to die.

Saber Alexiares tugged at the ties that bound him to the post, knowing that he was too weak from blood loss to break free or escape. As he glanced toward the eastern horizon, his heart sank in his soulless chest.

The sun.

That great ball of fire that journeyed every day from the east to the west...

Entire civilizations of humans had worshipped it throughout history; many more counted on it to give life to the trees and the plants of the fields today; but to his kind—the sons of Jaegar—it was an abomination, a scourge of nature to be feared above all else.

The sun was dreaded more than the vampire-hunting societies, the Lycans, or even the males in the house of Jadon—for its rays meant certain death. And not an easy or painless passing, but the slow, insidious cleansing of darkness by light. A

Tessa Dawn

purging by fire that was said to burn like acid flowing through the veins, like alcohol permeating an open wound, to pierce the skin and the internal organs like a thousand blades of steel, each one sharper and more finely honed than the last, rendering the dying vampire incapacitated by an agony that assaulted his mind, body, and soul without mercy.

It was a final reckoning that no one dared provoke. And even young boys were taught to flee from its light, to dive away from busted windows in desperation, to calculate their comings and goings from the colony with infinite precision for one reason and one reason only: to always, *always* avoid the sun. The fear of the sun was more than ingrained or conditioned; it was instinctive and all-consuming.

Despite his desperate attempt at courage, Saber's heart thundered in his chest, and he refused to meet the eyes of his accusers, not because the warriors in the house of Jadon intimidated him—and not because he gave a damn what they thought—but because his mind was too consumed by primordial terror to focus on who was in front of him. Eight hundred years of conditioning had stricken terror into his soul, and his vision was growing blurry beneath the onslaught of fear.

He hung his head forward, not wanting to meet the sun with his gaze when, at last, it rose over the horizon. From all he had been told, the first rays burned the orbs right out of their sockets, and then it began to penetrate the brain—

"Stop!" he commanded himself, helpless to get control over the fear. "Do not think about it."

In his debilitating state of weakness, he swayed where he stood, hanging from two posts like a sacrificial lamb, and then he prayed to the dark lord of his birth that the demon might take his soul before the sun began to scorch him: Even the tortures of hell were a welcome substitute compared to what would soon be rising over the canyon.

Saber felt a sickening wave of nausea wash over him, and he struggled not to vomit in front of his enemies, and then he saw the faintest glimpse of something he had never expected to behold in all of his 800 years.

Natural, solar light.

The sun peeking its blazing face over the horizon.

Terror seized him like a vise, and the air rushed out of his body. Every instinct, every ounce of training he had received over the centuries, assailed him at once, demanding flight. Demanding that he flee to the shade.

He had to get out of the sun!

Summoning whatever strength he had left, Saber succumbed to pure hysteria, his mind a red haze of insanity.

Get out of the sun! Get out of the sun!

The light! The light!

The sounds that came from his throat were inhuman; the contortions of his body, as he bucked and pulled and twisted and turned in a feverish attempt to break his bonds, were desperately grotesque. His arms snapped like twigs, and the vertebrae in his spine popped like corn behind the effort, yet he still continued to struggle mightily, his frenzied psyche driving him over a ledge from which he would never return. The flesh on his feet grew bloodied and torn, as the appendages tore against the stones on the ground. As he tried in vain to run...

Run!

But the air wouldn't move through his lungs!

His body wouldn't budge—not even when he broke his wrists in an effort to free his hands from the manacles.

Saber could not escape.

As his world became nothing but a living, breathing ball of fire, scorching away even the last remnants of what had been his sanity, Saber Alexiares descended into a world of madness where the sun was the devil, and he was the greatest sinner on earth.

Napolean Mondragon watched in morbid fascination as the macabre scene played out before him. He had sentenced Dark

Ones to die in the sun before, and the brutal taking of their bodies by the great ball of fire had never been a pleasant thing to witness, but this was beyond gruesome.

Beyond comprehension.

The male tied to the stake was suffering unlike any other he had ever seen, but not from the sun's rays, and not because his wicked body, soul, and mind were burning.

He was suffering because his flesh remained untouched.

Saber Alexiares was not burning in the sun!

And that simply wasn't possible.

Napolean turned to Nachari Silivasi and the council of wizards who sat beside him on the ground, those with a front row seat to the execution. "What is this?" he demanded.

Niko Durciak shook his head. "Milord, he isn't—"

"Burning?" Napolean clipped, his impatience getting the best of him. *By all that was holy, would somebody stop that screaming?* He had never seen the likes of it. "Why not?" he demanded.

Nachari Silivasi turned his attention inward and began to chant softly beneath his breath, trying desperately to divine what his sovereign lord requested. And then, in an abrupt halt, he raised his head and furrowed his brows. "I heard something, but I don't know what it means."

"You don't know what *what* means?" Napolean asked calmly. He had to keep his composure despite the ghastly display persisting in the canyon.

"The word that comes to me is *Serpens.*"

"Serpents?" Napolean asked, seeking clarification. "Snakes?"

"No, milord," Nachari answered. "Serpens. Like the Celestial deity of rebirth."

Napolean spun around, trying to make sense of Nachari's words. He stared at the spectacle taking place before him, his own heart now racing in his chest, while his mind processed what he had been told: *Serpens…the Celestial deity of rebirth.*

All at once, understanding dawned, and the earth stood still around him. "Who has the keys to the manacles?" he shouted.

There was a moment of confusion as the warriors searched

their pockets and coats. Finally, Ramsey Olaru stepped forward. "I have them, milord, but why…" His voice trailed off in disbelief. Clearly, he couldn't even form the question because the meaning was so absurd: *Why would they release the Dark One?*

Napolean gestured toward the keys and met Ramsey's stare head-on. "Get him down from there and take him out of the sun—before he kills himself with fright."

"Milord?" Ramsey's voice was harsh with disapproval.

"He isn't from the house of Jaegar, and he isn't going to burn," Napolean explained.

Nachari's eyes widened and he took a step back. "I don't understand."

Napolean blinked several times and slowly shook his head. "Somebody find Rafael and Lorna Dzuna; I believe this male is their son."

About The Author

Tessa Dawn grew up in Colorado where she developed a deep affinity for the Rocky Mountains. After graduating with a degree

in psychology, she worked for several years in criminal justice and mental health before returning to get her Masters Degree in Nonprofit Management.

Tessa began writing as a child and composed her first full-length novel at the age of eleven. By the time she graduated high-school, she had a banker's box full of short-stories and books. Since then, she has published works as diverse as poetry, greeting cards, workbooks for kids with autism, and academic curricula. The Blood Curse Series marks her long-desired return to her creative-writing roots and her first foray into the Dark Fantasy world of vampire fiction.

Tessa currently lives in the suburbs with her two children and "one very crazy cat" but hopes to someday move to the country where she can own horses and a German Shepherd.

Writing is her bliss.

Books in the Blood Curse Series

Blood Destiny

Blood Awakening

Blood Possession

Blood Shadows

Blood Redemption (Coming Soon…)

If you would like to receive notice of future releases,

please join the author's mailing list at

www.TessaDawn.Com